WEIGHTLESS

VIRGINIA DUAN

Letters to Artax Press

Book cover by Joyce Park
Developmental edit by Jacquelin Cangro
Copy edit by Melody Ip
Cultural edit by Diane Park
Author photo by Susanna Stroberg

Paperback ISBN: 979-8-9901853-2-6
EPUB ISBN: 979-8-9901853-3-3

1st edition 2024

Contents

Chapter 1

Dropped by old haunts and ran into ghosts.
>   - Katie Wu, X, January 2024

Park Jae-sung was seeing things.

The rapper could have sworn he just saw Katie Wu exiting one of SB Entertainment's conference rooms and heading down one of the carpeted hallways. Jae-sung would know Katie's body anywhere—average height and lean, but soft and curvy in all the right places. He had spent his twenties with her, worshiping her naked form. Sometimes, he still dreamed of her.

But that couldn't be. As far as Jae-sung knew, Katie was based out of Los Angeles now and wasn't slated to return to Seoul ever again. She had let her contract at SB Entertainment lapse a few years ago, choosing not to re-sign when her term had ended.

Jae-sung had been secretly relieved when he'd heard the news a year after she'd vanished. Even then, hearing her name had still stung. If he was honest with himself, it still did.

His body moved on its own volition, and before he knew it, Jae-sung was chasing what had to be Katie's doppelgänger, eager to prove his eyes wrong.

When he eventually caught up with Katie, her old manager Baek Ha-joon, and her friend Alton Kuang, Jae-sung couldn't help blurting out the first words to pop in his head.

"Katie, is that you?"

Katie turned at his voice and his heart stopped. She was still so achingly beautiful. The intervening years had been kind to her—her heart-shaped face still sharp, her skin still smooth, her hair still black and glossy. It didn't seem fair, though they were the same age and he, too, looked younger than his 30 years. She smiled gently at him. All he could hear was the blood pounding in his ears.

"Hey, Jae-sung," Katie said, polite and friendly, as if the past seven years hadn't happened. As if she hadn't shattered his heart when she ghosted him. He'd wanted to marry her—have babies with her—and then Katie had left without a word three years ago. "You remember Alton, don't you?"

Jae-sung's heartstrings snapped in familiar annoyance upon seeing the older man. He'd always suspected Alton'd had designs on Katie. Seeing her here with the wealthy heir, his arm possessive around her waist, Jae-sung couldn't help himself.

"I see you swooped in as soon as I was out of the picture," Jae-sung said in English. He was shocked at how bitter he sounded.

Alton grinned, wide and antagonizing. "Someone had to be there for her," the man said, his voice the epitome of lazy, rich, and cultured. Alton tucked Katie closer to him, gazed at her adoringly, and kissed her forehead.

Jae-sung wanted to punch Alton in his fucking smug face but held himself in check. Jae-sung was no financial slouch, but Alton could buy him several times over and was armed to the teeth with attorneys. As much as his pride smarted, Jae-sung hadn't survived years of scrabbling to the top of the global music scene as the leader of the K-pop septet DOYEN just to get slapped down by a spoiled Singaporean chaebol.

Katie sighed, small and fragile. "I am not a thing to be fought over and possessed," she said quietly. Her dark eyes dripped with reproach. "It was good to see you again, Jae-sung," she added in dismissal.

She was not going to escape again that easily. He deserved answers.

"That's it? That's all you have to say to me?" Jae-sung hated how desperate he felt.

Ha-joon cleared his throat. The stocky man glanced conspicuously around the hall and the doors leading to offices and conference rooms. "Jae-sung, perhaps now is not the time."

Jae-sung felt a surge of fury at Ha-joon, too. At the time, he had blocked Katie from Jae-sung. Ha-joon had been a wall, steady and unyielding, keeping her whereabouts secret—even disappearing for a year or so until her contract was up. Then he'd returned, quitting his role as manager and switching back to the A&R department where he'd started.

"When would be the time, exactly?" Jae-sung replied resentfully. "When would be convenient for you?"

Jae-sung could see the way Alton puffed up and grew slightly larger, stepping forward. He almost expected Alton to shield Katie physically with his body, but she was no shrinking violet.

This time, her voice was professional and clipped. "I regret to inform you that we're heading to the airport right now, Jae-sung. Perhaps the next time I'm in Seoul—"

"No. Not good enough. Who knows when that will be?" Jae-sung growled. "It could be another two or three years."

Jae-sung knew he was being unconscionably rude and obvious. But Katie's presence had ripped away the bit of healing he'd managed. He was scraped raw.

"Apologize," Alton said even as she tugged on his arm. The older man was as tall as Jae-sung's 185 centimeters, and though not quite as filled out, still a formidable person.

"Alton," Katie pleaded. "Let's go, Ge."

"Were you just going to waltz back here—to *my* fucking city—to *my* fucking company—and pretend we never existed? I woke up one morning and you were just gone." Jae-sung briefly registered that he was shouting, but he couldn't stop himself. Suddenly, he didn't care who could hear him. "Not just you yourself—but all traces of you. When I went to your apartment, it was completely empty. Your studio code was changed. Your number was disconnected. The company refused to tell me anything about you—and now you think you can just reappear and act as if nothing happened?"

"Jae-sung," Ha-joon said, his gruff voice a warning. "That's enough."

Katie's face had gone pale, and her knuckles had gone white as she dug her fingers into Alton's arm. "What I think is none of your concern, Jae-sung," she said icily, "just like what you think is none of mine."

"You're a cold-hearted cunt, aren't you?" he raged. He immediately regretted it, but the words were out, so Jae-sung owned them.

"Yes," Katie said. Then she abruptly turned heel and left with Alton following closely.

Ha-joon glared at Jae-sung. "I hope you're proud of yourself," he spat before also leaving.

Jae-sung just shook his head and felt hollowed out.

September 2015

Met my labelmates again today!!!! <3333333 In related
news: can one actually die of embarrassment?
                    - Katie Wu, Twitter, September 2015

K-pop singer Park Dae-jung was excited.

Dae-jung's band, DOYEN, was meeting Katie Wu again today, and even though they'd met before his band's concert in Taipei a few months ago, this time was different. She was going to be a labelmate! Actually, she'd been their labelmate for a few months already, but that didn't count because Dae-jung and his bandmates had been on tour. As a result, they hadn't been around to greet Katie properly when she'd first moved to Seoul.

Dae-jung wondered if Katie would fit in at SB Entertainment and hoped that she would. The agency was small and it would be fun to have a noona only a year or two older than his almost 20 years. He was the eldest of his family and had always wanted a big sister. Maybe Katie would be like one to him. After all, she had been friendly and enthusiastic back in March. If Katie stayed that way, she would be great to have around.

Katie's boyfriend who'd accompanied her backstage had seemed like a bummer, but from what Dae-jung had heard, they'd broken up—something about a scandal?—so even that wouldn't be much of an obstacle. Dae-jung only hoped she wasn't too sad about the breakup. Katie'd seemed too good for the guy anyway—even if he was as handsome as Dae-jung's eldest bandmate and fellow vocalist Lee Ye-jun.

Dae-jung could tell that Katie's ex had been at the concert for the clout and not for DOYEN. He'd clearly thought he was better than Dae-jung and his entire group. Fuck that guy.

When Dae-jung and his bandmates were herded into the small, dingy conference room to officially meet Katie, she was already there, passed out in a cheap, metal folding chair and slumped against her manager Ha-joon. Her mouth was wide open, and Dae-jung was tempted to throw something in it.

Upon seeing the DOYEN members trickle in, Ha-joon lightly nudged her. "Wake up, Katie."

"Go 'way," she mumbled in English, her hand blindly attempting to push him away. "Unless it's a cheeseburger. I'll fuck that cheeseburger up."

Ha-joon rolled his eyes. "No, it's DOYEN. They're here for the meeting."

"I'm not falling for that again, Oppa," Katie said as she pulled her UCLA hoodie over her face. "Unless it's a cheeseburger or Lambent, I'm not waking up," she hummed contentedly. "Lambent's a motherfucking snack."

Dae-jung was trying very hard not to laugh—as was the rest of his group—especially when Ha-joon gestured at rapper Hwang Woo-jin, who went by the stage name Lambent, to come over.

"You rang?" Woo-jin asked in careful, smirky English.

None of his members could keep it together as Katie bolted upright in horror.

"Oh my god!" she shrieked. "Why didn't you tell me they were here?"

Katie smacked poor Ha-joon repeatedly—and from the look on his face, it hurt. She jumped up from her seat and bowed haphazardly, hastily muttering a proper greeting in Korean from a hoobae to a sunbae. Dae-jung wasn't particularly hung up on ceremony, but he still enjoyed having juniors in the industry treating him with the respect due a senior—even if DOYEN had debuted only two years prior.

"Please excuse what I just said, Woo-jin-sunbaenim. I meant no disrespect," Katie said in English, tugging on Ha-joon's sleeve desperately so that her manager would translate.

"I can understand your English just fine, Katie," Woo-jin replied carefully in English and then switched to Korean. "I just prefer to respond in my own language. Why should I change to accommodate Americans?" Woo-jin cracked a sly smile. "Besides, I think you like me just fine the way I am, hmm?"

Dae-jung watched as Katie looked at Ha-joon again for a translation, waiting for her comprehension of Woo-jin's suggestive comment. Dae-jung's patience was rewarded when she flushed pink and refused to look in the rapper's direction. Katie instead picked at imaginary lint on her sweatshirt and mumbled something that sounded suspiciously like "motherfucking Hwang Woo-jin."

Katie was saved by one of Dae-jung's managers starting the meeting. Dae-jung was trying very hard to pay attention, but he was having too much fun observing Woo-jin bait Katie by pinning her constantly with stares of varying intensity.

She studiously ignored Woo-jin, instead acting as if manager-nim Kim Sung-mo was the most riveting person in the room. Dae-jung likely would have bought it except that Katie clearly didn't understand Korean, and Ha-joon was busy translating at her side. He wondered what it was like for her to be a foreigner in Korea, if it was as isolating as he'd found the experience of traveling to the States briefly for additional vocal, dance, and rap training.

Dae-jung surmised it was probably harder. After all, though his American teachers only spoke English, he was still able to learn how to use his baritone more soulfully. A few of his bandmates were fluent in English, as were some of his staff, and they helped with translating. As for Dae-jung and the members who weren't, they could speak Korean to each other and make do with the rudimentary English they'd all learned in school. Somehow, Dae-jung didn't think Americans learned Korean—rudimentary or otherwise—in their schools.

"Katie-ssi, would you like to introduce yourself?" Sung-mo asked after he re-introduced Dae-jung's bandmates: rappers Jae-sung, Woo-jin, and Jung Do-won, and his fellow vocalists Ye-jun, Kitahara Akihiro, himself, and Choi Soo-min.

Katie's eyes widened at her name, but understanding didn't dawn until Ha-joon explained. Dae-jung could see the instant she slipped into public-facing mode.

"Hello, everyone," she said in Korean, bowing slightly while still seated. "I'm Katie Wu and it's a pleasure to meet you all again. I hope that we can be good colleagues and learn from one another. Thank you for making room for me in your studio and your schedules. Please be patient with me as I learn Korean and strive to make improvements."

Dae-jung was pretty sure she'd memorized that whole bit, but he knew how it went. He had memorized plenty of lines in different languages that he didn't actually know how to speak.

He decided he would have to trick Katie into memorizing Korean phrases and insults to try on Akihiro. "Babo" would be too easy—she would likely already know that it meant "fool." He had to come up with something very creative. Ooooh! Maybe he could teach Katie some Daegu satoori swears! There would be no way an American would know curse words in a Korean dialect! That would be hilarious. He hoped Akihiro remembered them and would be adequately offended, but even if his same-aged friend didn't, the punchline would only be momentarily delayed until Akihiro asked someone else.

Dae-jung belatedly realized that Jae-sung had just finished his polite welcome to Katie in English. Jae-sung had spent a few years in New Jersey during elementary school, and not for the first time did Dae-jung envy his leader's language skills. Dae-jung figured he should resume paying attention. Thankfully, the meeting adjourned soon after, and they hung around, chatting with Katie as much as her limited Korean and their limited English could allow.

"What are you working on right now, Katie?" Jae-sung asked in English.

She smiled, bright and open. "I'm learning how to rap and I'm terrible!" She laughed, full and mouth uncovered in the unrestrained way of Americans.

Dae-jung decided anyone who laughed as unfettered as she did couldn't possibly be bad. He resolved to help her personally with her Korean—out of the kindness of his heart, of course.

"Oh, how, um, nice," Jae-sung responded.

Dae-jung resisted the urge to roll his eyes. Jae-sung wasn't as smooth as he prided himself on being.

Katie laughed again, eyes dancing. "I'm sure even the amazing King Ja$e was once terrible at rap." She winked at Jae-sung and gathered her things.

"*I* certainly wasn't," snarked Woo-jin in another rare show of English. "If you ever need any one-on-one help, let me know."

Though Dae-jung's second eldest bandmate could speak and understand English well enough, Woo-jin absolutely hated using it. Something about how western imperialism had robbed enough from Korea and he refused to be colonized any further. Dae-jung thought it was mostly bullshit for show, after all, here was Woo-jin giving proof to all the fan theories that he was secretly fluent in English.

Katie protested, "Woo-jin-sunbaenim—"

"Call me Oppa," Woo-jin cut in, a smirk gracing his feline features.

Katie's confident demeanor vanished as she turned into a sputtering mess. "I—um, that won't be—" she started before she gave up and ran out of the room.

Woo-jin grinned. "This is going to be so much fucking fun."

October 2015

Guess who dropped her completely full menstrual cup all over her pants and shoes and onto the public bathroom floor at work? :: soul cry ::

> \- Katie Wu, Twitter, October 2015

Also guess who had to wash her cup and pants in the bathroom sink bc she didn't bring a change of clothes? Sorry office unnies! Surprise!

> \- Katie Wu, Twitter, October 2015

Jae-sung arrived at the dance studio before the rest of his members showed up, expecting an empty room to practice and warm up in. Instead, he walked smack into Katie and her dancers having an impromptu dance party. He couldn't help but stare at the exposed skin under her cropped tee and low-slung joggers repeating infinitely in the mirrors lining the front and back walls of the small, square space. Katie glistened with sweat, and her taut belly rippled in appealing curves. He noted the sweeping black ink of what looked to be parts of tiger and dragon tattoos sinking low on her back.

"Oh," he uttered.

Jae-sung shook himself. Of course Katie was attractive. Everyone in the industry was attractive. He needed to get himself together.

"Jae!" Katie called as she reached out to him, her heart-shaped face open and welcoming. "Join us!"

She smelled faintly of sweat and effort. It was not unpleasant, and Jae-sung willed himself to focus.

"Uh," he replied brilliantly.

Jae-sung really wasn't quite prepared for the onslaught of just how dynamic Katie was in motion. She sparkled. He really needed to eat more—he was clearly feeling faint.

Before he could clear his head, he heard the opening for Tupac's "California Love" and Katie yelled a joyful, "AAAAAAAAAYYYYYYYYYY!!! THIS IS MY SOOOONNNNG-GGGGG!!!" and started dancing freestyle with her dancers. She was actually pretty good—but what really surprised him was how she knew all the lyrics to the classic Tupac track, although he supposed she was from California. Perhaps it was standard for Californians to know it. Maybe it was a regional anthem.

But when Jae-sung heard the iconic start of Craig Mack's "Flava in Ya Ear Remix," she knew all the lyrics to that, too. Katie and the dancers threw themselves onto the wooden floor, giggling as they all caught their breaths during the slower song.

"Thanks for being so patient with me today," Katie said in Korean as the group of dancers got up to leave. "See you tomorrow!" She stayed splayed out on the floor, exhausted but still bopping along to the track.

"Are you learning these songs to practice rapping with?" Jae-sung asked in English.

"Is that how you learned to rap in Korean? Practicing American '90s hip-hop classics?" Katie pinned him with a bemused gaze. "Jae-sung," Katie said in her low, smoky voice, "is it so beyond your imagination to think I know the lyrics because—oh, I don't know—I know hip-hop?"

Once she pointed it out in that dry tone of hers, Jae-sung realized how stupid his question was. His face warmed. "Just because you know the words to two songs doesn't mean you know hip-hop," he retorted.

Katie's face filled with abject disdain. "How disappointing." She got up, grabbed her backpack and water bottle, said a dismissive, "See you later, Jae-sung," and left.

Jae-sung felt like an asshole of monumental proportions.

If Jae-sung had worried Katie would hold a grudge, he needn't have. She was still her polite and friendly self every time she ran into him in their tiny shared studio, as well as around the dilapidated SB Entertainment offices.

It was a good thing for Jae-sung that she didn't because word had gotten out to the rest of DOYEN that Katie had mini dance parties after her practices. More than once, Jae-sung had found her dancing and laughing with Do-won or Akihiro before DOYEN's dance rehearsals. Soo-min would also be present and had often seemed as if he'd really wanted to join—but he'd still been too shy to really commit. He would blush, stutter, and touch his ears with his hands, and then run to the restroom or pull his hood over his head and sit in the corner.

It was so obvious their youngest bandmate had it bad for Katie. But she was always kind to Soo-min, trying to include him in her shenanigans—and she had a lot—and accommodate his shyness. Maybe it was because Soo-min was also an American and could understand her English better than Do-won or Akihiro. Whatever her reasoning, Katie seemed to be extra friendly to their maknae, as if she wanted to ease some permanently startled part of his soul.

Jae-sung found that endeared Katie to him more than he wanted to admit.

And so, it was not an unfamiliar sight to Jae-sung when he pushed open the door to the dance studio and found Katie and Do-won showing off for each other with Q-Tip's "Vivrant Thing Club Mix" blasting in the background. She was once again (as he'd discovered over the weeks) rapping along to the lyrics as her feet made light work of the floor. She was so confident and free—relaxed in a way Jae-sung had yet to master—that he envied her boldness, even if her rapping left much room for improvement. She wasn't even that swaggy—at least not in the way he could pinpoint.

Katie was just loose and unbothered. She didn't seem to care that she wasn't the best at dancing or rapping. She always just went for it, willing to play the fool if it meant she would eventually learn and improve.

She reminded Jae-sung of Ye-jun, who didn't pick up dance moves as quickly but put in the extra time to make sure he wasn't holding everyone else back. Jae-sung hated how this new piece of information also endeared Katie to him.

"Jae-sung hyung!" Do-won called out. "Noona was just showing us her new bars and moves. Want to check it out?"

"Oh, you really don't need to—" Katie started to say before Do-won cut her off.

"Noona, Jae hyung has been big in the underground rapping scene since he was 12 or something—and he dances and raps at the same time."

Katie cut Do-won a look after Ha-joon translated. Her manager really was the MVP in these social interactions. There was no other way for her to communicate unless her Korean improved logarithmically. (Do-won's English certainly wasn't going to.)

"You also dance and rap at the same time," she said. "I found your tips just fine and supremely helpful! I don't like it when you undersell your abilities, Wonnie."

Do-won beamed at Katie, his esteem broadcast in every minute detail of his body language. "Ah, Noona. It's not like that," he muttered bashfully. "It just never hurts to have more than one person give you feedback. Especially someone like Jae-sung hyung."

A dejected expression crossed her features. "I'm sure Jae-sung-sunbae-nim has better things to do than monitor an amateur rapper such as myself," Katie replied and then turned to Jae-sung. "Seriously, I'm really bad," she said, chuckling ruefully. "We may have to cut the song or change the title track if I can't get my shit together."

Jae-sung didn't quite like her implication that he was a snob, but he supposed she was justified. "I don't mind, Katie," he said, trying to sound as sincere as possible. (He *did* mind, but he knew how such social currency was built or lost. Also, Jae-sung knew better than to incur the wrath of Do-won.)

Katie seemed dubious but Do-won dragged her into the center of the room. Though her backup dancers had left for their next schedules, she still gamely got into position and waited for Ha-joon to cue the music.

A bright and infectious beat piped through the speakers, and Katie immediately launched into the hook and laid-back choreography. The song itself was a solid number—as to be expected from SB Entertainment's producers and her preceding reputation. Her singing was steady and the lyrics were compelling.

He could tell Katie was a bit more nervous than she likely wanted to let on, but that was also to be expected. Jae-sung hated being put on the spot during music show interviews—or interviews in general—and this felt like all of those situations but with slightly less pressure. Or maybe it was more pressure. Who was he to judge?

And then she switched from singing to melodic rap. It was a good choice by her producers since it was closer to singing than other kinds of rap, except she was only serviceable. It wasn't that Katie was bad per se. She just seemed to lack something, and he couldn't quite put his finger on it.

After the performance was over, Katie took one look at Jae-sung's face and laughed self-deprecatingly. "You look like you're scrambling to find a polite way to say, 'You're terrible,'" she said in English. "Go on, Jae-sung. Hit me."

The way her voice rasped that last "hit me" dug deep into all the pleasure centers of Jae-sung's mind. If only her rapping sounded like that. Actually—

"How is your non-singing rapping?" Jae-sung asked suddenly. "It's not that you're bad at melodic rap—I can't figure out why it's not hitting right."

"Ah, that might actually be worse," Katie lamented.

"Show me," he insisted.

Katie was not good. Oh, she tried. But she was not good. Not by a long shot.

"You're rapping, but it's not believable," Jae-sung critiqued honestly.

She sighed. "Yeah, I know. The producers told me it was a long shot to get good in such a short amount of time, but I love hip-hop and was hoping K-pop's famous training grounds could make something of me. So many idols can rap, sing, and dance—I was hoping that I could, too."

Jae-sung understood Katie's desire to be a triple threat. He, too, wished his dancing and singing were better—but unlike Katie, he had more realistic expectations. And though entertainment agencies did teach their trainees how to rap—Do-won had learned to rap at SB Entertainment, after all—the fact that she'd hoped to master a skill Jae-sung had spent the last decade honing was both laughable and insulting.

Do-won's mouth was a triangle and that never boded well. Perhaps Do-won agreed with him. "Noona, don't take this the wrong way, but did you understand what you were rapping?" he asked.

Katie waited for Ha-joon to translate, and then she flushed. "Well, seeing as I had to wait for Oppa's translation...," she sighed. "It's not that I don't understand what I'm rapping, but it's just so hard to internalize it when

I'm trying to perform and make sure I don't fuck up the pronunciation." She sighed again. "I memorized sounds. I don't know what I'm actually rapping as I rap it."

Of course she didn't. Jae-sung wondered if she had even written the bars. "Did you write the verses?"

Katie looked annoyed. "I wrote the original verses in English. But last I checked, it's my Korean debut. Mun.light PD translated the gist of what I was saying and took some creative liberties to make it flow and fit the beat."

"That might be the majority of the problem, Noona," said Do-won after her manager once again translated.

So much was lost in translation, and Jae-sung wondered if he was too harsh in his assessment. Maybe Do-won was right.

"Part of performance is knowing something so well that you don't have to think—but you haven't gotten to that point with the lyrics yet *and* you don't really understand what you're rapping as you're rapping it," Do-won continued, clearly in his element. The rapper was an electric performer, his teen years spent participating in dance battles as an underground dancer an obvious advantage to his career as an idol. "You don't feel grounded. You don't embody your words and so you end up sounding fake." At her moue, Do-won rushed to add, "You're not bad, Noona."

Katie took another peek at Jae-sung's face and said wryly, "I think your leader would disagree, Wonnie. But thanks for trying to make me feel less shitty."

"Can you perform it in English?" asked Jae-sung.

"I'd have to look up the original lyrics—I definitely don't have those memorized. And I'm not sure if what I wrote fits the beat and music now. It's been a while and I don't remember what we changed."

"We still have a bit of time before our rehearsal starts," Jae-sung replied. "It doesn't have to be perfect. I just want to test a theory."

After checking with Ha-joon if she had time, Katie shrugged and scrolled through her phone to see if she had the lyrics somewhere. Apparently, she was like Woo-jin and usually wrote a lot of her lyrics in various notebooks, but if she'd sent them to A&R, likely they were also on her phone.

"Ah," she cried, "found it!" She cued the music and tried again, this time with the verse in English instead of in Korean.

Jae-sung and Do-won shared a glance that only people who'd worked together for years could understand. Katie needed work and practice, but she was already so much more believable.

"Switch to the English verses," Jae-sung said. "You need polish and a lot of practice, but until your Korean gets better, you should rap in English—preferably bars you wrote yourself."

"Oh," Katie said softly, her eyes taking on a suspicious sheen. She cleared her throat. "Thanks, guys," she said in Korean. She blinked rapidly as she launched herself at Do-won and then Jae-sung in a fierce (and slightly sweaty) hug. "Thank you so very, very much," she said.

Ha-joon gave Katie a subtle jerk of his head, and she grabbed her things and disappeared out the door with her manager in a flash to her next appointment.

Jae-sung could still feel her heated breath on him and the echo of her squeeze through his body. No, he wasn't further endeared at all. Not one bit.

December 2015

His name is Sting—show some mthafkg respect!!!

- Katie Wu, Twitter, December 2015

Jae-sung entered the tiny studio DOYEN shared with Katie, fully intending to work on the lyrics for one of the B-sides of their next album. It was a compilation of their "War" duology called "War: Aftermath." Because DOYEN had just had their latest comeback in early November for "War: Hell," the second album in the series, Jae-sung had barely had time to write. The past six weeks had been filled with rehearsals, hair and makeup tests, costume fittings, music show appearances in the middle of the night, and press runs for the EP.

He was exhausted—they all were exhausted since their title track "FIGHT 4 U" from "War: Rumblings" finally topped the Korean music shows in April of this year. It had been unexpected, and their first win changed the trajectory of their career.

Everything DOYEN had done since then was ride the wave of the track's success and capitalize on that upswing as much as possible. The grueling K-pop music release schedule was untenable, but Jae-sung and his bandmates were two and a half years past debut and the average lifespan of a male idol group was typically seven years. The prevailing wisdom was to try and hit it big before Jae-sung and his Korean members had to serve their mandatory military service and their group's inevitable decline in popularity.

SB Entertainment was still teetering on the border of bankruptcy, but the success of "FIGHT 4 U" bought them more time. Hopefully with the addition of Katie on their roster, she could ease the heavy burden Jae-sung felt as the leader of DOYEN—even at his tender age of 22 years—for the hardworking staff and teams.

Speaking of Katie, she was already in their shared studio playing Nas's "The Message" on her Taylor Academy 12e-N nylon string guitar. She made a pretty picture on their old leather couch, an open notebook filled with her scrawls at her side. Admittedly, he only knew what sort of guitar it was because she had given him a long lecture about the difference between nylon and steel stringed guitars a few weeks ago. He was still smarting from it.

"Oh, I didn't know you liked Nas," he remarked in English.

Katie cut him a look of such scandalized horror that, for a second, Jae-sung thought he had gotten the song incorrect. But no, that was clearly "The Message."

"I'm playing Sting's 1993 classic 'Shape of My Heart'—which Nas *sampled* for 'The Message' in 1996," she corrected.

Jae-sung had known that—or at least he was pretty sure he had known it was a sample—but also, now who was the snob? He decided to let it slide, except he wanted to needle Katie a bit more.

"Who?"

Katie's back straightened. "WHO?!? WHO?!?" She glared at him, face incredulous. "You're shitting me, right?"

"No," Jae-sung said, totally shitting her. "Not at all."

"You can't be a Nas fan and not know that he sampled Sting. How is this even possible?" Annoyed, Katie ran her hand through her jet black hair.

"What's not possible?" asked Woo-jin in Korean as he entered the room.

Katie flushed even more, throwing flustered hands at Jae-sung and in the air in response.

Woo-jin threw her a smug, shit-eating grin. "How illuminating," he said in English.

His use of English threw Katie off even more, and she narrowed her eyes at the older rapper for a few moments. "Ask Jae-sung," was all she could say, clearly giving up on using any more Korean, and Jae-sung smiled internally. Katie was so easy to rile up—especially with Woo-jin around. It almost wasn't sporting.

"Hyung," Jae-sung asked, "have you ever heard of Sting?"

Never let it be said that Woo-jin didn't catch on quickly. He affected a purposely bewildered expression. "Who?"

Katie's mouth flapped open and just hung there, as if her mouth, too, was flabbergasted. "I hate it here."

Katie got up from the battered couch and tucked her guitar onto the stand in the corner of the studio.

"Y'all fuckers ruined my vibe."

She put on the poofiest jacket Jae-sung had ever seen on a person and looped a thick baby blue scarf around her neck, pulling the jacket hood over her head. He could barely see her—she was drowning in material. She pulled on matching blue gloves and slipped into thick fake fur-lined knee-high boots.

"Are you going on an Antarctic expedition?" Jae-sung asked.

Katie scowled. "My people are from a tropical island!" she justified heatedly. "Besides, I think the heat is still broken in the break room."

"Wait. Taiwan is considered tropical? I thought it was subtropical?" interjected Woo-jin, his cat-like eyes squinted in confusion.

Katie scowled even deeper. If she wasn't careful, she would get wrinkles.

"Just the southern tip is," she said huffily. "And as we all know, 'just the tip' really means the whole thing." Katie flounced out of the studio, and Jae-sung couldn't stop laughing—both at her indignation and her innuendo.

"Oh, you've got it bad, don't you?" Woo-jin asked after he was sure she wasn't coming back. Woo-jin's sly tease knocked all the humor out of Jae-sung.

"What?" Jae-sung bumbled as he realized Katie had left her notebook behind. Though he knew it was an invasion of privacy, he couldn't resist peeking at her lyrics. He loved catching glimpses of how other artists worked.

His eyes caught on a hastily scrawled stanza titled "Profit" with doodled frowny faces and broken hearts in the margin. He scanned the lyrics, idly noting how Katie's "g's" resembled "8's" and that she used ink gel pens instead of ballpoint.

What have you done to me / You've wrecked all my formulas / Switched around integers and lied with statistics / The ledger no longer balances / And now nothing nets / All I see are zeroes / Those worthless placeholders / Where my heart used to be

It was rough and raw and needed to be polished, but Jae-sung felt the bewilderment and fury of how the words hit. He had no idea she wrote lyrics like this. Since Katie's Korean debut was next month, he presumed these lyrics were for a future album, but still. He could not help but wish to hear the finished version.

When Jae-sung finally glanced up, Woo-jin's smirk widened. "If you want me to back off so you have a fighting chance..." His voice trailed off at the implication, and Jae-sung's pride was pricked.

"You'll have to try harder than that, Hyung," he lobbed back. "She won't even look at you. At this rate, Jun hyung will overtake your place as her bias. They're always texting back and forth and sharing inside jokes."

"Ye-jun's her wrecker and that's a wrecker's job: to cause trouble," Woo-jin said disaffectedly. "I'm not worried about my place as her ultimate bias."

"She's not my type anyway," Jae-sung said after a few moments.

"Too many male friends?" Woo-jin knew him too well. "You want to be her whole world?"

Jae-sung felt his face heat up. "Not exactly," he murmured. "She seems like she wouldn't get me. She's so bright and shiny—but you know how I get into my moods. I don't think Katie would get my dark side." He gestured toward Katie's notebook. "These lyrics don't even sound like her."

Woo-jin took the notebook from Jae-sung, quickly scanned the words and then stared at Jae-sung. He shook his head. "You really haven't checked out any of Katie's music, have you?" He dug out his big headphones from his bag and before he slipped them on, he added, "You really should. I think you'd be pleasantly surprised."

Jae-sung didn't know why he felt so chastised since Woo-jin wasn't actually scolding him, but he supposed he had judged Katie with the same harsh lens other people judged him and his group. After Jae-sung had debuted in the idol group, the hip-hop forums had lambasted his and Woo-jin's choices, claiming they'd sold out—that they weren't real rappers, just dolled up idol rappers who couldn't hack it.

He'd always felt that if their haters had given DOYEN's music half a chance, they would have realized that though Jae-sung and Woo-jin had chosen to become idols, they were still rooted in hip-hop. He supposed he could extend Katie the courtesy he desired from others and listen to her music.

He didn't know why his stomach dropped at the thought of getting to know Katie through her art, but his stomach dipped all the same. When Jae-sung thought back to this very moment years later, wondering where it had all gone wrong, he'd realize that it had been fear—fear that Katie would blow him away, that he would fall for her and be irrevocably lost.

He had been right to be afraid.

CHAPTER 2

January 2024

What does it mean to tell the truth? How does one deal with the consequences of doing so? Throughout her gut-wrenching memoir and debut, "Telling a Truth Is a Slippery Slope," Taiwanese American K-pop singer/songwriter Katie Wu details and reinterprets her trauma, meditating on its reverberations through her musical career and personal life. Wu holds no bars and pulls no punches.

> - Los Angeles Times, October 2023

Haunting. This comes as no surprise if you are at all familiar with Katie Wu's oeuvre and music. Like her best albums, her memoir hurts even as it provides healing.

> - Rolling Stone, October 2023

Fittingly titled "Telling a Truth" rather than "Telling the Truth," Katie Wu demonstrates how telling a single truth trig-

*gers an avalanche—not only a landslide of more truths, but
also the collapse of her personal and professional lives.*
- Publisher's Weekly, October 2023

*I spent so long swallowing my words that I forgot how to speak.
I hid, afraid of this ugly thing—this monster—and now, it was
out and I couldn't corral it back in. Was the monster my father
or me? Maybe it was neither; maybe it was we.*
- "Telling a Truth Is a Slippery Slope" (Red Lantern Publishing House, October 2023)

The air was tense between Katie and Alton as they rode the elevator down to SB Entertainment's lobby. "I'm sorry, Mei," Alton said, his face only slightly less smug than usual. He did sound contrite despite the thread of satisfaction in his melodic, tenor voice.

She sighed. "Must you be so petty, Ge?" She leaned against the cool metal panel and closed her eyes.

"He deserves to be put in his fucking place after what he said to you." Alton sounded unusually harsh. "I will never forgive him for what happened after."

"Ah, Alton. You know that wasn't his fault," Katie said quietly. Though she appreciated Alton's loyalty, Jae-sung didn't deserve his anger. "He didn't know. He would have never otherwise—or at least I hope he would have never otherwise."

"Never. Forgive."

Katie believed him, too. Despite how the two of them bickered, Alton was always her fiercest protector. Depending on the day, this immutable fact both comforted and discomfited her.

"Jae-sung's always had it in for me," Alton grumbled.

"Possibly because you tried to get in my pants from the jump."

"How was I supposed to know you were dating?"

"I didn't say he was reasonable," Katie replied wearily, "merely that you wanted to fuck me, and Jae-sung didn't appreciate it."

She sighed again as she recalled this old argument. But instead of disagreeing with Alton, she had argued with Jae-sung about Alton's intentions. As much as Jae-sung had tried to curb his jealousy of her male friendships, he'd never understood why she had so many. Well, it wasn't his problem any more.

Besides, Alton knew where they stood with each other.

Alton scrunched his handsome face in dismay. "He wasn't there! Someone had to save me from that mind-numbing wedding reception!"

"Um, hurtful. I was the emcee," Katie said, making a cursory protest. "And the bride was your cousin!"

Alton was unrepentant. "My least favorite cousin." He wasn't wrong.

"Yeah, Cece is, uh, a piece of work."

"I did back off once you told me you weren't interested," Alton wheedled.

Clad in a gray worsted wool suit, Alton cut a fine figure even while wheedling. Only two years her senior, Alton seemed intimidating to people who didn't know him. To Katie, he was just an annoying older brother.

"Right, as if not being problematic is something to be proud of," Katie scowled in exaggerated displeasure. "Do you want a fucking cookie?"

"I do indeed," he smirked, his velvety brown eyes dancing. "Oh! I should call ahead to the private jet and ask them to provide us some."

"Can you ask them to have something more substantial ready, too?" Now that Katie was leaving her old company's high-rise building, the appetite that had been missing all day returned with a vengeance.

"Of course, love." Alton sent a few texts and by the time they met his driver at the curb, everything was all set. After they settled in the sleek, silver executive S-class and the partition closed, he spoke up again. "You should tell him."

"About what? That we're not actually fucking?" Katie grimaced. She really shouldn't have let Jae-sung draw the incorrect conclusion, but some base part of her was glad for the additional barrier between her and Jae-sung. She didn't deserve his favorable opinion.

"Well, you can have him keep thinking that." Alton's eyes glinted with mischief and then quieted. "I mean, you should tell Jae-sung what happened. Why you left—and the aftermath."

"He can read the book," Katie said flippantly, wanting to talk about anything else.

Alton huffed in exasperation. "You know that isn't enough. Besides, for obvious reasons, you don't actually go into too much detail."

"You seem awfully persistent for someone who doesn't give a shit about Jae-sung."

"It isn't for him. It's for you." The older man squeezed her hand. "I want the satisfaction of him feeling like shit when he finally learns what happened."

"You're a bloodthirsty fuck, aren't you?" Katie observed.

He winked at her, his dark chocolate brown eyes sparkling. "It's part of my charm."

She nodded in solidarity. "Thanks for accompanying me, Alton," she said, changing the subject. "I don't know if I would have been able to make it through without you."

Katie rested her head on his steady shoulder and stared out the window at the Seoul traffic. Whether in Los Angeles, Singapore, Taipei, or Seoul, all traffic was the same. All those cars containing people going about their lives—churning and swirling around her—perhaps lucky enough to return to a loving family and children. She couldn't relate.

Alton kissed her lightly on the crown of her head. "You would have been fine, baby. I'm just sorry I can't join you in March."

"It's alright. I'll be busy recording the Korean audiobook anyway," she replied. "I'll see you for the Singapore leg of the book tour, right? Or one of the other stops? I don't think the Korean publish date is until June. Maybe you can make that media blitz, too."

Katie really hoped so. Alton was always distractingly fun to be around, and he was also her rock. Ha-joon had returned to Korea when her contract with SB Entertainment had ended, and Alton had spent the second half of 2022 with her in Los Angeles. She'd missed him last year when he'd returned to Singapore and knew Seoul, Hong Kong, Shanghai, Beijing, Taipei, or Kaohsiung would be way more exciting if Alton joined up.

She was grateful for the extra time she'd be spending with Alton the next two weeks in Singapore while she recorded the Mandarin translation of her book.

"Of course, Mei," said Alton congenially. "I wouldn't miss the acclaimed author of 'Telling a Truth Is a Slippery Slope' for the world. It's a guaranteed bestseller!"

"You better not buy the books in bulk, Ge. I don't want padded sales—I won't be accused of sajaegi."

"I wouldn't dream of it. When you're on the New York Times Best Sellers list, it won't be because of me," he assured.

Katie paused. "I hit that last week," she admitted shyly.

"No fucking shit!" Alton cheered. "Why didn't you tell me earlier?"

"I was too stressed about the trip to Seoul. It's what allowed me to get better terms at Firefly Publishing. I know they're a small indie publisher in Seoul, but hitting the best seller list made the risk more palatable for them," Katie explained. "Having Ha-joon oppa and your attorneys there advocating for me helped a lot, too."

"It's my honor, love."

"Your cow's, too," she quipped.

"I'd do anything for my cow," Alton agreed. "She's simply bovine."

She winced. "You go too far, sir."

Alton raised his eyebrows suggestively. "Is that how we're playing to-day?" He dropped his voice to a delicious baritone. "Tell me how far we should go, then."

Katie screwed her face up in distaste. "Does this actually work on people?"

"I have a very impressive success rate." He leaned back in the leather seat and grinned. "You're my only strike out."

"Well, I'd hate to ruin a batting average," Katie said dryly, "but we all have our crosses to bear."

"Anytime you want to stop punishing yourself and have someone else do it for fun, let me know, Mei."

"Isn't that incestuous? We're practically family."

Alton shrugged blithely. "Practically, but not actually." He peered at Katie, the full weight of his gaze slamming into her chest. "If I ever thought you'd have me, I would absolutely be yours."

Suddenly, Katie wished for the partition to open so that such a conversation couldn't be possible. She no longer knew how to love—not in the way people expected from a lover. She didn't even believe in it. And though Katie loved Alton, the tectonic plates of her soul had shifted. The ensuing oceanic trench seemed impassable.

"I—"

"Don't," he said, holding up a hand. "Let me have this. Let me have the illusion that it's possible—that it's just out of sight."

Katie stared at her friend—her beautiful, handsome, clever, and stead-fast Alton. She didn't know how she would have survived without him these past few years. He had been a good enough friend before she left Seoul—but after?

After, he had been her lifeline.

She owed him her life—and that was the problem. She always paid her debts, but this was one she could never fully remit. Her soul chafed at the power imbalance.

Except—

Katie canted into Alton's space, lids half-closed and lips hovering above his. She felt more than heard his sharp intake of breath.

"I can give you the illusion if you want, Alton," she murmured. "You can punish me for fun, and we can have a good time until we don't."

Alton cupped a hand behind Katie's neck and nudged her in those last few millimeters. His lips were soft, and he tasted of residual coffee. He smelled of petrichor and cedar, and she lost herself in the play of his mouth reshaping hers.

Katie opened, and he slipped his tongue into her invitation. And then, he was leaning away and brushing his thumb lightly on her bottom lip.

"Just once—I wanted to just once," he whispered.

Katie peered at him through lowered lashes and wished with all her might that she could give him what he wanted.

And then, Alton gently stroked the slope of her nose with an elegant finger and tapped the tip. The town car pulled to a stop. "Time to go home, Mei," he said, voice rough.

January 2016

Taiwanese American pop star Katie Wu thrills fans and critics alike in her hard-hitting Korean debut "Shameless" (SB Entertainment, 2016). Wu's musical fingerprints are all over the mini-album and not only does she wow us with her signature clear and bold vocals, she delights by also rapping on multiple tracks. Her delivery is surprisingly believable and we look for-

ward to how her rapping style will mature in future releases.

Opening with the heartrending breakup song "Reeling," Wu's gorgeous vocals reel us in while obliquely referencing Wu's ex, Taiwanese pop star Johnny Chen. With "Reeling" as the only nod to sentimentality and love, the rest of the album bristles with defiance and electricity. Title track "Shameless" is blatantly unapologetic, reclaiming the insult "shameless" and cleverly inverting the term into a symbol of pride. The anthemic hook stirs the soul—Wu's powerful verse and rap delivery mocking and provoking those who would humiliate her.

- The Korea Herald, January 2016

The entire album is a middle finger to Wu's detractors—and most assuredly, aimed at her famous ex.

- Taipei Times, January 2016

[1] Reeling [2:38]
[2] Shameless [3:24]
[3] Immutable [3:41]
[4] Even the Rock of Gibraltar Succumbs to Time [3:32]
[5] Fall Down 7, Get Up 8 [3:17]

- Track list, "Shameless" (SB Entertainment, 2016)

Cuz baby, I'm shameless (shameless), shameless (shameless)
Muthafuckas keep telling me I'm shameless (shameless)

I'm shameless (shameless), shameless (shameless)
Muthafuckas can't touch me cuz I'm weightless (weightless)
                      - "Shameless" (SB Entertainment, 2016)

Dae-jung loved Katie's Korean debut. It was so brash and ballsy, and she really came out swinging. He especially loved rapping along to her English because she wasn't a particularly fast rapper. What she lacked in speed or finesse, she made up for in power and performance.

Plus, Katie was honestly terrifying on screen. Her M/V for "Shameless" was sexy as hell, and he would be lying if a certain leather harness she wore hadn't appeared in his random daydreams (respectfully, of course). If he was only acquainted with Katie from her music alone and believed the public persona she projected in all her M/Vs and interviews, Dae-jung would for sure be super intimidated.

As it was, he'd tricked her into insulting Akihiro in satoori on such a regular basis that Dae-jung was beginning to think that she was in on the joke and just wanted an excuse to insult Akihiro. She was such a goofball around him and the maknae line—dare he say lovable idiot?—that it was impossible to take Katie seriously. She doted on Dae-jung, Akihiro, and Soo-min, always bringing snacks and asking them for help in Korean slang—especially the swears.

Dae-jung adored her.

So when Katie's debut album sold well, he was so happy and excited that he was gobsmacked when she became a lightning rod for controversy.

Apparently, word got out that Katie had donated a substantial amount to several feminist organizations in Taiwan and Korea. Coupled with the fact that many of her lyrics blatantly illustrated women's empowerment and clearly disdained the fragile egos of men—and perhaps contained thinly veiled criticisms of the church—well, that was all some people needed.

A pastor had denounced Katie as a modern-day Jezebel in a ranty sermon that went viral on Twitter. When Katie found out, she thanked the man and declared on the platform it was the perfect name for her fandom—and thus, the Jezebelles was born. This, of course, stirred up even more of a media frenzy and drew the attention of Korean incels and men's rights activists.

When rape and death threats started streaming in, much to Katie's bewilderment and dismay, management increased her security. Dae-jung thought if the incels had wanted to silence Katie, they had gone about it all wrong. She was now more vocal about her opinions than ever.

SB Entertainment had briefly considered locking down everyone's Twitter accounts because Katie was firing back at haters with ridiculous speed—really, debate was her natural element. But since she was mostly citing studies, academic journals, and other experts—and all in English since her Korean wasn't nearly good enough—and she wasn't going for ad hominem attacks, SB Entertainment had decided it wasn't necessarily a bad thing to be known for being pro-woman and having a highly intelligent artist on its roster.

Besides, they had known who Katie was when they'd approached her after her scandal with Johnny.

Dae-jung had asked around and learned that Katie's ex had gone on a shock jock radio show claiming Katie had traded sexual favors in exchange for winning the Taiwanese reality show "The Singer Songwriter." Since Johnny was Katie's mentor on the show prior to their relationship, many people had believed him.

How else could a non-Taiwanese native have won? How else would a pop star of Johnny's caliber stoop so low as to date a nobody like Katie? It didn't matter how vehemently both Katie or the show denied the allegations, stating that she and Johnny didn't start their romantic relationship until after she'd released her first album. Her reputation was in tatters.

Katie had fought back then, too, at least according to Woo-jin. Woo-jin was the one who had discovered her initially, and he and Ye-jun were the resident experts on Katie and her career. Although funny enough, no one had ever mentioned it when they teased Katie about Woo-jin and Ye-jun being her bias and wrecker, respectively.

Dae-jung needed to decide which would be more amusing: witnessing Katie's continued awkwardness in Woo-jin's presence or watching the tables turn on his two eldest bandmates. He would discuss it with Akihiro. Akihiro would know. Akihiro always knew the best way to shape things.

At any rate, Dae-jung thought the world of Katie. He loved how down to earth she was and how quick she was to laugh and make fun of everything, including herself. Katie was the noona he'd always wanted, and he would fight anyone (if he knew how to fight) should they dare slander her name to his face.

April 2016

Choose your fighter:
○ *Core 'ngrato - Luciano Pavarotti*
○ *X-Factor - Lauryn Hill*

- Katie Wu, Twitter, April 2016

Dae-jung and the rest of his members were busy chatting and congratulating Katie at her album's 100-day celebration dinner. SB Entertainment had rented out a local Chinese restaurant, and Dae-jung was trying to eat as much jjajangmyeon as humanly possible.

Katie's Korean was much improved—or at least she was much better at faking it—and she happily participated in the banter between shoveling jjambbong and palbochae into her mouth, sipping soju and griping that it was a travesty that Chinese restaurants in Korea didn't have beef chow fun.

Katie was mid-sip when Dae-jung heard a man say "Hey, Katie" in English. She dropped her shot glass, spilling liquor all over herself and the round table. Their collective security guards surrounded the familiar-looking man as he said, "Come on, Katie. Call your dogs off."

Katie was busy blotting up the soju with napkins Dae-jung and the rest of DOYEN had immediately offered and replied, "No, I don't think I will, Johnny."

Dae-jung bristled at the interloper, though he looked to his managers and the older members of DOYEN for how he should behave. Despite the men instantly being on high alert, they all remained seated, so Dae-jung forced himself to follow their lead.

"Babe, please," Johnny said, sounding exasperated. As if he had any right to be ruining her celebration.

Katie's face was serenely blank, though Dae-jung could feel the waves of fury spilling from her. "Security-nim, could you please ask this man to leave?" she requested politely in Korean after calling Chang Young-sik, her head of security, over. "He is making me extremely uncomfortable. Please be careful—he is very famous."

Young-sik relayed her request, and Katie and DOYEN's security detail began to politely (and aggressively) herd Johnny toward the exit when he suddenly yelled in English, "I see you're still a bitch. The only time you were tolerable was when you were on your knees."

Dae-jung wasn't fluent in English, but he sure understood that and the implication.

Katie smiled, eyes crinkling in amusement. "Oh, Johnny," she retorted huskily. "I was never on my knees for long. How you must have suffered." Her voice dripped with honey and Dae-jung tried to suppress a shiver.

She acted as if she promptly forgot all about Johnny and addressed the group, her countenance light and airy.

"Everyone, please carry on as if Johnny doesn't exist. Spout gibberish if you must," Katie rasped in Korean, her voice a promise of sin and secrets. Then she directed the full force of her intensity at Ye-jun. The older singer swallowed hard. "Oppa, tell me all about your day but say it like you want to fuck me," she ordered, chuckling dark and smoky. Her face was a sexual proposition.

Dae-jung felt a kick in his gut.

He had been so, so wrong. Katie was terrifying in real life, too.

"Is he gone?" Katie asked.

"He's gone," replied Ye-jun, his entire being resetting to his natural goofy state from the contrived, seductive persona Katie had asked him to take on just a few minutes before.

Jae-sung watched as Katie did the same to her own body. He blinked and she transformed from a languid, sensuous woman, to a young, vulnerable one.

Katie waved Ha-joon over and spoke rapidly in English. "How would Johnny know we were here?" she asked. "Do we have a leak at SB Entertainment? I can't imagine the restaurant would tell Johnny we had reservations here."

"I'm already on it, Katie," replied her manager as he crouched beside her chair. "I'll stay with you tonight just in case he comes by your apartment, too. We should look into moving you somewhere with higher security anyway."

Jae-sung had heard Katie'd received death and rape threats and knew that her security had increased, but he hadn't realized it was to the extent that she had considered moving. Come to think of it, he'd also heard rumors of her team considering no longer accepting fan gifts, too. She was getting a lot of inappropriate and downright scary shit in the mail and it wasn't worth the hassle of dealing with anymore.

"I should thank these insecure men for getting me better digs and more eye candy. One can never have too many strong men hanging around," Katie remarked. "At least half my shit is still in boxes so that should make it easier."

"I'll get the rest of your stuff packed up for you," her manager acknowledged while straightening up.

"Just be careful with my DOYEN merch!" Katie cautioned. "I have a signed 'Misfit Cavalcade Special Edition' that I bought off eBay. It may be the most expensive thing I own outside of my instruments."

"You literally see them all the time. All your albums could be signed," Ha-joon retorted.

Katie protested, "But that's cheating!"

Ha-joon rolled his eyes and Jae-sung felt a surge of solidarity with the older manager. Jae-sung had a hard enough time dealing with his bandmates and their ridiculous banter—especially when it came to Ye-jun sometimes. At least Do-won would help him make peace and often dealt with a lot of the performance-related logistics, leaving more of the liaising between management and their group to Jae-sung as their leader. Ha-joon only had himself, and Katie seemed like more than a handful.

As Ha-joon left with Young-sik to discuss additional security for future events, Katie turned back to her table.

"Sorry about that, guys," she said.

Katie stared at her empty soju glass for a second and then reached for a bottle, first pouring for the others at the table. Akihiro took the bottle from her and filled her glass in return, and she tapped her index finger twice on the table. Katie had once explained it was a gesture of thanks in Chinese tea etiquette, except she had transferred the habit to anytime someone poured her a drink.

"Gan bei!" she cheered in the Mandarin pronunciation. She then turned away from Ye-jun and Woo-jin, downed the shot, and then beckoned to Akihiro to pour her another when he finished his own.

"Are you okay, Noona?" Akihiro asked.

"Nope!" Katie replied with artificial cheer as she downed another shot. Jae-sung had never seen Katie get drunk, but he supposed her album celebration and its ensuing disruption were both good enough reasons to drink more. "But this is my party so Johnny can suck my dick." She sipped on her water, loaded generous servings of rajogi, nanja-wanseu, tangsuyuk, and palbochae on her plate, and then tucked into her shrimp fried rice.

Jae-sung and the rest of his bandmates took their cue from her and resumed their eating and random conversation. It helped that he loved jjajangmyeon, the only reason to go to a Chinese restaurant in his opinion. Katie took one look at how he was heaping his plate full of noodles and made a face of displeasure.

"The Chinese version is better. How can you eat that?" she disdained, wrinkling her nose.

Outraged voices chorused in denials and refusals to entertain Katie's hot take. "You just haven't had really good jjajangmyeon, Noona," Soo-min insisted, his Bambi eyes dripping with sincerity.

"Ah, Soo-min, you're probably right," Katie said gently, and the younger man visibly brightened. "But," she added, her eyes glinting, "noodles shouldn't be sweet." She cackled at how Soo-min seemed to deflate, but then squeezed his arm to show there were no hard feelings. She always softened herself for DOYEN's maknae, but apparently she drew the line at jjajangmyeon.

After that brief exchange, Katie joined in the conversation every now and then, but was mostly quiet and subdued. Thus, Jae-sung didn't notice she had slipped the waiter her card until Ye-jun protested.

"Katie, the company should pay for this!" Ye-jun cried.

She waved his concern away. "I'd rather not remind Song PD that I'm a negative line item just yet," she commented. "I've got it."

Jae-sung did some quick math and knew the dinner for that many people—including alcohol—was likely several million won. He never saw Katie spend large amounts of money and wondered—not for the first time—what her financial situation was. Was Katie floating this meal on debt or was she truly able to afford it?

But if such an expense was no hardship, why was Katie, for lack of a better term, so cheap? So few of Katie's clothes, shoes, and accessories were luxury brands and she dressed as if she was far less successful than she likely was. In fact, half the time, Katie didn't even recognize the brands he and his fellow members wore.

She was so very strange to Jae-sung.

Katie never seemed to care about the expensive purses and gifts her fan sites sent to SB Entertainment headquarters. He'd once seen her direct Ha-joon to sell the luxury items and distribute the proceeds to her team if no one wanted a particular item. She did, however, squeal in delight at a set of super cheap rubber pig cell phone grips, called them her porcine children, and named them Market, Home, Roast Beef, None, and Wee.

She'd even made sure to post pics of the piggies all over social media much to the delight of her fans—who started calling themselves "Samgyeopsals" or the "Pork Bellies"—a play on her fandom name "Jezebelle."

Jae-sung told himself that Katie's money was none of his business and, instead, thanked her for paying for dinner. As her party was about to leave,

Jae-sung noted how she tucked herself into the side of Young-sik. She was so small compared to that huge man, it completely startled Jae-sung.

All this time, Katie had taken up so much space that when she suddenly did not, Jae-sung found that he hated it.

He found himself wondering exactly what Johnny had done to her.

May 2016

Did you see Katie's reaction to the Tsunami M/V? kekekekekeke her horror at King Ja$e's hair and shriek at Blond!Jun thumbing his mouth!!

- Twitter user, May 2016

It was her wails at LAMBENT's "let's get wet" for me. Same, girl, same.

- Twitter user, May 2016

how desperate are they to build katie's youtube channel?

- Twitter user, May 2016

Stop giving us CHIMERA a bad name—we stan a stan! They're at the same label and are all friends—CTFO.

- Twitter user, May 2016

Jae-sung and his members were in the middle of their cramped studio, crowding around a tiny screen watching questionable porn on his old laptop. The man in the video was flat on his back and the woman was seated on his dick while facing the man's feet, her legs spread-eagled in the air, making a wide V.

He wasn't sure why he and his six bandmates were acting as if they were a group of hormonal junior high school kids. Jae-sung's only excuse was that he wasn't thinking because he was exhausted. Between the comeback for their latest album and preparing for KCON NYC at the end of June, Jae-sung was run ragged and, for some reason, clicked through on a link a friend had sent him on Kakao and here they were.

He wasn't even turned on.

"Jesus, guys," he heard Katie's amused voice say from over his shoulder. He slammed his laptop shut. "Oh, don't stop on my account—although, blurred bits? Use a VPN at least. This is just sad."

"We're so sorry, Katie," Jae-sung sputtered as he reluctantly turned to face her. Even dressed casually in a fitted gray UCLA T-shirt and navy joggers, she was stunning. "Please don't report us for sexual harassment."

Akihiro and Soo-min covered their faces with their hands, clearly dying of embarrassment. Ye-jun's ears flamed, but his face remained impressively impassive like his remaining bandmates.

"Oh, yeah. I suppose I could." Katie pretended to think, her pretty eyes flashing mischief. "I think the only thing I would report you for is bad taste. That poor woman looked uncomfortable—although her core strength is goals. Surely, you boys realize that's highly unrealistic. No one wants to fuck like that. Not a single person."

"Your Korean has really improved, Katie," praised Ye-jun randomly.

Jae-sung whirled around just in time to see Katie preen at the older man's compliment. "It's a work in progress," she replied.

Now that some of Jae-sung's panic had subsided, he realized Ye-jun was right. Katie had markedly improved.

"No one watches porn for realism, Katie-yah," drawled Woo-jin, his cunning eyes gleaming with predatory delight. "Pretty sure it's for the angles."

Katie's smugness faltered a bit as it always did around Woo-jin, but she pushed ahead. "What's the point? It's tragically pixelated."

Woo-jin dragged his gaze up and down her body as he crooked the corner of his mouth. "Some of us have excellent imaginations."

Katie rolled her eyes. "Some of us don't lack for partners."

Woo-jin snorted and his voice was so low, Jae-sung could barely catch what he said next. "How sad for you that your imagination isn't necessary even then."

Jae-sung felt Woo-jin's words explode, heavy and full of promise. Katie sucked in a breath. He hated himself for wondering what it would be like to affect her bodily the way Woo-jin seemed to on a regular basis. Her eyes flashed, but as always, she retreated in Woo-jin's presence—much to the older man's obvious amusement. He only had a year on Katie and Jae-sung, but Woo-jin had a way of carrying himself that made Jae-sung feel far younger than his 22 years.

"My loss, then. Clearly." Katie shifted her gaze from Woo-jin to the rest of the group, scraped out an "I'll let you seven get back to, uh, group bonding" and escaped the studio.

"What the fuck, Hyung?" groaned Akihiro, his numerous earrings and necklaces tinkling as he dramatically sank onto their battered couch. "You're lucky Noona is so easy-going. I thought I was going to die of embarrassment."

Dae-jung plopped down next to Akihiro and poked him in the ribs. "You're usually more open about sex than this, Aki-yah. I don't think I've seen you this shy in a long time."

"We were just standing there like idiot kids seeing porn for the first time," Akihiro protested, his plush lips pursing into a fetching pout. "It wasn't even good porn. Now she's going to tease me forever about my bad taste—and it's all Jae-sung hyung's fault."

Jae-sung stared at his younger members incredulously. "That's what you're worried about? That Katie will think you have bad taste in porn?"

Do-won moved from where he'd been leaning against the wall, threw himself on the other side of Akihiro and leaned over, squishing the vocalist's cheeks. "Aw, poor Aki-yah," Do-won cooed in a sugary, sweet voice. "Does my dongsaeng wish his pretty noona walked in on something truly filthy so she can know he's all grown up?"

Akihiro pushed Do-won away with an indignant "fuck off, Hyung," and the rapper cackled in delight.

Jae-sung didn't know whether he was relieved that his bandmates weren't truly upset or if he was worried there was something seriously wrong with them.

"Seriously, though," said Ye-jun, his clear tenor voice cutting through Jae-sung's whirling thoughts. "We really did luck out that Katie is a good sport about these matters and that we're good friends. If it had been Gyuri noona, we would be in big trouble, Jae-sung-ah."

Na Gyuri was the other female soloist at SB Entertainment, and though she was friendly with DOYEN, she absolutely would have reported them to management. It wouldn't matter that Gyuri hadn't put out a new album in a few years. She was older than them, good friends with management, and was considering going into their A&R department. Since proceeds from FL3X, the girl group Gyuri had been in, had floated SB Entertainment just enough so that DOYEN could train, she had a lot more power and influence than a low-selling artist normally would have.

Well, that and the fact that subjecting co-workers to pornography at work was violating a lot of rules set in place to keep people safe.

Jae-sung hung his head. "I'm sorry, guys," he said. "I really fucked up."

His youngest bandmate shuffled over and gave him a side hug. "We all watched along with you," said Soo-min gently. "Any one of us could have stopped it or left. It's not all on you."

Jae-sung openly stared at Soo-min. "That's surprisingly mature, Soo-min-ah."

"Someone has to be, Hyung," Soo-min grinned, his bright eyes holding entire galaxies. "Especially when you're all trying to corrupt me. What would I tell my mother?"

"YAH! You're so full of shit, Minnie!" exclaims Ye-jun as he flapped his arms about. "Don't think we don't know about your hidden porn collection on the shared computer at home."

"Maybe Aki should play that next time Noona's around. She'll finally look twice at him once she realizes he's grown some ball hair," quipped Do-won.

Jae-sung snorted in laughter along with the rest of his band members. He let their voices wash over him as his mind wandered back to Katie.

Ye-jun was right. Katie really was very open about sex with them—even though she only looked fondly on the younger members. She had some weird rule about not dating people who were younger than her—even if they were ten days younger than her like Jae-sung was!

That didn't explain why Katie never gave into the indisputable sparks between her and Woo-jin. The rapper was a year older than her and they clearly had chemistry and a lot in common. It was baffling, although Jae-sung conceded that likely, she was too busy to consider anything at the moment.

And while Katie was friends with his bandmates, they only overlapped briefly at the office. After all, he and his members were still promoting their latest album and Katie was supposed to be working on the Chinese version of her Korean debut in between dance classes and more rap lessons to get her skills up to par. As far as Jae-sung knew, Katie didn't know many people beyond their staff and colleagues.

He wondered if she was lonely.

July 2016

Los Angelessssssss I AM IN YOUUUUUUUUUUU!!
                                        - Katie Wu, Twitter, July 2016

Dae-jung was still struggling with jet lag and trying not to doze off in the back of the SUV when a thump shook him alert. The vehicle veered sharply to the right and he thought he caught a "shit" from their manager Sung-mo, who was driving.

"Is everything okay, Hyung?" Jae-sung asked from the middle row as their manager tried to pull over safely to the side of the road.

"It's probably a flat tire," Katie said. She was riding with them to save on space and car rentals. "LA's roads are notoriously shitty."

Sung-mo parked, turned on the hazards, and went out to examine what was going on. After a few minutes, he opened the door and said, "It's a flat tire. I have to call the KCON staff to tell them we'll be really late."

"Does the rental car come with roadside service?" Katie asked.

Sung-mo shook his head. "No. It was a rip-off to add."

"Ah, well, we'll have to call a tow truck and see how long it will take for them to get here—but it's LA," she said. "We'll probably have to wait at least forty-five minutes to an hour—especially since we do not belong to a roadside assistance company or have insurance."

"We're going to be really late and miss soundcheck," Sung-mo said, frowning.

Dae-jung watched as Jae-sung texted the group chat the band had with their managers. He could only imagine how poor Do-won was taking this setback. Do-won wasn't their official leader, but in terms of performance and keeping on schedule, his word was law. Though Dae-jung felt bad about the situation, he also knew there was nothing he could do about it. He might as well enjoy the bonus "free" time.

"Are we too far to walk? Can the other SUVs pick us up after they drop everyone else off?" asked Jae-sung.

"Oh, we're still at least thirty to forty minutes out," Katie said, "assuming there's no traffic."

"How do you know, Noona?" Soo-min asked, curious. "I used to live here and I didn't know that."

"Technically, you lived in Torrance, Minnie. Besides, you lived here as a child," she replied. "I lived here when I went to UCLA. It's different when you live somewhere as an adult. I had a car and I drove all over LA with my friends."

"That explains why I keep finding things familiar but in a vague sort of way. There's something about the light here, though. There's nothing like the California sun," Soo-min observed thoughtfully. "I guess I didn't get a chance to visit much when we were trainees," he added softly.

"At least you'll get to stop by your house for a night, right?" Dae-jung asked while patting their youngest comfortingly on the back. Poor Soo-min. Sometimes, Dae-jung forgot that Soo-min saw his family the least out of his bandmates. He had become a trainee so young. It was in great part why they doted on him so much. Dae-jung looked over at Sung-mo who seemed to be on hold and looked super annoyed. "Looks like Hyung is going to be a while."

Katie sighed. "I guess it's a good thing my hair is styled in braids today," she grumbled. She unbuckled her seatbelt, got out of the car, and shrugged off her white denim jacket to reveal the black sequinned triangle bikini top she had on underneath.

Dae-jung concentrated on keeping his eyes on her face, though he was sorely tempted to take more of her in. It seemed wrong to do even though she would eventually be performing on stage in the very same clothes.

"Katie, what are you doing?" croaked Jae-sung. His leader was so obvious.

"Can't get the stage outfit dirty now, can I?" she retorted. "Good thing these are camo pants. Everyone out of the car," she ordered. "I'm changing a tire."

Dae-jung's eyes widened but he obediently followed Katie out. She popped the back of the SUV, took some bags out of the trunk, and lifted the cargo-floor cover.

"They said it would be at least an hour before they could get here," Sung-mo said as he joined them behind the SUV. "What are you doing, Katie?"

"Noona's going to change the tire," said Dae-jung excitedly. He had never seen anyone change a tire.

"You sure you can do it?" asked his manager.

"I haven't changed one in a few years, but I should be able to. If I can't, we're no worse off than before," Katie replied reasonably.

And with that, she removed the car jack and instructed Soo-min to get out the tire iron and tire. She turned off the vehicle, grabbed the manual, pulled the parking brake, found a few large stones by the freeway and stabilized the tires with them. She then efficiently and effectively changed out the tire for a spare, occasionally asking Soo-min to help her loosen or tighten the more difficult lug nuts. He practically glowed when she praised him.

The whole process took about half an hour and by the time Katie carefully lowered the jack and replaced all the items, forty minutes had passed. She was a bit covered in grease, extremely sweaty, and her hair was attempting to escape her loose French braids.

Katie had never seemed hotter.

"Alright, guys. Hopefully that worked," she said as everyone got back in the SUV.

They ended up being about ten minutes late—but that was still better than if they had waited for the tow truck. Plus, Katie had saved the company a lot of money—and the company needed all the help it could get.

Though DOYEN's popularity was steadily rising and they were making more money, they had been in the hole for so long that it would take more than a year of steady sales to right the ship. Besides, in a company that had struggled for so long, it would be foolish to act as if they had more spending room than they did—or at least that's what Dae-jung heard Woo-jin and Jae-sung discussing late at night in their apartment.

Woo-jin, who had grown up poor, was eager to spend what meager spoils they had, unsure if he'd ever have another chance. Jae-sung, who had grown up in far cushier surroundings than either Woo-jin or Dae-jung, cautioned them to save their money just in case. Jae-sung could have saved his breath; he didn't understand how Woo-jin—and to a lesser extent, Dae-jung—almost never had nice things growing up. The burning envy and desire to signify "making it" was far greater than Jae-sung could imagine from his safe little suburb.

Dae-jung distinctly remembered the smirk on Woo-jin's face when he walked into the apartment after buying a Rolex Submariner watch. He smiled at the memory as he stared out the SUV, determined to make sure he and his hyung could buy many more expensive watches in the future.

A few hours later, Dae-jung and his members were resting in their company's designated area, a double white tent acting as their greenroom. He was decompressing after a particularly passive-aggressive interview conducted by a Korean American rapper. The guy obviously had a chip on his shoulder.

It wouldn't have mattered to Dae-jung much, but he saw how Woo-jin and Jae-sung kept up their polite facades while deflecting the barbs lobbed at them by the gyopo. It wasn't fair at all, but Dae-jung understood why his hyungs swallowed the indignities. Just let this rapper go back to Korea and see how their variety show hosts would treat him.

Dae-jung was lounging on an uncomfortable folding chair and marveling at how the dry heat in LA was so much more bearable than the humidity in Seoul when Katie entered the tent, practically dripping with sweat from her performance. Dae-jung's interest was piqued when he realized a pretty Asian woman he didn't recognize was with Katie. He would have noticed her anyway since she was a new face, but the woman was also emitting a very loud noise at a very high frequency.

"Guys, this is Ellie, my old college roommate," Katie said in English, only slightly wincing. "Ellie, this is the guys. Please stop screaming."

"Oh my god—I'm so excited to meet you all—I love you guys and I'm the reason Katie started listening to you—so really, Katie, you should thank me for everything I've done for your career—"

"Oh, wow. You're not chill at all. Jesus."

Dae-jung didn't want to go out on a limb, but he got the sense that Ellie was a lot of fun if not also easily excitable. He also found her a little hard to understand because she was speaking so fast and without any sort of discernible sentence structure.

"—and you're welcome, you bitch—oh my god, I swear I'm not a terrible person—I think you're all so talented and I LOVE YOU, 1DEL1GHT!"

Do-won beamed, said a bright "hello," and beckoned for Ellie to sit next to him. If possible, Ellie got even more excited. Dae-jung noted that Do-won didn't seem to mind the screeching at all—most likely due to Ellie's very short skirt and low-cut top. He didn't want to jinx things, but he was pretty sure that Ellie seemed amenable to whatever the rapper might have in mind—and since she was Katie's friend, Dae-jung was pretty confident that Do-won could make it happen.

Katie took one calculated look at Do-won and Ellie and grabbed a chair by Dae-jung. "I regret this life choice already," she groaned.

"How was your performance, Noona?" Dae-jung asked her. He had caught glimpses of her rehearsal, but because of the interview, could not attend her set.

Katie took a swig of water and held it to her neck to cool herself off. Dae-jung couldn't help but follow the bead of condensation dripping down her chest. He looked away as his pants suddenly felt too tight.

"Oh, it went well. American audiences are so fun," Katie mused. "And I got to see a bunch of my friends in the crowd so that was great, too."

"Will you get a chance to see them on this trip?" Akihiro asked, joining the conversation. "We had fun meeting your friends when they visited Seoul. You know a lot of people, Noona!"

Dae-jung thought back to last month when several of her male friends met up with her in Seoul and she took everyone out for dinner and drinks. He and Akihiro had begged her friends to tell embarrassing stories about her, and boy, had they delivered. His favorite had been the one about Katie breaking her arm trying to impress a guy by jumping up to grab onto a balcony and then failing to hang on.

Katie had idly commented that she only broke her bones in front of guys she crushed on. That had led to them finding out how she'd broken her foot in college trying to jump over a couch to once again impress a guy she had liked. Dae-jung had asked if she would end up breaking a bone in front of Woo-jin and then everyone, including Katie, had cracked up.

"How was your interview with K-Netic?" Katie asked after acknowledging that she did, indeed, know a lot of people in Los Angeles. Dae-jung fell back into the present. "Was he cool?"

Dae-jung debated how much he should share, but Akihiro beat him to the punch. "He was a dick, Noona," Akihiro said, his normally warm brown eyes fierce and furious. "He kept trying to imply that we were just a bunch of wannabes—Jae-sung hyung and Woo-jin hyung especially."

Katie sucked on her teeth. "He did what?"

"Yeah, he was trying to make it seem like he was joking, but we could tell he wasn't," Dae-jung added.

"How unfortunate," she said somewhat sadly. "I really liked his music. What an insecure little man." Katie seemed as if she was about to add another thought when Do-won cackled loudly.

All their heads whipped toward Do-won and Ellie, and Dae-jung tried to suppress a grin at Do-won collapsing in laughter over Katie's friend. From anyone else, it would have seemed calculated, but Do-won was effusive like that, always falling over people as he cracked up.

"No fair Wonnie hyung is the only one who gets to meet a pretty girl," Akihiro complained.

Katie flicked water at the younger man. "My friends are out of your league, baby," she teased.

"As if they'd be my first noona," Akihiro retorted. "Noonas love me."

She leaned forward, squeezed one of Akihiro's cheeks, and crooned. "What's not to love, Aki-yah? You're adorable! Noonas love to cuddle cute babies!"

Dae-jung laughed at Akihiro's scowl. "Ah, Aki-yah," he said slyly. "You know how we are to Noona—she only has eyes for Woo-jin hyung. She can't properly appreciate us at all."

It was true, too. Dae-jung knew he was a good-looking guy—they all were—but he knew better than to imagine even a hookup with Katie when she looked at Woo-jin with an equal mix of terror and lust.

"What?" Katie squawked, her limbs gesticulating in protest. "I—"

Woo-jin conveniently walked by and stopped in front of their group. "Katie, do you think these jeans look okay on me?" he asked as he turned around in his tight, ripped denim.

"I—"

Even under all her stage makeup, Dae-jung could see Katie's telltale blush.

True to form, he and Akihiro pounced immediately on this weakness. "Noona loooooooooooovvveessss how your ass looks, Hyung!" cried Akihiro, getting his revenge. "Bend over so she can get a proper eyeful!"

Dae-jung took advantage of the moment and smacked Woo-jin's ass. "So juicy! So bouncy!"

Much to his delight, Katie stood abruptly. "Ellie, I have to get to my fan meet. Did you want to come with?"

Ellie reluctantly got up from beside Do-won and said, "Sure! I would think you'd want to continue staring at Lambent's ass though—don't act like you haven't discussed it in excruciating detail with me! Something about it being perfect to squeeze and bite?"

Ellie's comment set off another round of laughter while Katie glared at her friend's faux innocent look. "Traitor," Katie growled, grabbing Ellie by the arm and bodily dragging her out of the SB Entertainment tent.

"Bye, boys!" Ellie called as she waved her delicate fingers while leaving.

Dae-jung loved America.

*TFW: you look at your amazing friends and wonder when they
turned into adults with real jobs and you're still just an idiot*
                                    - Katie Wu, Twitter, July 2016

"Park Jae-sung! Lee Ye-jun! Hwang Woo-jin! Jung Do-won! Aki jjang!
Park Dae-jung! Choi Soo-min! DOYEN JJANG!"

Jae-sung poked his head out into the carpeted hallway of the hotel only
to see Katie, Ellie, and two more Asian women staggering toward Katie's
room. He was suddenly thankful his company had reserved the entire floor
for their artists and staff. It wouldn't do to have rumors flying about how
a DOYEN member was having an orgy or something equally salacious.

"Shhhhh!" Katie admonished loudly. "You'll wake everyone up, Ellie!"

"But I wanna wake up Do-won's little 'Wonnie' and make him big!!"

"Ellie!" admonished her friend with the pixie cut.

"Oh my god, Ellie! He's an infant! An actual child!" Katie complained.

"Just because you have some stupid rule about not fucking anyone
younger than you doesn't mean the rest of us are dumb," Ellie yelled,
clearly drunk. "I don't know what your excuse about not hopping on
Woo-jin's dick is though—he's older than you."

"I learned my lesson with Johnny," Katie said quietly, almost too low for
Jae-sung to hear. "I don't shit where I eat anymore."

Ellie's face crumpled in remorse. "Ah, fuck, I'm sorry, Katie."

"It's fine," Katie mumbled, still rifling through her pockets.

Katie's other friend wasn't having it either. "Jesus, what is the fucking
hold up?"

"I can't find my keycard," she said. "I swear I had it when we left—it's
like I'm channeling Jae."

Well, that was rude.

"Katie," Jae-sung found himself saying. The four of them jumped, all startled. "I was going to offer you my room until you said that."

"Oh," Katie said. "Um, that would be super nice of you if you did, though, Jae-sung."

"We have snacks and alcohol!" offered her friend with the pixie cut.

"And Katie will buy you dinner," added Ellie, her eyes glittering with trouble. "A fancy one—when you're back in Seoul—if you can get Do-won to join us."

Jae-sung grinned. Do-won owed him big time. "Done."

Ellie pumped a triumphant fist and he opened his door wider so the four women could traipse into his room.

"Jae-yah, it's a mess in here. How can we sit anywhere?" Katie nagged as she took in his standard issue hotel room with double queen beds as he busily texted Do-won and the rest of DOYEN.

"If you don't like it, the outside is through the door," he replied.

"Hmph," Katie grumbled. "This is Sarah," she said, pointing to her friend with the pixie cut, "and this is Angela. And you already met Ellie."

Jae-sung nodded and said, "Nice to meet you, Sarah and Angela. Good to see you again, Ellie. Wonnie is on his way."

"AAAAYYYYY!!!" Ellie cried, throwing him a high-five. "If you ever need a favor, Jae-sung, I've got you! Katie's got my number."

"How did you end up without a roommate, Jae?" Katie asked as she plopped on one of the queen beds, her voice only slightly slurred. "Did you win rock, paper, scissors?"

Jae-sung ignored the twinge of desire at seeing Katie sprawled on a mattress. "Nah," he answered. "Soo-min went home tonight. He'll be back tomorrow, but he wanted to spend time with his parents."

Katie threw an arm over her eyes. "It must have been so hard on him to leave for Korea on his own as a kid. I can't believe his parents let him go so young."

"We looked out for him," Jae-sung reasoned.

"You were also a child!" she exclaimed indignantly, abruptly sitting up and staring intently at Jae-sung. He resisted the urge to gulp. "At least I was 17 when I left for college. Still too young, but almost an adult. Minnie was a baby and so far away from home." She sniffled, her pretty eyes taking on a suspicious sheen.

"Are you...crying?" Jae-sung asked incredulously.

"Katie gets soft when she drinks," explained Angela as she sank onto the bed next to Katie. "It's the only time we can get anything resembling human emotions from her."

Sarah threw herself down on Katie's other side. "You make her sound like a robot," she complained. "Just because she has self-control and isn't messy like the rest of you bitches."

"Right, because Johnny wasn't messy," Angela sniped back.

Angela tossed her long black hair and examined her bloodred nails before grabbing a bag of gummy candies from a plastic grocery bag. She stretched out her hand to offer Jae-sung some and he politely declined. He did not enjoy the way the candies stuck to his teeth.

"Johnny can fuck all the way off," Ellie contributed from her place by the hallway mirror. She was touching up her makeup and putting on a slutty lipstick color. Jae-sung wasn't sure how a lipstick could be slutty, but this one sure was. "Katie was too good for him. His dick game was bad, too."

Sarah and Angela guffawed. "That is not what Katie told us and you know it," Sarah corrected.

"Any middle-aged man who has to pressure innocent girls into doing shit they don't want to automatically has bad—"

"I'm literally right here," Katie piped in before Ellie could finish her sentence. "Besides, without Johnny, I wouldn't have had the opportunity to work at SB Entertainment and then what would Jae-sung do without the pleasure of my company. Now tell me how pretty and talented I am."

"Yeah, yeah. I'm pretty sure you could have worked with DOYEN at some point even without Johnny fucking up your career," Ellie said, sitting after finally being satisfied with her appearance.

Katie's friend was right. SB Entertainment had started making overtures to Katie even before the scandal had hit, but before Jae-sung could say so, Angela added, "Sorry for bringing him up, Katie. No more rehashing old news in front of company."

Jae-sung felt an unexpected sting at Angela's comment. He wasn't close to Katie, but neither was he a stranger. He wanted to think of himself as a friend—after all, would strangers offer their rooms in the middle of the night? He chose not to dwell on his feelings and nodded his thanks when Sarah handed him a cold bottle of Pacifico. He easily twisted the cap off and poured the Mexican beer down his throat.

"You are forgetting the most important part," Katie complained. "Someone tell me how hot I am!" She'd clearly picked up some of Ye-jun's antics.

"You're so needy," Ellie said fondly even as Sarah obliged Katie by saying, "You're the prettiest. I'd leave my girlfriend for you."

"At least make it believable! Who in their right mind would leave Melissa for me?" Katie chuckled. The four women laughed good-naturedly.

The rest of the night got blurry as Akihiro and Dae-jung showed up with Do-won—who really was only there long enough to say hello and leave with Ellie. Jae-sung quietly watched and finished his beer, moving onto tequila as Katie and her friends danced and drank with Akihiro and Dae-jung to '90s pop music. Though Katie had beckoned for him to join them a few times, he was content to just watch as Katie and her friends got more and more inebriated.

By the time Ha-joon showed up with new key cards, Akihiro was actively shoving his entire tongue down Angela's throat and Dae-jung was far too snug (and smug) in between Katie and Sarah as the three of them continued grinding to Nelly Furtado and Timbaland's "Promiscuous" in a progressively more suggestive manner as the beer loosened inhibitions and limbs.

Ha-joon took in the scene as he passed the key cards to Jae-sung in the doorway. "Well, isn't this wholesome," Ha-joon said.

"Is that what we're calling this?" Jae-sung quipped. "I think wholesome left the chat about an hour ago."

"Do any of you need condoms?"

Jae-sung eyed his and Katie's friends with a sobering eye. "I guess it never hurts to have some just in case. Not for me, of course. I mean—"

Ha-joon rolled his eyes. "Please, I don't need details." He huffed as he pulled a plastic bag from his bomber jacket pocket and handed a flat cardboard box to Jae-sung. Jae-sung caught a muttered "What was the point of me getting her so many new key cards?" as Ha-joon made his way back to the door.

Jae-sung walked back to the bed and sipped on more Jose Cuervo even as he winced at the burn. Although he knew he'd likely have a lot more fun if he drank more, he didn't know Katie's friends well enough to be so uninhibited. Katie trusted them, but he had more to lose than she did if pictures of their night leaked.

"Scoot over, Jae," grumbled Katie as she stumbled toward him. "The room is all bendy."

Jae-sung moved over as she collapsed face first onto the pillow. Next thing he knew, her friends were shaking Katie lightly, giving her bleary goodbyes as they slipped out of his room super early in the morning. Katie immediately fell back asleep next to him, and Jae-sung fell back into a deep slumber a few breaths later.

Well, that could have gone better. (Could've gone worse, too.)
                                    - Katie Wu, Twitter, July 2016

Jae-sung woke up to a raging erection and someone soft and warm in his arms. His brain scrambled to recollect last night's events and after several laggy moments, he realized he was holding Katie. He vaguely recalled her whimpering in her sleep after her friends had left. When he realized he had hogged all the blankets, he'd felt bad and had pulled her into his embrace so he could warm her. Katie had settled shortly after and had gone limp almost immediately.

And now, now she was snuggled against him, and her ass was pressed against his dick, which explained why he was hard and—oh, fuck—Katie was awake. He could tell because she had suddenly stiffened—and no, that was not a dick joke.

"I know you're awake, Katie," he said, his voice low and growly.

Katie expelled a little gasp and he felt her relax just a little, as if she was wishing to press back into him—but that would be crazy talk—and then she did. She went pliant and shifted so her ass brushed his dick even more.

It was too much.

He flipped her over onto her back.

Katie closed her eyes and held out her hand in the universal signal for "stop."

"I'm gonna barf."

Welp. Jae-sung scampered off Katie and thankfully, located the waste-basket one of her friends had helpfully placed next to the bed. "Here you go, Katie," he said as she proceeded to vomit.

It was just as well. No good could come of fucking her.

K-pop singer and UCLA alum Katie Wu performs a surprise set for advanced music seminar students with friend and fellow alum, film composer Tony Vu.

- The Daily Bruin (July 2016)

For many Asian Americans, going back to Asia to pursue music or acting is a no-brainer. Yes, there are cultural and linguistic barriers—but at least we have a shot. In America, we're invisible.

- Katie Wu, The Daily Bruin (July 2016)

Jae-sung had thought Katie would address what had almost happened between them, but he'd thought wrong. As it was, after she threw up and rinsed her mouth, Katie took one look at her reflection, shrieked, and promptly ran back to her room.

His dick had long gone soft, and now, his brain was in overdrive. Was Katie into him? Would she have fucked him if she hadn't been so hungover? What did it mean? And did it mean anything other than she had woken with a dick pressing into her ass and had wanted to press back?

If he was honest with himself, Jae-sung knew that he rarely thought too much about who he was fucking. If Katie had been willing, he absolutely would have fucked her and enjoyed himself. He held no romantic notions about their industry. Though people thought it would be easy for idols to find willing partners—and that was true to a certain extent—the difficulty lay more in discretion and coordinating schedules long enough to trust someone well enough to date.

Jae-sung was far more familiar with hooking up with people who worked in the industry due to ease of access and similar scheduling difficulties.

Katie working at his company only made life easier for him—especially when he knew it was more in her interest to keep things quiet. The casual sexism of the entertainment business was awful, but it did benefit him, so Jae-sung rarely protested it, except in theory.

After he'd showered and eaten breakfast, Jae-sung checked the group chat with his managers about plans for their day off. Sung-mo had mentioned Katie was doing a Q&A with the music department at UCLA, as well as performing a small set with live instruments, and did any of them want to tag along?

Jae-sung found himself replying in the affirmative along with Woo-jin. He told himself it was because he wanted to check out the famous UCLA campus and wanted to support Katie. It had nothing to do with how she'd felt in his arms and how much he wanted to get to know her.

No matter how long it's been since I've last visited, UCLA is always under construction. Go, Bruins!

        - Katie Wu, Twitter, July 2016

Best "Caruso" cover?
◯ *Luciano Pavarotti*
◯ *Metallica*

        - Katie Wu, Twitter, July 2016

Katie was amazing. Jae-sung had known, of course, that she could play a lot of instruments. He'd seen her playing the keyboard and the guitar at the studio, but he had never seen her play anything close to a live set. And Katie—she came alive.

She'd come in about two hours early for a quick run-through with her friends—which, considering they hadn't played these arrangements of her songs together before, Jae-sung was fascinated that they meshed as well as they did. According to Ha-joon, several of them were session musicians and the fact that Katie could keep up with them was impressive.

He watched as Katie performed her songs and then answered complex musical questions from senior music students. Some of them were clearly trying to show off or trip her up, but for the most part, the students were respectful and curious.

It helped that Katie was so diplomatic and learned in her answers. It was obvious she knew her shit, both about the Taiwanese and Korean music industries and the specialized aspects of producing music. She spoke at length about how her art was supported by highly technical musical theory, but also how art did not necessarily require high musical literacy. She preferred the former, but cautioned it was easy to slip into snobbery and sophistry.

Katie cited Tchaikovsky, Debussy, and Chopin as her main classical music influences, adding that she had a soft spot for super sad opera arias. She casually referenced famous composers—and was clearly familiar with their body of work. She drew modern allusions to bands like Tool, Metallica, and Radiohead, and mentioned that she hadn't even touched on her alternative, hip-hop, and pop influences—her brain was just so sexy.

How had Jae-sung never realized what an agile musical mind Katie possessed—the way she connected all sorts of genres and blurred boundaries? He wondered at what sort of music she would create in the future and found himself curious as to how she approached her lyrics and if she did other types of written art forms, too.

"Did you have a good time, guys?" Katie asked from the middle row of the SUV on the way back to the hotel.

"I did, Katie," Jae-sung said, "thanks for having us along."

"Of course! I'm glad I could show you the Sculpture Garden and where I used to go to classes," she enthused, turning around and leaning over the back of her seat to look at him more closely. "Too bad we didn't have time to check out the botanical gardens—I think you would've really enjoyed them, Jae."

"Maybe next time."

Katie hummed happily. "Maybe! What about you, Woo-jin?"

"It was really cool," agreed Woo-jin. "Your friend, Tony, was really cool, too. He was explaining to me how the Vietnamese film industry worked."

Katie giggled lightly. "He has a boyfriend already," she teased Woo-jin. "They're probably going to get married."

Woo-jin just rolled his eyes and leaned back against his seat nonchalantly. "Just because I also like men doesn't mean I am always on the prowl, Katie."

"Oh, I wasn't—I'm sorry, Woo-jin oppa," she stammered, chastened.

"I'm just fucking with you, Katie," the older rapper drawled. "Besides, I'm seeing someone right now anyway."

"Still," Katie doggedly continued. "I didn't mean anything by it, but I can see how I could have hurt you."

Jae-sung had to give it to Katie. She was a lot quicker to apologize about misunderstandings than he had ever been. He wasn't proud of how he'd initially reacted to Woo-jin's sexuality, but after Jae-sung had gotten his head out of his ass, Woo-jin had helped him work out some of his internalized homophobia. It was thanks to Woo-jin that Jae-sung was better equipped to deal with Dae-jung and his other queer friends.

It had also helped when Woo-jin stated in no uncertain terms that Jae-sung was emphatically not his type. It still shamed Jae-sung sometimes at how relieved he'd felt, but he tried to do better.

"Don't worry about it," Woo-jin said, clearly wanting to change the subject.

Katie sent Woo-jin one more glance and said, "Tony is so fucking talented. He helped me with a lot of my early cover songs on YouTube. He taught me so much." She suddenly leaned forward and tapped Ha-joon in the driver's seat. "Oh, Oppa," she said. "Can we stop by Fatburger? I need a runny yolk on a cheeseburger right the fuck now! Seriously, guys, you have to try it. My treat, okay? It's so fucking noms!"

"Alright," Jae-sung said. He rarely refused food if someone else was treating. "Should we get some for the rest of the guys, too?"

Woo-jin chuckled as Katie sighed. "Bet you're regretting that offer now, aren't you?"

"I guess I should add fries and milkshakes for everyone, too. Go big or go home, right?"

Jae-sung couldn't help but smile at Katie, allowing himself to pretend they were just regular people, grabbing burgers and fries for their friends. He let himself enjoy the relative anonymity in America, knowing that when they returned to Korea, the scrutiny would immediately increase. Though he was grateful for their rising status, he missed the days when they were just nameless idiots pursuing their music dreams.

August 2016

The only proper response to "Never get involved in a land war in Asia" is "Never go against a Sicilian when death is on the line!"

- Katie Wu, Twitter, August 2016

"What are you up to today, Noona?" Dae-jung asked from his spot on the worn couch of their shared studio, taking a quick break from memorizing lyrics for DOYEN's upcoming concert.

The couch was ugly, but it was comfortable, so he tried to sprawl on it as much as possible whenever his daily schedule allowed. Unfortunately, he was only half-sprawled on it today because Woo-jin had gotten there first. Dae-jung threw his legs over the unoccupied portion and dug his feet into the rapper's lap as a pointed reminder of who the sofa actually belonged to. Dae-jung never said he was mature about it.

Katie looked up from her Korean study materials spread across the folding table in the center of the room. She sighed. "A rep from my old label is coming in to discuss signing over part of the rights to some of my old songs."

"Oh?" asked Woo-jin. "Do Taiwanese labels do that very often?" Woo-jin was mindlessly scrolling through social media on his phone and thoroughly unbothered by Dae-jung's feet. Dae-jung didn't let that disrespect phase him though.

He noted with no small amusement at Katie's slight flush from Woo-jin's direct question. Even after all this time spent in the older man's presence, she always seemed slightly dazzled by him. Nevermind that they often discussed music and songwriting and both seemed to know the most random information. They often had conversations in English, losing Dae-jung almost immediately. He really should have paid more attention in school, but how could he have predicted his need for the foreign language to chat with a pretty noona?

More often than not, Ye-jun joined the conversation despite knowing almost nothing about the topic except how to derail a conversation and steer people toward complimenting his handsomeness. The three of them would huddle in the studio, Ye-jun and Katie bickering in rapidly raising voices with Woo-jin as the ultimate enabler, egging them both on from the sidelines. Dae-jung found their antics almost as amusing as when Katie goofed off with him, Akihiro, and Soo-min. He loved how Katie treated them like they were slightly dumb puppies—not that she was wrong. Dae-jung acknowledged they definitely radiated yappy puppy energy.

"Not that I know of," Katie replied. "It's really bizarre because I never thought I'd get them. The majority of the credits went to Johnny since he was the bigger name, even though I wrote most of the songs. I think he changed a word or a note, but he got the lion's share of royalties."

"That sucks," Woo-jin commiserated. "I've totally had beats stolen from me when I was starting out. Too bad for them I'm fueled entirely by spite."

"Spite has definitely carried me far, that's for sure." She laid her pen down in her workbook to mark her place before closing it. "The weirdest thing is that *they* reached out to *me*. It makes no sense, honestly," Katie mused.

"Maybe they grew a conscience," Dae-jung suggested.

They all burst out laughing. "Right, they probably want me to hand over my firstborn in exchange," Katie said. "They can keep the rights. I'll just write better songs."

"That's the attitude," Woo-jin encouraged, flashing her a gummy smile. "Never look back."

Dae-jung returned to memorizing lyrics and only looked up again when Ha-joon popped in the room.

"Auspicious's rep is here, Katie," said Ha-joon, his voice calm, but sounding a warning. "And I just need you to know that we're doing everything we can to get a different one—but for now, it's up to you if you want to meet him."

The combination of Ha-joon's voice and the look on the large man's face gave Dae-jung a bad feeling.

"Who is it?" Katie asked, her voice uncharacteristically muted.

"They sent Johnny."

Happy Birthday, Katie. I miss you every day.
- Johnny Chen, Twitter, August 2016

New phone, who dis?
- Katie Wu, Twitter, August 2016

"No," Katie balked, "absolutely not."

"Come on, Katie," Johnny wheedled from across the folding table of SB Entertainment's tiny conference room. "Max four to six months and then we can break up amicably, citing living in different countries and being geographically challenged. We don't even have to be seen in public much."

Katie remembered how Johnny used to get his way all the time by using this tone of voice with her. Back then, she hadn't been able to resist. She'd thought he'd been so cute and vulnerable. How refreshing it had been to her, after her college boyfriend Gary, to have a man try to persuade her by being adorable instead of dictating what he wanted from her.

Except in the end, it was only a more subtle form of manipulation. How many times did Johnny convince Katie to give more than she was comfortable with, blowing past her boundaries by using his age and previous mentorship against her?

She was no longer that innocent naif anymore. Johnny had ensured that.

"I don't want to be seen in public with you at all," Katie replied. She leaned back in the metal folding chair. "Keep the fucking rights you stole, Johnny. I'll just write better songs. SB Entertainment isn't greedy. They pay their artists fairly."

"I don't see the big deal, Katie. It's just business. We don't actually have to fuck unless you want to." Johnny scowled upon seeing her full body grimace. His fingers drummed angrily on the tabletop, silver rings on his fingers occasionally glinting.

She used to love his fingers, the way they caressed piano keys, plucked guitar strings, and fiddled with engineering soundboards. His light touch on instruments had translated well on her body, too. Johnny was an ass, but he had been an excellent teacher.

"Even if I weren't fundamentally opposed to even one more second's association with you, I don't understand why you're offering this at all. You made clear your contempt for me on national radio." Katie paused in thought. "Unless—"

Johnny's scowl deepened.

"Ohhhh, I get it." Katie had the temerity to laugh. "How badly did your plan backfire, Johnny? Trying to do a bit of image rehab?" Katie laughed more. "Who came up with this farce? Evan? Tell your brother that you need a new manager."

"I told him it wouldn't work."

"Of course not! Who would believe this obvious PR stunt?"

"So, it's a no?"

Katie shook her head at the audacity of Johnny and his team. "Yeah, it's a no."

Johnny pushed back from the table and thundered, "Well, thanks for wasting my time."

Katie was about to lay into him again except he had opened the conference room door just as all of DOYEN passed by. She bit her tongue and watched Johnny leave.

TFW the trash you took out keeps coming back.
- Katie Wu, Twitter, August 2016

Jae-sung and the rest of his bandmates were walking down the hallway to attend a meeting with their managers, passing through a carpeted corridor lined with windows into all the conference rooms. As they passed the one in which Katie was ensconced with Johnny and Ha-joon, Jae-sung saw Johnny stand abruptly. He yanked open the glass door and stalked out into the hallway, leaving Ha-joon and Katie at the conference table.

The singer took one look at DOYEN, recognized Woo-jin and Ye-jun, and sneered. "Katie used to scream about you two all the time. You're lucky I broke her in for you," he snarled crassly in English. "Best thing about virgins, you know. You don't have to train them out of any bad habits. They're brand new."

Jae-sung could see through the glass windows how Katie's jaw clenched and her hands formed into fists.

"It's not a shame to be inexperienced," she said with as much dignity as she could muster. She pushed back from the table and stood in the doorway as Ha-joon mirrored her actions. "The real shame is a 31-year-old man stealing from girls more than ten years their junior."

"I didn't have to steal shit," Johnny ridiculed, his attractive features twisting. "You gave it all up so easily."

Jae-sung wanted to physically shield Katie from this horrible man and edged closer in case he had to intervene. Logically, he knew Ha-joon could more than hold his own against Johnny. The older man was definitely shorter, but what he lacked for in height, he more than made up for in heft. He was barrel-shaped and looked like he could form a good barrier between Katie and Johnny if it came to a fistfight. Jae-sung could sense his own willingness to commit violence boil to the surface and felt the same sentiment emanate from each of his bandmates.

"I did," Katie conceded, eyes bright. "I loved you, Johnny. I would have given you anything you asked for if I had it to give. I gave you everything because I loved you. There is no shame in that."

Regret flashed over Johnny's face and disappeared as quickly as it came. "As if you ever had anything I would want." His face hardened. "That was your problem. You always thought so much of yourself. You think just because you won some songwriting show, you're hot shit?"

"Oh." Katie inhaled a deep breath, her hand fluttering to her mouth.

"I've always hated you. Hated your smug mouth."

Katie's pretty face crumpled. "What?"

Jae-sung wished he could physically stop Johnny from speaking. Katie was the same age as Jae-sung so she must have been so young when she was with Johnny.

"From the very beginning, all I could think of was putting you in your place. As if someone like me needed someone like you."

Katie flinched as if she'd been hit. "I see," she said.

"I hope you do." Johnny leered, cold and calculating.

Tears slipped from Katie's devastated eyes. She did not bother to wipe them off her face. "I suppose I should thank you for the early and very thorough lesson on vipers in the industry. I hope you find what you're looking for, Johnny." Katie drew herself to her full height, and though she was a mere slip of a thing, she seemed to loom larger than she had before. "Now get the fuck out."

Jae-sung had to give it to Katie. After Jae-sung's manager Sung-mo politely and firmly escorted Johnny out, Katie held it together longer than he thought she would. She made it through Johnny disappearing around the corner. She made it through all their concerned questions and attempts at small talk. She made it through Ha-joon telling her he would make sure her old record label would never fuck her like this again. She made it back to their shared studio without falling apart.

And then, Woo-jin—of all people—growled, "You want me to kill him for you?"

Katie barked in surprise, and then next thing Jae-sung knew, she was hysterically cracking up until sobs erupted from deep within her soul. Woo-jin pulled her into a tight embrace, and she wept into his chest. He soothed her with shushes and nonsense comfort sounds. When she was all cried out, he called her sweetheart and kissed her softly on her forehead, setting off another round of weeping.

Jae-sung felt an irrational surge of jealousy. What would it be like to be Katie's person—to be the one she relied on for her dark side? He wondered if he would ever find out.

October 2016

While Katie Wu's previous album "Shameless" (SB Entertainment, 2016) lightly touched on criticisms of the Church and religion, her first studio album "Gain All the World" (SB Entertainment, 2016) clearly castigates the hypocrisy of Christianity and its dogma. Wu compares both religion and relationships to inherently unfair contracts between unequal parties.

Her greatly improved rapping and rapid-fire cadence browbeat the scathing lyrics so hard and so blisteringly that the listener will beg for atonement all the while petitioning for more. Standout tracks are "Pulpit Fiction," a swanky piece calling back to old-school gospel music, and "Love: A Series of Progressively More Demanding Transactions," a hilarious yet sobering view of love made all the more poignant by Wu's surprisingly good mandolin playing.

- IZM, October 2016

Cerebral and fierce, "Gain All the World" is a study of power and an apologetic for secular spirituality. Incisive and polemic, the album is a comfort and solace to the disaffected.

- The Dong-a Ilbo, October 2016

[1] Profit [2:51]
[2] Bad Faith, Bad Terms [3:07]

[3] Pulpit Fiction [3:16]
[4] Mammon [2:58]
[5] Love: A Series of Progressively More Demanding Transactions [4:20]
[6] Of All the Seouls [3:15]
[7] No Refunds, No Returns [2:34]
- Track list, "Gain All the World" (SB Entertainment, 2016)

Never change I love everything about you
Except could you please
Just breathe a little less loudly
And could you—for fucking once
Remember to turn off the lights when you leave
- "Love: A Series of Progressively More Demanding Transactions" (SB Entertainment, 2016)

Did you think I'd never audit
That I cared only for profit
Would accept improper fractions
Instead of the integers I'm due

You lied with statistics
Plied circular references
Wrecked my formulas
Now my cells are askew

Hidden rows and invalid syntaxes
My ledger no longer balances

Nothing nets zero
And my interest no longer accrues
                              - "Profit" (SB Entertainment, 2016)

And in that same breath of love unconditional
They hurtled a book full of bonds and decrees
Turns out nothing can separate, can tear, can sunder
Like a man in the pulpit to me, me, me
                         - "Pulpit Fiction" (SB Entertainment, 2016)

"Katie?"

Katie was on the carpeted floor of the shared studio, head resting on her knees, hands balled into fists by her face, back to the battered couch. Jae-sung could hear her harsh and shallow breaths from where he was by the door. She looked like she was in a bad way.

"Katie, are you okay?" he repeated as he walked closer, whatever had brought him to the studio forgotten. He saw tracks of tears on Katie's face and he swore he heard her muttering between gasps, "523, 541, 547, 557, 563..."

Was she...listing prime numbers? And, if so, how long had she been listing them—and how did she know so many?

"Katie, are you having a panic attack?" At her tight nod, Jae-sung willed his voice calm. "I'm right here, Katie. I will stay with you unless you want me to leave. Do you want me to leave?" He crouched in front of her and stretched out a hand.

Katie reached out and grabbed his fingers, her grip a tight vise. His fingers hurt.

"Okay, Katie, I'm right here if you need my help." He took a deep, cleansing breath. Jae-sung had enough experience with Woo-jin's panic attacks to help ground her. The older rapper used to get them regularly as a trainee and still got them occasionally on really bad days. "You're safe, Katie. You're safe and the panic attack will pass soon. I promise."

"Okay," she answered, her voice quavering.

"I want you to focus on my voice, Katie. Can you do that for me?" At her nod, Jae-sung continued. "Follow my breath, okay? Here we go. Breathe in, two, three, four."

Katie breathed in, following his instructions.

"Hold, two, three, four, five, six, seven."

She held her breath as he counted.

"Exhale, two, three, four, five, six, seven, eight," Jae-sung counted while Katie breathed out. "Let's try it again," he said, knowing it would take several rounds before her system would reset.

Jae-sung continued to inhale, hold, and exhale until Katie's death grip on his hand finally loosened and her breathing eased. She slumped against him, spent.

"Thanks," she whispered.

"Anytime, Katie," he replied. "I'm here for you."

She remained lightly pressed against him, letting his words sink in for a few beats.

"Please don't tell manager-nim," Katie requested after a few moments. "He does so much for me, and I don't want him to worry."

"Do you want to talk about what triggered it?" Jae-sung asked gently. "Maybe it will help?"

Katie was quiet for a bit and Jae-sung wondered if he'd overstepped. They weren't friends like that. If anything, she rarely let anyone in beyond her bright exterior. Although, after Woo-jin had suggested he listen to her music, Jae-sung realized that Katie contained so much more depth than he had ever thought possible.

"My uncle just sent me a text telling me I was going to hell and that I'd better repent. Otherwise, he'll cut me out of his life like he did to my father," she said, still not looking at him. Such confessions often seemed easier when given side-by-side rather than face-to-face.

"Wow," replied Jae-sung. "That's awful."

"Yeah," Katie said glumly. "The thing is, my father is an asshole, but like, my uncle—he's a pastor in Chicago—my uncle is, too. Like, talk about not being motivated to change if repentance is having him in your life?"

Katie laughed forlornly as tears squeezed out the corners of her eyes.

"I'm sorry, Katie."

"I'm used to it. My dad's side sucks." Katie wiped her face with the hem of her shirt, revealing a sliver of smooth skin. "It's so stupid. I don't even consider myself a Christian anymore—but it's just so hard to—" she paused, struggling to find the right Korean words. "It's just so hard to divest myself of the toxic Christianity and patriarchy I was steeped in for my whole life," she continued in English.

Jae-sung was thrown momentarily as he tried to switch gears. But as her words sank in, he understood why she switched to English. He liked that she could do that around him—that if she felt hamstrung by Korean, she had the option of a language she was far more comfortable in.

"The way purity culture made me feel as if I was garbage or worthless—it's so deeply ingrained inside me," Katie continued. "It doesn't matter how much I tell myself it's all bullshit—that it's all ways men try to control women. Sometimes, I just spiral."

"You're not garbage," he said firmly in English. He could smell the light grapefruit scent of her shampoo and had to repress the urge to breathe her in deeply.

She smiled sadly. "I wish I had your confidence." Katie got up and brushed off her clothes. Her dark eyes were filled with an unnamed emotion. "I know we're both promoting albums right now, but maybe we can grab dinner sometime? I think I still owe you a night out at a fancy restaurant, right?"

"Oh, Katie. You don't have to. Your friend was just joking."

"A contract is a contract," Katie teased. "And I always keep my end of the bargain."

Jae-sung was a little thrown by how quickly she seemed to revert to her bright and friendly persona, but he also understood the need to cling to normalcy in the face of heavy feelings. He grinned. "Alright. But only because I am helpful and don't want to ruin your reputation."

"That's my Jae. Always helpful."

Loathe as Jae-sung was to admit, he couldn't help but bask in the afterglow of her praise. He didn't know what it was exactly about Katie that made him feel both vulnerable and protective, but she made him feel like the sort of king he claimed himself to be.

If he wanted to chase that feeling, well, he was only human.

The way Katie kept covering her eyes during "In Harm's Way" every time Soo-min came on and screamed, "Not the baby! Not the baby!"

\- Twitter user, October 2016

I couldn't stop laughing. Katie actually choked on her own spit when a bound and gagged Akihiro glared directly at the camera.

\- Twitter user, October 2016

Aki-yah! :: Katie flails :: :: Katie punches air :: Classic!

- Twitter user, October 2016

**Woo-jin enters the chat* Did Katie just say she needs a sandwich? Something about needing to sink her teeth into some meat?*

- Twitter user, October 2016

when lambent did that finger beckoning thing and she whimpered lolololololl

- Twitter user, October 2016

OMG SHE REBUKES THIS HAHAHAHAH SHE REBUKES DAE LICKING HIS LIPS

- Twitter user, October 2016

What did she throw when King Ja\$e blew cigarette smoke into 1DEL1GHT's face? Did she hit PD-nim?

- Twitter user, October 2016

I live for Katie's DOYEN reactions. Relatable QUEEEEEEEEN! I don't know how she works with them and doesn't spontaneously combust.

- Twitter user, October 2016

Her full body cringe when Jun leans into the camera and slowly licks his lips while staring seductively—comedy gold!

- Twitter user, October 2016

Can SB Entertainment please make Katie react to EVERY MV and dance practice bc this is GENIUS

- Twitter user, October 2016

"WHY IS THIS MV SO SEXUAL?!?" BWAHAHAHAH Katie in distress at sexy DOYEN is my new sexuality.

- Twitter user, October 2016

"Thanks for making time to have dinner with me, Jae-sung," Katie said as they waited for appetizers. They were seated in a hidden alcove at one of Seoul's top high-end steakhouses at the end of a long day. "I'm sure you're exhausted."

"I'm just glad a time slot opened up!" Jae-sung responded cheerfully. He inhaled the distinct smell of sizzling meat and let it hit the pleasure centers of his brain. After years of only eating bland chicken breasts during their time as trainees, Jae-sung was always grateful when he could indulge in quality and flavorful meat.

He really was glad, too. The fact that they both happened to be free tonight and impromptu decided to have dinner—when otherwise, the next opening likely would have been after award season in early Febru-ary—it really was serendipitous that they each had last-minute cancellations and were in the mood to go out. Even better that Ha-joon had procured reservations at the hottest new steakhouse in Gangnam.

He happily soaked in the stylized ambience of the restaurant, admiring the dark wood paneling, red velvet and metal-studded high-back dining chairs, green and gold geometric-patterned fabric booths, crisp white tablecloths, and heavy cutlery on the table.

Granted, they were both in their casual work clothes, although even Jae-sung's casual work clothes were designer or expensive streetwear. He was currently decked in a Junya Watanabe jacquard cardigan, a SUPREME T-shirt, Acne Studios denim, and pristine limited edition Nike Air Force 1s, whereas Katie was decidedly not in anything designer or streetwear. She'd changed out of whatever the stylist noonas had put her in for her schedule that day and was comfortably in her go-to oversized UCLA sweatshirt, San Francisco Giants hat, generic navy joggers, and scuffed white and navy Adidas classic sneakers.

The maître d' had looked askance at Katie when he let them in through the restaurant's back entrance as if he were going to bar them from entry, but they were still both celebrities. Katie still had on her glam make-up—though even barefaced, she was a stunner—and the man had led them to their table, immediately sending over a bottle of merlot on the house.

"Katie, I meant to ask you what college was like in America. I've been wondering ever since I attended your Q&A at UCLA."

Katie looked a little puzzled, but she seemed willing enough. "I can't say I speak for everyone's college experience, and I have no idea how it compares to college in Korea, but I guess I can try? Did you have a specific question?"

"What was your major? Did you like it? What was college like? Is it the same as they depict in the movies?" Jae-sung was a little embarrassed at how quickly his questions rushed out. It was too late to recall them, so he just went with it. "Sometimes, I wonder if I hadn't gone the idol route, if I would have applied to American universities instead of trying to get into

SKY. I remember American schools being so much easier than my Korean ones."

"SKY?" Katie asked.

Sometimes, Jae-sung forgot that there was still so much Katie didn't know about Korea. Especially since most of her education was music industry-related and not so much everyday life.

"You know, Seoul National University, Korea University, and Yonsei University," he explained. "SKY."

"Oh, duh," Katie replied good-naturedly. "I actually knew that. I don't know why it didn't register." She sipped some water and dabbed her lips with the white cloth napkin. "Well, I don't know how easy American universities are—don't pretend you aren't a genius with your 153 IQ, Jae-sung. But to answer your question, I was an Asian American studies major and minored in history. I had to drop history to graduate early, but I did like it for the most part. It was a lot of reading and term papers though."

Jae-sung was surprised. He had assumed Katie would have chosen a music or performance major, but he supposed she was Asian American. Her parents probably wouldn't have let her. Except, Asian American studies and history seemed equally unconventional. "Your parents let you study that?"

She smiled ruefully. "They weren't happy, but I told them it would help me get into law school. UCLA has an amazing law program, you know."

"You were going to be a lawyer?" It wasn't that Jae-sung thought Katie was dumb, but she didn't seem to be the lawyer type. "Don't lawyers have to be, like, super smart?"

Katie cackled. "Wow, Jae-sung. Tell me you think I'm stupid without telling me you think I'm stupid, I guess."

Jae-sung felt his face get hot. He'd bungled that badly. "That's not what I meant, Katie. I mean, I'm sure you're smart enough." Katie choked on her bite of bacon-topped deviled egg and laughed even harder. Jae-sung's voice cracked as he doggedly continued, desperately trying to extricate himself from the hole he'd dug. "You're just so good at music, I can't imagine you doing anything else."

Katie was now laughing so hard that her entire face scrunched and her mouth hung open and uncovered, uncaring about how rude it was in polite Korean society to show the inside of her mouth. Jae-sung glanced around guiltily, noting the looks of distaste from some of the neighboring tables.

When she finally stopped cracking up, she said, "Jesus, Jae-sung. You have no idea how condescending you are all the time, do you?" Katie didn't sound mad. Her voice was definitely tinged with amusement. "I know you're super smart, but that doesn't make you special. It doesn't even make you unique—especially not at this table."

"What, are you going to tell me you have a genius level IQ, too?" he quipped sardonically.

Katie winked saucily at him. "Did you know that IQ tests are culturally biased?" she asked instead of answering him. "And what use are tests that only value and measure—inaccurately, I might add—one type of intelligence?"

"This sounds like something someone who is not a genius says to comfort themselves for not being one," Jae-sung returned smugly. He didn't even know why he was arguing with Katie. It wasn't as if he put a lot of stock in such outward markers of intelligence and success.

Katie chuckled quietly. "Of course you would say such a thing, Jae. It's always a pleasure when you're on brand."

Jae-sung resisted bristling at her observation. He wasn't as smug an asshole as she depicted. And besides, she was one to talk!

Katie was about to comment when a waiter interrupted them with their entrees. Katie's face lit up as she gazed lovingly at her prime rib and caramelized brussel sprouts with bacon. She inhaled deeply, her body practically wriggling with anticipation. Jae-sung couldn't help but be charmed. He enjoyed food, but Katie loved food on a level that rivaled Ye-jun.

She impatiently waited for Jae-sung to be served his filet mignon and then eagerly cut into her prime rib. She blithely took a bite and moaned decadently, all the while happily bouncing in her chair.

Jae-sung decided he'd change the subject back to the conversation prior to Katie's attempt to take him down a peg. "So what were you like in college?"

Katie swallowed and replied, "Uh, I was super Christian and insufferable."

He was learning more about Katie in one conversation than he'd had in the last year or so. Granted, he'd been busy with writing and recording DOYEN albums, practicing for comebacks, and preparing for concerts and performances, but he supposed he could have tried harder to show interest in her.

"So other than the Christian part, you're the same?" Jae-sung jested.

Once again, Katie laughed with her whole body. "Pretty much," she agreed. "Overall, it was a good experience. I made a lot of good friends—I should keep in touch with them better—and had fun."

"What made you stop being a Christian?" The closest thing Jae-sung had to religion was his love for hip-hop and music. Even when DOYEN had seemed like the biggest mistake, he couldn't imagine doing a 180 and walking away from his band or his fans.

Katie's eyes hardened.

"I decided that any god who allowed suffering and injustice on such a mass scale didn't deserve my worship. That any god who answered Job's question of 'Why do bad things happen to good people?' with their presence instead of a real answer was using their power to overwhelm a puny human and dodging the question." She sucked in a deep breath. "I got tired of making excuses. Either god was powerful enough to fix things and chose not to, or they were well-intentioned but powerless. Neither depiction inspires my respect or devotion."

"Oh, wow," Jae-sung stammered. Not that he hadn't come to his own similar conclusions, but to Katie, it seemed deeply personal, as if god had personally failed her.

"Not that it matters anymore," Katie immediately said, seemingly embarrassed at what she'd inadvertently revealed about herself. "What were we talking about before I derailed our conversation so spectacularly?"

Though Jae-sung wanted to know more about how Katie had come to this worldview, he did what was expected of him in the social dance. "Did you date or attend a lot of parties? What was that like?" He really had consumed way too many movies about this idealized American college experience.

"Sorry to disappoint, Jae-sung," she said, flashing him a grateful smile. "Other than a brief slutty period my first year, I mostly didn't date."

Intriguing. "Slutty period, huh?"

"Yah! It's so pathetic when I think back about it," Katie mused mournfully. "Didn't even get to fuck anyone yet still felt all the guilt."

"You don't strike me as a sexually conservative person." Jae-sung really wished he did not say that part out loud.

"You think about me sexually a lot?" Katie laughed again. She really did laugh a lot. He couldn't tell if he was funny or if she was just generous. "I guess I'm not anymore. But like I said, I grew up super Christian—and, you know, there weren't that many Asians at my school when I was a kid. All the popular girls were white. I wasn't unpopular, but I definitely wasn't considered pretty—let alone hot."

Given how striking Katie was despite her execrable fashion sense, Jae-sung called bullshit. "I find that hard to believe," he said.

"I know, right?" Katie's mouth twisted self-deprecatingly. She played with her wine glass, swirling the base over the tablecloth. "But seriously, it's difficult to find yourself beautiful when none of the beauty standards look like you. I'm glad I ended up at UCLA. There's a reason they called it University of Caucasians Lost among Asians."

"No!" Jae-sung cracked up. "That's awful. And amazing!" He paused to let the server refill his water. "But college is when you realized you were hot?"

"I really didn't know what to do with guys showing interest in me. I think I was so surprised I just did stuff with whoever was willing." Katie cut another piece of her prime rib and took another ecstatic bite. "I love meat," she sighed.

Jae-sung decided not to make a dirty joke though he was positive Katie would appreciate it. "I could have sworn you had a boyfriend at one point?"

"Ah, yes. Gary. That was a dark time." She shoved more prime rib into her mouth.

"With a name like that, I can see why."

Katie switched to English. "He was so controlling, and worst of all, I let him. I thought it was the Christian thing to do—to let the guy lead and be the head of the relationship." She rolled her eyes and sipped her merlot. "I'm not saying all Christians think this way, just the particular brand I was in. What a load of shit."

"I really cannot imagine you letting anyone control you—let alone a man." Katie was full of surprises tonight.

Katie shrugged. "Perfect storm of daddy issues, toxic Christianity, people pleasing, and low self-esteem."

"I'm sorry, Katie," Jae-sung said. "I'm really sorry you had to experience that."

"It's okay. Hymns and church music were foundational in my upbringing. Church allowed me my first few opportunities to play live music and write songs. It wasn't all terrible."

"Well, I'm glad for that, then."

"I still hear hymns in my head sometimes and get the urge to sing their alto lines. They comfort in a way no other music can touch."

"What's your favorite hymn?" Jae-sung did not grow up with a Christian background—considered himself an atheist—so he really wouldn't know what the hymn was, but he wanted to check them out on his own. Just to see what formed her musical sensibilities. That wasn't weird, was it?

"So many. 'O, the Deep, Deep Love of Jesus,' 'Come, Thou Fount of Every Blessing,' 'How Great Thou Art,' 'Be Thou My Vision,' 'The Old Rugged Cross,' 'Just As I Am.'" Katie's eyes got a far off look.

"You'll have to sing them for me sometime," Jae-sung said quietly.

"I'll think about it." Katie quirked her lips. "Oh, this reminds me. All your dating questions have me wondering: How do you date? How do you even meet people?"

"You mean other than people in the industry? Cuz we meet people all the time."

"Right. But like, you can't really get to know people at industry events. I am not the type to go on a date with someone just because they're hot." Katie cleared her throat and took another sip of her wine.

"Really!"

She sniffed and lifted a haughty brow. "I'm a walking friends-to-lovers trope. There is no other explanation for Gary."

Jae-sung did not expect her to ask him of all people. "I'm surprised you didn't ask Ye-jun hyung."

"Oh my god, no. He's so nosy—he would demand to screen all my dates and then I would have to murder him. Awkward."

"Ah, I see. I'm not sure I can help you though. I meet women at music shows and we figure it out."

"You only date people in the business?"

"No, but it's much easier. They can understand my lifestyle a lot better and know how to be discreet." Something was bugging Jae-sung. "Wait, have you just not been dating?"

"I mean, I haven't really had the time," she deflected.

"Right, but what about just, like, fucking?" It occurred to Jae-sung that he could have perhaps phrased that better. Clearly, he had gotten too comfortable with his labelmate.

Katie chose that moment to take another bite, likely to buy herself time before she answered. "I had a string of one-night stands after Johnny, but I didn't particularly care for it. Then I was in Seoul and trying to learn Korean and debut and I just—I just never got around to it."

"What about Woo-jin hyung?"

Katie blushed a bright pink. "What about him?"

"The two of you obviously have chemistry. He's your bias, right? And he flirts with you constantly. Just fuck him. I'm sure he'd be down for it."

Katie just stared at Jae-sung. "No."

"I mean, yes, he's at the same company—I know that's a thing you don't do—but maybe you could? Woo-jin hyung's a good guy. He wouldn't fuck you over like Johnny did." Shit. Woo-jin was going to owe him big time if this worked. Jae-sung really did not know what possessed him to suggest such a thing. As far as he knew, Woo-jin was no longer seeing anyone, but that didn't mean he wanted to see Katie. "Not just because he isn't a dick—well, now anyway—but because it would kill his reputation and that of our entire group."

"No."

"Why not?" Jae-sung pushed.

Katie glared at him. "Because! Woo-jin oppa is like the sexiest person alive! What the fuck, Jae?"

"I don't see the problem?"

"If Hwang Woo-jin tried to fuck me, I would just cry. I would uncontrollably sob and be completely worthless. Who wants to fuck a person who can't stop crying? That sounds terrible—mostly for Woo-jin oppa because I would probably still like it—but no! I will not subject myself to such humiliation! I would have to leave the country!"

"Wow."

"If you tell him I said any of this, I will cut your heart out with a spoon."

Jae-sung was still catching up. "So your reasoning is that Hyung is too sexy? I can assure you, he's just a normal dude. You see him all the time. Really?"

"No. I mean, yes. I don't know how to answer this question properly, and I'm really confused." Katie finished her glass and reached desperately for the open merlot bottle on the table.

"He really is your bias."

Katie poured herself a very generous pour. "I don't want to talk about fucking Woo-jin oppa anymore. Truly, a terrifying prospect. Especially after hearing 'Death Before Dishonor' and Oppa's line about making all the boys and girls go dumb on his tongue."

"That song was in 2014."

"I said I don't want to talk about it."

"Wow."

"Shut up and eat your food, Jae-sung."

Jae-sung shut up and ate his food, but his mind wouldn't stop churning. Before he could stop himself, he asked, "What about me then?" Oh, Jae-sung was just pushing all the envelopes tonight, wasn't he?

"What about you?" Katie glowered.

Jae-sung raised an eyebrow.

"No."

"I have the same need to be discreet, and you already know me," he reasoned. "We work at the same company and can hang out without much suspicion."

"One, you're a baby fuckboy," Katie explained. "Two, I'm older than you. And three, I would eat you alive."

Jae-sung sucked in his cheeks in annoyance. "One, there's nothing baby about me. Two, technically, you're only ten days older than me, and in Korea, we're the same age." He pushed up the sleeves of his cardigan slightly and noticed how Katie's eyes followed his every movement. "And three, you just said you would sob uncontrollably if Hyung tried to have sex with you."

"Yes. Keyword: Woo-jin oppa. Nowhere was your name mentioned. I would destroy you."

"I have a pretty strong sex drive, Katie. I think you would tap out before I would." Jae-sung crossed his arms and gazed at her through his dragon eyes.

"Only because of chafing, Jae—which wouldn't be a problem if you could get and keep me wet." Katie's voice dropped low and growly, hitting Jae-sung straight in the dick.

"There's really only one way to settle this, Katie."

"I'm a complete pillow princess, Jae-sung. I'm sick of catering to men—and I'm not saying I wouldn't ride good dick—but I'm out for me and only me. If you happen to come, good for you—but I honestly don't care if you do."

"You truly make no sense to me." Sometimes, Katie really confounded him in the most aggravating ways.

"What do you mean? All you have to do is find my clit—and if you can't, I will move you." Katie was so incredibly provoking.

"First you say you're a walking friends-to-lovers trope. Then you say Woo-jin hyung is too intimidating to fuck. And now you say you're a maneater? Make it make sense."

"Clearly you didn't understand Whitman's line, 'I contain multitudes.'" Jae-sung hated how hot this statement made Katie. "The first is for dating and relationships," she explained. "The second is Hwang Fucking Woo-jin aka sex god Lambent. The third is just fucking."

"I only have one more question," said Jae-sung. "When do you want to start?"

Chapter 3

December 2023

When my mother called me, the first thing I thought was: He can't hurt me now. It has been years, and still. Still I flinch. Still, my first instinct is to cower. To protect my face. To protect my vital organs.

I tell myself he can't hurt me now. I am safe. And yet. Every day, I hurt.
- "Telling a Truth Is a Slippery Slope" (Red Lantern Publishing House, October 2023)

Dae-jung was seeing things.

He was lounging in bed with Kim Ha-rin, his girlfriend of the past three and a half years and reading his new favorite webtoon when he could have sworn he just saw Katie Wu's name pop up in his KakaoTalk notifications. He used to receive daily texts from her—gossipy, breezy, and sometimes bossy missives that crackled with good humor and unsolicited advice to the maknae line. She had even changed her contact information on his phone to "my favorite noona" and he'd never changed it—even long after she'd disconnected her old number and vanished.

Katie had ignored him and his other members for so long that he'd thought she'd blocked them all.

Hey guys, she texted, *I'm going to be in Seoul next month and dropping by SB Entertainment offices to see Ha-joon oppa. Would any of you be open to meeting up? I totally understand if you would prefer not to.*

Dae-jung's heart leapt. "Fuck," he breathed as he sat up.

"What, jagiya?" Ha-rin asked as she sat up, her long black hair falling into her face. "Everything okay?"

Instead of answering Ha-rin, Dae-jung immediately clicked on the group chat participants to see who she'd messaged. A quick scan made him sigh in relief and sorrow. Jae-sung was not included, and though Dae-jung understood the reasoning, he could not help but feel as if he were betraying his hyung.

Did you see Noona's message? Akihiro's text notification popped up in their side chat group—the one Ye-jun had created for everyone minus Jae-sung after Katie and Jae-sung had broken up. *What do we do?*

I'm going to say yes, replied Soo-min almost immediately.

Of course he was. Soo-min had always loved Katie with an adoring sort of puppy love. It didn't matter that she was Jae-sung's girl. Soo-min could never be dissuaded no matter how much water was under the bridge or how many years had gone by. Sometimes, Dae-jung wondered if maybe in some other universe, Soo-min would end up happily ever after with Katie. He found himself fervently wishing for such a timeline for the maknae.

"Dae," Ha-rin said, interrupting his train of thought. "You know I hate it when you drift off into your own little world. I asked you a question."

"What?" Dae-jung asked even as he carefully texted, *Even after what she did to Jae hyung?* Dae-jung missed Katie, of course, but his loyalty was to his leader first.

We don't even know the whole story, argued Soo-min, *and we won't unless we ask her. Didn't it seem out of character for her to just up and leave? Like,*

Hyung must have either done something terrible or something must have happened to her.

Hyung would never, Dae-jung fired back.

We've hashed this out over a million times in the last few years, Akihiro interceded before the disagreement could devolve into a full-blown fight. *Hyungs, what do you think we should do?*

I always have time for you, Katie, Ye-jun texted instead of replying to Akihiro. It was just like Ye-jun to reply so nonchalantly—as if Katie still texted them all the time—and without consulting the rest of them. He always did what he wanted.

"Dae-jung!" Ha-rin said, this time with much greater force. She poked him in his shoulder. "Park Dae-jung, I am speaking to you."

He finally tore his attention from his phone and registered his girl-friend at his side. Ha-rin was fuming, her eyes squinched into twin brown daggers. "Sorry, Ha-rin," he said placatingly. He could not engage in war on two fronts. "Katie noona just texted us."

Ha-rin's eyes went wide. "Jae-sung oppa's ex? After all this time? What does she want?"

"She wants to meet up," Dae-jung shared, "and Ye-jun hyung already said he would."

"Of course he did. Let me guess, Woo-jin oppa was right on Ye-jun oppa's heels," she observed caustically. "Those three were always thick as thieves."

Dae-jung glanced at his screen again. Right on cue, Woo-jin also popped into the chat to say, *Same.* Dae-jung stared incredulously at his screen. Woo-jin never responded to texts, but Dae-jung should have known. Ever since Woo-jin first found Katie on Twitter, thanks to their fans tweeting about any celebrity who was a DOYEN fan, the two eldest members had ever been in her pocket.

"You got it," he said.

Ha-rin snuggled into his side, his previous inattention set aside for gossip. "What are you going to do?"

Thanks for consulting with us, Hyung, Do-won texted sarcastically in their side chat. *Maybe some of us need some time to think things over, and now you made us look like assholes.*

I didn't have to do shit. You did that all on your own, Ye-jun replied.

"Well, they really forced our hand," said Dae-jung.

Ha-rin rolled her eyes as she returned to her side of the bed. "Just because the rest of your group agrees to something doesn't mean you have to."

Dae-jung sighed wearily. Ha-rin's pretty face screwed into the stubborn set he recognized. Three years with a person made him wonder if there were any mysteries left to discover, but he pushed the disloyal thought aside. He knew Ha-rin wasn't actually talking about Katie anymore, but he didn't have it in him to argue with her tonight.

"Ha-rin-ah," he voiced with a warning note. "Don't be like this, baby."

"Like what? Like I want to go out in public with my boyfriend like a normal person?" She crossed her arms. "My parents are getting impatient, Dae-jung." Ha-rin was not going to let the subject slide, especially if she was going to mention her parents. She never let him forget that they were constantly parading chaebols around her in case her fling with a mere pop singer didn't work out.

It was this stubborn streak that had initially drawn Dae-jung to her when they'd met at a modern art gallery opening right before the pandemic had shut everything down. Jae-sung had dragged him as his plus one because Katie'd refused to fake interest in what she considered such blatantly bad art.

Dae-jung had thought Katie was exaggerating; he'd actually purchased two pieces that night. It would have been three except Ha-rin had snatched up some weird, splotchy mixed media composition before he'd had a chance to make an offer. He'd counted on his charm and starpower to convince her to sell to him at a considerable markup. Instead, Ha-rin had just laughed in his face and told him that denying him the pleasure of owning the piece only added to its value. However, for the price of an intimate dinner, he was welcome to swing by her place to look at it after.

He'd instantly been smitten.

Of course, that stubbornness was now their biggest source of conflict. Dae-jung could barely concentrate on his current texting crisis let alone attend to Ha-rin's obvious ploy to pick a fight.

"This isn't the best time, jagiya," he said, hoping to delay the inevitable.

It was the absolute wrong thing to say. "It's never a good time for you, Dae-jung," she bristled.

Dae-jung resigned himself to the inevitable. He tossed his phone onto his dark chocolate-colored comforter and turned to face Ha-rin square on. "You know we can't go out together. I'm stalked by paparazzi and there's no point in courting scandal after being so careful all these years."

Ha-rin gaped in fury. "I'm not a scandal, I'm your fucking girlfriend, Dae-jung," she hissed.

"Ha-rin-ah, what does this have to do with me meeting up with Katie?" Dae-jung held up his palms to appease her, but this was an old fight.

Though Ha-rin's perspective on his life had initially been refreshing, her worldview soon lost its shine. She was used to a privileged life, so his money and idol status didn't impress or intimidate her. As an only child, she was used to getting her own way, and it baffled her at how often Dae-jung downplayed his own desires for the good of the team at large. Of course, she understood deferring to familial pressures, but DOYEN wasn't family. In her eyes, they were merely business partners—and overly demanding ones at that.

She always fought him on DOYEN-related decisions.

They'd fought when he'd chosen to enlist at the same time as Do-won instead of delaying his military service until the last moment. As the youngest South Korean DOYEN member, he would have been the only remaining DOYEN member who still had to serve his mandatory military service. Akihiro was a Japanese citizen and Soo-min was Korean American, so they were exempt.

Ha-rin got up from the bed. "Don't 'Ha-rin-ah' me, Dae-jung," she huffed. "You know it's all connected."

"Must we do this?"

She grabbed her pillow and her phone charger. "If you're too stupid to see how easily you fall in line like a good little DOYEN member every time your hyungs say 'jump,' then I can't help you. Don't you have a will of your own?"

"Ha-rin," Da-jung said. "That's not fair."

"Grow a spine, Park Dae-jung. I'm going to sleep in the guest room—I have an early morning." Ha-rin flounced out dramatically and Dae-jung knew better than to follow her.

She would not be swayed.

It hadn't mattered then to Ha-rin that if Dae-jung had done what she'd preferred regarding military enlistment, it would have screwed up the timing for so many of DOYEN's future albums and touring options. She had known their fans wanted to see all the members together—and that his position as one of the most popular members meant that his absence would affect ticket sales.

His bandmates had counted on him enlisting before he technically had to so they could reunite earlier. In hindsight, Dae-jung acknowledged that they should have all enlisted during the pandemic, but there had been no way of knowing that it would last as long as it did.

Besides, if he had, then DOYEN wouldn't have topped the American Billboard charts for as long as they did with "Party Up" and "Baby, Baby"—and Dae-jung would have missed the opportunity to star in two separate popular dramas, as well as film a supporting role in a movie that had released while he was in the service.

He was surprised that Ha-rin and he had stayed together during his enlistment, but once Dae-jung had finished, he'd foolishly hoped things would get better.

And now, Ha-rin had so many more demands for him. She wanted him to stop giving fan service—to stop indulging his fans' beliefs that they were the most important people in his life. It didn't matter that the rest of his group saw no harm in it. He was one of the most popular members—had some of the craziest fans, but he still loved them. Their fandom CHIMERA gave him everything he had. How could he turn his back on them?

Dae-jung slumped against his tufted leather headboard and picked up his phone. His members had been busy texting with Katie while he'd been arguing with Ha-rin.

Soo-min had immediately asked for Katie's schedule without waiting for Do-won, Akihiro, or Dae-jung to chime in. After some back and forth, they'd settled on a date. Apparently she was coming into town to negotiate with a Korean publisher for the translation of her book. A quick scan of their separate chat informed him that Do-won had already found the book and that it was a memoir.

Though Do-won had already expressed his concerns, Dae-jung chimed in, too. *Are you sure we have nothing to worry about?* he asked.

If there was something scandalous in it, wouldn't we have already heard about it? reasoned Akihiro after a few moments. *Besides, Ha-joon hyung would have given us a heads up, right?*

Dae-jung supposed Akihiro was right. He usually was.

I'm in, Dae-jung replied to Katie's chat. *Sorry it took so long to reply, Noona. Got sidetracked.* He felt foolish adding the clarification, but he didn't want Katie thinking he had to be convinced to meet her, though it was true.

No apologies needed. If anything, I owe you all many apologies, Katie replied.

Dae-jung felt it was an exercise in self-control to refrain from replying that she really owed an explanation to Jae-sung, but he remembered himself and didn't. He didn't want to scare Katie away before they got some answers.

Thankfully, Soo-min chose that moment to text, *I'm telling Ha-rin noona you called her a sidetrack instead of the main event.* The cheek of him.

Yah! You're a menace, Soo-min-ah, Dae-jung texted. He knew an out when he saw one.

Tell Ha-rin I said hello, came Katie's polite response. *Thanks for chatting with me. I'll let you guys go and circle back to confirm.*

Wow. You've really been sending business emails in Korean, haven't you? teased Soo-min. *"Circle back"? Kekekekekeke.*

Lol, yeah, that was pretty cringe. It's been awhile since I've texted in Korean. I'll try to brush up on my rusty language skills!

We have all new slang to teach you, said Akihiro.

Can't wait. <3

Dae-jung didn't feel great about Jae-sung being the only one left out of the dinner, but what else could they do? Katie clearly wasn't ready to include Jae-sung—and they really wanted to know what happened. They couldn't even properly warn Jae-sung since he shut down every time her name was mentioned.

Better for them to find out first and figure out a game plan. Involving Jae-sung and his still very much unresolved feelings was a bad idea.

Dae-jung thought of Ha-rin stewing in the guest room. Katie and Jae-sung had been relationship goals, and Dae-jung was just as shocked as everyone else when she'd disappeared three years ago. It had seemed, from the outside looking in anyway, that she and Jae-sung had been perfect.

Dae-jung supposed that perhaps perfection wasn't all it was cracked up to be.

October 2016

IYKYK:
○ *first date*
○ *third date*
○ *what's a date?*
○ *stop conforming to arbitrary (and patriarchal) timelines*
        - Katie Wu, Twitter, October 2016

Jae-sung realized he'd never been to Katie's place before and was surprised by her sparse decor. Other than a large bookshelf in the corner with a collection of K-pop albums and every DOYEN album and DVD, along with a prominently displayed Lambent fan and an autographed "Misfit Cavalcade Special Edition" in pride of place, her living space was bare and utilitarian. He found it odd that none of her own albums were on display.

Katie had Korean books and notebooks scattered all over her IKEA coffee table, a guitar resting against her couch, and a cozy, burnt orange blanket thrown to the side. No art graced the walls and no knickknacks littered the surfaces. There were no framed photos or other comforting touches of home. The only decoration was a large scroll of a Chinese character he couldn't read.

"What does the hanja say?" Jae-sung asked.

Katie looked up from putting her things in their proper places. "That's the character 'yì.' It means righteousness or justice."

"Why did you choose that particular hanja?"

She regarded him carefully for a few moments, and Jae-sung wasn't sure why he felt so lacking under her sharp gaze. "It's a reminder." Katie paused. "But let justice roll down like waters, and righteousness like an ever-flowing stream," she finally said in English.

So curious. Katie never struck Jae-sung as someone who was driven by justice or righteousness. "Where's that from?"

"It's from Amos 5:24, a book in the Old Testament of the Christian Bible." She smiled sadly. "You can take the girl out of Christianity, but you can't take the Christianity out of the girl. It shaped me so irrevocably."

"What does it mean?"

A queer look crossed Katie's face and she sighed. "Amos was a Hebrew prophet who was passionate about justice and criticized corruption. Right before this verse, he talks about how God hated Israel's offerings and festivals—that instead, God wanted justice and righteousness from his people."

Katie looked somewhat embarrassed, as if she didn't want Jae-sung to see this deeply into her.

"It reminds me that outward markers of success and faith are meaningless and, in fact, despicable if we don't pursue justice for the poor and the oppressed," Katie continued.

"Is this why you don't spend your money on luxury clothes and accessories?" Jae-sung didn't know why he asked, except that he wanted to know. And for some reason, the more he caught glimpses into Katie's lissom mind, the more he wanted her.

"Is this your way of saying I dress like I have no money?" Katie laughed. "No. I don't give a shit about fashion or brands, but not because of any moral reason. I just find most of it ugly and a waste of money."

Jae-sung cocked an eyebrow at her. "Is this your way of saying you find my clothes ugly?"

"Yes. Please take them off so I don't have to look at them anymore," Katie said nonchalantly, gesturing her hand to indicate that he should get going.

He snorted. "If you wanted to see me naked, all you had to do was ask."

"I have no idea what you're talking about," Katie replied loftily.

"Is that how we're going to play it?"

Jae-sung was amused. He got the feeling that Katie wasn't nearly as confident as she had projected at dinner just an hour ago. That she did not have a lot of experience in the way of casual encounters.

"If you don't feel comfortable, we don't have to do this," he reassured as he leaned against the arm of her couch.

Katie bristled. "I'm comfortable," she replied somewhat defensively. She was such a proud creature.

"You sure?" Jae-sung wasn't sure why he goaded Katie except that if she needed to react to him—needed him as a foil to protect her pride—he could provide that for her.

He saw the instant Katie slipped into whatever public-facing persona would help her get through this moment.

"The question you should be asking, Jae-sung, is if *you're* ready."

Katie's voice was heavy, and her eyes glinted with seduction. And though he knew it for an act, his stomach still dropped in response.

Jae-sung crossed the room in two broad steps, yanked her into his embrace, and crashed his mouth into hers. Katie briefly stiffened in his arms and he almost stopped, but then she melted and kissed him back.

She was intoxicating. It wasn't just the remaining notes of the merlot on her tongue or the lingering effects of her intellect. She was the perfect amount of insistence and reserve, of bite and soothe, of tease and retreat. Jae-sung's blood roared for more.

"Katie," he gasped as he licked into her mouth, losing whatever he was going to say when she sucked on his tongue.

Katie's hands were as greedy as her mouth. She snaked her fingers through his hair, directing him to kiss deeper and—fuck, if she fucked like she kissed, then fuck.

"Ready to see if you can get and keep me wet?"

Oh. *Oh.* Insufferable woman.

Jae-sung couldn't help it. His competitive streak reared its ugly head and he wanted to impress Katie, to wipe that posturing smirk off her face. He had known many women, and from what he'd gathered at dinner, she hadn't known much more than a handful of men.

He knew the way of women much more than she likely knew the way of men—amazing kisser or not.

"Any hard stops?" he asked.

"No degradation," Katie replied in English. "And if you want to fuck me in the ass, I will need more notice."

He gulped. "You'd let me fuck you in the ass?"

"I mean, it's not my preference." Katie shrugged, "And really, you would need to give me a lot more time to prepare. There is no way I'm letting you do that to me after the dinner we just had."

Jae-sung nodded vigorously. "Okay. No ass play tonight—but in the future is a possibility with enough heads up."

Katie rolled her eyes. "Men are always the same. A perfectly good pussy in front of you and yet, you must try the back entrance if it's on the table." She snickered. "What's the matter, Jae-sung? You gonna cream your pants at the thought of sticking it in my ass alone?"

Katie's English was filthy. It actually tracked that she wouldn't know how to say most sex stuff in Korean. If he was honest with himself, Jae-sung was excited by the prospect of her being an apt pupil to all the nasty shit he was already planning to teach her. And if she was on her knees during part of the instruction, all the better.

He wanted to hear Katie choke.

"What about you?" she asked. "Is that hole in play for you, or are you more of a 'do as I say and not as I do' kind of guy?"

"Oh, um," Jae-sung stumbled out. "I—I don't know. No? Probably no for now."

Katie stepped back and appraised him with a heated once-over, lingering on the swell of his crotch. "Come on, Jae. It's been a long day and I want to lay down."

She turned and pulled off her hoodie and shirt in one smooth motion. Jae-sung saw her bare back, uninterrupted ink swirling in Chinese calligraphy style—a snapping dragon taking up the majority of her back, a cyborg rooster, a crouching tiger, and four hanja characters at the base of her neck. He belatedly realized she hadn't been wearing a bra this entire time.

Fuck.

Katie felt so good beneath him. After she'd informed him that no outside clothes were allowed on the bed, she'd kicked off her joggers, underwear, and socks, and unceremoniously spread herself on her bed. She hadn't been kidding about wanting to lie down.

Jae-sung had stripped himself as fast as he could and climbed on top of Katie, careful to settle his weight between her legs and on his forearms. He'd immediately reclaimed her lips as her hands had wandered, exploring the planes of his body. His own hands had wandered back, caressing her curves.

And now, Katie was panting and arching into him as he fucked into her softness. She sounded so good that he was grateful the condom dulled his sensitivity.

"You like that, baby?" Jae-sung asked as he rolled his hips into her. At Katie's encouraging moans, he switched up his rhythm, determined to wow her with his stable of signature moves.

Katie's moans faded to light sighs and then to quiet as she bit her lip. He nuzzled her neck and breathed heavily into her ear. She sucked in a breath and let out a whispered "fuck." Jae-sung grinned, pleased with himself as he changed his pace once again and began to thrust shallowly into her as Katie tried to chase him. He had stunned her into silence and Katie wasn't a really loud lover anyway, so he wasn't worried.

"Harder, Jae," Katie murmured as she grabbed Jae-sung by the ass and pulled him deeper into her. "I like it hard and fast."

He obliged her, and Katie resumed a steady stream of "yeses" and "mores." But Jae-sung was getting close and he didn't want to come so fast—not when Katie hadn't come yet—so he altered his tempo once again, eager to show off. After that, he changed up his moves every few minutes—even flipping Katie onto her stomach and then to her back again—until finally, she pushed him off.

"Katie?" He was confused.

Katie sat up, looking thoroughly annoyed. "Do the girls you usually fuck enjoy being flipped from front to back every seventeen thrusts?"

Jae-sung felt his cheeks heat up. "I've never had any complaints."

"Well, they lied." Katie looked semi-regretful at that blistering assessment. "Sorry, Jae-sung. Even K-pop songs only have eight to nine change-ups max, and it was starting to hurt."

She kissed him gently on the cheek and got up from her bed, picking up her clothes from the floor to throw in her hamper. She walked out of her room, presumably to the bathroom, and Jae-sung was left alone—naked and with a rapidly wilting boner.

After a few moments, Jae-sung shook himself out of his shock, pulled off the condom, and tossed it in her wastebasket. He gathered his own clothes and put them back on. He didn't know what to do. Usually, he left after fucking and only rarely cuddled—mostly because they were both rushing to get back to their living quarters.

But this time, while he supposed technically Katie was finished fucking, he couldn't imagine just creeping out of her apartment while she was in the bathroom. Jae-sung wasn't sure how he was going to be able to work with her in the same studio the next day, but he dutifully went to her living room and sat on her light gray sofa.

When Katie finally emerged, still naked, she took one look at him and sighed. "Gimme a second, Jae," she said as she strolled to her bedroom, changed into pajamas, and came back out.

"I guess I was right," joked Jae-sung through his extreme embarrassment. "You did tap out first."

"Ah, I suppose I did," Katie acknowledged. "Even though one could make the case that I did stipulate you had to get and then keep me wet."

Jae-sung wanted the floor to open up and swallow him whole, but he wasn't the leader of DOYEN for nothing. He was good under pressure and excellent at taking feedback and criticism. (Not that his ego enjoyed it. And never had it been about his sexual performance.)

"Are you hurt?" he forced himself to ask.

"Nothing that I can't recover from." Katie flashed him a wry smile. "Listen, I didn't think you were literally going to fuck my pussy 'til I'm battered and bruised—"

"Katie!" Jae-sung's face went up in flames even as his brain automatically supplied the next line of "a bitch like you only begs to be used."

He didn't know whether he should be mortified or flattered that she'd dredged up his horrifyingly problematic Soundcloud track he'd posted as a teenage trainee. He had been trying so hard to be cool and push back against the emasculated image of male idols that he'd tread into toxic misogyny instead. He was lucky that he'd learned from the justifiable outcry instead of doubling down.

Katie took pity on him and cupped his face kindly, thumbing his cheek. "As impressed as I am by your stamina, an hour and a half is a bit excessive, Jae-sung."

"Edging is a thing, Katie," he huffed.

"But that requires getting a person close."

Jae-sung let Katie's words sink in and tried to quell his defensiveness and shame. He supposed she did not have to tell him the truth, that she could have lied to save his feelings. Perhaps it meant something that she didn't fake an orgasm and then ghost him. And then, Jae-sung horrified himself with the thought that all the other women he'd been with in the past had faked it. Surely, he would be able to tell, right?

"I can see you are having an internal crisis," Katie said in English as she sighed again. "I concede that I could have been more obvious in my cues and given you more direct feedback."

"Please tell me you don't actually talk like this after sex," sniped Jae-sung. "I'm getting flashbacks of trainee evaluations."

Katie ran a hand through her mussed hair. "Look, I don't know how to do this, okay? Johnny was the only person I had sex with enough to even need to give feedback to. He had a lot more experience, and I just went along with it. I eventually figured it out."

It was lowering to be compared to a man as awful as Johnny and be found wanting. "Is that why you stayed so long with him? He was good at fucking?"

Katie winced. "Nine months is a long time in your world, huh?" she fired back. "I stayed because I loved him. And yes, he was generally good at fucking, and when I didn't like something, he was very persuasive." Regret flashed across her face. "So perhaps, I am not as good at communicating what I want in the same way you are not as good at delivering dick as you'd like to be."

Jae-sung was appropriately chastened. "I'm sorry, Katie. That was shitty of me."

"Yeah, well, I suppose I could have been a bit easier on your ego," Katie replied. "I'm sorry I was insensitive."

"Can I make it up to you?" he asked.

Katie chuckled. "Buy me some bungeo-ppang and we'll call it even."

"Let me eat you out," he begged, uncaring of his ego. "I promise I'm really good at that."

A careful wariness returned to Katie's eyes. "You don't have to make it up to me, Jae-sung," she said quietly. "You don't have to prove anything to me. I'm—I'm sorry I made it seem as if you needed to impress me and do all the work."

"What are you saying, Katie?"

"Look, I'm terrible at this casual business," Katie said as she finally joined him on her couch. "I don't have any clue how to be nonchalant and whatever about fucking—especially with people I consider friends."

"But you said—"

"I think you and I both know that I'm full of shit, hmmm?"

Katie was right. He had suspected, but now he knew. "Then why?"

"I—I would like to be different. I would like to be the kind of person who just fucks and takes what she wants." Katie shrugged and seemed to shrink in front of him. "I'd like to think it's just something you practice..." Her voice tapered off as she fiddled with her fingers. "My mother always said 'Practice makes permanent,' and I was hoping it would be true."

"And you were going to practice on me?" Jae-sung asked.

"You seemed as good a person to start with as any," Katie replied. "You're hot, you're smart, and you seem a decent sort."

"You think I'm hot?"

Katie's eyes swept over Jae-sung's body and lingered on his mouth. "The ash gray hair is a look." She did not elaborate.

Jae-sung paused to think. And then. "Let me take you out on a date."

"Jae, you really don't have to do this."

"Please."

"What, you think the third time's a charm?" Katie asked in a mix of English and Korean.

"Third time's a charm?"

Katie's lip quirked in amusement. "It's an American idiom. Like, if something's already failed two times, you try one more time because maybe the third time will succeed."

"But it would only be twice?"

She speared him with a glance. "Oh, I guess your dick pressing into my ass was just my imagination."

"As I recall, you pressed back."

"A moment of weakness."

It was Jae-sung's turn to level her with his dragon eyes. "Would you have let me fuck you if you hadn't been so hungover?"

"I don't know," Katie said as she averted his gaze.

Liar. "How long have you been wanting to fuck me, Katie?"

"Time is a construct."

Jae-sung barked a laugh. "Alright, be like that."

"I don't need your permission," Katie muttered.

"Baby, let me take you on a proper date."

Katie's eyes narrowed. "I am not your baby."

"You could be, though. If you wanted." He watched as his words hit. Jae-sung could be smooth if he wanted, too.

December 2016

Do you:
◯ believe in life after love
◯ know where you're going to
- Katie Wu, Twitter, December 2016

Something was different with Jae-sung. Dae-jung wasn't sure exactly what, but something was different. He was gone a lot during their limited free time and he seemed to be perpetually in a good mood—like he was finally getting his dick sucked on the regular.

Oh. That must be it.

Dae-jung made a mental note to confer with Akihiro about this development. Akihiro probably already knew who the other person was despite Dae-jung being Jae-sung's roommate.

Akihiro knew everything.

Regardless, Dae-jung was exhausted with preparations for all the year-end shows. Though he didn't have much to do with their company's relocation to a bigger building, he still felt the stress permeating their staff as everyone rushed to prepare so many stages and logistics.

Though Katie wasn't performing in any of the shows, she was busy rehearsing for her upcoming Asia tour. Occasionally, when Dae-jung had a sliver of free time, he would sneak into her space to watch her dance or practice playing her songs solo in conjunction with a looper pedal.

While Katie was a decent dancer and performer, Dae-jung found her use of the looper pedal the most fascinating. She'd explained to him how after a lot of fiddling and work with the SB Entertainment sound engineers, they'd built her a custom looper pedal, and she was constantly rearranging her music to be played live by her array of instruments on stage.

No matter how many times he'd seen Katie record a line of music or vocal effect on the machine and then incorporate supporting melodies and countermelodies, it was like watching magic. She was masterful with the intricate timings. The joy that spread over her face was contagious as she live-built the supporting audio track anew every performance.

Sometimes, Katie would even let Dae-jung fuck around with the machine and record his own little loops. If he was honest, those were the moments he most looked forward to during the slog of endless rehearsals. That and witnessing Katie's face radiate delight. She was luminous.

And thus, he was confused when he popped by their shared studio for his usual dose of her playing and saw Katie curled up on the floor hyperventilating.

"Noona?" he asked. "Noona, are you okay?"

With her eyes shut tight, Katie shook her head lightly. "No," she gasped in English.

"Oh, shit," Dae-jung said. "Let me go get manager-nim."

"No!" she cried.

Katie sucked in another breath and tried to hold it in an attempt to regulate her breathing. Dae-jung could see wet tracks of her tears seeping from the corners of her eyes.

"Noona, I don't know what to do. I don't know how to help," he said as calmly as he could. "Can I text the members for help?"

At her terse nod, Dae-jung texted the group chat. *Noona is hyperventilating or maybe having a panic attack? I don't know what to do—can someone please come to our studio and help?*

Be right there, Jae-sung replied.

"Noona, Jae-sung hyung is on his way," Dae-jung said, breathing a sigh of relief. "You're going to be okay."

Katie squeezed her eyes shut and resumed counting random numbers in English. When Jae-sung finally arrived a few minutes later, he immediately ran to her side and said, "I'm here, baby."

Dae-jung's mind tripped over the endearment, but his brain really had trouble processing when he heard Jae-sung ask, "Can I hold you?" At her nod, Jae-sung scooped Katie into his arms and kissed her temple.

Dae-jung tucked that information to unpack at a later moment, all the while noting how Jae-sung told Katie to inhale, hold her breath, and then exhale. Her fists were still clenched tight though Jae-sung had wrapped himself around her, reminding Katie how to breathe. He assured her that it would pass soon, that she wasn't dying, and that she was safe.

When Katie's panic attack finally passed and she finally realized how close she was to Jae-sung, she startled a bit and pulled away, much to Jae-sung's obvious disappointment. Fascinating.

Katie shot Dae-jung a wan smile. "Thanks, Dae," she murmured. "Sorry for worrying you."

"I'm just glad you're okay, Noona." He paused. "You are okay, right?"

"Yeah, I should be fine now," she reassured.

Jae-sung stroked her hair tenderly and she shivered. "You want to talk about it?"

Katie folded her knees under her arms, and shook out another breath. Dae-jung hated seeing her so small and vulnerable. It seemed so at odds with how she was normally that it broke his heart.

"I texted my father to let him know I was going to be in Hong Kong next month for the tour," Katie finally said. Dae-jung had never heard her mention her father before. "He lives across the river in Shenzhen," she explained, "but it's been two weeks. He still hasn't responded."

Her eyes welled up again.

"Maybe he's just busy?" Jae-sung suggested.

Dae-jung wanted to smack his leader. Sometimes, he was pretty dumb for a genius.

Katie's eyes shuttered and she retreated. "You're probably right," she said placidly. "I'm sure he's fine, and I'm just worried for no reason."

Katie was lying. It was obvious to Dae-jung that she hadn't been worried about her father's well-being, but he didn't want to call her on it. Clearly, she wanted to keep it to herself.

He shot her a questioning look and she just stubbornly set her chin and glanced away.

"Anyway," Katie said airily, "I tried to rehearse my concert set with the loop pedal but I kept getting the timing off. Then I couldn't stop thinking about it failing spectacularly while live and, well, you get the idea."

Jae-sung pulled Katie into another embrace despite the alarm crossing her features. "Baby, you're going to be amazing. You just got thrown off today."

Katie cleared her throat and distanced herself from Jae-sung, shooting him an unreadable warning as Jae-sung started guiltily.

It was too late, however. Dae-jung knew with sudden clarity that Katie was the reason Jae-sung was in such a good mood lately and couldn't wait to tell Akihiro. He was a little surprised that it was Jae-sung and not Woo-jin she'd ended up with, but this development was definitely far more titillating due to the surprise factor.

Dae-jung excused himself, but they weren't slick. Or rather, Jae-sung wasn't slick. Katie on the other hand? Dae-jung had a feeling she was exceedingly good at hiding in plain sight.

January 2017

HONG KOOOOOOOONNNNNNNNNNNGGGG I AM IN YOUUUUUUUUUUU Xiānggǎng wǒ zài nǐ lǐmiàn~~~!
- Katie Wu, Twitter, January 2017

gimme all the carbs & meats ~ pineapple buns, egg tarts, boba, noodles, zongzi, roast goose, duck, pork, dim sum, char siu ~gimme gimme gimme
- Katie Wu, Twitter, January 2017

Katie had just finished throwing up in the restroom backstage and was hopped up on pre-show jitters when someone knocked on her dressing room door. "Come in," she called.

"Hey, Katie," said Ha-joon, dressed in all black as always. "Someone claiming to be your father is at the door and threatening to start a scene."

Katie's stomach sank. "Does he have any ID or did anyone take a picture? I thought I put my father's name on a list to allow him backstage."

"Ah, yes. The thing is, the names don't quite match—it's likely because of the different kinds of romanization—but since you're still getting shit from those incels, we wanted to make extra sure," explained her manager. "Here's his picture and a picture of his American passport."

Katie stared at the familiar face. Thomas Wu looked as if he'd aged a lot since she'd last seen him—but she knew never to trust her own eyes or ears with him. Her father always lied.

"That's him," she said. "How much time do I have before I need to go to hair and makeup?"

"About thirty minutes."

Katie knew it was a bad idea, but she really did not want her father to cause an incident outside her venue. Plus, she wanted to see him despite the lack of notice. The last time she'd seen him was when she'd left for "The Singer Songwriter" reality show.

She gave Ha-joon the go-ahead and before she knew it, Katie was hugging her father for the first time in at least four years.

"Of course," Katie said dully, the roar in her ears threatening to drown out all sound.

"I knew I could count on you," her father praised as he clapped smugly. He was always jovial when he got his way.

"Oh, that's not what I meant," she choked out as her father's face changed like quicksilver. "I can't give you the money. It's too much, Baba. I barely just finished paying off your Taiwanese debts."

Katie wasn't strictly lying. She *had* just finished paying off the debts, but she did have some money. She just didn't want to hand it over to her father.

"Ah, wá," her father said, his voice taking on a conciliatory tone. "Those people took advantage of you, bǎobèi. They were investors, not lenders, and they shouldn't have gone after you."

Katie couldn't believe her ears. She had seen the contracts—had had her lawyers and her grandfather's lawyers check the veracity and validity of the contracts her father had abandoned in Taiwan.

It was just like him to gaslight her.

She bit down on her tongue until she could taste blood, for once listening to her brother and her mother.

"But these men—these are bad men, bǎobèi," her father said. "They will go after me, your mother, and even you and Mattie."

A chill slithered down Katie's spine.

"I don't believe you." She did not *want* to believe him. She hardened her voice. "How much do you owe?"

"A million dollars."

"U.S.?" Katie felt faint.

She recognized the curt nod her father executed. Hers was its exact carbon copy.

"Take it out of the house."

He laughed, mocking and empty. "No bank will loan us any more money. It's already mortgaged to the hilt."

"Ask Nǎinai or Ah-Gong."

"I already have. I refuse to beggar my mother, and your mother's father won't take my calls."

Katie wanted to scoff. Her father had no qualms about beggaring her or *her* mother's family—but didn't want to take his own mother for everything—because he already had, stealing his own brother's inheritance. She did not blame her ah-gong for disclaiming her reprobate father.

"Mommy already has me covering Mattie's tuition and the mortgage—"

"Your mother doesn't know."

Katie was going to pass out. She couldn't do this. "What?"

"I didn't want to stress her out—her health hasn't been the best lately," said her father.

She did not buy his concern for one second. In the end, that's what tipped it. She simply did not believe him. Her father was never credible. He had cried wolf one too many times, and she was tired.

"No," Katie said.

"No?" Her father's face deepened to a purplish-red.

She stood and moved out of his reach. "No," she repeated.

"You worthless whore," he hissed.

"I'm not your daughter anymore, remember? What do I care if you lose your home? It's not as if it's mine anymore. You threw all of my things out after the scandal with Johnny, remember?"

Her father surged to his feet. Katie had forgotten how he used to loom over her, his six-foot frame and muscular build blocking out the light. He was an ox of a man. She resisted the urge to step back or cower and steeled herself for what would happen next.

"If you don't, I will go to the papers and sell your story to the highest bidder."

"What story?" Katie could not resist taking his bait. "There is no story."

A wicked smile spread over her father's features. "Johnny reached out to me a few months ago."

All the blood drained from her face. "What?"

"He was very respectful and apologetic. Begged for my forgiveness and for my help to win you back."

He paused for dramatic emphasis. Katie was helplessly ensnared.

"Johnny enlightened me on so many things—both about your stint on the show and how you got that contract at SB Entertainment." Her father paused again. "Really, Kǎi Tíng-ah. I approve of using whatever assets you have, but stop reusing the same play every time. Sex can't always get you whatever you want. I didn't raise you to be so common."

"Johnny lied."

"I know. But the press doesn't care, does it?"

Katie did not know her father could still break her heart. "You would ruin me. You could never get any money from me again after. You wouldn't kill your golden goose."

"Who pà who, bǎobèi? Who pà who?" he sneered.

His words triggered an immediate desire to fold. Katie had been conditioned since her childhood to choose a safer strategy when her father would declare "who pà who?" or "who's afraid of who?" right before he was about to win at cards. Later, he started to say it arbitrarily. It wasn't until later that she'd realized he was bluffing—except by then, it was too late. The dread that he was going to destroy her hand could not be rooted out.

What kind of father groomed his child to yield in something as trivial as a card game?

Katie capitulated. It had never been about cards.

"I can only spare fifty thousand," she said, and her father knew he had won.

Katie could see the triumph lighting his dark eyes. She knew he would ultimately take more than the fifty she opened with. It was never about the dollar amount; it was always about bending her to his will.

February 2017

The way our girl full on ugly cried watching the Return to Me MV. Same, girl. Same.

          - Twitter user, February 2017

Did she just say she wanted to be a table because of the way Lambent stroked it?

          - Twitter user, February 2017

Her face got all dreamy and googly-eyed every time Jun showed up on screen. So hilarious to watch someone get wrecked in real time.

          - Twitter user, February 2017

Oh, she hype! Katie screaming RUN ME MY MONEY with her whole chest!

          - Twitter user, February 2017

WAS THAT LAMBENT AT THE BEGINNING OF THE VIDEO HANDING HER A BULDAK RAMYEON SAYING THAT SHE'LL NEED IT? IT SOUNDS LIKE HIM!!!

          - Twitter user, February 2017

OMG HER SCREECH WHEN THE CAMERA OPENS ON LAMBENT

- Twitter user, February 2017

lol so much screaming! how many times did she rewind that part where lambent thumbs his nose? i lost count. lololololol

- Twitter user, February 2017

the way this poor woman refuses to look directly at the screen whenever soo-min is the focus. kekekekekekekeekekke

- Twitter user, February 2017

Did they give her a buldak ramyeon so they don't have to bleep out as many swears? Maybe that's why Lambent delivered it. He knows what he did.

- Twitter user, February 2017

Katie aggressively slurping and chewing those noodles and then immediately regretting when the spice hits every time she's triggered by Lambent is fucking brillz. I hope it becomes a thing.

- Twitter user, February 2017

"Did you miss me, baby?" Jae-sung was currently lying naked on Katie's bed and hadn't bothered pitching his voice higher. At Katie's shiver, he knew he'd made the right choice.

Katie kissed lazily down his neck and chest. "I'm still so mad I didn't get back in time for your Seoul concerts," she complained. "I almost committed a crime." She nipped his pectoral and then soothed the sting with a pulsing suck. "Wait, is watching illegal streams on Periscope committing or being an accessory to a crime?"

"Hmmmm?"

Admittedly Jae-sung had stopped paying attention when he realized she was kissing a slow path down to his dick. All the blood rushed out of his brain at the prospect of getting brain.

Katie's chuckle rumbled low and throaty. "From what I saw, you were dripping, and all I could think of was licking you clean. Even in 144p."

Jae-sung's cock twitched. "Oh?" He placed a heavy hand on her head and was rewarded with a moan.

For all that Katie seemed domineering and intractable in real life, she was surprisingly pliant in bed. It wasn't that she was submissive in the BDSM sense. More so that she liked direction given by a firm and steady hand. She had likened it once to decision fatigue. Katie just wanted to shut off her mind and sink into someone who was not her—and Jae-sung didn't mind being that person.

"I missed your cock so much, Jae," she said in between kissing and sucking along his hip bones. Her hot breath graced the sensitive skin of his inner thighs.

"Did you?" His voice was already blown.

Katie's answer was to sink her wet, wet mouth down his dick. She was not in the mood to tease anymore now that her prize was in sight and, quite frankly, Jae-sung approved of the decision. He gathered her hair into a messy, faded blue ponytail and held it by the roots.

All Jae-sung could register was how deep she took him, how he hit the back of her throat, how she pushed him in even more, how he could feel the flex and constriction of her muscles as she accommodated him. He could hear the slick and squelch and spit. Before he could give her a warning, he shot, thick and gushy into her throat.

When he lifted his head to really look at her, Katie was a mess. Tear stains down her cheeks. Slobber and come down her chin. Flyaway hairs framing her face.

Katie was a vision.

Later, when Jae-sung was getting ready to return to the apartment he shared with his bandmates, Katie casually tossed out a "Hey, I know you're leaving on tour in a few days so..." from where she sat on the bed, uncertain amidst her cream-colored sheets.

Jae-sung paused gathering his things and took in her affected indifference. For all that Katie was open to him with her body, she was still so very much a mystery.

"So, what?" He lifted a singular brow at Katie and took immense satisfaction with how that simple motion affected her.

"If you want to see other people while you're traveling, I'm cool with it," she said.

"You'll have to be more specific. I see a lot of people."

Jae-sung didn't know why he always provoked Katie, except that maybe he wasn't sure of where he stood with her either. Jae-sung wasn't sure if he liked what that said about him.

The slight crease in Katie's forehead was the only indication of her feelings. "Oh. Right. I—well, now I feel dumb—you never needed my—we never—" She smoothed her countenance. She took a deep breath. She continued, "I'll see you when you get back."

Jae-sung didn't know how Katie did it. How could she vanquish him with just a few words? How did she not know how much she meant to him? Wasn't it obvious in his every action?

"Katie," he said. Her dark eyes darted to his. He caught only a glimpse of the panic before she tamped it down. "Katie, I'm crazy about you."

"Oh."

"Oh?" Jae-sung could not help the lilt of amusement in his tone. "Unless you were telling me so that you could fuck other people?"

Katie's eyes widened in shock. "What? No—no! I—I don't want to fuck other people. I—" She shut her mouth.

Jae-sung took pity on her and sat on her bed, ignoring Katie's unspoken protest about his outside clothes on her green-checkered duvet.

"Katie, if you're trying to tell me I can fuck whomever I want when I'm on tour—which I appreciate your, uh, concession to my needs—then you better be prepared to come on tour with me. You're the only one I want."

"Oh," Katie said, eyes shimmering. And then, it was as if his words finally sunk in. "Oh my god, Jae-sung—I can't go on tour with you—I have to make money—" She physically clamped a hand over her mouth.

"Didn't you just sell out a tour?" he asked, confused.

Did Katie have money troubles? Is that why her living quarters were so spartan? Why she brought all her meals to work and rarely ordered in? Why she was constantly sending out her songs to other studios and trying to improve her production skills?

"I did," Katie said as lightheartedly as she could manage. "You know we're only as successful as our last hit."

Jae-sung knew she was evading his question, but he let her lead him astray. "Is success that important to you?"

Katie was dodging something important, but he couldn't pinpoint what it was. But he supposed her money was none of his business.

"Isn't it to everyone?" Katie replied, answering his question with another question. She flicked her blue-blond bangs out of her eyes. "Wait, so are you my boyfriend now?"

The abrupt change in topic surprised a laugh out of Jae-sung. He grinned, knowing full well his dimples were out on display and that they made Katie weak.

"I can be, if you want. I can be whatever you want me to be."

"In that case, can you be a pastrami sandwich?"

Katie was infuriating. He leaned in to kiss her. "Stop running, Katie," he said against her lips. Jae-sung deepened his kiss.

"Be my boyfriend, Jae," Katie whispered into his mouth as she leaned back, pulling him on top of her.

He never did make it back to his apartment that night.

June 2017

Katie Wu's new LP "Crossroads" (SB Entertainment, 2017) continues examining the spiritual bargains we make to live in a secular world, a theme that was previously explored in "Gain All the World" (SB Entertainment, 2016). Showcasing her astonishing versatility throughout, Wu's contemplative lyrics, lyrical and raging rap styles, soaring vocals, haunting melodies, exciting ad-libs, and excellent production value create a brilliant rendering of the morality play "Faust" and is absolutely fantastic.

Unfortunately, it's highly unlikely the general public will appreciate this complex, operatic album. More an epic tale in song form, "Crossroads" is not easy fare. Opening with the annunciatory "Mephistopheles," Wu grabs you by the throat and never lets you breathe. Each successive track builds on the former until the climactic "Hermes, You Cheat," a piercing introspective on the choices we make in the pursuit of our ambitions. Ending on the resolute "There Is Only Forward," the piece is not necessarily hopeful so much as it is fatalistic. Oddly enough, the most relatable piece is "A Crone, Filled With Potential," which is a master class on fear, yearning, and despair.

- The Korea Times, June 2017

An intellectual tour de force, "Crossroads" is a visceral account of temptation, moral quandary, ambition, fear, surrender, and perseverance. That Katie Wu conveys all of this through killer beats, challenging orchestration, and agonizing lyrics is a miracle. Not radio-friendly in the slightest, "Crossroads" is a must-listen.

- The Hankyoreh, June 2017

[1] Mephistopheles [2:36]
[2] Sleepless Nights [2:47]
[3] Liminal Spaces [3:29]
[4] A Crone, Filled With Potential [3:41]
[5] Faustian Bargain [3:30]
[6] No Relation to Morals [3:24]
[7] Reputation Killer [2:09]

[8] Hermes, You Cheat [3:13]
[9] There Is Only Forward [2:58]
                    - Track list, "Crossroads" (SB Entertainment, 2017)

Got me laid low
And buried deep
When they root us out
That fall is a killer
                    - "Reputation Killer" (SB Entertainment, 2017)

Will I look back on the road untaken
Rue the rusted sword and spear
Made a decision by never making one
Not even a plowshare or pruning hook to show

Frost, a robber corroding my still full clip
Better to be even half-cocked
Than this careful, shrinking perfection
Of nothing ventured, nothing gained
- "A Crone, Filled With Potential" (SB Entertainment, 2017)

Jae-sung was in the middle of soundcheck with his bandmates in Saita-ma when his phone wouldn't stop vibrating in his pocket. When he finally checked the caller ID backstage, he frowned. Katie knew his schedule and almost never called during work hours.

Something must be wrong.

He found a tucked away corner and called her back. "Hey, baby. You okay?" asked Jae-sung.

"I'm so sorry to bother you, Jae." Her voice sounded muffled and wet.

"You're never a bother, baby. Are you okay?"

Katie was quiet, as if mustering up the courage to talk to him. It was such an odd stray thought that Jae-sung's mind snagged on it and refused to let it go. Fear was never a word he would use to describe her.

"No."

"Do you want to talk about it? I have a few moments before they need me."

"I don't know if I can stay in music, Jae," Katie said, her voice coming out in small sobs. "My album isn't doing well—and I don't know what to do."

"I thought the reviews were all raving?" he asked.

"I don't care about reviews, Jae-sung-ah," she replied. "Who cares if critics love my shit if no one is buying it? If it doesn't get played on the radio? If I'm labeled too erudite and intellectual for the masses?"

"Didn't you say the pre-orders were encouraging? That your fans were streaming and posting?"

Katie sucked in a ragged breath or two and held it, as if she was trying to control her breathing. Jae-sung could tell his words weren't hitting. He didn't know what to say.

"It's not enough. The numbers are lower than the projections—and SB Entertainment's bottom line is going to take a hit," Katie said quietly. "I don't think I can tour on this album."

"Your album is amazing, Katie," Jae-sung said. He meant it, too.

"It doesn't matter. Amazing doesn't keep the lights on—and it just puts more pressure on DOYEN to carry the company." She sniffled. "It would be smarter for PD-nim to cut his losses."

"Has PD-nim said anything to you?"

Katie went quiet again. "He said, 'Good work.' And then told me he loved the album and that he was proud of me."

"PD-nim said that?" Jae-sung was floored. Song Byung-ho wasn't like other producers and CEOs, but still. This seemed extra soft, even for him. Maybe it was because Katie was American. "That doesn't sound like he plans to cut you."

Katie was silent for so long, Jae-sung wasn't sure if she was still there. "Katie?"

"Yeah?"

"It will be okay, baby. You will be okay." He really wanted Katie to know that deep in her bones.

"I don't know if it will be okay in time, Jae," she whispered.

Klaxons blared in Jae-sung's brain. "Wait—what do you mean, Katie? Are you—you're not thinking of self-harm, are you?" He wondered just how quickly Ha-joon could get to her.

"What? Oh my god, no!" she replied quickly. "No, oh my god, no, Jae. I'm not—Jesus—I'm not *that* dramatic about sales. Fuck."

"Oh, thank fuck," he said. But then what did she mean? "In time for what though, Katie?"

"I don't think I'm out of the probationary period of my life insurance anyway. It wouldn't work," Katie mused, as if she hadn't heard him.

"The fuck, Katie?"

She occasionally slipped into morbid humor, but Jae-sung hated it. Hated that he couldn't tell if Katie was really that dark. Hated that if she was, she hid it so well and so often that it only leaked out occasionally.

Katie paused. "It's a joke, Jae-sung."

"It's a shitty joke."

She sighed. "I'm sorry for worrying you."

"S'okay," he pouted.

"Thanks for listening to me, Jae-sung. I'll let you go," she said and then hung up.

It wasn't until after his concert that night that Jae-sung realized two salient points: Katie had never told him what it would be too late for, and she needed money. Badly.

CHAPTER 4

March 2024

> *I was always afraid. Every time my father was home, I was afraid. Every time I received a call from an unknown number, I was afraid. Would this be when they told me he'd finally killed her? And yet, my mother always chose him. Why could she never choose me? What was so wrong with me that my own father and mother could walk away from me so easily?*
> - "Telling a Truth Is a Slippery Slope" (Red Lantern Publishing House, October 2023)

Jae-sung was seeing things.

No way was this happening again. Surely after the last time, Katie Wu would know better than to show up unannounced in his city. In his company. In his life.

Except there she was. Again. Sitting on one of the butter yellow easy chairs in the artists' lounge—of all places—and surrounded by his bandmates. Traitors.

All he'd wanted was an Americano from the fancy coffee machine in the lounge kitchenette and there Katie was, dressed head to toe in excessively warm clothing. She and her thin blood could never handle the cold.

"What are you doing here?" Jae-sung asked icily.

Katie flicked her gaze to meet his, her eyes as dark and challenging as they ever were. "I work here," she replied, voice neutral and devoid of any warmth, but also missing his abject hostility.

"Bullshit."

Ye-jun glared at him, his normally warm, brown eyes full of admonishment, evident even from across the room. "Show some respect, Jae-sung," he said.

"How can you say that after what she did to me, Hyung? What she did to all of us?" Jae-sung exclaimed.

"Jae-sung, that's enough." Woo-jin's voice cut through Jae-sung's emotional haze, the eldest rapper's tone brooking no argument. He stood and crossed from his place on the slate gray sectional against the wall to the side of Katie's chair. She looked up at Woo-jin, a hint of a sad smile at her lips.

"Why does everyone keep saying that to me?"

"Because if you'd just pull your head out of your ass, you would figure it out!" Ye-jun scolded from a matching yellow chair by Katie. Even though his hyung was dressed in a soft lavender sweater, there was nothing soft in his demeanor.

Did their thirteen years of history together mean nothing to them? It hurt Jae-sung that both his hyungs were so blatantly on Katie's side, even after all she'd done to him. Newly finished with their mandatory military enlistment, Ye-jun and Woo-jin had seen firsthand what a drunken mess he'd been when she'd disappeared.

The only reason Jae-sung hadn't done anything more stupid was that he'd had to enlist for his own military service shortly thereafter. The grueling boot camp and regimented military schedule had provided a lifeline. When his eighteen months of service were finished, he'd finally wrestled his emotions into a more acceptable form.

"Our company just bought Firefly Publishing, the indie publishing house that Noona is signed with in Korea," Do-won provided helpfully. "It was literally announced at the last company-wide meeting, Hyung."

Katie was surprisingly silent, although Jae-sung supposed he didn't know her enough anymore to make a judgment about what would be surprising or not. He found her unnatural stillness disquieting.

"I didn't know Katie was published by them," Jae-sung said woodenly. He resisted the urge to fidget and pull on the hem of his oversized A Bathing Ape hoodie. "I didn't even know she'd written a book."

"She's been on the New York Times Best Sellers list for months, Hyung," Soo-min said softly, as if he was trying to soothe a wild animal. "Noona's here to record the Korean audiobook."

"At our studios?" It was ridiculous. As if SB Entertainment was the only studio in Seoul.

Akihiro sighed from the sectional as he ran a hand through his black hair. "SB Entertainment owns the publishing house now, Hyung. And because they're so small, they don't have their own recording studios."

"You all knew this whole time and no one told me?" Jae-sung was furious. He was hurt. He was—he didn't know what he was.

Woo-jin scoffed. Loudly. "And how were we supposed to have told you, Jae-sung? We can't even bring her up around you."

"Hyung, do we really want to discuss this right now?" Dae-jung interjected, gently placing a hand on Jae-sung's shoulder.

"I should go," Katie finally said. She stood up and bent down to heft her very practical army green cross-body bag over her shoulder. He recognized it from their years together. "It was good to see you all again," she said, belatedly adding a formal-sounding "Jae-sung." Clearly she did not include him among the people she found good to see.

Jae-sung once again was unable to control his mouth. "Go on and run away again, Katie. It's what you're best at isn't it?"

He heard the sharp intake of breaths all around. He was not sorry.

"Apologize to Katie, Jae-sung," Ye-jun said, flexing his rarely exerted hyung status.

Jae-sung should have expected this from Ye-jun and Woo-jin. They'd made clear they were her staunchest supporters. The three of them had always had some weird bond, which he'd supported when they were dating. It had meant a lot to him that Katie was so close to the people he loved more than anyone else in the world.

Katie sighed. He recognized the patient forbearance in it. Had always hated the sound. "He doesn't have to apologize, Oppa," she said roughly.

"I'm not sorry anyway."

Katie chuckled mirthlessly. "Yes, I can see that."

"Were you going to tell me you were here? Or did you lie last time, too?" queried Jae-sung, voice wobbling.

"Let's give them some privacy," Jae-sung heard Do-won say. Do-won was always looking out for him.

"I was considering it," Katie said as the rest of his members shuffled out of the lounge, "but obviously, I decided not to."

"Why not?"

Katie's face gave very little away. He'd never realized she could be so empty of expression. She was so very changed. His heart grieved for the woman he used to love even as he tried to armor himself against her. She did not deserve to be mourned.

"I'm here to do a job, Jae-sung. I have limited time in the studio, and I don't have the emotional bandwidth to record this book and also deal with you."

"I don't care. You will deal with me now."

Katie raised a single eyebrow at him. He hated how he used to watch her practice that lift in the mirror for hours until he couldn't stand how infuriatingly hot it would make her. He'd always take her to bed for hours after.

He hated how his memories of Katie were still so clear and brought into all the starker relief because of her presence.

"Very well, Jae-sung. Let's go."

July 2017

SINGAPOOOOOOOOORRRRRRRRREEEEEE I AM IN YOUUUUUUUUUUU Xīnjiāpō wǒ zài nǐ lǐmiàn~~~!
- Katie Wu, Twitter, July 2017

Best first dance wedding song:
◯ El Tango de Roxanne - Moulin Rouge soundtrack
◯ I Write Sins Not Tragedies - Panic! At The Disco
- Katie Wu, Twitter, April 2017

Katie was bored out of her goddamn mind. This was the fifth socialite's wedding she was emceeing this month alone, and she wanted to stab herself through the ears with a very sharp stiletto. Granted, she was doing a favor for her grandfather's business associate, but what was it with rich Chinese families demanding that celebrities host their wedding receptions? And what did it mean that she was resorting to such measures?

She supposed she should be glad for the work and that at least this wedding was at a lavish hotel with a fully stocked bar (where she currently sat) and not a stuffy restaurant banquet hall where her only alcoholic options were Hennessy XO Cognac or some other awful concoction.

This could not continue.

"My cousin sure knows how to throw a party," Katie heard an amused masculine voice say in perfect American Standard English behind her. She wanted to sway into the buttery and cultured sound.

"But?" Katie replied as she turned around, mouth curving up in appreciation at the tall drink of water standing before her.

His eyes were warm and velvet mahogany. He looked as if his trim figure was poured into his suit, which clearly cost more than her entire wardrobe combined.

"But it's still a wedding, and if you've been to one, you've been to them all."

"I suppose it's different if it's your own," Katie allowed graciously. She never knew who was listening.

"I'm Alton Kuang, by the way. Cousin to the bride." Alton stuck out his manicured hand for a handshake, and she was pleased to note that his grip was as strong as his hands were smooth.

"Katie Wu," she replied.

"Thanks for subbing in at the last minute," said Alton. "Cece was about to call off the wedding."

"That seems extreme," Katie observed neutrally as she sipped on her vodka soda and lime. She examined Alton surreptitiously in one of the many mirrored walls of the bar. He really was just her type: tall, rich, and extremely good-looking.

"It's bad math is what it is," harrumphed Alton.

Katie took another sip. "Can't have bad math. One should always derive carefully."

Alton's eyes lit up, his generous mouth twisting into a smile. "Can I buy you a drink?"

"Sorry," Katie replied, barely concealing a smirk, "I don't drink and derive."

"You can stop now," he said, rolling his eyes.

"I think it's great that you know your limits." This time, Katie could not help but cackle.

Alton crooked his mouth and leaned deeper into her space. "I walked right into that one."

Katie felt effervescent and sparkly in his presence. All of a sudden, she missed Jae-sung something fierce.

"How long are you in Singapore, Katie? Perhaps I could show you around?"

Katie raked her eyes over his pleasing form and smiled regretfully. "I would love that, but full disclosure: I have a boyfriend."

"Ah, I should have known someone as clever as you would already be taken," Alton replied, disappointment evident on his handsome face. And then he brightened. "I'd still be happy to show you around, though. You're worth getting to know beyond just as a potential romantic partner."

"Oh, smooth," Katie jokingly approved. "This isn't some nefarious plot to prise me from my boyfriend's very capable hands, is it?"

The beautiful man winked. And then he got very serious.

"You are the granddaughter of my shú gong's close friend and business associate," Alton said. "There is no way I would ever fuck with my granduncle's people. That's not how the Kuangs do business."

And just like that, Katie knew.

She couldn't explain how, but like a bolt of lightning, Katie knew that if she let him, Alton would love her and care for her all the days of her life. He was a man of honor and to have someone like him in her corner—she would have to earn it every day for the rest of her life. Maybe it was fate.

"I accept your offer, Alton Kuang," she said, matching his mien. "It's an honor for me and for my family."

"Don't forget your cow," he teased.

Katie howled. "Let's get down to business," she started, because what were her other options? Her heart burst in happiness when Alton chimed in with the rest of the lyrics from "I'll Make a Man Out of You."

But what really sealed their friendship was when Alton went on to denounce the patriarchy as well as postulate that Li Shang was clearly bisexual because he was attracted to Mulan when she was pretending to be Ping.

Before Katie knew it, she was back on the dais thanking all the distinguished guests for attending, with Alton's number in her phone and a sense that she should end the wedding emceeing on a high note.

August 2017

Have you eaten yet?

- Katie Wu, Twitter, August 2017

"No" is a complete sentence.

- Katie Wu, Twitter, August 2017

"How was your meeting with Song PD today?" asked Jae-sung over the remnants of their Italian takeout. He leaned back in Katie's somewhat rickety kitchen chair and idly noted how he should replace it with a sturdier one.

Katie's head jerked up abruptly from the nonstop texting she had been doing on her phone. "How did you know I had a meeting with him?" she asked.

"Oh, I was supposed to meet up with PD-nim today, and he asked me to reschedule because of a conflict with your appointment," replied Jae-sung.

He wondered why Katie seemed so defensive but then dismissed it as her being extremely private about her personal details. She was such a strange mix of openness and vulnerability while being a completely closed book.

Even during the few months they had been together, Jae-sung learned quickly that certain topics with Katie were to be avoided. Topics like her family and money. Despite Jae-sung trying several times to check in on Katie about her album sales or seeing if she needed financial assistance, she always subtly redirected the conversations.

He watched helplessly as she hustled, writing and selling her most commercially viable hits to other artists. She constantly flew back and forth from Seoul to Taipei and, for some reason, was often in meetings all day—meetings Katie refused to talk to him about. When he asked, all she mentioned was that it was boring and related to her family's business.

He didn't even know what kind of business her family was in.

He did not understand how meetings about family business involved Song PD, her manager, and a whole fleet of outside lawyers and consultants.

Katie scowled at her phone while furiously texting.

"Is everything okay?"

"Yeah," she replied absentmindedly.

Her phone buzzed.

"Hey, Jae. I'm sorry—I have to take this. Do you—do you mind heading home?" Before waiting for his response, Katie got up and headed to her room while answering her phone. He heard a muffled "Hey, Unnie. Yeah, PD-nim told me...," and then she closed the door and he was forgotten.

Jae-sung just sat there, shocked.

If he was honest, his pride stung. He missed Katie and she was so shut off and distant lately that he didn't know why he bothered. He had been gone for most of the year on tour and he was constantly in rehearsals for DOYEN's September comeback and the last leg of their global tour that he just wanted to be with her in the little spare time he had.

Jae-sung couldn't stop wondering who Katie was talking to. He suspected it had to do with her meeting with PD-nim earlier that day and whatever money issues she refused to speak to him about. She was his girlfriend, and it hurt when Katie did not trust him, constantly shutting him out.

He sulked all the way home.

October 2017

TAIPEEIIIIIIIIIIIIIIIIIIIIIIIIIIIIII I AM IN YOU-UUUUUUUUUUU~~ Táiběi wǒ zài nǐ lǐmiàn!!
- Katie Wu, Twitter, October 2017

OMG did you see Katie in the VIP section going crazy with her friends? FLEX!
- Twitter user, October 2017

Remember when Katie and Johnny met DOYEN back-stage? It's all come full circle!
- Twitter user, October 2017

Katie was drunk—drunker than Jae-sung had ever seen her.

She was normally so contained, drinking just over the edge of buzzed and then stopping—even when she was with just him. When Jae-sung had asked about it, Katie had replied that she hated losing control. Drunkenness had never appealed to her.

Katie had maintained that she was inappropriate enough sober. No need to get herself into more trouble than she normally did.

Her mouth ran a good game, but Jae-sung had never thought Katie was anything but tightly leashed. Everything about her was just enough. Just enough irreverence. Just enough rebellion. Just enough challenge.

When they were physically intimate, Katie never lost herself. She had a good time, but she was always in control—even when ceding some of it to him. She was never undone.

Even in Katie's music. Critics and fans alike commented on her rawness—but even then, her rawness was refined and distilled, like in her song "Profit." The original lyrics he'd stolen a glance of were rough and unpolished, but they had hit him emotionally more than the final version—though the album cut was sleek and clever. Her essence was so pure in a sea full of fakers, but she was deliberate all the same.

But tonight, Katie and her college friends Ellie, Sarah, and Angela were dancing up a storm in her hotel room to old Britney and Justin songs from the 2000s and, like that night in Los Angeles several years ago, Jae-sung was sitting on the sidelines and watching them rile up any hot-blooded male.

"You're in a good mood tonight, Katie," observed Ellie. "Is it because you're finally letting KJ rail you into the mattress?"

"Christ, he's right here, Ellie," scolded Sarah. "At least have the decency to ask when he's out of earshot."

Ellie grinned. "Where's the fun in that?"

"I'll tell but only if you tell us about Do-won first," Katie slurred as she slunk up to where Jae-sung sat in an upholstered chair, a bottle of Taiwan Beer in her hand. She started grinding in his lap. "If you're good, I'll give you a demonstration."

"Katie," Jae-sung replied, somewhat scandalized and aroused at the same time.

"Ooooooh! Voyeur kink activated!" squealed Angela. "Ellie, start talking!"

"But I already told you what happened," protested Ellie. "And besides, I was hoping for a repeat performance. Katie, you were supposed to invite Wonnie!"

"He's coming over later. I think he wanted to shower and eat first," Katie said before she decided to straddle Jae-sung instead of continuing to grind. He was already getting hard, and if Katie kept it up, he supposed he really wouldn't mind fucking her in front of her friends. "Wanna eat you, Jae-sung-ah," she whispered into his ear. "You were so fucking hot tonight."

"What's gotten into you?" he murmured back. "I've never seen you like this."

"You've never seen me after illegally streaming your concerts on Twitter," she replied. "Plus, I got some great news today."

"Yeah?" Jae-sung nuzzled Katie's neck and grabbed her ass, ignoring her friends' catcalls. "What was it?"

"Just finalized some contract details, and pretty soon, I'll be free."

Jae-sung sobered up really fast. "Are you leaving SB Entertainment?"

Katie giggled. "No, silly. Just tying up some loose ends with my family." She downed the rest of her beer and placed the empty bottle on the floor.

Jae-sung figured this was as loose-lipped as he'd ever find Katie so he decided to push his luck. "What sort of loose ends?" he asked.

She cupped his face in both her hands and devoured him with her entire mouth.

"Get a room!" Angela hollered.

"This is my room!" Katie hollered back.

"Go to KJ's room!" yelled Sarah.

"But I wanna watch!" complained Ellie. "If I can't be fucking Wonnie right now, I wanna see at least one of my friends fuck a DOYEN member."

At that moment, there was a knock on the door and in came Do-won, Akihiro, and Dae-jung. Katie's friends exchanged greetings with the guys and Jae-sung vaguely registered Do-won leaving with Ellie while Akihiro and Dae-jung cast mischievous grins at Katie riding Jae-sung.

Katie and Jae-sung weren't a secret, but neither were they terribly open about their relationship. It was the first time his members had seen her so physically affectionate with him, and Jae-sung was 100% positive that he'd be the butt of teasing for the foreseeable future. But at the moment, he did not give any fucks who saw what because all he knew was that he needed to be inside Katie, fucking her until she saw stars.

"Time to go, baby," Jae-sung growled. The way he almost shot his load when Katie purred in response. Shit.

Jae-sung did not know how he got Katie back to his room, but it perhaps involved tossing her over his shoulder like a sack of rice—much to the amusement of his members and the cheers of her friends.

Katie also perhaps implored her friends to pray for her pussy on the way out. He couldn't wait to hear the shit she'd get because of that.

"Katie," Jae-sung rumbled as he pounded into her heat. "Fucking love your pussy, baby."

Her only response was unfettered keening. He had never heard Katie lose it quite like this, and it only made Jae-sung want to fuck her harder.

"*Fuckfuckfuckfuck,*" Katie gasped as he thrust. "I love you, Park Jae-sung."

"I love you, too, Katie Wu," he replied automatically, his voice rough with exertion.

She kissed him hard, all tongue, teeth, and no finesse. "I fucking love you, Jae. Love your cock. Love your face. God, I love you so much, you make me stupid."

And while it wasn't the first time Katie had told him she loved him, it was the first time she had declared it with such wild abandon. How could

Jae-sung help but come? He made it up to her by licking up every last drop from her cunt as Katie cried out his name.

July 2019

Katie Wu returns to her esoteric roots with the scathing "Whore of Babylon" (SB Entertainment, 2019). While her previous two albums were more mainstream and still managed to hit hard and fun, longtime fans (including this critic) are euphoric at what seems to be Wu revisiting the deconstruction of patriarchy and Christianity. We missed her skewering society while couching it all in brilliant barbs and badass beats.

The album opens with "Revelations," a wordplay on how Wu bares all, as well as the closing book of the Christian Bible where she gets the title "Whore of Babylon." Wu examines how patriarchy punishes ambitious women who buck expectations and seize what they want. Wu references Lady MacBeth and gumihos on their own tracks, and in "Harlot's Portion," name drops famous biblical fallen women such as the woman at the well and Rahab, the prostitute who helped the Israelites capture Jericho and became the ancestor of Boaz and thus, Jesus.

But without a doubt, "Defenestration" is a love song and rallying cry for her fandom, which is also called the Jezebelles. While the Bible paints Jezebel as the harlot queen, used throughout history to vilify beautiful women and those who used makeup, Wu flips the insult much as she did with her Korean debut album "Shameless." Instead, she tells a story of a rightful ruler who resisted a coup and whose son was murdered, but was ultimately thrown out a window by the followers of a power hungry prophet who claimed to be on God's side.

Smashing.

- Rolling Stone Korea, July 2019

After two mini-albums that clearly catered to trends and veered away from Katie Wu's signature "fuck you" to main-stream tastes, Wu is back in fine form. "Whore of Babylon" (SB Entertainment, 2019) is everything we hoped the previous two releases would be: experimental, speaking truth to power, and a slap in the face to incels and religious conservatives.

Fucking fantastic.

- NME, July 2019

[1] Revelations [1:06]
[2] Harlot's Portion [3:48]
[3] Out, Damned Spot! [4:07]
[4] Se7en [3:15]
[5] Casting the First Stone [2:56]
[6] Pluck Out Your Eye [4:22]
[7] Gumiho [3:39]
[8] Until the Stars All Fall [4:30]

[9] I'm Glorious [2:45]
[10] Defenestration [3:27]
  - Track list, "Whore of Babylon" (SB Entertainment, 2019)

Score us victorious
I am utterly meritorious
Notorious, uproarious
I want you to adore us

No abstentions or declensions
Predicated on inflections
Apprehensions, dimensions
You have no comprehension

Excoriated, excruciated
Your vision's become corrugated
Adjudicated until I abdicated
I shall not be eradicated

Censorious, spurious
Dismiss the vainglorious Greek chorus
Implore us, laborious
The weight of story is glorious
                    - "I'm Glorious" (SB Entertainment, 2019)

Oh shit! Our girl's going off!
                              - Twitter user, July 2019

Can't wait for the backlash from tiny, insecure men and the religious hypocrites. Jezebelles, go!

- Twitter user, July 2019

oh fuck the mv for im glorious is glorious

- Twitter user, July 2019

*all the leather and corsets and chains and boots and bursts of color and lingerie and tiddies and ass cheeks and *faints**

- Twitter user, July 2019

i'm glorious is pretentious drivel. y'all need to stop pretending it's anything more than shitty rapping on top of an overused duran duran sample.

- Twitter user, July 2019

Katie reading thirst tweets on BuzzFeed is everything! The way she isn't phased by a damn thing.

- Twitter user, July 2019

I love how Katie doesn't need any fucking explanations. And shit, that low chuckle of hers combined with her eyebrow raise? STEP ON ME, QUEEN!

- Twitter user, July 2019

SHE READ MY TWEET SHE READ MY TWEET FUCK SHIT SHE WINKED AASKJFADSKDF ASDF;LKJAS-DF;KLJASDKFJS

- Twitter user, July 2019

DID SHE ACTUALLY TELL THE PERSON TO OPEN THEIR MOUTH AFTER THEY ASKED FOR HER TO SPIT ON THEM OMG FUCK ME

- Twitter user, July 2019

"Oh, shit."

Dae-jung looked up at Jae-sung's comment and noted how flushed his leader was. He looked around the greenroom of the Kyocera Dome to make sure they were alone and asked, "You alright, Hyung?"

"Katie dropped her new M/V," Jae-sung replied from the makeup chair, voice cracking.

Soo-min, who was sitting in the makeup chair next to Jae-sung, lurched at their leader's phone. "I wanna see! Is it good? Noona wouldn't send us any pictures from the set and made us promise not to watch teasers." When Jae-sung wouldn't relinquish his phone, Soo-min's face lit up in mischief. "You do know we can just look it up on our own devices, right? Where's my iPad?"

"No—it's inappropriate!" Jae-sung choked out even as Soo-min searched through his black Supreme backpack.

Woo-jin smirked from his perch on the arm of a generic black leather sofa. "You can't stop us, Jae. It's on the internet, and we're all of age."

"That's beside the point. She's my girlfriend."

"Oh, fuck. Now I really want to see," quipped Ye-jun. The singer was looking particularly handsome today with his violet bangs swept off of his forehead. "Hurry up, Minnie."

Dae-jung and the rest of his members knew that Jae-sung tried to keep his jealous streak in check, and it rarely reared its head enough for them to take advantage. So, of course, Dae-jung crowded around Soo-min with the rest of his members to watch Katie's latest M/V. Dae-jung knew from Jae-sung's lack of further protest that his leader knew it was a lost cause anyway.

From the opening black and white shot of Katie's back—naked except for a tiny leather waist cincher—Dae-jung did not quite know how to react in an appropriate manner. The inky dragon, prowling tiger, and cyborg rooster tattoos rippled down her toned back while the hanja at her neck stood out, bold and fierce. He'd never paid much attention to Katie's tattoos, but this time, he was mesmerized.

Plus, the swells of her ass were pert, round, and bare. Fuck.

"Is she rapping 'I'm Glorious' over a sample of Biggie's 'Notorious'?" Do-won asked, his smile wide and bright. "Oh, Noona's fucking amazing."

"What does her tattoo say? Is that new?" Woo-jin paused the video and squinted at the screen.

Now that the video was stopped, Dae-jung stared closely, too. He followed a beautiful script up the length of Katie's inner thigh, except it was either too hard to read or he was too distracted by the lines of her shapely leg.

He heard a burst of laughter from Woo-jin. "Taste and see that the Lord is good," he read in English. "Katie is fucking hilarious." At Jae-sung's grumble, Woo-jin added, "Well, Jae. How does the Lord taste?"

"Is it real?" Akihiro couldn't resist asking, his earrings tinkling as he leaned closer to Soo-min's iPad. "When did Noona get it?" At Jae-sung's sputtering, Akihiro collapsed over Soo-min's shoulder, cackling. "You haven't seen it yet, have you? You didn't even know!"

"We've been on tour!" Jae-sung defended hotly. "Katie said she had a surprise for me and—ah, fuck. I won't even see her until next week. She did this on purpose," he groaned. "She knew we'd be in Osaka today. Why is she like this?"

Dae-jung joined his bandmates in their good-natured ribbing. "Doesn't seem like you mind the way she is, Hyung."

"So, what's this BuzzFeed thirst tweet video with Noona that YouTube is recommending next?" asked Do-won.

"NOOOOOOO!" cried Jae-sung in despair. "Why does Katie do this to me? This is her revenge on me being on tour this past year and half, isn't it? She just gets hotter and adds secret tattoos and flirts with her fans, and I can only watch through a screen."

"Stop pretending that you hate it," Ye-jun snickered. "You love that you're the only one she lets touch her."

Dae-jung ignored the twin twists of desire and envy roiling in his belly as he watched the BuzzFeed video, only understanding some of the references. He understood enough, though. Many of the tweets sounded similar to what he saw in response to their tweets from their DOYEN account.

He divested his body's response from his mind. Katie was Jae-sung's girl. Had been for years. He knew better than to lust after her. They all knew better. And yet, sometimes Dae-jung could not help but wish for someone like Katie in his life.

His hyung was the luckiest man alive.

August 2020

Our girl is too good to us! It's her birthday except us Jezzies get the gift!!

- Twitter user, August 2020

What did we do to deserve a Sweet Child of Mine cover? Katie killing the guitar solo!

- Twitter user, August 2020

"Happy Birthday, Katie," Jae-sung said as he entered Katie's studio in the new SB Entertainment headquarters. She always had the lights so bright, he didn't know how she could make music with everything so well-lit.

Katie turned around in her Herman Miller Aeron office chair and upon him handing her a tiny velvet box, cut him a suspicious glance. "I thought we agreed on no presents!"

"I heard you say a bunch of words. I don't recall getting a chance to say any back." He grinned, making sure she could see his dimples. "Open it, baby."

"If this is an engagement ring, I will punch you."

"I would never." Jae-sung leaned over to kiss Katie on the cheek.

"Good. Only selfish narcissists would subvert a day meant for me and make it about them, and you're not a selfish narcissist, right?"

Jae-sung laughed and sat on her red sectional couch. Katie was such a stubborn ass. "Open the fucking present, Katie."

She shot him one last grumpy look and then obliged him. Next thing he knew, Katie was crying.

"What's wrong, baby? You don't like it?"

"Oh, Jae, it's beautiful!" Katie cried, slipping on the custom ring. "This must have cost a fortune."

Katie held out her hand to better see the sparkling aquamarines, sapphires, and diamonds arranged to suggest the swirl and eddy of a crashing wave. She was right, too. She was always right when it came to jewelry—a fact that had surprised him when he'd first gotten to know her. It had cost him a fortune to match the gradient shades just right and design it so that it resembled moving water.

Katie crossed her studio to Jae-sung and threw her arms around him. "Thank you, Jae-sung," she said, voice thick with emotion. "I love you so very, very much."

"I love you, too, baby." He cleared his throat. "It's not just a birthday present, though."

"Park Jae-sung, you told me it wasn't an engagement ring!"

"And it isn't, love. It isn't." Jae-sung cupped Katie's chin and stared deep into her dark eyes. "It's a promise."

"You gave me a promise ring for my birthday? That's so high school virginity pledgy of you."

He chuckled. "No. It's just a birthday ring that comes with a promise."

Katie cocked a judgmental brow.

"I love you, Katie," he said in English. "And I promise that if you let me, I will love you for the rest of my life."

Katie was crying again. "Goddammit, Jae-sung!" she sobbed as she grabbed him by the shirt and dragged him in for a wet and dirty kiss. "I love you, Park Jae-sung. Of course I will let you love me."

She kissed him again and showed him exactly, in detail, just how she would let Jae-sung love her.

May 2021

Thank you for all your love and condolences. I appreciate everyone respecting my family's privacy during this difficult time.

- Katie Wu, Twitter, May 2021

After receiving the news that her father had passed away, our artist Katie Wu quickly left the set of "Konglish With Kyrie." Due to family circumstances, Katie is unable to attend her remaining schedules for the month. May Thomas Wu rest in peace.

- SB Entertainment, Official Press Release, May 2021

Jae-sung couldn't understand Katie. Katie, who cried during commercials, hadn't shed a single tear (at least none that he'd seen) over her father's death. Her actual father who, though she claimed was an asshole, was still her father.

Sure, Katie almost never mentioned the man, and in fact, they were estranged—for reasons Jae-sung was never clear about—and yet, he'd still thought she would have some sort of reaction. Instead, Katie just went about her life as if nothing had happened. Shockingly, she'd complained about SB Entertainment canceling all her schedules and having to go along with it to keep up appearances.

She wasn't even flying back to the US for the funeral.

When Jae-sung had asked her about it, Katie had merely hardened her features and said that she wasn't going. When he'd pressed, she'd just walked away and left the room.

He stopped asking.

The hardest part was that Jae-sung just couldn't reconcile the Katie that he knew—the warm, caring, considerate woman who got along with his parents, gossiped with his younger sister, and mothered the maknaes—and the Katie whenever her family was mentioned. It was as if they were completely different people. As if Katie had no past and had sprung whole from some long-dead god's head.

He'd once seen a photo album of Katie's that was full of happy pictures of her, her family, and friends. From what he'd pieced together, her family was extremely well-off. Her house was huge, filled with art and expensive furniture. They even had a pool, and she had received a new silver BMW for her sixteenth birthday. And yet here, in Seoul, her apartment was still as stark and bare as it had been when he'd first visited—despite all his attempts at the contrary.

Katie had clearly grown up around wealth and luxury, yet she still lived so simply, only allowing Jae-sung to indulge her on rare occasions. Though she did not begrudge Jae-sung ordering takeout and often took turns paying, she still cooked so many of her meals—he couldn't believe that she still brought her lunch to the office most days. What also surprised him was that Katie made many of her meals last more than a day or two. He remembered from his trainee days how Woo-jin showed them which ingredients could make a little go a long way.

It annoyed him—and quite frankly, troubled him—that after four years, he still didn't know where Katie's money went. He fully intended to marry her, but if she was bad with money or had a lot of debts, he would need to know before he tied himself to her forever. He wanted to tell her that she could trust him with her finances. He wanted to freely spoil her without any pushback.

He wanted to know why she didn't attend her father's funeral.

He hated how Katie was still such a black box even after all these years.

Jae-sung wondered if he would ever truly know her.

July 2021

Glad they finally released Katie's reactions of Miss Me Like That and Baby, Baby! I get that they were trying to respect her loss—but it just wasn't the same without her.

- Twitter user, July 2021

Nothing like hearing Katie whimper in pain. Poor girl was nomming that spicy tteokbokki throughout and ate so many she had to beg PD-nim for milk.

- Twitter user, July 2021

The way she full on let loose a string of expletives so long they just muted the entire elevator scene.

- Twitter user, July 2021

Still hilarious when she refuses to look directly at SM BWHAAHAHAHAHA

> - Twitter user, July 2021

Katie angry eating bc DOYEN is too hot is a mood

> - Twitter user, July 2021

oh Katie does NOT fuck with Baby Baby lolololol

> - Twitter user, July 2021

her face when she hates a track but is trying to be polite + professional is pure comedy

> - Twitter user, July 2021

"I don't see the big deal, Katie. Why are you so upset?" Jae-sung said exasperatedly.

They had been arguing over Pokémon—of all stupid things—and it had gotten so heated that Katie had started yelling, calling him names. She was throwing a tantrum over his "addiction" to collecting Pokémon bread in his living room and he felt as if he were having an out-of-body experience.

"Just like a fucking man," Katie seethed as she paced around his furniture. "Of course you wouldn't see the big deal. It's not that difficult if you just considered it for a moment."

"Hey, watch your fucking tone with me," he snapped.

She stopped in her tracks. "Do not. Tell me. To watch. My. Fucking. Tone."

Jae-sung didn't know what to do. He was trying to be patient and understanding—Katie's father did just die less than two months ago—but she was impossible.

He had been so busy with "Miss Me Like That" and "Baby, Baby" promotions and then preparing for their virtual fan meeting, as well as all the content he was banking for when he enlisted in the military in September. Katie spent all day shut inside her apartment or studio, not talking to anyone. Granted, they were still in a pandemic, but she also wasn't eating. She wasn't writing music. She was barely speaking to him, and when she did, she constantly lost her temper.

Jae-sung was at his wit's end. He felt guilty all the time about his career and all the opportunities that were opening up despite the eldest members being enlisted in the military. It was unheard of—all the record-breaking sales in the US, invitations to American award shows—and all the while, Katie was obviously so unhappy about her father's passing, but still adamantly insisting she was fine. She refused to talk about it with him or any of her friends.

"What do you want me to say then? You're yelling at me," he protested.

"Just because my voice is loud doesn't mean I'm yelling, Jae-sung." She carded a hand through her recently chopped hair. "I can't help that my voice projects."

Jae-sung wanted to scream.

"It's abusive! You're abusive!" he blurted out in frustration.

"I—" Katie slammed her mouth shut. Her face went blank. She clenched her hands tightly and left the room.

Jae-sung considered himself lucky that Katie didn't immediately leave his apartment.

Later that night, he curled around her in his bed and whispered, "I love you, baby. I'm sorry."

Katie didn't respond, but she also did not push him away when he held her and stroked her belly with light then insistent touches. Jae-sung kissed her neck and shoulder and begged forgiveness with his lips on her skin. And when he eventually slipped his hardness into her softness, and he thrust languorously until he heard her quiet sigh as her cunt clenched around his cock, he fervently hoped his love could travel from his seed to her bones.

The next morning, Jae-sung woke up to an empty bed. Katie's side was cool to his touch and he wondered how early Katie had risen. He reached for his phone and froze.

There, on his nightstand by his phone and wallet, laid the ring he'd given Katie for her birthday only a year prior.

CHAPTER 5

March 2024

I constantly feel as if I'm on trial—as if I have to justify myself to everyone—but most especially to my gentle giant. I left him like a thief in the night, stealing myself from his life so completely that surely he must have questioned if we ever existed.

The thing of it was: I was never his.

Oh, I loved him. I loved him as much as I was able. But he never knew me. How could he? I had been stealing myself away from him since the beginning.
- "Telling a Truth Is a Slippery Slope" (Red Lantern Publishing House, October 2023)

Jae-sung led Katie to his studio, and though he knew it wasn't fair, that it wasn't remotely neutral territory, he did not care. He needed all the advantages he could get.

Katie followed him silently, a far cry from the endless stream of chatter and conversation they used to share. Granted, much of it had been bickering—especially on the topics of art and literature—but there had rarely been tension or meanness.

Jae-sung's heart throbbed with phantom pain. Katie had thrown it all away. She had thrown him away and had never looked back.

When he finally entered his studio, Katie merely hovered at the precipice. For a moment, Jae-sung thought she would bolt down the hall, and then the moment passed. She took a breath. She clenched and unclenched her hands. She stepped into his sanctum.

She waited at the edge of the room until he indicated his sofa—a new rich brown upholstered one since the previous seat had been imprinted with one too many memories of Katie soft and mewling, Katie panting underneath him, Katie grinding above him, Katie coming into him as if he were home.

"Oh, shit," Katie said suddenly. "I have to let the sound engineer know."

Jae-sung nodded as she called the engineer and apologized profusely, promising to come back tomorrow ready to work. A sense of shame washed over him as he realized how he had not only hijacked her entire schedule, he was making her look bad to her colleagues and fucking up the process for her team.

He was fucking with her money. With his company's money.

He shrugged it off. What did he care about Katie's reputation? Did she not kill his when she suddenly upped and vanished? Everyone—especially the members of her creative team who had chosen to stay in-house—had looked at him for months after, all secretly wondering what he had done to instigate such a drastic move on her part.

Jae-sung himself had wondered. *Maybe he was a monster?*

Katie sighed as she finally crossed over his green area rug. She settled primly into the leather sofa chair across from where he was on the couch. How dare she act as if she were the one being put out and put upon.

"I'll try not to take up too much of your time."

"How considerate of you," Katie replied.

Katie was full of shit. Jae-sung didn't know her anymore, but her sarcasm was obvious.

To his surprise, Katie fished out a silver flask from her bag, unscrewed the cap, and took a generous swig. She briefly considered him and then extended the flask in his general direction.

"Scotch," she clarified when he eyed her proffering suspiciously. "Macallan 18-year-old Sherry Oak."

Jae-sung winced and shook his head. "I thought you hated scotch."

"I do. Macallan is more tolerable than others, though," Katie said. "Smoky, citrusy, and reminds me of dark chocolate."

"Sounds, uh, delightful." It did not. It sounded awful.

Katie snorted inelegantly. "It's just enough for Dutch courage," she said in English, "but horrible enough to deter me from getting blotto."

"I thought Macallan was Scottish whisky?"

"It is," she acknowledged. "It's an idiom for getting courage from alcohol."

"Blotto is drunk, I presume?" Jae-sung asked. He had missed absorbing from her the kind of English he could never learn from books. For all his fans seemed to praise, his few years in New Jersey as a child had not been enough to get his English to near-native level.

"Extremely."

"You have a great need to get wasted?"

Katie sipped a markedly more measured sip and grimaced. "Every fucking day." She regretfully screwed the cap back on her flask and slipped it into her purse. "I suppose you have questions," she said in Korean.

Jae-sung almost laughed at the careless way Katie threw that acknowledgement in there. As if his questions hadn't plagued him every day since that morning he woke up without her. When he saw his rejected promise of forever on his nightstand.

They hounded Jae-sung every time he thought of pursuing another woman. *Maybe he was a monster? Maybe she would one day leave him, too.*

"Why?" His voice broke. He supposed all things considered, it was a wonder he wasn't a worthless sobbing mess.

"Do you want the short answer or the long answer?" Katie sighed again. "I suppose you want both." She pulled at her thick scarf and unwound it from her neck. "I'm sorry, Jae-sung. I'm so sorry for what I did to you. I had my reasons, but in the end, the reasons don't really matter. They may help or they may not, but they happened. And I'm sorry. For all of it."

Jae-sung didn't know how he thought it would go, but it was not like this. "Go on," he clipped out. He was not inclined to absolve Katie from just a mere sorry. She had so much to answer for.

"Please understand this is very hard for me," Katie said. "I know it's also been very hard for you—and I'm not trying to minimize the consequences of my actions. And still—still, this is very difficult for me."

"Just tell me, Katie. I deserve answers." Jae-sung hated how rough he sounded. He wanted to sound unaffected but he supposed the game was up a long time ago.

"Okay," she said, as if psyching herself up. "Here we go."

May 2021

Can't wait to catch up with the baddest bitch Kyrie!
                                    - Katie Wu, Twitter, May 2021

Katie was hugging Korean American singer and YouTube show host Kyrie Ko goodbye when her phone wouldn't stop ringing. Her afternoon shoot for "Konglish With Kyrie" had run long and it was probably her boyfriend asking about dinner plans.

"I'm so sorry, Unnie," Katie said. "Let me check who's blowing up my phone. Maybe it's Jae-sung telling me about some other record DOYEN fucking broke."

"Tell him 'hi' for me, Katie," laughed Kyrie. "And tell him no one likes a braggart."

When Katie realized she had ten missed calls from her mother, her stomach dropped. It was close to 2 a.m. in California. She fervently hoped Mattie and her mother were safe and sound as she found a quiet corner on set.

"Mama, is everything okay?" Katie asked as soon as her mother picked up.

"Baba had a heart attack—"

"What?" Katie cried, almost dropping her phone. "Is he okay? Do you need me to fly to Shenzhen?"

"He's gone, Katie."

"What?" Katie gasped. This could not be true. "What do you mean? Is he not in Shenzhen? Is he in Hong Kong? Beijing? Shanghai?"

"He's dead, Katie."

Katie's brain ground to a halt. Her blood roared in her ears. She did not understand how she could feel so heavy and weightless at the same time. She was floating.

"Baba was so stressed about money all the time, and it finally killed him," her mother accused over the phone. "He came to you for help, and you turned him away while you lived your life of a spoiled pop star in Korea."

"How can you say that, Mama?"

Katie could not believe it.

Katie had bought the house from her parents so that her father couldn't steal it from under her mother's nose. It had taken a lot of maneuvering to get him to sign over the house—but she had done it. She had worked herself to the bone negotiating terms and paying down the multiple liens against their home.

She had done this all while paying for Mattie's college tuition, as well as setting aside money to restore whatever her father had stolen from her uncle.

The debt kept piling up. It was never enough for her mother. Katie was never enough.

"Don't bother coming home."

"Mama, you don't mean that. You're just upset. Please," Katie begged, willing her panic to stay at bay. "What would people say?"

"They will say you have no filial piety. That you have no honor. That I have lost both a husband and a daughter today," her mother replied coldly.

Katie couldn't believe her ears. "Mommy, please."

"You killed him," her mother stated icily. "You think I didn't know about the Lau family and how much your father owed them?" she berated. "You left him to die. You cut him off, and you might as well have pulled the trigger. I have no husband anymore and now, I have no daughter."

The line cut abruptly.

Katie's chest felt as if it was going to explode, and she fervently wished it would. Her own mother wished she was dead.

She wanted to be wiped clean from the earth.

July 2021

I was so small. I always forget that I was a child trying to hold my own against a grown man. How could I have ever hoped to succeed when even my own mother couldn't?
- "Telling a Truth Is a Slippery Slope" (Red Lantern Publishing House, October 2023)

Due to unforeseen circumstances, Katie Wu is canceling all remaining schedules for the foreseeable future. We ask that fans and the media respect her request for privacy. We express our apologies and will be refunding all event ticket holders as quickly as possible.
- SB Entertainment, July 2021

Abusive. She's abusive. Jae-sung had called her abusive. How dare he call her abusive. Katie slipped out of Jae-sung's bed, careful not to wake her sleeping boyfriend. *How dare he compare her to her father. She was nothing like him.*

Katie quickly found several large trash bags and old shopping bags under the kitchen sink and began to systematically clear the drawers Jae-sung had set aside for her. She sifted through the dirty laundry for what was hers. She swept all her expensive toiletries into a trash bag along with her emergency stash of feminine hygiene products. It was a good thing Jae-sung could sleep through an apocalypse.

If Jae-sung brought over other women after, they could buy their own shit.

Abusive. Abusive. She was just like her father. She was not fit for a relationship. She was not fit to live.

Oppa, she texted Ha-joon. *Oppa, are you awake?*

Within a few minutes, her manager texted back. *What's up, Katie?*

Can you pick me up from Jae's? I need your help.

It's 3 a.m., Katie, he replied. *Can't it wait until morning?*

I have to leave right now, Oppa. We broke up, and I have all my things. It wasn't technically a lie. She and Jae-sung were through. There was no coming back from this. Her heart was a stone.

I'll be there in 20. Even when her world was collapsing, she could always count on Ha-joon.

Katie swept through Jae-sung's place, grateful that she generally owned few possessions. She stashed all her shoes and slippers into another trash bag and found a few of her winter coats, too. She grabbed her spare Taylor 912ce acoustic and gently laid it in its case, broke down the guitar stand, and tucked that into another bag. She searched for all her notebooks and Korean books and, finally satisfied that nothing was left, she went through Jae-sung's penthouse one more time.

She was just like her father. Look at her, abandoning Jae-sung just like her father had abandoned her. Abusive. Abusive. She was abusive. Jae-sung thinks she is abusive.

Katie's phone lit up with Ha-joon's text saying he was parking and coming right up.

Text me when you're at the door, I don't want to wake him.

Katie got up and surveyed the small pile of her things by the door, mentally preparing to never return to a space that had felt like home for years.

When Ha-joon texted again, she opened the door and held a finger to her lips. Her manager looked at her sadly, held out his arms and instead of the hug he likely expected, she handed him her guitar and a few of the heavier trash bags.

"Can we go to a hotel?" Katie whispered and breathed a sigh of relief when Ha-joon nodded.

As she was about to step over the threshold, Katie glanced down at her right hand and saw Jae-sung's promise to her twinkling under the hall lights. She stopped.

"Gimme a sec, Oppa," she said softly.

Carefully, very carefully, Katie went through rooms and hallways lined with art and back into Jae-sung's room. She gazed at his handsome face and for a moment, regretted her decision. Surely, all they had to do was talk it out. This was not the first time they'd fought. They'd always recovered.

And then, Katie heard it again.

Abusive, her mind insinuated. *She was just like her father. Abusive. She destroyed all that she touched. She would ruin Jae-sung. She had ruined Jae-sung. Better to leave him now before they were married and had kids.*

Katie twisted her birthday ring off her finger as tears spilled from her eyes. She placed it right next to his phone and wallet so there was no way he could miss it. She leaned over Jae-sung's sleeping form and kissed him lightly on the lips.

"I love you, Park Jae-sung," Katie breathed.

"I love you, too, Katie Wu," Jae-sung muttered back automatically in his sleep.

Katie almost lost her resolve then and there, but she girded herself. She could not stay with someone who thought she was abusive. She could not protect him from herself.

She was a monster. An endless maw. An all-consuming fire. She was a rip current, tearing Jae-sung from land into the open ocean, wearing him down until he drowned.

Katie took one last look at the love of her life. She hardened her heart and turned away. She gathered the remaining bags and stepped over the threshold. She closed the door and walked away.

Hey, Hyung, do you know where Katie is? All her things are gone, and she won't pick up. I just need to talk to her, Hyung. Please. I can fix it.
- Text from Park Jae-sung to Baek Ha-joon, July 2021

Hyung, her apartment is empty, and her studio code has been changed. What the fuck is going on?
- Text from Park Jae-sung to Baek Ha-joon, July 2021

I'm begging you, Hyung. Please tell Katie I love her. I don't know what I did but I'm sorry. Is she okay?
- Text from Park Jae-sung to Baek Ha-joon, July 2021

Hyung-nim, please just let me know if she's safe?
- Text from Park Jae-sung to Baek Ha-joon, July 2021

Hyung-nim, please tell Katie that I can take a hint. I won't bother either of you anymore. I wish you both well.
- Text from Park Jae-sung to Baek Ha-joon, July 2021

"I don't understand," said Ha-joon, sitting in the office chair of her hotel room. "You want me to what?"

"I need to leave Seoul," Katie repeated from her perch at the edge of one of the queen beds. "And I need my apartment empty by morning."

"That's impossible," he replied, crossing his arms.

"It really isn't. Just throw everything away," Katie replied. She absently stroked the sateen bedsheets. "I won't need it where I'm going."

Ha-joon went rigid. "Where are you going, Katie?" her manager asked carefully.

"It doesn't matter."

Ha-joon looked Katie directly in the eyes. She had never seen him so serious. "I need you to tell me exactly what you mean, Katie," he said, voice firm and unyielding.

Kate averted her gaze. "I need to disappear, Oppa. I need you to help erase all traces of me."

"What happened, Katie? Are you in trouble?"

"Jae-sung and I are done, Oppa. And I don't want to be here anymore," Katie replied dully. "And if you don't want to or can't help me, I'll do it myself." She stood up and grabbed her purse.

Ha-joon went on high alert. He rose quickly and positioned himself between Katie and the door. "Katie, I need you to tell me exactly what you mean by 'disappear,' as well as why it doesn't matter if we throw everything away," he said.

Katie stalked to her manager. "Let me by, Oppa," she demanded, her finger pushed into his sternum. "I have an apartment to pack. I don't want to cause anyone trouble after I'm gone."

"Katie, I think you need help," Ha-joon said sadly and held out his hands in an effort to placate her. "I know it feels like your life is over because Jae-sung broke up with you but—"

"I broke up with him," she cut in.

"What?"

"I said I broke up with him. I can't stay with him. I don't feel safe." Katie's voice pitched higher, her panic leaking out.

Ha-joon inhaled, sharp and abbreviated. "What did Jae-sung do? Did he hurt you? Do we need to file a police report?"

"Oppa, I need to hide. I don't want him to ever find me again," Katie sobbed. "I can't be around him anymore. Please, Oppa!" She sounded hysterical even to her own ears.

"Please, Katie," begged Ha-joon. "Do we need to file charges? I need to know how to protect you and what to tell the company."

"Protect me by hiding me," Katie pleaded. "I promise, he didn't hurt me. He didn't touch me."

"Then I don't understand. Help me understand," Ha-joon pleaded.

She tried to go around him, but Ha-joon was intractable.

"If you don't let me by, I will scream," Katie threatened. "I don't want to do it because you have always been kind to me, but if you don't let me pass, I will scream so long and so loud that it will look very, very bad."

By the expression on Ha-joon's face, Katie knew she had just broken something precious. Of course she did. She did not deserve someone as good as Ha-joon. Better he knew exactly what she was.

All the fight went out of him.

"I'll make some calls, Katie," Ha-joon said. "Let's go."

Katie, Ha-joon, and several very grumpy and tired staff members who were sworn to secrecy helped her pack up her entire life in Korea.

Ha-joon promised he would store the majority of Katie's things in a self-storage unit until she was ready to ship her stuff to wherever she wanted. He even promised to empty her studio when the time came, but until that moment, he would only change the door code.

"What should I do with all of this?" one of the staff members asked about her bookshelf full of DOYEN memorabilia.

"Throw it away," Katie said.

She pretended not to see Ha-joon shake his head, indicating the boxes he had provided. As far as Katie was concerned, it didn't matter anyway. She didn't want to create even more work for everyone, but she didn't want Ha-joon to suspect anything either.

Kaite had never been more grateful for her complete lack of home decor and sparse furnishings. As it was, it still took the five of them three or four hours at top speed to clear the whole place. She was relieved Jae-sung had a late schedule today so he would sleep in.

And then, just like that, six years of her life had been crammed into boxes and trash bags and unceremoniously loaded into an SB Entertainment van by more staff members sworn to secrecy.

Katie was curled up in the hotel bed, pretending to sleep. She felt Ha-joon's concerned eyes bore into her, and she didn't blame him. She knew her behavior these past three days was highly erratic, except she could not stop herself.

She had holed up, never leaving her modest room. She was terrified that someone who knew Jae-sung would see her and tell him her whereabouts. Though it was highly irregular, her poor manager insisted on staying with her, adamantly refusing to leave her alone.

Katie's thoughts eddied and oscillated, crashing against the hidden boulders of intrusive thoughts.

All she could think of was the millions her father owed the Lau family. Millions. Plural.

She did not understand how it was possible—how the Lau family could continue to throw good money after bad. She did not understand how the Laus could be so pathetic at financial decisions except that somehow, they thought they could either ensnare her or her ah-gong's steel company in some bizarre form of hostile takeover as a result.

When Mattie had told Katie the total amount, she had become paralyzed. She was already so bowed down from the payments for everything else that this new number seemed insurmountable. Thankfully, Mattie had graduated two years ago, but even with that minor relief, there was just too much.

Katie had known that she'd need to quickly produce a lot more music or go touring and perform at more fan events, but SB Entertainment had canceled them all out of respect for her mourning period, not knowing the lost income was piling an even greater amount of stress on her.

Nevermind that Katie hadn't been able to bear playing or listening to music since her mother's phone call. Nevermind that she couldn't pen a single word. Nevermind that she was afraid to open her mouth lest she scream until her voice blew out—and even then, she wouldn't be able to stop.

The sky was falling. The walls were closing in.

Katie knew it wasn't her responsibility to cover her father's debts, except now they were her mother's debts—and eventually hers and Mattie's. If she didn't take care of these matters now, they would only accrue into even more impossible amounts later. And perhaps, the debts were her fault after all. If only she had been a more filial daughter. If only she had not drawn such a line in the sand. If only she had asked for more help earlier. If only she had been more successful. If only she had not fucked it up so royally.

If only, if only, if only.

Katie's two life insurance policies totaling $20 million seemed her only way out.

She could still feel the weight of Ha-joon's regard, but she allowed herself to be patient. Ha-joon had to sleep some time.

March 2024

What if tapping into your inner genius didn't mean pain but healing? Joy, not hurt?

- Katie Wu, X, March 2024

"Please tell me you didn't, Katie," Jae-sung cut in, his stomach cratering.

"Tell you I didn't what?"

"That you didn't try to… I can't even say it. Thinking about it makes me sick."

"You want me to lie to you?"

Jae-sung's whole world was spinning. He had known Katie hadn't been doing well—but he hadn't known it was to that extent. His heart was in pieces all over again.

"You could have told me, Katie," he said bitterly. "I had more than enough money."

Katie refused to look at him. "It wasn't your problem to solve. How could I ask that of you, Jae-sung?"

Jae-sung wanted to scream, to implore for Katie to stop. He wanted to cover his eyes at all the scary parts—but hadn't she done that all those years she'd been with him? What had that gotten him but a lie?

He had asked for it; he would see it through.

"What did you do, Katie?"

Katie's fingers were trembling. "I don't remember most of it. Oppa told me about it months later." She shoved her hands underneath her thighs, sitting on them. "He saved my life. I still don't know why."

"Because he loves you, Katie. Because you're a person," Jae-sung said.

He hated Katie, but he also really wanted her to know that. He wished she could see what he had seen. What they all had seen.

"Oppa woke up as I attempted to leave the suite. I didn't want to burden him with finding me in the morning."

"Ah, fuck."

"He said I had emptied a bottle of sleeping pills, and that he had forced me to vomit as much as I could. He'd even had activated charcoal ready just in case." Katie's voice had turned robotic, as if she was reciting a grocery list. "I have no idea how much money SB Entertainment paid to hush this all up, but Oppa got me to a hospital. Afterward, they had me committed to a suicide recovery center just outside of Seoul."

Never in Jae-sung's most fervid speculations had he ever imagined such a possible outcome.

"They had me on suicide watch for a few days. I was so disoriented and unresponsive that they were really worried."

"Did they call your mother?"

"No. I was adamant she not be told anything. I—I couldn't handle them telling her and her not caring." Katie wrapped her arms around herself. "They called Mattie, and he, in his distress, called Alton. Mattie told Alton everything."

"Ah."

Jae-sung had wondered when Alton figured in. Had wondered since January why Katie had turned to Alton and not him. Had wondered how he had fallen so short of the Singaporean magnate.

"Alton convinced Oppa to take me to an in-patient recovery center in Santa Barbara—it's just outside Los Angeles—where no one knew me and I could understand the language better."

Katie reached for her purse again and stopped herself. She resumed sitting on her hands.

"He coordinated everything: the plane tickets, the treatment center, the health insurance, the living situation once I was in out-patient treatment. He played hardball with the Lau family and negotiated—then settled—the debt. Alton and Ha-joon oppa saved my life. They saved my family."

No wonder Katie loved Alton. No wonder she was so loyal to the older man. No wonder she belonged to him as she had belonged to no other.

"Alton must really love you," Jae-sung forced himself to say, his anger and shame twisting his emotions into churning knots. "I hope you've found happiness with him, Katie."

Katie's lips twisted wistfully. "He does."

Jae-sung tamped down his grief. Katie was right. Knowing simultaneously helped and did not. His wounds were still there, entrenched and gaping. He still didn't understand. She was still so frustratingly opaque.

"Why didn't you tell me? I loved you, Katie. I was going to marry you." His voice cracked along the faultlines of his soul. Tears streamed down his face. "What did Alton have that I didn't? You never even gave me a chance."

"It wasn't you, Jae-sung." Katie's eyes filled with tears of her own. "I want you to know that. It wasn't you. And I'm sorry."

"You're sorry," he sneered.

"Yes. And I know it's not enough."

"It really isn't."

They stared at each other from separate corners of Jae-sung's studio, both breathing hard. Jae-sung wanted to yell. To curse. To throw his expensive KAWS figurines.

"I tried, you know," Katie finally said. "I tried—but you were so perfect, Jae-sung."

Jae-sung laughed savagely. "Me. Perfect."

"You are so good, Jae. I know you say that you don't believe people are inherently good—but you are. You really are." Katie swallowed, her hands wringing. "Your parents are so kind, so nice, so supportive. I know you struggled and suffered for your art—that you didn't have an easy time with debuting." She shifted in her seat, leaning toward him as if to plead her case. "I know you got shit from the hip-hop community and from the music industry at large, but your life, Jae—your family. To me, you were perfect, and I didn't—I didn't want to sully you. I didn't want to poison you, to infect you with my family. I didn't want my father to know of you—to ruin you, too."

Katie started to sob. Jae-sung did not move.

"I didn't want to see the way you loved me change. I didn't want your pity."

"Well it changed anyway, didn't it? Now, I don't love you at all."

Jae-sung immediately wanted to recall his harsh words. He'd gotten what he'd wanted. Why was he still so angry?

"So you would accept his money but not mine, huh?" he seethed. He knew he sounded as petty as he felt, but he did not care. He could not stop himself. "I was too perfect to help you, but Alton came running and you took it. You didn't seem to care about sullying *his* family name."

Katie turned to him in disbelief, her face puffy from crying. "Jesus Christ, Jae-sung. It's not a pissing contest," she croaked. She narrowed her eyes at him. "I want you to really think things through. Just what do you think would have happened if the press not only got wind of us dating, but the fact that you had to pay off my father's debts from shady business dealings?"

Jae-sung was heated. He wanted to argue more, but Katie was right. The scandal would have ruined him and possibly taken DOYEN down with him. That didn't make it better, though. Not by a long shot.

"I just don't know why you couldn't talk to me about it—why you thought the proper response was to disappear," he continued doggedly. "I don't even know what I did."

"You called me abusive!" she shouted, as if it had been obvious when nothing about her was. "How could you not get that?"

Jae-sung reeled. "I was frustrated. It was impossible to talk to you about anything. You had to have known that—you remember, don't you?" he shouted back. "I misspoke, but you should have known that! I would never have called you that had I known about your father—but you never even gave me a chance to apologize. To prove myself."

Katie pressed her fists against her eyes. She gulped in a huge breath and held it. She exhaled and sucked in another breath. She clutched her chest, eyes still shut tight.

What had he done?

"Katie—" he started.

"I'm fine," Katie gritted out. "I—just—give me a moment and I will get out of your way. You have what you wanted?"

Katie reached blindly for her purse and dug around until she found a tiny bottle of prescription medication. She popped two in her mouth with shaking hands and though she also had a water bottle on her, she downed the pills with a swill of scotch.

Jae-sung was a fucking asshole. He did not deserve Katie's love and adoration. No wonder his members were on her side. No wonder she had left him.

"I'm sorry, Katie. That was—that was uncalled for."

"It's fine," Katie dismissed too quickly with a wave of her slender, ring-clad fingers. "You're right. I never gave you a chance to prove yourself," she admitted. "I'm sure there are a lot of things you want to say to me. Go ahead. I'm not stopping you."

Katie seemed so defeated, so beaten down. All the fury blazing in Jae-sung for the last three years snuffed out. Instead, he was over-whelmed with sorrow.

"I loved you so much, Katie," he said.

Her face was full of heartbreak and sorrow. He didn't understand how she could be even more beautiful than ever. "I know, Jae-sung. I loved you, too."

"Was it even real? Did I even know you?" Jae-sung shook his head. "I gave you all of me, and you threw me away. You threw us away."

"I did."

"You lied to me. You didn't even tell your family we were dating—did I get that right?"

Katie nodded miserably.

"All this time, I thought you'd never introduced me to your family because of the physical distance." He was gutted. When would her body blows stop hitting so hard? "I had assumed that you had at least told them about me."

"Mattie would have called you if he'd known," Katie said softly. "He's always liked you."

Jae-sung had always liked Katie's younger brother, too. He was a few months younger than Soo-min and from what he'd seen, had given Katie almost as much shit as the maknae had. No wonder she had always harbored such a soft spot for Soo-min.

"You know what I don't get? I understand you obviously couldn't call me and break up with me when you were in the hospital or during your in-patient treatment," said Jae-sung. "But after? You had years, Katie. I waited for years."

"I'm sorry."

Jae-sung wondered if either of them would believe or accept Katie's apologies if she said sorry enough times. He did not think so.

"You couldn't even tell me to my face. You wrote a whole fucking book and told my members, but you didn't even have the balls to tell me." Jae-sung took a long, calming breath. He didn't want to say anything else he didn't really mean. "You could have at least had the company pass along a message to warn me. I didn't even know you had a book until today."

"Manager-nim wanted to tell you, but I wouldn't let him. I wouldn't let the company tell you anything." Katie paused. "Don't blame the guys, either. I only recently told them, and they respected my wishes to let me tell you myself—which, obviously, I did not do until you pushed the issue."

"You're a coward, Katie." He watched as his words hit like a whip.

"I am," she agreed, shrinking into herself. Katie cleared her throat. "Anything else you want to get off your chest?"

He was done with her. "No."

Katie got up and gathered her scarf, shoving it into her bag. She straightened her clothing and then held herself erect. "Goodbye, Jae-sung. I wish you well," she said.

Jae-sung watched hollowly as Katie left, and at the click of his door, he sank his head into his hands and wept.

Chapter 6

February 2022

Daepyo-nim, just checked Katie out of the recovery center. She seems out of it, but I am hopeful that with the proper care, we should be back in Korea by the end of the year or early next year at the latest.

- Text from Baek Ha-joon to Song Byung-ho, September 2021

She won't eat. She won't talk. She won't write. She won't sing. She won't let me play music. She just lays in bed and refuses to move. She stares at the wall—she doesn't even cry. I don't know what to do.

- Text from Baek Ha-joon to Alton Kuang, September 2021

She keeps complaining that Santa Barbara is too white and that if she has to be subjected to microaggressions, cultural igno-rance, and being othered one more fucking time by the staff she

*will make sure she's much more thorough on her next attempt.
Are there any out-patient programs in Los Angeles?*
- Text from Baek Ha-joon to Alton Kuang, October 2021

She's a wreck.
- Text from Baek Ha-joon to Alton Kuang, November 2021

*Daepyo-nim, I don't think Katie will be back in Korea this year
or even the next. I am recommending she not renew her contract
with us in June.*
- Text from Baek Ha-joon to Song Byung-ho, December
2021

*We need to start making plans for who will take care of Katie
when her contract ends in a few months. Unfortunately, I will
not be able to stay. I am not confident that she will be able to
live on her own safely.*
- Text from Baek Ha-joon to Alton Kuang, February 2022

"Everyone keeps asking me if I'm in LA and if I can meet up with them in K-town. I don't know what to tell them, Oppa," said Katie to Ha-joon one late afternoon as she entered the kitchen.

The fading southern California light barely filtered through one of the bay windows and Katie switched on the lights. She slid into one of the counter-height chairs at the long kitchen island, propped her elbows on the granite counter, and followed Ha-joon around the open kitchen with her gaze.

"Who's everyone?" Ha-joon asked as he stared into the open refrigerator. "And technically, you're not in LA. You're in San Marino, so you wouldn't exactly be lying if you said you weren't."

Katie and Ha-joon were staying in Alton's understated mansion in San Marino, a wealthy suburb of Los Angeles. She loved the sleepy little town and how it almost felt as if they had no neighbors, with the house set far back onto the 2.3-acre property. Old oak, bay laurel, lemon, and California sycamore trees on the property further created a sense of privacy that a stone wall around the home already provided.

"You know, industry friends." At Ha-joon's snort, she mumbled, "Like Soo-min and Woo-jin."

"No Ye-jun?" asked Ha-joon as he pulled out Napa cabbage, daikon, bean sprouts, and other produce and pork to start dinner.

"I think he's still mad at me," Katie said. "Not that it makes a difference anyway since I'm not replying to any of them."

"Do you want them to know?" Ha-joon asked carefully, as if she was fragile and he was always breaking her.

"No," Katie replied.

Katie noted Ha-joon's small sigh even as he began washing the vegetables. She hated herself for turning her once open, confident, and tough love manager into an anxious, guarded person. She knew he was exhausted, and she was the cause of his burnout. Katie was the reason he was going to be without a person to manage in three months. She was the reason Ha-joon was switching departments at SB Entertainment. She was the reason Ha-joon now hated his job.

How he must despise her.

"Do you want me to tell them to back off?" Ha-joon offered kindly. Even now, he was doing his best to take care of her. Katie did not deserve him.

"You shouldn't burn your bridges, Oppa," Katie said softly. At his bewildered expression, she continued. "If you make DOYEN members mad, I'm sure it would affect your career prospects."

"Aish," Ha-joon replied brusquely as he started chopping the vegetables, "Song PD and I go way back. Don't worry about me. I don't want any sort of nonsense clouding the time I have left with you. I only have you a few more months, Katie-yah."

Katie merely stared after him, brain fritzing. "Oh."

Everything in her being rebelled at accepting his words as truth. Katie didn't realize she was sobbing until Ha-joon enveloped her in his strong, dependable arms.

"Ah, Katie," Ha-joon murmured. "Oppa will miss you so very, very much. But don't cry just yet—we still have plenty of time together."

Katie nodded into his chest and didn't move for some time. Lies circled her overwhelmed mind like vultures, except—for once—she allowed herself to sink into the hope that Ha-joon was here because he loved her and not because he wanted a return on his company's investment.

She vowed as she always did that tomorrow, she would make it up to Ha-joon and Alton. Katie would make them proud one day; she would repay all the sacrifices they had made for her.

The next morning, Katie woke up feeling as she always did: grayed out. The world was muted as if she was underwater and all she could hear was the pounding of her pulse. It did not matter that she was surrounded by luxury.

She spent her day like she did every other day, refusing to budge from her bed until her bladder could no longer hold and then crawling back under heavy blankets. She zoned out on mobile games until her elbows hurt. If she sensed Ha-joon down the hall, she would toss the covers over her head, pretending to sleep.

One day slipped into the next, and once again, time lost all meaning.

"Stop avoiding me, Katie," scolded an impeccably dressed Alton through the tiny screen of her phone. Katie could just see Singapore's skyline behind Alton so she guessed he was at his office. "And before you lie to my face and say you're not, I have it on good authority that you spend all day locked in your room pretending to sleep."

"Who says I'm pretending?" Katie scowled even as she burrowed deeper into the pillows propping her up in bed. "I have years of sleep to catch up on."

"I don't think that's how it works, Mei."

Alton sounded so disappointed. He had to be. He'd settled millions of dollars on her behalf and Katie repaid him by wasting away her life in bed. Nevermind that she had no idea how to settle the debt, given that the thought of singing or performing made her want to vomit. Nevermind that Alton waived it away as if it was nothing. Even if it was nothing to him, it was not nothing to her.

Mattie couldn't understand why Katie wasn't more relieved. She didn't dare confide in him about her sense of despair and indebtedness. The one time she had when he'd visited, Mattie had flown into a rare temper.

"Why can't you just accept this good thing, Katie? Why do you always have to be such a martyr? As if you're the only person in the world who can save us?" They'd been sitting on a bench in the stone courtyard of Alton's home. The fact that Mattie—calm and collected and easygoing Mattie—had raised his voice at all had thrown Katie into disarray. "Don't you fucking dare do anything stupid to pay Alton back. I will never forgive you if you do."

He had sounded near tears. "I promise, Mattie," she had said, turning to face her younger brother. She grabbed his hand. "Could you clarify what you mean by 'stupid' though?" she had teased, trying to lighten the mood. Mattie had not been amused.

"Anything that jeopardizes your life is stupid, you get me, Katie?" her brother had growled, his voice flinty and hard.

"I get you."

"I know you sacrificed for me so I could have an easier life, but I don't want it. I'm 24 years old and I don't need it. What I need is my fucking sister to be alive." Mattie had glared, his hands fisted at his side. "I need you to live, Katie."

Katie had stared at him and perhaps had seen him for the first time. Mattie was no longer a child. He did not need her to take care of him anymore. Perhaps he never had.

Guilt coursed through her as she thought of what she'd put her brother through this last year. "Okay, Mattie," she had said.

Mattie had stared back, unsure if he could trust her. Katie hadn't blamed him. "Okay," he'd replied as he pulled her into a tight embrace. "Okay."

Her little brother, who'd established that he was no longer quite so little, had held her for a long time. Somehow, the weight of living had seemed even more ponderous than all her other debts.

Katie was dragged back to the present when Alton said, "I have a proposal, Mei." He looked as if he was trying not to seem worried and settled on nonchalance.

"I don't even get a fancy dinner?" she quipped.

"Dinners are for ladies who put out."

"Problematic."

"Just checking to see if you were feeling more like yourself," Alton replied. "Glad to see you're still putting me in my place."

Katie grunted. Even this little bit of banter took a lot out of her. She wanted to lay back down, but she didn't want to face Alton's judgment.

"What's your proposal?" she asked. Anything to move the painful conversation along.

"I know you hate feeling like a charity case—"

"Well, I wouldn't if you would just tell me why you saved my ass," she retorted. Alton shot her a look of disbelief and Katie added, "Okay, I would still feel awful, but at least it would make more sense to me."

Alton assessed her carefully through the screen. "My family owes yours—so much more than what I paid for your father," he said, his face uncharacteristically serious.

"What are you going on about?" Katie asked, confused.

"Your ah-gong and my shú gong's families were super close—and during World War II, your grandfather lent our family some money at a crucial time. He wouldn't even accept any interest when my family started paying him back. Without him, we would have been wiped out."

Katie was quiet for only a moment. "I sincerely doubt my ah-gong lent your family 3.2 million dollars, Alton. Don't make it more than it was," she dismissed.

"Don't disrespect your grandfather or my granduncle, Katie," Alton snapped, his usual warm eyes now blazing and fierce. "How do you put a price on a life—let alone multiple generations of lives? Everything we have is because of him."

Katie could not bear it. "Is that what I am to you? A debt to be repaid?" Her voice wobbled. She covered her face. "I'm sorry," she muffled through her fingers. "I know it's not about me—it's just—it's a lot."

She risked a glance at Alton. His gaze once again dripped with concern and sorrow.

"This is why I didn't want to tell you, Katie," he said softly. Alton leaned closer to his phone and ran his fingers through his perfectly coiffed hair. "I wouldn't love you out of obligation. I love you for who you are—and also, my family owes yours a debt we can never repay. They can both be true, love." He smiled ruefully, turning his boyish charm back on. "Of course, I can assure you until we're old and gray and still, you would not believe me."

Katie nodded at his assessment. He wasn't wrong.

Alton took a deep breath and forced a bright smile on his handsome face. "So, hear me out," he said, pitching his voice light and mischievous. "If you want to earn your keep, then I have a list of demands."

"Demands?" She raised a questioning eyebrow.

"Alright, alright. Suggested work specs," Alton amended.

"I really can't work on music, Alton," Katie whispered, worried once again that she'd fail Alton in providing the right response. "So if that's the work, you'll be even more disappointed in me."

Alton rolled his eyes. "I'm only allowing this bullshit about you disappointing me slide—as if you could ever—because I'll be there in person in June and I don't want to fight before I get to LA," he said.

Katie gestured for him to continue.

"Your work is to physically get out of bed—and stay out—before noon every day." Alton held up a hand to forestall her burgeoning nitpicking. "And yes, including weekends. And no, you cannot just use another bed."

"Spoilsport."

"I also will need you to eat at least one nutritionally balanced meal a day, as well as do some sort of physical activity twice a week. Oh, and spend at least fifteen minutes in the sun every day."

Katie narrowed her eyes at him. "You ask too much. You know how I feel about the sun."

"Katie, I'm worried about you." Alton's face softened. "You spend too much time in your head."

She had nothing to say. Panic pulsed at the edges of her mind. Surely, Alton wasn't asking too much of her, and yet, it felt like too much.

"I love you, Katie. You know this, right? Please tell me you know this."

Katie nodded, a curt, abbreviated motion. "Just know I'm making you pay for the laser treatments if I get sun spots."

"I wouldn't expect anything less." Alton smiled tentatively. "I'll call you tomorrow?"

"If you must," Katie sighed, hoping Alton could tell she was teasing even if the tone didn't sound quite right.

"I must," he insisted.

After Alton ended the call, she sank back under her covers and thought of his blatant ploy to get her back into the motions of living. If Katie was to start working tomorrow, she might as well get in one last wallow.

Katie did not know the way out, but she hoped maybe duty and obligation to Alton would carry her through.

January 2024

TFW old friends refuse to let you accept judgment instead of grace.

                                        - Katie Wu, X, January 2024

"It's good to see you again, Noona," Soo-min said as he wrapped Katie in a tight hug, his oversized black T-shirt drowning her in excess material. "Don't let it go so long next time," he added, leaving unsaid so much of what Dae-jung and the rest of his members had wanted to say for the last few years.

They were in one of the private rooms at Heiwa, the Japanese restaurant co-owned by Ye-jun and his older brother, Ye-sung, and had always been one of Katie's favorite places to eat. Dae-jung appreciated that even after all these years, she still remembered to support them—even their family members. It reminded him that though she had dropped off the face of the earth, she still cared in tiny, ingrained ways.

Katie flushed prettily, eyes remorseful and shimmering. "Thanks for agreeing to have dinner with me," she said as she took turns hugging everyone.

Woo-jin and Ye-jun insisted on her sitting between them, and for a moment Dae-jung flashed to a version of them all at a similar long table. Katie looked like a fluffy chick flanked by a raven and a sparrow, her pale yellow and white striped cashmere sweater contrasting with Woo-jin's black button-down shirt and Ye-jun's heather gray henley. Do-won grabbed a spot next to Woo-jin, and Dae-jung, Soo-min, and Akihiro took up the other side.

The seven of them made slightly strained small talk. Katie asked about their year-end performances and families while steering clear of mentions of her own. Dae-jung could not help but notice her near constant sipping of hot sake. She obviously felt ill at ease, holding her body tight and aloof when she used to lean into his band members casually and take up their space. His heart twinged at the years lost between them. He couldn't stand it any longer.

"I'm sure you don't really care about how we feel about the weather and our schedules, Noona," Dae-jung broke in gently. At Soo-min's shocked gasp, Dae-jung wondered if perhaps he was not as gentle as he'd thought.

Panic flicked across Katie's countenance before she shut it down, smoothing over her features. "I suppose you're right, Dae-jung," she said, her voice trembling while she tucked a loose lock of hair behind her ear.

Dae-jung pretended he didn't hear the quaver. He loved her, but he owed it to his leader to ask. Her elusiveness had gone on long enough. "Where have you been, Noona? What happened between you and Jae-sung hyung? And why did you come back?"

"Dae-jung!" rebuked Ye-jun.

Katie placed a hand on Ye-jun's arm. "It's alright, Oppa. You deserve answers. Just please let me tell Jae-sung myself?"

At their nods, Katie downed the remainder of her sake and launched into the most heartbreaking story Dae-jung had heard in a long time. He wanted her to stop but it was as if now that the dam was released, she couldn't. Dae-jung wondered if he had ever known her.

"Noona," breathed Soo-min after she finished. "Oh, Noona. I'm so sorry." His eyes welled over again and Katie squeezed his outstretched hand across the table.

Woo-jin stared stonily at his food and looked as if he wanted to punch something or someone. Ye-jun couldn't stop touching Katie in small ways, as if to reassure himself she was really there. Do-won kept dabbing his eyes, and Akihiro looked eerily calm.

"I'm sorry for laying it all on you like this," Katie said. "I suppose there's no way to ease into it—at least not when I have so much to answer for."

"We would have helped you, Noona. Surely you know this?" accused Akihiro.

Dae-jung could tell Akihiro was seething just underneath his calm exterior. An angry Akihiro was terrifying to behold. Katie sighed. Dae-jung could tell she'd likely heard this from any number of her friends—especially Alton. She knew enough wealthy people.

"I know," Katie said, fiddling with her napkin. "I don't know if you've noticed, but I am perhaps a little too proud."

Akihiro barked a startled laugh. "I suppose you are," he conceded, his expression immediately softening.

"I saw you ask for help all the time though," Dae-jung observed.

"Family's different," Katie said. "You all have such good and kind families—how could I even begin to tell you what my father was like? I—" she swallowed. "My mother disowned me," she continued dejectedly. "What if—what if I told you everything and you wanted nothing to do with me? If my own parents didn't want me—how could any of you?"

Her voice broke and she threw her napkin into her lap. She gazed longingly at her empty sake cup and it seemed to Dae-jung that she'd come to a decision. Katie picked up the cup and settled it back on the table upside down.

"Don't be an idiot," Ye-jun blustered. "If I can love these idiots, I can most certainly love you."

"We love you, Noona," Soo-min said, resolute. "You're good through to your core."

"I—I really am not," Katie croaked.

"You think we can't read people after over a decade in this business?" Soo-min continued. "We're not naive children anymore, Noona. We can't afford to let the wrong people in our circles—and you're good people. That's why it hurt so much when you disappeared. We couldn't understand how all seven of us—especially Jae-sung hyung—could have gotten it so wrong."

"It doesn't matter what your father did or what your mother said. We're only upset because you had to go through it alone and without us. We love you," declared Akihiro. His tone brooked no dissent.

Dae-jung figured it was time for him to say something lest she thought he disagreed. "I'm glad you finally told us, Noona. And I'm glad that writing your memoir was healing. I look forward to reading the Korean translation."

Dae-jung's subject change brought the conversation back to safer territory, and he was relieved to see Katie's body finally relax, even as she cast a worried look at Woo-jin, who still had not said anything. They chatted a bit more until she looked at the time.

"I know it isn't even close to midnight except the jetlag is still kicking my ass. But before I forget, I have something for you." Katie got up and handed them each a gift bag from the shopping bag she'd brought with her. "It's nothing fancy, but I—uh, I hope you like it."

Dae-jung took out the tissue-wrapped package and ripped it open. He found a thick cable-knit scarf in a deep forest green shot through with silver-gray embellishments. When he looked carefully, he noted a cuddly otter embroidered on both ends. He caressed the soft cotton fibers and felt himself choke up.

"This is beautiful," murmured Akihiro. "Where did you find it?"

Dae-jung looked up to see the rest of his members holding up similar scarves. Soo-min's was charcoal gray with red accents and embroidered puppies, Akihiro's was a rich indigo blue and silver-gray with embroidered ducks, and Do-won's was bright yellow and pink with embroidered butterflies, coincidentally matching the vibe of his lime green beanie. He tried to look at Ye-jun and Woo-jin's scarves, but neither of them had taken theirs out of their bags.

"Ah," Katie hemmed, flushing slightly. "I knit them. I hope you like them."

"Noona, I didn't know you knew how to knit," gushed Soo-min. "I love it."

Katie's mouth twitched ruefully. "I had a lot of spare time," she said. "I made one for each of you—if you don't mind?"

"Thank you, Noona," Do-won said as he hugged her again, his voice still thick with emotion.

She let Do-won go and said, "I—I don't know if Jae-sung would want—he must hate me but I, I didn't want to leave him out." Katie's voice faltered and she cleared her throat. "Maybe if I—if you could hold onto his until you think it's the right time?"

Akihiro looked torn and Soo-min's face was filled with anguish.

"Of course, Noona," Dae-jung said, wanting to relieve some of the burden from his members.

"It was good to see you again, Noona," Akihiro said as he stood to hug Katie, his voice breaking. "Don't be a stranger in March, okay?"

Katie nodded, blinking rapidly. She looked a little lost when Woo-jin and Ye-jun got up without saying much. Woo-jin often kept his own counsel, but Ye-jun was uncharacteristically subdued. Dae-jung and the other members chattered among themselves, gathering their things to give her a moment with their two eldest.

Still, he couldn't help but overhear when Ye-jun pulled Katie in tight to his chest, his typical flippancy gone. "Ah, my brave little poppet," he choked out. "I swear if you ever do anything this foolish ever again, I will follow you into the next life and hound you until my voice is so embedded into your brain that you will never doubt just how precious you are."

"I don't know whether to be touched or terrified, Oppa," Katie eked out against Ye-jun's chest.

"Of course terrified," the singer grumbled, "as if there was ever a question." Ye-jun glanced at Woo-jin, who was scowling on their periphery. "Oh, for fuck's sake, Woo-jin-ah. Just join our group hug and ride the coattails of my soul-stirring declaration. The last thing Katie needs is your emotional constipation."

Woo-jin sighed and allowed himself to be pulled into Ye-jun's embrace, and in turn, covered Katie in a hug with his surprisingly broad frame.

"Don't fuck with my family, Katie-yah. You're my family and I won't have this disrespect," Woo-jin muttered in his low drawl. "Besides, you know my father was not always kind. I know how it can go."

Katie burst into tears, and Ye-jun glared down at Woo-jin. "What is this disgusting display of sentimentality? The two of you are such disasters! You're lucky I have enough sense for the lot of you."

Dae-jung couldn't help but feel as if he'd trespassed, but his heart was fuller than it had been a few moments ago.

When they were outside, Akihiro requested one last group photo, and Dae-jung was hit once more just how much he'd missed Katie over the last three years. She had been like a big sister to him, and he had relied on her steady and indulging presence for so much. She had kept him grounded.

He watched as Katie caught a cab and waved as the car pulled away.

It still smarted when he thought of how much of herself she'd hidden away out of fear and a misguided attempt to shield them. Maybe it was time they protected Katie for a change.

March 2024

The chickens have come home to roost.

- Katie Wu, X, March 2024

What does it mean when the man you've spent your life with calls you abusive? Does that mean he saw something inside you—something you thought you'd hidden?
- "Telling a Truth Is a Slippery Slope" (Red Lantern Publishing House, October 2023)

Dae-jung almost ran into Katie as she rounded the hallway corner at top speed after, he presumed, leaving Jae-sung's studio. "Noona, are you okay?"

It was a stupid question. Katie obviously was not. Her eyes and face were swollen, and there were still tear tracks on both cheeks.

"Do you want me to sit somewhere with you?" Dae-jung asked, though if he was truthful, he was more worried about Jae-sung. If Katie was a wreck, then how was Jae-sung faring?

"No, I—I'm fine. Really," Katie lied.

Dae-jung chose to believe it and let her go as he hurried down the corridor to Jae-sung's studio.

"Hyung?" Dae-jung said as he opened the door right after knocking.

All he needed to see was Jae-sung slumped on his couch, his head buried in his hands, and Dae-jung was at his leader's side, throwing his arms around the older man. He just let Jae-sung turn into him and weep on his shoulders. Dae-jung felt it was about time Jae-sung let others carry his burdens, too.

"I suppose you know what happened?" Jae-sung grated out after collecting himself.

"Just now? Or in Noona's missing years?"

"I guess everything." Jae-sung shrugged. "You must hate me."

Dae-jung wrapped his arms around the older man again and squeezed. "Why would I hate you, Hyung? You didn't know. How could you be blamed for something you knew nothing of?"

"Am I a monster?" Jae-sung choked out. "Is that why Katie didn't trust me? She tried to explain, and I only said horrible things." Jae-sung started sobbing again. "I'm just so, so angry. I thought if I just got a reason from her, I would feel better, but I feel worse. I'm even angrier, and I didn't think it would be possible."

"Ah, Hyung," Dae-jung soothed. "Of course you're angry. It's a terrible situation in general. You both did the best you could."

"Did I, though? I don't think I did the best of anything today except be a dick." Jae-sung wiped his face on his shirt.

Dae-jung smoothed his hand over Jae-sung's back in small, comforting circles.

"You're allowed to be angry. You're allowed to be a dick and not have a perfect response," said Dae-jung. "You're a person and it's all been a shock to you. It doesn't matter even though now you know what happened. She still hurt you, Hyung."

"She really did." Jae-sung sighed a wet breath. "And the worst part is that I still love her. I love her so much, Dae."

Dae-jung just gazed at his friend sorrowfully. "I know, Hyung. I know."

"I'm so stupid. Katie's clearly moved on. As soon as Alton saw an opening, he took it," Jae-sung scowled. He pushed himself off the couch and paced around the studio.

"What?"

"You remember Alton. I always hated him. It was her perfect revenge," mumbled Jae-sung.

"Noona's not with Alton. She's not with anyone," Dae-jung said carefully. "She hasn't dated anyone since she left."

"Katie's not dating Alton? But—but she made it seem like she was?"

"Did she ever say that or did you assume something and she didn't disagree?"

Jae-sung paused in his pacing. "Oh." Jae-sung met Dae-jung's gaze and Dae-jung hated the spark of hope in his friend's eyes.

"Oh, no. No, Hyung. No."

"What?"

Dae-jung snorted. "You think you're slick, huh? Whatever you're thinking, forget it." He leaned back against Jae-sung's very comfortable couch, his fingers stroking the rich fabric.

"I don't know what you're talking about." Jae-sung stopped at his workstation and fiddled with the half-empty soda and water bottles haphazardly littering his desktop.

"I thought you were angry. Angrier than you were before," reasoned Dae-jung.

"I am. But that doesn't negate how much I still love her." Jae-sung shoved his hands into the pockets of his corduroys and hung his head again. "I'm pathetic."

"I thought you were going to try and love yourself a little more, Hyung," Dae-jung said gently. He hated when Jae-sung was too hard on himself. "You feel what you feel, and what you feel is real."

"It's been years. Why are you still quoting 'Frozen 2'?" Jae-sung asked as he sank into the leather sofa chair.

Dae-jung shrugged. "I can't help that it's valid."

"I don't know what to do." Jae-sung's entire body crumpled into a sad ball.

"First, give yourself some time to absorb this new information and process your grief and anger," suggested Dae-jung. "And then possibly consider that the Noona you love is not the same as the Noona she is now—and perhaps she never was."

Jae-sung rubbed his eyes with the heels of his palms. "When did you get so wise, Dae?"

"I've always been this way," Dae-jung chuckled. "It's just that you finally realized it."

"I suppose you're right," conceded Jae-sung. He leaned back into the chair and spread his legs. "Thanks, Dae."

"'Course, Hyung," he replied. "We've got you."

"Yeah, you really do."

June 2024

Love you, CHIMERA! Your love throughout the years has seen me through rough and easy times. I can't believe it's been 11 years and still you love us. #Dae-jung

- DOYEN Official, X, June 2024

Dae-jung opened his front door to Ha-rin staring at him from his living room couch. She had called him that morning, asking him to come home early from work. He'd had a sense of foreboding so strong that though he normally would have blown off her request, he'd rescheduled a meeting with a producer he wanted to work with.

He slipped off his shoes and gave Ha-rin a stilted hug and kiss before he sat opposite her in his favorite leather easy chair.

"I can't do this anymore, Dae-jung," Ha-rin said before he could even get some small talk in. She was wound so tight, her arms crossed and defensive.

He resisted the urge to immediately ask for clarification. Ha-rin would hate the interruption.

As he suspected, she proceeded to inform him without delay. "All these rumors about you and other idols—even your own members!" She shuddered in revulsion and Dae-jung tried to let the comment go. He knew it had less to do with his sexuality and more to do with her feelings about his members, but it still stung. "They're parking under your staff's social media handles and commenting vile shit. It's too much. I know I wanted us to go public, but I don't want to be stalked by your sasaengs."

"They won't find out, jagiya," Dae-jung protested. It had become automatic, but he knew he couldn't promise anything. He'd taken great pains not to have his phone upload to the cloud due to possible hackers, but then, his entire phone was at risk if he didn't remember to manually back it up onto a personal computer. "I've been careful. We've been careful."

"It's been years, and it's only getting worse," Ha-rin insisted, her fingers twisting a shiny bauble Dae-jung had bought her years ago. Her eyes shimmered with unshed tears. "My parents want me to get married. They're worried you're just stringing me along until someone better comes along."

Dae-jung noted that she didn't mention how her parents constantly paraded better options for her to consider. They hated him because though he was rich now, he wasn't born with a silver spoon in his mouth and had the temerity to be in entertainment. They wanted someone respectable and from their world for their only daughter.

He would never be good enough for them.

"Ha-rin," he soothed, though it angered him that her parents could be so casually cruel. "Don't listen to your parents, baby, please. We're only 28, and I'm going to be gone a lot on tour this year. It's just not the right time yet."

"That's the problem with you," Ha-rin said, so soft and deadly. "You're always promising me 'maybes' and 'in the futures.' But it's never the right time, Dae. You're always asking me to wait another month, another year."

Dae-jung wanted to scream in frustration. It wasn't that he didn't want to marry Ha-rin. He did—one day. But she refused to understand how whatever he did reflected on the rest of DOYEN. He was sure his true fans would be happy for him when he eventually got married. He hated how it felt like Ha-rin was pressuring him even as she complained he was pressuring her.

"You know what my job entails, jagi," Dae-jung mumbled as he slumped in his chair. "You know how my fans get. It's safer keeping you a secret until we're actually married. Besides, no one our age is getting married yet."

Ha-rin glared at him. "I've given you four years, Dae-jung. If you don't have any intention of marrying me, you should have told me from the beginning so I didn't waste my youth on you."

"You think our relationship has been a waste?" He reeled. "Ha-rin, I love you. You love me, too, right?" He'd known she was unhappy, but he hadn't realized that she was unhappy enough to end things. He was floundering and Ha-rin just watched him drown.

"I don't know anymore, Dae-jung," she replied coldly. "It was cool at first, you know? The secrecy was kinda sexy and mysterious." She pierced him with deadly brown eyes. Her bloodred nails tapped against her cream Celine cardigan. "But I want to show you off. What's the point of dating Park Dae-jung from DOYEN if I can't even tell my friends?"

Dae-jung felt as if she'd slapped him. Ha-rin was many things: opinionated, stubborn, and spoiled, but she had never been a clout chaser.

Ha-rin sighed, her face softening for just a moment. Dae-jung wondered when the last time she'd seemed soft around him. He couldn't remember. "I want to do normal things like go on dates with you. I want to walk along the Han River instead of hiding in a parked car looking at it."

"Ha-rin, baby, I'm so sorry. I know it hasn't been easy for you—and you've been so good about it," Dae-jung pleaded even though he knew it was a lost cause. He knew very well all that Ha-rin had given up to be with him. "You know I love you, Ha-rin. You're my entire world. I want to spend the rest of my life with you."

"It's not enough, Dae-jung," Ha-rin replied, her spine steeling once more. "I just want to show off my boyfriend," she said, her voice laced in bitterness. "Instead, I have a stack of NDAs gathering dust in the corner. Your staff combs through my phone sporadically to make sure I'm not leaking confidential information. Your lawyers breathe down my neck, warning me not to fuck things up for you. It's like you don't exist at all."

He did not need Ha-rin to say the rest. She broadcasted her resentment in the way she closed in on herself, holding herself apart from him, as if they were already two separate beings instead of the one he'd thought they were for so long.

"I'll respect whatever you want me to do," Dae-jung said resignedly. What else could he do? He could at least give Ha-rin that.

Ha-rin scoffed, animosity evident on her face. "You let me go so easily, huh, Dae-jung? You didn't even have to think about it. Didn't even consider giving up DOYEN for a second."

"Is that what this was, Ha-rin?" Dae-jung asked, his heart breaking. "Was this a test?"

"I don't know. I had hoped—" Ha-rin paused. "It was stupid of me. Your DOYEN members say 'jump' and you ask 'how high?' You give them everything that should be mine by rights." Her pretty face was skewed with defiance.

"Everything I have is because of DOYEN. I will always be a part of DOYEN, and I don't want to leave it behind," Dae-jung said evenly. "And I could never leave CHIMERA behind."

"CHIMERA," Ha-rin sneered, the hate open on her face. "Those demanding people who want every piece of you. They would tear you apart if they knew about us. They would tear me apart, and you would defend them."

"Real CHIMERA wouldn't care. They would be happy for us," he insisted. It was yet another worn argument, one neither of them would win.

"That's what you always say. You don't get to pick and choose who CHIMERA is," Ha-rin volleyed back. "I guess we'll never find out. I'll arrange with your managers and staff to return your stuff. I already asked them to start processing the paperwork of divesting myself from you." Ha-rin got up from her seat.

Dae-jung was gutted. "You told them before you told me?"

"I just want it to be over as quickly as possible, Dae-jung," she replied, evenly meeting his gaze. "I want to be free."

"I see," Dae-jung said even though he didn't.

He understood, even though he didn't. If he was honest with himself, deep down, he was surprised they had lasted as long as they had. Dae-jung had thought it was because they were meant to be, instead of them holding on despite their innate incompatibility. What they had wasn't true—and god, he longed for true.

"Goodbye, Ha-rin. Thank you for everything."

She flinched when he reached to hug her, so in the end, Dae-jung just watched helplessly as Ha-rin, the woman he thought would bear his children, walked out of his apartment.

He wondered if there would ever be someone for whom he wouldn't be too much. He wondered if there would ever be someone for him who was true. Dae-jung wasn't quite sure what true looked like, and had been tricked a few times already, but he had faith that one day, he would find it. And when he found that true, he would never let it go.

Former singer Katie Wu is back in Seoul after a three-year absence, but this time, it's as an author. The Korean translation of her New York Times bestselling book, "Telling a Truth Is a Slippery Slope," has surprisingly flown off the shelves and has even broken records in Korea for books written by a celebrity. Likely, many gossip hounds are curious for clues about who her mystery boyfriend of four years was.

They will get more than they bargained for. "Telling" is a gorgeous piece of writing—and utterly heartbreaking. Wu said she hoped her book would shine a light on domestic violence in Asian American households as well as break stigmas about mental health and suicide. She wished to give courage and hope to those who are suffering.

- The Korea Herald, June 2024

No surprise, Katie Wu is in the headlines for stirring up con-troversy again. Men's rights activists and multiple government officials are calling for a ban on "Telling a Truth Is a Slippery Slope" because Wu promotes harmful feminism and lacks fil-ial piety. Extra security is being hired for her reading events and local authorities are recommending attendants proceed with caution.

- JoongAng Ilbo, June 2024

I'm so excited!! I won tickets to Katie's book tour stop in Seoul!! I wonder if her old labelmates will attend to support her?

- X user, June 2024

[+ 107,892, - 12,389] Katie is a disgrace. A real man would have kicked her to the curb years ago. She had an entire album called "Whore of Babylon" a few years back and now she's back with this shit. Why do we keep allowing a self-admitted prostitute back into this country? Send this Chinese slut back to where she came from.

- internet user, Pann, June 2024

It never failed to surprise Dae-jung when he saw all the security and protesters surrounding Katie's events. In theory, he understood it. After all, he was constantly protected by a detail due to his international celebrity status, but Katie was markedly more low-key. He could never grasp what it was about her that enraged so many men.

Could these men not see how Katie was a warrior artist of unparalleled caliber? Or maybe that was the problem; they could and were terrified.

He half-heartedly followed his bandmates into Starfield Library and gazed at the 13-meter book display. Though he didn't think it was Katie's style of bookstore, he understood that the venue was chosen to accommodate DOYEN, AQ9, and other SB Entertainment groups as they supported Katie. The floor was full of press and fifty lucky raffle winners chosen from Katie's fan club members.

"I thought we were supposed to be a surprise," whispered Soo-min. "But it seems the press already knew?"

"Of course the press knew," Jae-sung remarked acidly. "How else could they drum up publicity for Katie's book? We're here to do our part. Otherwise, we wouldn't have flown back from Japan and just continued with the Asia leg of our tour."

Though Dae-jung didn't voice his opinion, he agreed with Jae-sung. Granted, he didn't feel like doing anything lately outside of performing. He didn't know what to do with himself now that Ha-rin had left him. The free time that had seemed all too short during the four years they dated now loomed endless. He supposed supporting Katie was better than moping alone in his hotel room, stuck in a foreign country.

"Why did everyone tell me it was a surprise then?" Soo-min pouted, his thick eyebrows two dark slashes on his scrunched forehead.

Jae-sung sighed loudly. "Because it's a surprise to the general public, Soo-min. They probably didn't want us to spoil it."

"Like I'm the one they need to worry about," Soo-min grumbled back.

"Are you going to be okay?" asked Ye-jun quietly. "Woo-jin or I can speak if they ask for our opinion. I can be extra ridiculous today if you want."

Dae-jung's heart warmed at the gesture. Even though he knew Ye-jun loved Jae-sung, he also knew how much his eldest hyung adored and passionately protected Katie. Between Ye-jun, Woo-jin, and Soo-min, she was well defended among his bandmates.

It was good to see Ye-jun remind his leader at a critical moment that he was on Team Jae-sung, too.

"I'm fine," Jae-sung snapped. He took a deep, calming breath. "I'm fine, Hyung," he tried again, this time with more care. "Sorry for being a dick, Minnie."

"'S fine, Hyung," replied Soo-min, eyes wide and full of concern. "Let's grab a seat, yeah?"

Dae-jung and the rest of his bandmates joined the section where all the SB Entertainment artists were expected to sit and chatted with the members of boy band AQ9 in the row behind them. He glanced over and saw Katie sitting by herself in the very front, back erect and proper. He took a moment to take Katie in and understood exactly why Jae-sung still wasn't over her.

Katie had buzzed the sides of her hair into a perfectly faded undercut leaving a shaggy mohawk that was styled like the rock star she used to be. Her ears were covered in so many piercings they resembled armor, and Dae-jung mused they probably were meant as such. He couldn't see the rest of her outfit, but it was black and framed the shape of her back in flattering angles.

He wondered why Katie was alone and was about to discuss with his members about greeting her when all 185 cm of Alton Kuang swept in, clad in Tom Ford and looking every bit the chaebol he was. Alton crushed Katie to him in a bruising hug and after, she melted into his tender and intimate touches.

Maybe Jae-sung had been right and it was another omission of hers that they'd missed. Or maybe it was a recent development. With Katie, they could never really be sure. She sure seemed like Alton's girl through and through.

Their palpable tenderness sent a pang through Dae-jung as he thought of Ha-rin and wondered if other people had seen any tenderness between them. Ha-rin had been all sharp edges. He had hoped to be soft enough for them both, but in the end, she'd left him holding his own bleeding heart.

Dae-jung flicked his gaze to Jae-sung, who had stiffened in his seat and was being comforted by Do-won, who had tasked himself with occupying their leader. As much as Dae-jung wanted to support Katie, he really wished it didn't have to be in such a public setting and at the expense of Jae-sung. The whole situation just made him sad, and he wasn't even a main participant!

Dae-jung decided to peruse the program instead, and before he knew it, the event started. He clapped politely in all the expected places, waved when DOYEN was acknowledged and thanked along with the other SB Entertainment artists, and then, it was Katie's turn to read.

Katie walked up, head held high and looking regal in a sweeping modern Tang Dynasty-style jacket embroidered with white cranes. Her movements revealed glimpses of a lacy bralette and black silk harem pants paired with black satin stiletto boots.

Dae-jung's breath caught. He'd forgotten just how devastating Katie could be and sent up a prayer for Jae-sung. They would all need one.

I don't know why you're here, but I know why I am, Katie began.

Dae-jung found himself seduced by her reading voice, a resonant contralto so different from her normal speaking pitch. If he had heard Katie reading without context, he would have never connected the sonorous, rich timbre with her. She was so deep, and he was lost.

I write this book as an altar; it is my pile of rocks in the middle of the Jordan, Katie continued. *In the future, my children will ask me, "What do these rocks mean?" I will tell them, "The water almost swept me away, but the people who loved me would not let me drown. These rocks will always remind me: I was here. I am here. I made a promise, and I will continue to be here."*

Dae-jung had always appreciated Katie's lyricism before, though he'd paid more attention to her vocal abilities and musical stylings. It wasn't that her words hadn't been important—it was more that he had never been a lyrics guy. That was more Jae-sung and Woo-jin's thing. And now that Dae-jung heard Katie's unvarnished prose, he realized, perhaps for the first time, that she was an extraordinary writer.

By the time Katie was done with her excerpt, there was not a dry eye in the house.

The emcee made a few remarks and the program switched to the question and answer portion from both members of the press and the audience. All seemed to be going smoothly until a male journalist representing a conservative paper got the mic.

"Some say that you're just desperate for attention—that your suicide attempt was faked and that your book is an attempt to revive your lackluster singing career," the man stated. He was sharply dressed in a button-down, navy slacks, designer glasses, and leather shoes—his staid outfit a striking contrast with the bright pink lanyard holding a press pass around his neck. "That as per usual, you relied on the sensationalism of sex instead of actual talent to make headlines. What would you say in the face of such observations?"

Dae-jung saw Do-won place a placating hand on Jae-sung's knee and he forced himself not to react. He would not give the press any satisfaction of provoking any drama from him or his members.

The corner of Katie's mouth lifted and Dae-jung knew to brace for impact.

"I would say that it seems as if you're projecting," she replied serenely as people in the audience stifled nervous snickers.

The man sneered. It didn't matter how nicely put together the journalist was, Dae-jung thought uncharitably, character mattered more. He and his members had been condescended to enough by well-heeled journalists to know. "Don't think you can dodge the question with a quippy remark. We know what you really are."

Katie's face was unfailingly polite. "And what am I?"

"An opportunistic upstart leveraging all your scandals in the absence of talent," he said.

All the oxygen snuffed out of the room.

"Is that right?" Katie drawled, her eyes belying her lazy calm. "Then it is as you say."

"That's it?" the man challenged, his eyes bulging and face purpling. "That's all you have to say?"

Katie shrugged, her earrings tinkling with the movement. "Let's not pretend you care about facts or truths or my interpretation of them. We all shape our own narratives and you have already chosen yours. It's always nice to see new fiction writers make a name for themselves."

Dae-jung wanted to cheer and some audience members actually clapped as Katie dismissed the man and said, "Next question?"

The rest of the time continued without incident. Of course, there were several requests for spoilers about Katie's mystery boyfriend, but she accepted them good-naturedly and skillfully sidestepped the attempts. There were even several moving moments where fans and readers explained how she comforted them in their hardship or gave them courage to ask for help.

Before Dae-jung knew it, the emcee was explaining logistics for the ensuing book signing and then ushering DOYEN and the other groups into promotional photos with Katie. Dae-jung waved quickly to her as he was shepherded out of the venue and the last he saw was her signing one book after another.

He wished they had more time to properly celebrate Katie's book, but they were rushing back to Japan to resume the Asian leg of their first world tour since all DOYEN members had finished their military service.

Dae-jung did not realize that he wouldn't see Katie again for another two years.

CHAPTER 7

Has Katie signed with another label? I miss her.

        - Twitter user, June 2022

Glad to see that SB Entertainment finally came to their senses and dropped that wh0r3. B1tch was sniffing around DOYEN a little too much.

        - Twitter user, June 2022

It's been over a year since we've had new Katie content. The music scene just isn't the same without her.

        - Twitter user, June 2022

I hope Katie is okay wherever she is, whatever she's doing.

        - Twitter user, June 2022

Ha-joon—I don't know how you did it, man. I've been here a week and we're going to starve. I had to buy a new house because we're worthless and spoiled and cannot get our shit together. Why didn't you tell me you were doing all the cooking and cleaning? If you ever decide you need a change in career, there will always be a place in my organization for a logistics and solutions king such as yourself.

- Text from Alton Kuang to Baek Ha-joon, June 2022

Forced Katie into all sorts of outside and physical activities. I think your sister hates me. Actually, I know she does because she tells me at least ten times a day. This is awesome.

- Text from Alton Kuang to Mattie Wu, June 2022

Please take lots of videos and send them to me. Ohohohoh make her go hiking and visit museums. She despises nature and art.

- Text from Mattie Wu to Alton Kuang, June 2022

HALP I'M GONNA MURDER ALTON HE'S THE WORST HE MAKES ME GO OUTSIDE YOU KNOW I DON'T BELIEVE IN WATER OR THE SUN AND THE AUDACITY TO CALL THIS GARBAGE ART

- Text from Katie Wu to Mattie Wu, June 2022

"Get up, Mei," said Alton as he threw Katie's weighted blanket back and then opened the blackout curtains, letting in the early gray light of Los Angeles' June Gloom. "We're moving to the beach house."

Katie sat up, bleary-eyed and annoyed. "You have a beach house?"

"I do now," he replied. "There's no furniture yet, but whatever. We don't really need it."

"Why wouldn't we need furniture? I like furniture."

It was too early for this sort of nonsense. Katie was still hungover from sobbing her fucking brains out when Ha-joon left for Korea yesterday, and unless Ha-joon was at the beach house, she didn't have any fucks to give.

Alton tsked and hauled her out of bed. "Come on, come on. We're going to be late."

Katie squinted at the weak light coming from the window. "Alton, it's barely light out. What do you mean we're going to be late?"

"I signed us up for surfing lessons." Alton was practically vibrating with excitement.

"No."

"YES!"

Katie thought her eyes were deceiving her as she saw one Alton Kuang bouncing and clapping out of happiness.

"I don't believe in water," she grated out.

"You what?"

"You heard me. I don't believe in water."

"Like, in its existence?"

Katie huffed. "Like, as a lifestyle choice. Especially if it's cold and requires me to be wet."

"I mean, you might not mind," Alton smirked.

"You're disgusting."

"You're doing it wrong."

"Just give it a try, Mei," whined Alton. "For me. Please?"

Katie regarded her friend and sighed. "Fine. But just know this is under protest."

"Yes, yes. Under protest. Under duress. But still, you'll do it?"

Katie forced herself out of bed. For Alton, she would get into the cold, polluted Pacific Ocean.

"You do know that the water is cold here, right?" she sniped after she stretched her aching muscles. Katie didn't care what people said, staying in bed all day was effort and her body protested the lack of movement in her life.

Alton scoffed. "Of course I knew that." He paused. "Wait, did I know that?"

"What's gotten into you anyway?" Katie wondered. "I never found you a particularly sporty person."

Katie crossed her room into the adjoining ensuite to wash her face, then thought twice. What was the point when she was going to be a drowned rat?

"I have a six-month sabbatical and I'm going to do all the things," replied Alton from the bathroom doorway. "I've never had a sabbatical before," he mused. "And I've really never made time to do the things I wanted to do. So now, I'm going to do all the things—and you're going to join me because nothing's better than forcing your friends to like the things you like."

"Erm, I can think of a few," Katie grumbled, but Alton's effervescent mood was contagious. There was no heat to her words. She decided she could pretend to be a decent person. "What are some of the other items on your list?"

Alton's handsome face broke out into a grin.

"I want to learn Krav Maga and kick ass! And learn to cook—like fancy cooking! And skydive! And bungee jump! And run a marathon! And maybe do a triathlon! And learn to scuba dive! Use a bow and arrow! And all the things, Mei! All the things!"

Suddenly, Katie felt unmoored. It never occurred to her that Alton, of all people, had things left undone. That Alton, breezy billionaire Alton, could possibly feel trapped by his life—although the more she thought about it, of course he would feel that way.

Alton wasn't the oldest of his extended family, but certainly, he was the most responsible and the most capable. All his siblings and cousins had no interest in the family hotel and import and export businesses and only wanted to fritter away their fortune. It had somehow fallen upon Alton to step up for his generation and keep the empire going.

And it wasn't that Katie had never seen Alton happy, but she'd never seen him quite so youthful or exuberant. Katie decided that for Alton, she would help leave no stone unturned in his life. If Alton wanted it, she would give it to him.

Two weeks later, Katie was with Ellie, her college roommate, staring out at the beach from the balcony connected to Katie's bedroom. Katie had initially debated reaching out to any of her Los Angeles friends—had spent the last six months avoiding anyone who wasn't Ha-joon, Alton, or Mattie. But after spending a single fortnight with Alton and his inexhaustible enthusiasm, she decided that she needed some feminine energy in the mix. That Ellie was also exceedingly vibrant and could match Alton's verve and vim was a bonus.

From her seat on the newly purchased wicker furniture, Ellie exhaled an impressive amount of smoke into the ocean air. Katie idly admired Ellie's lung capacity as she took in her friend's profile in the golden light of the setting sun.

"When did you start vaping?" Katie asked. "I didn't know you needed the nicotine hit."

Ellie chuckled. "Oh, you darling lamb. I'm vaping weed, honey."

Katie tried to be cool. "Oh," she gulped.

She was no longer in Korea, and though she had known people who smoked marijuana during college, Katie had never been tempted to try it. The idea of getting high and losing control had seemed anathema even then. When she tried to reason out how it was any different than how she currently used alcohol, Katie came up at a loss. But either way, she'd been in Taiwan and Korea where cannabis was highly illegal. She did not fuck with it.

"I know you're judging me," Ellie said, still staring over the balcony and now down at the pool instead of looking at Katie directly. "It helps me chill the fuck out—you know how I get anxious."

"Ah," Katie grunted.

"It got really bad after Ryan left me."

"Fuck, Ellie. I'm sorry." Guilt flooded Katie's brain. She was the worst of friends.

Ellie took another hit. "Just another casualty of COVID," she cracked. "Apparently, I was a workaholic and emotionally unavailable."

"He's a fool." Ellie was the best of people. Katie had liked Ryan, but he couldn't hold a candle to her friend.

"He wasn't wrong. I did work too much and was emotionally un-available." Ellie sighed. She brushed away loose strands of hair the light summer breeze had blown into her face. "Nothing like being forced in your husband's presence 24/7 to make you realize that you've grown apart and that one of you no longer wants to try and work things out."

"I'm sorry I wasn't there for you, Ellie," Katie said, resisting the urge to castigate herself even more. "I'm sorry you had to go through such a hard thing alone."

"You had your own problems, Katie. And I wasn't alone. Sarah and Angie were there. Don't worry, silly." Ellie beckoned Katie to squeeze in next to her on the egg-shaped wicker chair. Katie dutifully allowed herself to accept Ellie's graciousness.

They sat in silence as the sun continued setting and the sky slowly darkened.

Katie asked, "Does it work? You don't feel too high to function or out of control?"

"You know those times when your brain is just a bundle of anxiety and is useless, and you have to wait until the voices quiet so you can finally think?"

"Yeah."

"It's like that. Antidepressants made me feel too wonky and I hated it, so I tried cannabis instead. You'll have to figure out what works best for you—or if it's not your bag—but it's been the only reason I could make it through the day sometimes." Ellie passed Katie the vape pen. Katie didn't even like the feel of it in her hands. "Wanna try? I know it was hard to ask me to come."

"I love having you here," Katie protested.

Ellie hummed. "They can both be true."

Katie stared at the innocuous-looking pen. She'd vaped regular e-cigarettes before—was this really any different? "Is it going to make me hungry all the time?"

Ellie laughed. "Maybe. But more likely you'll get super horny."

"Hungry for that dick, huh?" It was immature and stupid, but that's all Katie had in her. She wasn't sure if dealing with emotions would ever get easier, but it wasn't going to be tonight. She returned the vape to Ellie.

"At least you live with Alton. He looks like he'd be more than happy to help you with that." She sighed dreamily. "He's funny, rich, and hot. The perfect man and just your type."

"You know we're not like that, Ellie."

"Your birthday is in two months, and he bought you a Lamborghini for an early present. I don't know what you're like." Ellie took a long hit from her pen.

"Not like how you're implying, s'all." It had been too long without Ellie in Katie's life. She'd forgotten the roundabout way Ellie could be sometimes; she connected the dots. "He's all yours. Don't break his heart too badly."

"The only thing I plan on breaking is his bed," Ellie retorted. "I don't know how you've been able to resist him all these months. Like, I get before—you were with Jae-sung. But now? I would have been on his dick as soon as he arrived in LA."

"I could barely get out of bed when Alton got here," Katie said in a rare show of transparency. "Now he's the source of all my pain and suffering. His dick is the last thing on my mind."

Ellie snorted in disbelief.

"It's true. You know he's making me take surfing lessons with him?" Katie took a pull from her beer. "He makes me go on hikes and then roped me into playing beach volleyball with him and some of his bros. All that salt and sun—I'm going to spend a fortune on skin care."

"Remember when you used to start off every morning writing morning pages?" Ellie asked, abruptly changing the subject.

"You mean when I'd write three pages of crap every morning? I recall hating it," Katie remarked. She was not sure where this was going.

"I decided to try it this last year. You might want to take it back up," Ellie said. "You seem near to bursting with all the words you refuse to say."

"I don't understand what you mean," Katie replied, stomach churning.

"You keep so much inside now—it's not good for your health," Ellie replied sadly. She stood up, brushing her clothes absentmindedly. "I know you don't want us to worry—and perhaps your thoughts aren't coherent enough to speak out loud. But morning pages might help when the voices are on loop or the lies in your head get too loud."

"What would I even write about?"

"Whatever you want, Katie. There are no rules except that you fill three pages." Ellie bent over and wrapped Katie in a tight hug. "I love you, roomie."

Katie's throat constricted. "Love you, too."

Ellie slid open the balcony door to Katie's room.

"You forgot your pen," Katie called after her.

"Keep it, babe. You seem to need it more than I do."

March 2026

Katie Wu's memoir, "Telling a Truth Is a Slippery Slope" (Red Lantern Publishing House, October 2023) has been optioned by SB Entertainment, Wu's former entertainment company. This will be SB Entertainment's first foray into moviemaking, and industry insiders are simultaneously doubtful and hopeful that this will mark the beginning of new voices in the movie industry.

- Deadline, August 2024

I can't believe they signed Katie as the lead for the movie based on her memoir. This will either be perfect or spectacularly bad. TBH, I'm hoping for the latter.

- X user, May 2025

Rumor has it that Park Dae-jung is attached to play the male lead and romantic interest in SB Entertainment's yet untitled movie based on Katie Wu's memoir. The power of DOYEN is undeniable and anticipation mounts for the project.

> \- The Hollywood Reporter, September 2025

Lambent is attached to write and produce the soundtrack of "Landslide," the movie based on Katie Wu's life. SB Entertainment is pulling out all stops and risking big on Wu's little memoir that upended the K-music industry.

> \- Billboard, February 2026

Bad news for DOYEN CHIMERA hoping for a new comeback. Park Dae-jung is in preparations for filming "Landslide" and other members are otherwise occupied until at least December. Never fear, though. Park Jae-sung recently dropped hints of KJ 4 coming soon.

> \- Koreaboo, March 2026

By now, Jae-sung knew he wasn't seeing things, and still—still it threw him for a loop when he saw Katie Wu with a woman he did not recognize, chatting and eating at the SB Entertainment cafeteria. He'd heard Katie was in Seoul to work with Woo-jin on the soundtrack to her movie and had known it was just a matter of time before he ran into her at the office.

He'd had years to think and work through his issues and still—still, his stomach dropped when he saw her. Her long glossy black hair was tied back in a high ponytail and she wore a light blue summer dress, with shimmering crystals hanging from her ears.

Katie was still so, so beautiful.

Without his own volition, Jae-sung found himself at her table, opening his big, stupid mouth. "Hey, Katie."

Katie's eyes panicked for a quick moment before she tamped that down and forced herself to smile. She even managed to inject some pretense at joy in her voice. "Hey, Jae-sung. You look good."

"So do you, Katie."

He meant it, too.

"Oh, Jae-sung, this is my friend, Ahn Mi-ran. She's a visiting professor of theology at Yonsei University," Katie said. "Mi-ran, this is Park Jae-sung of DOYEN."

Until she'd made introductions, Jae-sung'd had his eyes trained on Katie. But as soon as he focused on Ahn Mi-ran, his brain went blank. Mi-ran was a knockout. Beautiful, tawny skin. Curves upon curves. Gorgeous curls. Laughing eyes.

"Um, nice to meet you," he bumbled in English.

"A pleasure to meet you, too," Mi-ran replied in perfect Korean.

"Wow, your Korean is so good! You don't have any accent at all," he babbled. "It's better than Katie's."

Katie cracked a wry smile. "It should be. Mi-ran was born and raised in Seoul."

"Oh! I'm so sorry—I thought—I thought you were African American? I just assumed you chose your Korean name based on the actress Ra Mi-ran."

"I think I'm a little too old for her to be my father's inspiration, but I appreciate you thinking I am young enough," Mi-ran cracked.

Jae-sung just kept fucking up. He really wished the earth would swallow him whole, but then, he'd miss out on Mi-ran's gorgeous face and hazel eyes.

"My father is Korean and my mother is Black," Mi-ran continued patiently, as if she was used to this line of questioning. Actually, she probably was. Jae-sung instantly felt shame. "I split my time between Seoul and Los Angeles, where my mom's family is from," she added generously.

"Ah, that's so cool," he said.

"I suppose it was cool," Mi-ran said, shifting so the mixed metal bangles along her wrist jangled, "if you like being bullied for being different and having people constantly question your right to exist."

Jae-sung could feel his entire face heat up. Suddenly, his oversized tee and baggy shorts felt too stuffy and tight. He did not know what to say. "I'm sorry," he said instead. "That's awful and you didn't deserve any of it."

"I'm just fucking with you, Jae-sung-ssi."

"Oh," Jae-sung responded, voice cracking.

"I mean, I was bullied and people were awful and continue to be awful—but that's not what I normally lead with." Mi-ran's eyes danced at him.

Jae-sung nodded stupidly. "Ah, I see." Jae-sung threw a desperate look in Katie's general direction, and he heard her audibly sigh.

"Mi-ran, Jae-sung is hungry and has low blood sugar. Let's let his poor little brain catch up," Katie said in English, adding, "Don't let his 153 IQ fool you—Jae-sung's dumb but sweet. He means well and generally tries not to be problematic."

Mi-ran arched a mocking eyebrow. If that was Katie's version of a rescue, Jae-sung wasn't sure he wanted it. He summoned all his years of leading DOYEN and rallied forward. "How do you know each other?"

"Katie was a guest lecturer at Yonsei University and I happened to attend her session," replied Mi-ran. "I made the mistake of asking a question and she hasn't given me a moment's rest since then."

"Not my fault it was a good question," Katie huffed. "I fuck with deep thinkers."

Mi-ran winked at Jae-sung and his collar felt too tight.

"What was the question?" he asked.

Mi-ran grinned and cast a savage glance at Katie. "I asked if perhaps Katie hated a false Christian god made in the image of white supremacist patriarchy. And that perhaps the face of god is a Black woman."

"I find it hard to believe that Katie's Korean was good enough to have this discussion," Jae-sung said, his brow wrinkling. By the time Katie had left him, her Korean was reasonably fluent, especially when discussing music and its related topics, but theology? Highly doubtful.

Katie burst out laughing, as always, only half-covering her mouth even after so many years in Korea. "Always underestimating me, I see," she commented at the same time Mi-ran said, "I explained in English," which set off another round of raucous laughter.

Relieved Katie wasn't insulted, Jae-sung asked, "What did she say?" He had always loved the way Katie's brain worked and was pleased the years had kept that intact.

"I said that if I were ever to believe in the Christian myth again, that the Black womanist liberation interpretation appealed to me most," Katie answered in Korean. At Jae-sung's puzzled expression, she added, "What? Like it's hard or something?"

Mi-ran quipped in English, "I made her flashcards. She's been on my dick ever since."

"It's a nice dick," Katie replied serenely. "Besides, making flashcards for someone is practically declaring your undying love."

"I didn't realize you two were together—" stammered Jae-sung. This entire conversation kept shifting like quicksand; he could not get his bearings between the changes in tone, topic, and languages.

"Oh, Jae," Katie giggled. "My poor spring lamb. Mi-ran is stunning and if I could ever deserve her, I would fall at her feet in worship. As it is, I could never and so, I do not."

Jae-sung's head hurt. "Katie, could you please just speak like a normal person?"

"I'm not dating Mi-ran, Jae-sung," Katie replied drily. "I'm strictly dickly, remember? Also, Mi-ran is single at the moment, and if you play your cards right, I'll put in a good word for you. But no guarantees—she has standards."

"Katie!" Just once, Jae-sung wished he had a better sense of self-preservation. And yet, he could not bring himself to regret greeting Katie if it meant he'd meet Mi-ran.

"Where have you been hiding him, Katie?" laughed Mi-ran, her voice going smoky. "He's adorable."

Katie rolled her eyes. "As if I could hide him. He's gotten even huger—Jesus, Jae-sung. What have they been feeding you?"

"I—just, um, normal food things?" Normal food things. Jae-sung was going to have to move and switch industries. "I have to go."

He abruptly turned and exited the cafeteria and made it all the way to his studio before he realized he never bought his lunch.

"You naughty bitch," Mi-ran hissed as soon as Jae-sung was out of earshot, her hazel eyes sparking with glee. "Is he your gentle giant?"

"I don't know what you're talking about," Katie replied, as prim and proper as she could manage.

"He *is*," Mi-ran crowed. "Did he look like *that* when you ghosted him?"

"Jesus, no," Katie acknowledged, grateful that Mi-ran's comment didn't sting quite as much as it would have even a few months ago. Maybe that meant Katie could finally move on. "He was on his way, though. No fair his revenge bod is better than mine."

Mi-ran stopped and gave Katie a careful once over. "I'd call it even. You still keeping up with Krav Maga in Seoul?"

"Haven't really had the time, but I do box occasionally with Soo-min's trainer. He goes easy on me but I don't mind." Katie took a bite of her egg tart. It wasn't quite as good as the ones in Taiwan, but she gave it points for trying. "Mostly I'm attending as many dance classes as possible to prep for filming."

"You should get Do-won to give you one-on-one lessons." Mi-ran waggled her brows.

Katie winced. "No, thanks. Do-won is exacting but kind and I can't bear his disapproval."

"I don't know how you ended up fucking only one member after all these years."

"They're hot but so dumb," Katie responded good-naturedly. "Like a pack of overgrown puppies. It's hard to consider them anything but family."

"How are you going to deal with Dae-jung playing the romantic lead?" Mi-ran asked, once again asking the hard questions. "Aren't there full-on sex scenes?"

"We're both professionals," Katie replied primly. "And it's not like there will be any nudity. There's going to be an intimacy coach and we'll be surrounded by staff. It'll be like any other job."

When Song PD had first broached the possibility of casting Dae-jung as Choi Eun-seong, the character based on Jae-sung, Katie had balked. But after personal reassurances from both Dae-jung and Jae-sung, she acquiesced. She would far prefer the comfort and safety of Park Dae-jung in the love scenes than trusting some complete stranger.

"HA!" Mi-ran guffawed. "Jesus knows you for a liar!" Some workers at the adjacent wooden tables looked over with poorly disguised judgment.

"Look, I've got eyes! I'm not saying Dae-jung or the rest of them aren't ridiculously attractive!" Katie held up both hands in surrender. "I'm just saying that I've been down that road—and I have no intention of doing so again. I should have learned from Johnny before that, but I clearly didn't."

Katie worried that she'd killed the mood, but then, Mi-ran hummed sympathetically. "It's hard not to shit where you eat when the menu looks like Park Jae-sung," she mused.

She knew Mi-ran would understand. "It wasn't even his looks, Mi-ran. He was just so goddamn good," Katie said softly. "He is still such a good man."

"You okay?"

Katie glanced up to meet Mi-ran's incisive gaze. Despite often being on the sharp end of her tongue, Katie knew Mi-ran loved her. It didn't matter that she'd only known Mi-ran a year or so—and that most of the friendship had been conducted over KakaoTalk. Something about Mi-ran called to Katie.

Katie knew it must have been so difficult growing up Black in Korea—colorism and blood purity was definitely a thing. Add the general anti-Blackness in America and choosing academics and theology of all emphases—Mi-ran knew what it was like to be an outsider. Mi-ran knew intimately how lonely life could get, how her very existence was used against her. She knew the violence of being erased.

Katie could not help but be drawn to Mi-ran's brilliant mind. That Mi-ran was a badass and hysterically funny was a bonus.

"Yeah, I'm okay," Katie replied.

Mi-ran's entire demeanor softened. "Was I too hard on him? Was it too soon to tease you?"

Katie chuckled. "It's been years, Mi-ran. I know you rode him so hard because you actually want to ride him."

"Hoes before bros, Katie. I would never." Mi-ran reached across their lunch table and touched Katie's arm lightly.

"You know...," Katie's voice trailed off for a few seconds. "It's not a terrible idea."

"What's not a terrible idea?" Mi-ran asked as she dug back into her cheesecake.

"You and Jae."

"He wouldn't be able to handle me."

Katie shrugged.

"You yourself just told me he was a big, dumb baby."

Katie shrugged again.

"I do like them big and dumb, though," Mi-ran deliberated after half a beat. "You sure you wouldn't mind?"

Katie lifted both brows.

"I'm in. Tell me everything."

April 2026

Pick your poison:
◯ Nuthin' but a 'G' Thang - Dr. Dre and Snoop Dogg
◯ Gin and Juice - Snoop Dogg
- Katie Wu, X, April 2026

Round 2:
◯ The Rain (Supa Dupa Fly) - Missy Elliott
◯ Get Ur Freak On - Missy Elliott
- Katie Wu, X, April 2026

Round 3:
◯ *Sober - Tool*
◯ *Judith - A Perfect Circle*

- Katie Wu, X, April 2026

Round 4:
◯ *Winter - Tori Amos*
◯ *Cruel - Tori Amos*

- Katie Wu, X, April 2026

Round 5:
◯ *Calaverada - Gipsy Kings*
◯ *Bamboleo - Gipsy Kings*

- Katie Wu, X, April 2026

Round 6:
◯ *Just Like Your Tenderness - EggPlantEgg*
◯ *Love You One More Time - EggPlantEgg*

- Katie Wu, X, April 2026

Round 7:
◯ *Rock Me Gently - Erasure*
◯ *A Little Respect - Erasure*

- Katie Wu, X, April 2026

Round 8:
◯ *Control - Janet Jackson*
◯ *If - Janet Jackson*

- Katie Wu, X, April 2026

i don't even know half of these artists

- X user, April 2026

OH SHIT OH SHIT OH SHIT IS KATIE MAKING MU-SIC AGAIN SHE ONLY POSTS POLLS WHEN SHE IS OH SHIT OH SHIT FUCK

- X user, April 2026

"I'm not feeling it," said Woo-jin, pushing back from his workstation.

Katie collapsed onto the slouchy black leather couch in his studio. She never understood why so many studios had black leather couches. With all his money and interest in interior design, Katie thought Woo-jin would've chosen something far more interesting like a bright teal or orange, but not everyone had taste.

"You've been saying that for the last few weeks," she complained instead.

"And I mean it every time." Her old friend grumped and sank down next to her.

She refused to look at him, determined to cut the conversation short. "I don't know what you expect from me—you're the musical genius."

"If you would just listen to them and give me your feedback—"

"No."

"It would work better if we could work on it together," Woo-jin insisted.

Katie's stomach tightened. "They hired you, Lambent of DOYEN, to write the soundtrack to the movie. They didn't hire me."

"Which also makes no sense." Woo-jin shook his head. "Why won't you sing on it at least? Dae-jung is."

"I told you. I don't do music anymore." Woo-jin needed to mind his own business.

Katie stood up and examined the Mr. DOB and Futura collectibles that both Woo-jin and Do-won favored over Jae-sung's KAWS figurines. In her unsolicited opinion, they were all ugly. It merely proved to Katie that most people had more money than sense—her friends included.

"Right. You're a serious author and actor now." Woo-jin's tone bordered on mockery. "What are you going to do when they need you to sing and dance for the film?"

Katie hated how Woo-jin brought up very good points. She had not thought that far ahead—only that she would figure it out eventually, and eventually hadn't happened yet.

"I don't know. Probably lip sync."

Woo-jin scoffed. "You're shit at lip syncing."

"You're one to talk. I have never seen a group of K-pop singers be so shitty at a basic skill." Katie was ready to pick a fight and she could tell Woo-jin knew it.

"Stop deflecting." The rapper tongued his cheek and she ignored how infuriatingly hot he was. All these years and still, the man was a menace. His tongue was a menace.

"Put your tongue away before you hurt yourself," Katie sniped without thinking.

A predatory light instantly flashed in his dark feline eyes. "Got any suggestions for where I should put it?" Woo-jin taunted. He casually leaned an arm against the back of the sofa and crossed a leg over the other, forming a number four.

Katie sucked in a breath as her blood thrummed with desire. She forcibly quelled that hollow ache. This was Woo-jin—this was how he was with her. Provoking. Tantalizing. Frustrating.

Clearly Katie needed to end her self-imposed moratorium on sexual relations, get fucked, and get fucked good.

It had been so long since Katie had been with a man—she sometimes couldn't believe that the last person she'd slept with had been Jae-sung. She'd held out this long, though. She was not about to bend to the sheer charisma of Hwang Woo-jin.

As always with Woo-jin, Katie retreated. She capitulated to his superior sexual dominance.

"No," Katie whimpered. That was not how she was supposed to sound.

Woo-jin's pupils blew out and the pink of his tongue slipped between his lips.

She tried again. "No." There. She sounded a smidge more resolute. Granted, the sheer speed at which Katie shot up from Woo-jin's sofa belied her attempt at being cool.

"You sure about that?"

The vocal fry in Woo-jin's voice made him sound like ground gravel. His mouth lifted at a dangerous angle. She needed to get the fuck out of Dodge.

"Yup!" Katie insisted brightly.

"Bullshit."

The door beeped and Dae-jung slammed his way through Woo-jin's studio door. "Hey, Hyung." Dae-jung paused as he took in the scene before him. "Um, am I interrupting something?"

"Nope!" Katie squeaked just as Woo-jin narrowed his eyes and said, "Yes."

Dae-jung tilted his head and widened his eyes at Woo-jin. Katie ignored whatever sort of look Woo-jin was sending back and slipped out the door.

"This isn't over!" Katie heard Woo-jin holler after her.

"It most definitely is!" she trilled back, her equanimity returning now that Woo-jin was safely ensconced in his studio and nowhere near her person. "Byyeeeeee!"

Now, Katie just had to convince herself.

Lambent was a vision in his classic airport styling: black on black, chic messenger bag, and black snapback. Dae-jung joined his bandmate in loose golf shorts, sandals, and a flowy, patterned button-down. Katie underwhelmed as always in a Warriors cap and gray sweats. We wish everyone a safe flight to Los Angeles.

- Soompi, April 2026

"Excuse me, miss," Dae-jung heard Katie say to the flight attendant as soon as she'd sat down in first class. "Could I trouble you for a vodka soda? Heavy on the vodka, easy on the soda?" At the attendant's murmured assent, Katie said, "Actually, can you make it two? No ice?"

Dae-jung stowed his personal items to the side and took out his tablet, queuing up the latest dramas and movies he wanted to catch up on. Woo-jin already had his headphones on in the seat next to him, while Katie had already kicked off her Adidas Samba OGs and was currently downing two glasses of alcohol in quick succession. He did not recall Katie being a nervous flier but perhaps things had changed in the intervening years. He watched as she inserted her earbuds, pulled the hood over her cap, and drew the brim down over her face.

"Is Noona okay?" Dae-jung leaned over to ask Woo-jin.

Woo-jin slipped his headphones around his neck and cupped a hand over his ear. "What?"

"Is Noona okay?" he repeated. "She just downed like three shots of vodka."

Woo-jin raised an eyebrow. "Maybe she doesn't like flying," he observed.

"She didn't used to be like that. Noona's been unusually quiet since the company sent us on this bonding trip to LA. Does she not want to be with us?" Dae-jung swallowed his worries. "Does she not want me to be in the movie?"

"I don't think it's you, Dae-jung," Woo-jin reassured. "You know she loves you."

"She may love me, but that's not quite the same as wanting me to play her love interest." Dae-jung didn't like that line of thought, though. If Katie didn't want him in the semi-autobiographical movie based off her life, Dae-jung hoped she would have told him when he was first cast.

"It's probably because they're making Katie be on the soundtrack, and she really doesn't want to be. That or the fact that they told me to tap into her sound and inspirations or some shit." Woo-jin cleared his throat. "I can't quite figure it out. Katie would have jumped at the opportunity back in the day. She loved to go on about her process and influences."

Dae-jung assessed his hyung. "Hmmm, maybe it's you she doesn't want to be around."

"Is that right?" Woo-jin chuckled. He settled into his seat and readjusted the pillows behind his back. "And why do you say that?"

"I see you feeling her out." Dae-jung nodded sagely. "Noona is likely sick of your thirsty ass."

"It's how we are, Dae," Woo-jin said. "It's how we've always been."

"And it doesn't bother Jae-sung hyung?"

"A little too late for that—it's been ten years." Woo-jin grinned. "Besides, he's smitten with Katie's professor friend. He'd be fine if anything ever happened."

Woo-jin's outrageous flirting never used to bother Dae-jung. After all, they all used to rile Jae-sung and his easily provoked jealousies. It was likely Dae-jung's own uncertainties about taking the role, but Jae-sung had given his approval.

Dae-jung shook his head. "I wouldn't be too sure of that, Hyung. Just because he's into someone new doesn't mean he'd be cool with you and Noona."

"What did he say about you playing her love interest?"

Dae-jung had to give it to Woo-jin. He always knew how to land a clean hit.

"Hyung knows it's just acting." At Woo-jin's smug simper, Dae-jung colored. It had been super awkward and weird—likely for Jae-sung, too—but Jae-sung had said he wouldn't want anyone else portraying a fictional version of himself.

Whether that was actually true or not, Dae-jung wasn't entirely sure, but at the time, it was what he'd wanted to hear. Maybe Jae-sung could tell and had given in out of some misplaced sense of guilt, or maybe Jae-sung had agreed because he didn't consider Dae-jung a threat to his ego. Dae-jung had wanted the role so badly that he hadn't bothered digging into it at the time.

"It *is*," Dae-jung insisted. "I would never—"

"Tch," the older man interrupted. "Don't make promises you can't keep, Dae."

"But—"

"But nothing," Woo-jin replied. "You have to create a shit ton of chemistry with Katie and if it doesn't read well on screen, the movie is dead in the water. You know this, right?"

"Of course. I can have chemistry with a paper bag."

"You probably could." Woo-jin laughed for a second and then got serious. "There's a reason co-stars often become couples in real life, Dae-jung. Be careful with your heart."

Dae-jung felt unexpectedly rebuked. It stung that his hyung had so little faith in him. "Please, I'm not an amateur, Hyung. I've fucked plenty of people without falling in love—and this isn't even real fucking. It's all pretend."

"Right," snorted Woo-jin. "Maybe you're judging me this hard because you secretly want to practice the love scenes ahead of time."

"Why are you like this, Hyung? I don't think of Noona like that, I just have to act like I do," Dae-jung said exasperatedly. "That's why it's called acting."

He didn't like the knowing way Woo-jin looked at him, as if Dae-jung had auditioned for the role with ulterior motives. If anything, he'd wanted the role because it was through SB Entertainment and he could use his connection to Song PD to secure the role of Choi Eun-seong easily. That it was a chance to do justice to both the role based on Jae-sung and the story based on Katie's memoir—that had been icing on the cake.

Of course, Song PD had required Dae-jung to ask Jae-sung for permission first. The CEO was no fool. DOYEN was SB Entertainment's biggest cash cow and Song PD wasn't willing to cause tension between DOYEN members over an optional movie role.

Whatever. Dae-jung was a vibes person, but that didn't mean he was an idiot, either. He'd had a gut feeling about the movie—the same feeling that had him choosing SB Entertainment over the larger entertainment companies he'd auditioned at. Hadn't that worked out beyond his wildest dreams? Dae-jung didn't think lightning could strike twice, but maybe this movie could come close.

The rapper shot him a lopsided smile. "Katie's easy to fall for, Dae-jung," he said softly. Woo-jin repositioned the headphones over his ears and left Dae-jung with more questions than he'd started with.

"Noona, could we stop for food before we go to Alton hyung's place? I'm really hungry."

Dae-jung could tell Katie was trying very hard to be accommodating. In fact, he was surprised she was even coherent. He had never seen a person be so determined to be conscious for as little time as possible. If he was honest, Dae-jung was more than a little impressed. Katie had clearly had practice in keeping her blood chemistry at a preferred level of intoxication for an extended period of time.

"What do you want to eat? We can swing by a drive-thru or something," Katie offered as they all boarded the chauffeured black SUV with Ha-joon, while Dae-jung and Woo-jin's longtime managers Sung-mo and Park Chang-nam were picking up a rental car for their stay.

Dae-jung felt bad, but after the eleven-hour flight, he really wanted something more substantial. "Could we get Korean barbecue?"

"Are you fucking serious?"

Shit. Katie sounded a lot less accommodating now. "Yes?" Dae-jung responded as Woo-jin said, "That sounds amazing."

"You literally just arrived from Korea. Fucking Koreans!"

"And?" challenged Woo-jin. "Is there a problem with us being Korean?"

"An entire world of different cuisine—and we're in Los Angeles of all places—and all you want is Korean food!" Katie removed her cap, ran a hand through her hair, and placed the cap back on. "You guys are seriously just like my parents. Oh, we're in Wisconsin? Chinese food, please! Oh, it tastes terrible? I fucking wonder why!"

"But we're in LA and it has a K-town," Dae-jung protested. "The food is just like home!"

"You've been in America for less than two hours!"

"I thought you liked Korean food, Katie," Woo-jin needled. "I didn't realize our people's food was so objectionable."

"I *do* like Korean food, Oppa," she scowled, "I just like other food, too. Did it ever occur to you that I might be homesick, too? I've been in Korea for months now."

He pouted and made puppy eyes at Katie. His weren't as effective as Soo-min's, but they still worked more often than not. Dae-jung started to feel a little bad, but then, Katie sighed and dug her phone out of her purse.

"It looks like Ahgassi Gopchang is currently closed for renovations," she said, referring to DOYEN's preferred restaurant in LA. "Let me ask a friend what they recommend."

"How do you not know the best K-BBQ places in K-town?" questioned Woo-jin.

Dae-jung wanted to kick Woo-jin for not knowing when to stop, but he was also curious. He was also wondering why Ha-joon wasn't the one making the call, but maybe it was easier for Katie to deal with things herself in the US.

"I'm almost never in K-town," Katie replied as Ha-joon nodded silently in agreement. "I mostly stick to the San Gabriel Valley or the Westside. It feels more like home."

"What's in the San Gabriel Valley?" Dae-jung asked.

"Taiwanese people," Katie said, forming a wry smile. "I guess we all stick to what is familiar." She inhaled a deep calming breath. "It's where Alton's house is—unless you want to stay at his beach house in Malibu instead. But I think Ge only built a recording studio at the San Marino residence."

"Maybe we can check out the beach house on a day off? If that's okay with you, Noona?"

Katie nodded as she stared at her phone. "Cat unnie says we can try Chosun Galbee—it should be open by the time we get there. It's a classic and they should have a private room, too. Let me call ahead."

Dae-jung wasn't sure who Cat was or why he found it so strange to see Katie doing all the legwork. She wasn't incompetent, and it wasn't as if he didn't take care of things back in Seoul. Katie just seemed more in charge in America—as if she had a better grasp on how things worked—and well, Dae-jung supposed she did.

Not for the first time did he wonder which of Katie's aspects were country-dependent.

"Katie, we only have four weeks to bang this soundtrack out, and you've already wasted three days being hungover."

Dae-jung hadn't heard Woo-jin this stressed in a long time. He couldn't quite hear Katie's response, but he definitely heard Woo-jin's. He poked his head out of his room.

"I don't fucking care if it's been awhile! I know you know how to make music. If you're not going to help with the actual writing then I need you to at least give me *something*! I can only get so much from your discography." Woo-jin thunked his head against her closed door. "Please, Katie," he added, voice low and desperate.

Katie cracked open her door.

"Okay," she said. She sounded awful. "I just—I just need about thirty minutes."

"Okay," replied Woo-jin, relief evident. "I'll be in the kitchen—we can walk over to the studio together."

Dae-jung gathered that Woo-jin did not quite believe she was going to follow through, so he joined Woo-jin downstairs in the airy kitchen. They were chatting about nothing in particular when Katie stepped through fifteen minutes later with a lighter and—was that a joint?

"I didn't know you smoked," Woo-jin said in a tightly controlled voice.

Katie eyed them warily. "Is that a problem?"

"You won't do this in Korea, will you?" Dae-jung asked worriedly. He knew marijuana was legal in the US, but Korea didn't fuck with it—and many an idol's downfall had been because of smoking the drug. He didn't think Katie's career could survive another scandal. "Does the company know?"

He needed to know if he had to hide it from their managers. It seemed difficult to do so because they were all staying at Alton's house together, but the managers had gone sightseeing for the day. Woo-jin had kicked them out, saying he was too old to have so many babysitters. Dae-jung secretly believed Woo-jin had done so for Katie's sake and not his own.

"Relax. It'll be out of my system long before we get to Korea." Katie flicked the lighter a few times. "If the smell is a problem I can switch to a vape pen." She sighed. "The smell really is revolting. I would have taken an edible but I never know when it will hit. It's much easier to time this way."

Woo-jin's face mirrored Dae-jung's. "Why do you need to time it?"

"Because I really cannot fucking deal with the noise in my head *and* write music or whatever the fuck it is you want me for without it, Oppa." Katie flicked the lighter a few more times. Woo-jin was right. It wasn't Dae-jung. "I would take a shot or two but I'd rather not. It kills the rest of my day."

"I—I didn't realize," Woo-jin said. He looked crestfallen.

Katie threw the lighter and the joint onto the granite counter in frustration. "Yeah, well, now you realize."

"We don't have to do this, Katie. I can figure something else out." That's what Dae-jung always loved about Woo-jin. The rapper always acted like a curmudgeon, but in reality, he was a tenderhearted softie.

"I don't need to be coddled," Katie ground out as she pushed up the loose sleeves of her zippered San Jose Sharks hoodie.

"Why did you agree to helping me with the soundtrack if you didn't want to do it in the first place? I know nothing was hitting right for me, but I would have found my way eventually," Woo-jin protested, conflict written all over his face. "I don't want to traumatize you."

Katie gritted her teeth. "You won't. You specifically requested to the company for help. I won't be told I'm not pulling my weight. I will not be the reason this project fails." Katie was always too stubborn for her own good.

"You said it's been awhile. When did you last write music?" Dae-jung asked, hoping to pre-empt an argument.

"Before my father died." Katie stared morosely at the counter. "I haven't written anything since then. I barely listen to anything now unless it's unavoidable. I—I just can't bear to."

"Noona," he gasped. "That was five years ago."

Katie scooped up her lighter and the joint. "Yeah. Yeah it was," she said as she went through the French doors to the courtyard in the center of the house.

Dae-jung's eyes ached while he rubbed his chest. "Hyung," he started to say and then stopped. What was there really to say?

"Fuck," Woo-jin muttered. "I guess I get to be the asshole for the next four weeks, huh?"

He stood and went straight to Alton's liquor cabinet, rifling about until he found a bottle he liked. Knowing Woo-jin, it was probably a whisky.

"I can sit in with you," Dae-jung offered.

Woo-jin poured himself a generous three fingers in a crystal cut glass and took a sip. "Yeah, okay."

This was not looking out to be the breezy bonding month Dae-jung had thought it was going to be.

It was painfully awkward.

After hours trapped in the pool house turned studio, Dae-jung could tell Woo-jin was done prying information out of Katie. He'd spent hours questioning what music meant to her, asking about artists she loved—even the stories behind her songs or how she felt about certain scenes in the screenplay. It was obvious Katie was unable (or unwilling) to be real with him. Woo-jin was a patient man, but even he could not prevail.

"I don't understand why this is so hard, Katie," Woo-jin finally sighed. They were all in the common room of the studio and he was sprawled on the vermillion divan while Dae-jung and Katie sat on the more comfortable navy modular couch. "We used to talk about music all the time. For hours. Don't you remember?"

Katie crooked her mouth. "It was a long time ago, Oppa." She reached for Woo-jin's almost empty tumbler on the teak coffee table and slammed the remains, wincing. Dae-jung sympathized.

"It's a waste when you don't savor it."

"All whisky is wasted on me," Katie retorted. "If we used to talk about music so much, why do you even need me right now? You know me, Oppa. You know my music. You know what I sound like. Just do your thing."

"Don't you think I've been trying to do that all these months? I started as soon as I got signed! Except everything sounds derivative. I sound like I'm trying to sound like you."

"Then sound like yourself! It's supposed to be music inspired by the movie, not necessarily a carbon copy of me." Katie handed Woo-jin a full glass of Kavalan whisky as a peace offering. Somehow, that tiny consideration eased the worry in Dae-jung's mind. "Who cares if it sounds like me—I don't even know what sounds like me anymore. I don't even know what music sounds like anymore."

Woo-jin slumped even lower on the divan. "Everyone I've asked for feedback from sends it back saying it's good, but not right."

Katie grimaced. Dae-jung hated how stilted it felt between the three of them. Later, when he thought back to the evening, he wouldn't know what had possessed him to ask—but he was grateful for the nudge anyway.

"Why Jae-sung hyung, Noona?" he asked. "I always had my money on you and Woo-jin hyung."

"This idiot?" Katie scoffed as she gestured at Woo-jin, who was slumming it in a faded, oversized Fear of God shirt, basketball shorts, and a ratty bucket hat. "Please."

"Oh, come now. You said I was your bias! You could barely meet my gaze half the time we spoke." Woo-jin chuckled even as Dae-jung noticed the rapper's pallor and dark circles under his eyes. "You were too busy checking out my ass."

"I was not!"

Dae-jung laughed. "You really did stare at Hyung like you wanted to eat him. Like all the time."

"I will not tolerate such slander!" Though Dae-jung knew it for an act, he still appreciated how over-the-top Katie reacted. Perhaps they would be okay after all.

"It was particularly funny since Hyung was crazy about you." Dae-jung slid his eyes to Woo-jin and held in a smirk. "He's the reason our A&R team invited you backstage at our Taipei concert—and how Song PD knew to buy out your contract."

"What?" Katie cried as Woo-jin sputtered, "There's no need to go into detail about it. It's been over a decade!"

"Hyung used to spam us with links to your content all the time. He made us all buy your albums and stream when you had comebacks." Dae-jung was enjoying Woo-jin's flushed face too much for his own good. "Come to think of it, both he and Jun hyung were obsessed with you."

Katie straightened her spine, curiosity lighting her eyes. "How come no one ever told me?"

"Jae-sung hyung probably liked the fact you were terrified of Woo-jin hyung. It worked out to his advantage, right?" Dae-jung conjectured. He didn't know if that was the case, but it sounded like something Jae-sung would do.

"He actually suggested I fuck Woo-jin oppa first," Katie revealed, refusing to look over at Woo-jin. "Said Oppa would be the perfect fuck buddy."

"Did he really?" exclaimed Dae-jung, leaning forward on the couch. "And you passed? So interesting!"

Woo-jin scowled. "Even if Katie had decided she wanted to fuck me, it doesn't mean I would have reciprocated."

"Oh, that's hilarious, Hyung," Dae-jung said. And then, because he really was curious, he asked again. "If Hyung told you to go for Woo-jin hyung first, how did you end up with him? What was it about Jae-sung hyung that made you choose him?"

"Honestly?" Katie's eyes misted over in memory. "I think it's just because he offered."

Dae-jung and Woo-jin both tried to cover their laughter with coughs. "He offered?" stammered Dae-jung as Woo-jin couldn't hold it in anymore and doubled over the settee. "That's it?"

Katie shrugged. "He was hot. He was willing. I trusted him and he offered. End of story."

"That lucky fuck," cackled Woo-jin into one of the suede throw pillows. "I am never letting him live this down!"

"Wait—seriously? You're telling me if any of us had offered, you could have ended up with one of us instead?" questioned Dae-jung. Soo-min was going to cry when he told him.

"What? No—that's not what I said at all!"

"Oh, come on! We were hot, willing, and you trusted us, right?" insisted Dae-jung.

"I doubt you were all willing," Katie hedged, "but also, you weren't quite hot at the time."

Dae-jung could not believe what he was hearing. "What?"

"I mean, yeah, you're top-tier now, but back then—when you debuted especially—you and Soo-min were kinda funny-looking."

"Are you drunk or high still?" accused Dae-jung.

"I'm not saying you two were ugly—just that you had yet to grow into your features," Katie placated. "Whoever scouted you should be given multiple raises because look how hot you and Soo-min turned out. Like, no credit needed for scouting Jun oppa because he was always beautiful. But Minnie grew into his nose and you—well, you improved."

"I can't decide if I'm being insulted."

Woo-jin had not ceased cracking up. He choked out, "Oh, you're definitely being insulted."

Dae-jung glowered. He wasn't a vain person, but he also owned a mirror. He knew he was objectively attractive—and not just regular attractive. He was *superstar* attractive. It was his actual job to capitalize on his looks and talents—and he was exceedingly good at his job.

Katie was clearly mistaken.

"Dae-jung-ah, you obviously grew out of your awkward phase. Some people never do. Look at poor Woo-jin oppa."

To his credit, Woo-jin barely acknowledged the dig. Easy for him—it had always been obvious how much Katie lusted after the man.

"Okay, now I know you're full of shit," Dae-jung asserted. He would not stand for this assault on his character. On his very being! "The way you used to crumble around Woo-jin hyung—fuck, aren't your reaction videos still on YouTube?"

Katie's eyes widened as she suddenly realized it would be a relatively easy task to prove she'd been completely sprung over Woo-jin.

"Um, I don't know?"

Dae-jung pulled up YouTube on his phone. "Hyung, you think we can cast onto the TV?"

"I don't think this is necessary," Katie scrambled as she made grabby hands at Dae-jung's phone. "Also, it doesn't prove anything other than I know what kind of reactions your fans love to see from me. It doesn't have any bearing on the fact that you were definitely funny-looking from debut up through the 'Peace' era."

"Hurtful, Noona," Dae-jung pouted even as he stood and held his phone over Katie's head.

"I'm not trying to be hurtful! I'm telling you that you're super hot now—why do you also have to be hot as a child? That's inappropriate!"

Woo-jin still hadn't stopped laughing. He was huddled over, holding his stomach. All Dae-jung could see were his hyung's crinkled eyes and gummy smile. Dae-jung felt unexpectedly fond.

Dae-jung scrolled through a playlist of Katie's old reaction videos all while dodging Katie's lackluster attempts at stopping him.

"I didn't know you reacted to my solo song 'Event Horizon,'" he said.

Katie tilted her head. "I don't remember doing so, but I guess I must have. I reacted to all the DOYEN title songs and sometimes the other M/Vs when I had time." She squinted at the screen and then scanned the area until she found her glasses. "Which Simulation Trilogy album is 'Event Horizon' part of again? 'Veil,' 'Chimera,' or 'Intimacy'?"

Dae-jung feigned dismay. "Noona, I thought you were our number one fan? How could you not remember it was the leading track to 'Simulation: Chimera'?" He lifted a limp hand to his forehead in exaggerated drama. "I'm going to have to ask for your CHIMERA card back." He handed his phone to Woo-jin as Katie tried to make a last ditch effort at stealing it.

"You'll have to pry my Cute Humble Independent Musically Evolved Radical Aspect card out of my cold, dead hands," Katie teased back. "It's not my fault you guys get stuck on a concept like the pretentious asses you are and beat an idea like a dead horse."

"Actually, that's mostly Jae-sung and Song PD's fault," Woo-jin drawled tonelessly. "You of all people should know that, Katie-yah." He fussed with

Dae-jung's phone and the wifi settings, muttering to himself in satoori the way he did when he was frustrated or slightly intoxicated.

"This should put to rest your theory that I was funny-looking," Dae-jung stated.

Katie huffed and crossed her arms. "It will do no such thing, Dae. This was after your man-face already came in."

"My man-face?"

"Yes, yes. Your man-face. You know, when your jaw squares and you fill out and..." Katie waved her hand in the air vaguely. "You know what it is—your man-face!"

While Katie had been giving him the vocabulary lesson, Woo-jin had figured out how to cast her "Event Horizon" reaction video onto the television screen. Suddenly, they were confronted with Katie's younger self grumbling at the camera.

Dae-jung quipped, "You were grumpy even then, Noona."

"Probably because I was being forced to react to my ungrateful labelmates all the time," Katie blustered.

Dae-jung plopped down next to Katie and threw a companionable arm around her shoulders. "Right. Forced." As the song opened with a heavy R&B bassline and classic R&B snare and cymbals, he hummed along to the familiar melody.

Oh, shit. This song is sexy! the Katie in the video immediately said. She squinted and leaned closer to the laptop. *What's DJ doing with his hands? Dude, that finger choreo is sexy—*

"Did you just say 'dude'?" asked Woo-jin incredulously. "What are you, a frat boy?"

"I'm from California, okay? Dude is all-purpose. Don't you shame me!" Katie defended.

Dae-jung smiled indulgently at their bickering. He felt transported back to their early years when he often heard Katie and Woo-jin mocking each other in the corner of that cramped studio. She was so easy to egg on even after all these years.

On screen, Katie paused the video, stared off camera, and complained to the PD in English. *What is going on? Why is this video so sexy? Why does this sound like it's baby-making music? Is Dae old enough to be singing this sort of song?*

"How many times are you going to say 'sexy,' Katie?" Woo-jin pointed at the screen and criticized. "I thought reactors were supposed to be more interesting than this."

"It's not Noona's fault I was so sexy," Dae-jung smirked as he got more comfortable on the sofa. He even dared to poke Katie in the side, eliciting a gratifying shriek as she scrambled away from him.

Katie visibly devolved on screen, letting out a steady stream of *Why! What? How? Dae-jung? Dae-jung!* interspersed with *What are you doing with your face? You stop that! How dare you!* Katie's fists pressed against her mouth as she hunched over the screen, wincing every few moments.

"You seem distressed," observed Woo-jin.

Dae-jung snorted.

"Shut up," Katie retorted.

They continued to watch and Woo-jin continued his bored takedown of Katie's reactions. "Your vocabulary seems lacking, Katie. I thought your Korean was better than that."

Dae-jung was definitely amused. If Katie wailing his name had catapulted Dae-jung's thoughts in a decidedly less innocent direction, he pretended not to notice. It was a natural reaction to an attractive woman losing it over his stage presence. This happened all the time. He was used to it.

"Wow, they're bleeping you out a lot. Can people even hear the track at this point?" he said in an effort to distract himself.

Katie cut him a hard glare. "Everyone knows that's what the fans want. You know how it is."

"Right." It was too difficult for him to keep the smirk off his face, and so Dae-jung didn't.

Right when the choreography had him dipping low, Katie pushed away from the table and walked away with a loud *No! Who allowed this? How is this allowed on the internet? This is illegal!*

Woo-jin and Dae-jung could not contain their snickers.

"Still think I'm funny-looking, Noona?"

"I told you! This was after your man-face already came in! Why can't we watch my 'Rapture' reaction? I think I complain about your haircut the whole time!"

"Oh, look. The top comment under this is a link to your 'Madness' reaction," Woo-jin interjected, ignoring Katie completely. "We definitely need to watch that next."

The horror crossing Katie's face at the prospect of watching her reaction to Woo-jin's most famous solo hit was almost as fantastic as her freaking out in the "Event Horizon" reaction video.

"This was the best idea," sighed Dae-jung.

"The worst!" Katie whined as she tried to leave.

"The best," grinned Woo-jin as he pulled her back down, wrapping her in a hug. "The absolute best."

From Katie's lack of resistance, Dae-jung could tell she agreed.

Dae-jung woke up with a groan. His neck hurt and his entire spine felt like it was crunched into awkward angles. In the background, the television was playing some arbitrary reaction video on mute. Katie and Woo-jin were slumped to the side of the couch, with Katie curled under the crook of the older man's arm.

They looked so cute together, Dae-jung thought affectionately. It seemed to make perfect sense if they ended up a couple—as long as Jae-sung was okay with it.

He didn't know why he kept trying to pair Katie with his members. She had shown no sign of wanting to be in a relationship with his members or otherwise. Maybe it was the new knowledge from last night of just how amenable she would have been to any of them—and that Jae-sung had simply been in the right place at the right time.

Poor Jae-sung.

Though the genesis of their relationship may have been proximity and ease, Dae-jung acknowledged that Katie and Jae-sung ended up being wild for each other. The way she'd been in Jae-sung's pocket despite being a rather prickly sort—she had clearly fallen head over heels in love by then. It's what had made Katie's sudden disappearance all the more surprising and painful.

He reminded himself to find out what exactly made her love Jae-sung—for research, of course. It would be foolish of him to become her next fling due to the proximity and ease filming the movie would provide.

Dae-jung stumbled to the bathroom to relieve himself and wondered if he should wake Katie and Woo-jin. He decided that it wasn't worth the years of his life they'd take off and chose instead to return to the main house and shower.

After he felt human again, he made himself a quick egg scramble and scarfed it down directly from the pan.

"You didn't make any for us?" Katie's scratchy voice startled him.

"Didn't want it to get cold," Dae-jung replied easily. It was a lie, but who would it hurt, really?

"Liar," Katie scolded. She blearily climbed into a counter-height chair at the kitchen island and stared blankly at him. "It's like old times, isn't it?" she asked softly.

"What is?" Dae-jung asked as he slid her a mug of hot water and a container of loose leaf tea.

"This," Katie replied, gesturing at him. "Reminds me of all the times I slept over at your apartment—except I suppose there were always more of you guys underfoot making noise somewhere."

"If I recall, you made a decent amount of noise, too."

Katie flushed. "Like Jae and I were the only ones fucking in that place."

"Point taken," Dae-jung sniggered. And then, as if picking up the thread of his earlier thoughts, he asked, "When did it change to something more with him? What made you love him?"

Katie was quiet for several long beats. "Jae-sung's easy to love, Dae-jung. He was just so big—not like that, you pervert—and so floppy."

"Floppy? Are you sure we're not talking about—"

"Like a big, dumb golden retriever." Katie smiled wistfully and sipped her tea. "Jae was just so—is so—earnest. He was such a poet, Dae-jung. Who could hold out against such an onslaught?"

"Do you ever want to get back together with him?"

Dae-jung knew he was overstepping, but he could not help himself. He told himself it was research for the film, but even he sensed it was not the full truth.

Katie shook her head regretfully. "No."

"No?" he prodded gently. "Isn't Hyung still very much the same?"

Katie chuckled. "Well, first of all, he fucked the brains out of my friend Mi-ran."

Dae-jung choked a bit. "You're okay with this? I can't believe he'd tell you."

"Oh my god, no! Mi-ran texted me saying that he'd fucked her stupid—which means something because she's brilliant."

"That wasn't weird?"

"That's the thing, Dae. It wasn't weird at all." Katie reached over and scooped up some of his egg scramble with her fingers. "It's not like the movie version of us. We're not getting back together like they wrote us in the script. That book of my life is closed, and I have no intention of reopening it."

Katie tucked the eggs into her mouth and sucked her fingertips, casting about for a napkin before Dae-jung had the presence of mind to hand her one. He clearly needed to tug one out or something because his brain kept going to the most inappropriate places with Katie.

He blamed Woo-jin for planting the idea of her in his mind like that. Of course he'd always found Katie hot, and yes, there were moments where he allowed his mind to wander in less platonic areas. But for the most part, he'd been staunchly aware of his place in her life. He was her dongsaeng. A hot dongsaeng, but a dongsaeng nonetheless.

"And second," Katie continued, blissfully unaware of the detour his inner monologue had taken, "the balance of power would be too skewed."

"What do you mean?" Dae-jung forced his traitorous thoughts back in line.

"I would feel like I owed him—that he was doing me a favor by being with me again. That I would never be good enough for him." Katie shuddered. "I hate owing people. I always repay my debts."

Dae-jung had a flash of understanding. "Is that why you and Alton hyung never...?"

Katie's face clouded over. "I would lose myself with him," she murmured. "How could I ever feel like I had any right to anything? I literally owe Alton my life. I owe him everything."

"Alton hyung and Jae-sung hyung don't seem like the types to use your past against you, Noona," Dae-jung said softly. "They would never."

Katie's lip curled in a sardonic smile. "People always say they 'would never' until they do, Dae-jung." She held up a hand to forestall more comments. "Not on purpose—or at least not consciously. But how could it not always be in the undercurrent? How could it not always be there: unspoken but so loud nevertheless?"

Dae-jung's heart twanged as it often did around Katie. He continued questioning his reasons for signing onto this project, except deep inside, he knew he wanted her story done right. He wanted to handle Katie and her story gently. Reverently. He did not trust anyone else to do so.

He did not know what that meant except that Katie was precious to him. She was precious to all his bandmates, really. How he wished that she could internalize their love for her.

"Why did you agree to do the music if it hurts you so much, Noona?"

Katie flicked her dark eyes to his. "Everything always hurts, Dae-jung. What's one more?"

She slid off the chair and paused as if conflicted.

"My father was my first love, you know. He was like the sun: so bright." Katie wet her lips. "He loved music and performing. Sometimes, I wonder what he would have been like if he'd had the option to pursue those talents instead of making himself into what others expected."

Katie blinked rapidly, and Dae-jung followed a tear as it curved down her cheekbones.

"I painted him as a monster, but the more I think about it, the more I realize I was unfair. He wasn't a monster; he was just a man." Katie swiped at her face. "I wanted him to love me so much that I thought if I pursued the things he loved—if I made myself into what he wanted—that he would stay. That he would find me and my brother enough. That he would choose us instead of some woman or new get-rich-quick scheme."

Dae-jung wanted to stop Katie—to tell her that she didn't have to share if it hurt too much—except he was immobilized.

"Somewhere along the way, I fell in love with music and performing, too." Katie chanced a glance at him. "Don't you see, Dae? My father is the reason I love music. He is the reason I have what I have—and when he needed me, I abandoned him. I let him die," she whispered, "and when he died, all the music in me died, too."

Dae-jung's chest cracked wide open.

"You know it's not true, right?" asked Dae-jung.

"What's not true? That the musical parts of me are broken? I think I would know."

Dae-jung carefully gentled his voice. "The part about you letting your father die. You didn't abandon him." He refrained from going to her and stayed behind the kitchen island. Katie did not seem as if she'd appreciate his touch. "He made his choices."

"I abandoned him."

"You freed yourself," he insisted. "You're right: he wasn't a monster. But your father, the man, was killing you."

Even from several feet away, Dae-jung could see Katie tremble as she turned to face him.

"It was just money. Let's not overdramatize." Katie sounded so mean, and Dae-jung almost flinched.

"What would have happened if you were beholden to the Lau family in your father's stead, Noona? Alton hyung told me—"

"Since when do you talk to Alton?"

"You think he just lets anyone stay at his home with you? You'd think Woo-jin hyung and I were common criminals with the way he investigated us."

Dae-jung never wanted to go through such an experience ever again. He shuddered at the memory of Alton's congenial demeanor as he had threatened Dae-jung with utmost and complete destruction should either of them harm Katie. Even the unflappable Woo-jin hyung had seemed rattled. Either that or he'd been aroused. Dae-jung wasn't sure.

"At any rate, Hyung said that the entire Lau family was dangerous—especially their youngest son," he continued. "Hyung said that the guy was a known abuser of women and had been uncommonly obsessed with you."

"I would've handled it," Katie replied.

Dae-jung wasn't so sure about that. "Maybe," he acceded. "But at what cost to yourself?"

Katie's hands tightened into hard fists. "We'll never know," she grated out.

"Thank you for telling me, Noona," he said, attempting to mollify her. That, and he really was grateful. "I won't tell anyone."

"You can tell Woo-jin oppa," Katie replied. "I—I don't know that I can say it again."

"Okay," he replied. He decided he would ask if she wanted a hug. "Noona, could I hug you?"

"I—I don't think I can handle that right now, Dae," Katie said, voice tiny. At his disappointment, she added, "I appreciate you asking, though."

"Of course, Noona," Dae-jung said. "You know we love you so very much, right?"

Katie gave him a brief nod and left him alone in the kitchen. Dae-jung tried not to feel discouraged or wonder how she was going to play Vikki Yu, the character loosely based on Katie's life. How was Katie going to act as if she were in love with him—let alone enact the love scenes—if she couldn't even let Dae-jung hug her.

May 2026

Sometimes the idea of a multiverse is comforting. Out of my infinite versions, surely there exists a me who is happy. Other times, the thought that there are countless iterations who are just as miserable—if not worse off—I can't breathe.

                                              - Katie Wu, X, April 2026

"Do you want to go home?" Dae-jung inquired in Katie's ear as he slid next to her on the patio by the outdoor bar, noting that the white man speaking to her bristled when Dae-jung's fingers possessively grazed her bare arms. It always amused Dae-jung how differently secure and insecure men reacted to him.

Katie shook her head lightly. "Dae-jung, this is Gary," she introduced in English. "Gary, this is Dae-jung."

"Nice to meet you," Dae-jung said in careful English as he extended his hand in the way of westerners.

Gary's handshake was unnecessarily firm. Poor Gary, so eager to prove his masculinity.

"How do you know Katie, Dae-jung?" Strange how Gary sounded so petulant and oddly clingy.

"We work together," Dae-jung said, sticking to the agreed-upon script.

Though Katie had assured him that her college friend Allen Tsao had only invited their mutual college friends—most of whom were already married and had kids—the longer people didn't realize who he was, the better. Dae-jung was banking on the racist nature of Americans assuming all Asians were the same, though most of Katie's college friends were Asian, so perhaps this man wouldn't actually be confused.

Dae-jung just hoped that Allen was used to high-profile guests due to being a movie producer. Katie had mentioned Allen was someone to watch, producing edgy indie and Asian American films. It certainly seemed like Allen was a big deal due to the fact that there was a live trio playing light jazz and pop in the corner of the patio as well as a manned bar for a simple backyard party—well, as simple as the backyard of any Malibu mansion could be.

"For the movie?" Gary asked. "You said it starts filming soon?"

"Something like that," Katie replied cagily.

Gary seemed on the verge of asking Katie something but clearly didn't like the fact that Dae-jung was present. Dae-jung could always tell who was a social climber or if they had ulterior motives. Gary definitely was one or the other; Dae-jung did not like his face.

"Am I in it?" Gary asked, sharp and unsure.

"In what? The movie?"

What a weird question. Oh, unless—

"I have a family now, Katie," Gary said, his pasty face pinched. "I'm an elder in our church."

Dae-jung recognized the way Katie's face scrunched in annoyance—she didn't even bother trying to plaster over it with politeness.

"It's not an actual biopic, Gary. It's just a movie loosely based on my memoir—like how '8 Mile' isn't really a biopic of Eminem." Dae-jung could tell Katie was sick of explaining away the common misconception. "Besides, you weren't even in the book, why would you be in the movie?"

Every bit of Katie vibrated with irritation. Dae-jung suddenly wished Katie hadn't told their managers to take the night off. They would have some official-sounding bullshit at the ready and produce NDAs for people to sign. That usually deterred even the most stubborn, but their managers were out in K-town and unavailable.

Dae-jung cast about for Woo-jin, but he was talking to Allen in the corner. Woo-jin tended to unruffle Katie's feathers better than most—although perhaps she didn't need unruffling so much as this man needed a rescue before his imminent death.

"How do you know Allen?" Dae-jung interrupted. If Woo-jin couldn't save Gary, Dae-jung would.

Gary seemed startled, as if he'd forgotten Dae-jung was still there. "Oh, Allen and I lived in the same dorm at UCLA, and we hung out occasionally. A few of our friends overlapped, and we hung out a lot more after college."

"Fascinating," said Dae-jung. "What do you do for work?"

"Ah, I'm between jobs right now. I decided to take some time off to help my wife with our new baby," replied Gary.

"Oh, congratulations on the new baby! How old are they?" Dae-jung asked. He knew how to make polite small talk despite it boring him to tears.

"He's 3 next month."

Dae-jung barely caught his face in time, and before he could ask some more banal questions, Allen tapped the mic, gathering everyone's attention.

"Hey, everyone! Let's have a round of applause for my intern and his band, The Rice Rockets!" Allen paused to let everyone chuckle at the name and then cleared his throat. "As I'm sure you've all seen, our very own Katie Wu is back with us and gracing us with her presence after years away."

Dae-jung sensed Katie's entire body tense as she painted on a good-natured grin and waved.

"It's been years since we've heard you sing—would you play us a little something, Katie?" Allen added.

Katie flushed and waved both her hands in an obvious attempt to duck this unwelcomed spotlight. Dae-jung thought he could see a slight tremor as she fluttered in embarrassment.

"You're not too good for us now, are you?" Gary asked, voice pitched to carry. "You never used to be so modest."

Katie's eyes flashed violence, but all she did was smile. "It's been a long time since I've sung anything," she croaked. "I would hate to subject anyone to that."

"Oh, nonsense," encouraged Allen. "What do you say, everyone? Do we want to hear Katie?"

The twenty to thirty people in Allen's backyard cheered and chanted her name.

Dae-jung wanted to reach out and comfort her, but he could already tell that Katie was at maximum tension. He did not know if she would break.

Katie crooked a wry smile. "Ah, alright. You've twisted my arm." She giggled as if she was secretly pleased. "But don't blame me if it sucks."

She sucked in a deep breath and whooshed it out, and then sashayed to the makeshift stage, periodically bowing and clowning around. If Dae-jung hadn't just spent a month with Katie trying to squeeze music out of stone, he would have never known she was desperately attempting to seem normal.

Katie asked for the acoustic guitar from Allen's intern and bought herself some time tuning the instrument—as if the man hadn't just been playing on it. She took one more deep breath and began playing. The notes were incredibly familiar to Dae-jung and then she began singing about blackbirds singing, their broken wings, and taking flight.

Dae-jung watched as Katie sang in her lower register, her voice husky with disuse and smoke. Though he was angry that she'd been publicly manipulated into singing and playing again, he had missed her. When Dae-jung snuck a glance at Woo-jin, the older man seemed visibly moved—and no small wonder. The famous Beatles song was already intimate and moving, but something about her energy imbued it with even more poignancy.

He wanted to cry.

When Katie finished, she bowed and tried to wave off the whistles for encores. She laughed nervously into the mic. "Unfortunately, I haven't picked up a guitar in over five years, so that will have to do."

Her friends groaned in what Dae-jung considered friendly disappointment until he heard Gary's now familiar voice heckle, "Maybe we're just unsatisfied because you chose something every beginning guitarist knows!"

A smattering of "fuck off, Gary" and "Jesus" and other disgruntled murmurs peppered the yard.

Allen hovered by the mic, looking as if he was going to rescue Katie, but ultimately, giving her the choice to continue or not.

Katie sighed and went through the motions of tuning the guitar again, taking the moment to think. "Will John Mayer's 'Neon' suffice, Gary?" She huffed a colorless laugh as she shook her head. "Ah, fuck it."

Dae-jung didn't recognize the song but he assumed by the rising buzz from the group that it must be difficult.

"Here goes nothing," Katie hummed.

She began to play a complicated slap rhythm guitar with syncopated beats and elaborate fingering. It was dizzying, and by the whistles of appreciation, her college friends agreed that Katie was amazing. And then, she started to sing, too.

Dae-jung could not understand how Katie could keep track of all the different rhythms and fingering as well as carry a tune—let alone remember the words. And this was after five years of not touching the guitar? Who knew how long it had been since she'd played this particular song.

Minutes later, the makeshift audience gave Katie a standing ovation. She bowed with much brandishing, twirling, and exaggerated good cheer, and made her way out of the limelight. Dae-jung and Woo-jin beelined it to her and all seemed well until he noted her face as Allen was apologizing to her about Gary.

"Don't listen to him, Katie," Allen begged. "He's an ass and we only keep him around out of misplaced nostalgia. Honestly, we only invite him because we like his wife."

"Don't worry about it, Allen," Katie assuaged, despite clearly wanting Allen to actually worry about it. "I know it's an awkward situation. All the same, I'm—I'm going to head out." At Allen's protest, she added, "I appreciate the invitation, friend. It was good to see you all."

It took at least another hour before Katie could leave due to her endless goodbyes, all of her friends telling her to stay longer.

As it was, the drive home was in stilted silence. By the time they got back to Alton's San Marino residence, she was unable even to fake a smile.

Katie didn't even say goodnight as she closed her bedroom door.

"Noona," Dae-jung said as he knocked on her door. "Noona, please come out. It's been three days. The managers are worried, and I don't know how long Hyung and I can keep them from calling Song PD."

He heard some scuffling and shifting weight on her bed. After a few moments, her door cracked open. Katie looked awful and was wrapped in her blanket despite the heat of the day.

"Noona? Are you okay?"

Katie shook her head.

"Do you need a hug?"

Katie winced but nodded. That was all the permission Dae-jung needed as he bounded into her room and enveloped her into an embrace that was perhaps erring on the side of too tight. But Katie knew he was a human octopus, so she knew what she'd been doing when she'd agreed to terms.

Or at least, that's what Dae-jung was hoping would be the case. At any rate, he was hugging Katie and she was not pushing him away. That seemed to be a good sign.

When Dae-jung's arms were starting to cramp, he said, "Noona, don't take this the wrong way, but you need to shower." At Katie's sputtered indignance, he added, "Not because you smell—well, not only because of that—but because you'll feel better. Honestly, we'll all feel better."

Katie shoved him lightly. "Rude," she complained. "I smell delightful because everything about me is a delight and wonderment for all humankind."

Dae-jung only stared at Katie balefully. "You learned all that Korean just to what? Spout words that make Ye-jun hyung sound modest?"

"My goal is only to make Oppa sound reasonable," Katie replied, adding in English, "I can do all things through Oppa who strengthens me."

It all sounded vaguely ominous to Dae-jung. "I have no idea what that means," he admitted after a few beats.

"Don't worry about it. It's only funny if you can quote the Bible ironically."

"I can see why you're no fun at parties." He hoped he wasn't pushing his luck.

Katie sighed as if even her bones ached. "Fair."

Suddenly, she leaned over to remove her sleeping shorts and Dae-jung squeaked. "Noona! Wait until I leave first!"

Katie huffed a bleak little puff of air. "We're supposed to be fake naked with each other in a few months, Dae. I'm sure I'll be even less dressed then."

"But we'll have an intimacy coach present—and only after we have blocked out the scenes!"

Dae-jung did not want any of his members—especially Jae-sung—to accuse him of swooping in on Katie's vulnerable state. He would maintain proper decorum because it was the right thing to do. She deserved all the respect—especially after the way her so-called friends had manipulated her the other night.

Katie stopped and pierced Dae-jung with her unfaltering gaze. His insides churned with guilt despite him having done nothing to merit it.

"You're right, Dae. I'm sorry for making you feel uncomfortable. I forget that not everyone wants to see me naked."

He promptly shoved images of Katie spread out underneath him from his traitorous mind. Utmost. Respect. "You're really giving Ye-jun hyung a run for his money, huh?"

Katie shrugged. "Some days, it's the only thing giving me purpose." She sighed again. "Come on, now. Get out and let Noona rid herself of this scaly dragon skin and finally emerge a human again. It requires sharp claws and teeth and perhaps may shed some blood."

"You're speaking Korean, and yet, I don't understand a single word out of your mouth," he mused.

"They probably translated C.S. Lewis into Korean differently than I phrased it," Katie replied.

Despite not knowing who this Lewis person was, Dae-jung merely harumphed an acknowledgment as he left her room. It probably was some literary reference that Jae-sung would have immediately recognized.

Dae-jung wasn't stupid, but he certainly was no genius like Katie and Jae-sung. They were not only talented, they were book smart, too. Not for the first time did Dae-jung feel out of his depth around Katie. He resigned himself to the fact that it would not be the last.

June 2026

I'm sorry, Oppa. I hope you at least got the bones of songs for future usage.
> - Text from Katie Wu to Hwang Woo-jin, June 2026

Don't worry about it. Technically, I have until a few weeks after they've finished filming and editing before I have to hand anything in.
> - Text from Hwang Woo-jin to Katie Wu, June 2026

Then why did you insist on coming out to LA and making me feel bad?
> \- Text from Katie Wu to Hwang Woo-jin, June 2026

Free trip to LA. Also, I'm a dick.
> \- Text from Hwang Woo-jin to Katie Wu, June 2026

You were hoping Alton would come out and visit, huh?
> \- Text from Katie Wu to Hwang Woo-jin, June 2026

I don't know what you're talking about.
> \- Text from Hwang Woo-jin to Katie Wu, June 2026

I'm depressed, not stupid. You think I don't see you creeping in on my video calls with him?
> \- Text from Katie Wu to Hwang Woo-jin, June 2026

Also, because I'm awesome, he loves it when people talk interior design to him. Like, REALLY likes it.
> \- Text from Katie Wu to Hwang Woo-jin, June 2026

Like, wainscoting? Enfilade? Etagere? J-box?
> \- Text from Hwang Woo-jin to Katie Wu, June 2026

Watch your fucking mouth, you heathen. I'm a good girl, I am.
- Text from Katie Wu to Hwang Woo-jin, June 2026

Anytime you want to watch my fucking mouth, baby. I can make you bad if you want.
- Text from Hwang Woo-jin to Katie Wu, June 2026

No quippy rejoinder? That's what I thought. Coward.
- Text from Hwang Woo-jin to Katie Wu, June 2026

Hyung, I'm remodeling my spare penthouse. Was debating between trompe l'oeil or coffered ceilings. What are your thoughts?
- Text from Hwang Woo-jin to Alton Kuang, June 2026

Oh? Talk square footage with me, friend.
- Text from Alton Kuang to Hwang Woo-jin, June 2026

Quick. Tell me everything you know about Hwang Woo-jin.
- Text from Alton Kuang to Katie Wu, June 2026

Dae-jung and Katie were sitting in the courtyard at the center of Alton's home, enjoying the spring air from the shade of an old oak tree. He loved being outside, and though Katie hated it because of her allergies, she still sat with him. It was nice and comforting to be in her presence.

"Noona, I feel like I need to see where you grew up. Walk the streets you walked. Breathe the air you breathed."

Dae-jung didn't know what quite possessed him to ask Katie, but ever since the idea seized him one late night as he watched her and Woo-jin battle it out morosely over the MIDI, he couldn't let it go.

Katie flicked her gaze up at Dae-jung, the tightening of her grip on her hot tea her only tell.

"Oh?" she murmured. "I will have to find out from Mattie when my mother will be out of the house. But I suppose I can take you to the country club, and you can get in a few rounds of golf."

Dae-jung's eyes lit up. "Really? I didn't even know you could play golf, Noona!"

"My parents made me take lessons as a kid. I wasn't very good," Katie muttered. She shifted on the stone bench. "And then Alton made me golf with him, so I got better under protest. Let me make some calls." Katie paused. "Do you want a tour of UCLA, too? A lot of the dorms have changed but we can do that before we go up north, unless you want to wait until we film there."

"Yeah, let's do it!"

"It will have to be a quick trip, though," Katie added. "Filming starts in two weeks."

"Should I ask Sung-mo hyung to book flights?" Dae-jung asked. "He and Ha-joon hyung don't need to come with us, right?"

It was technically a work trip, but Dae-jung really wanted to spend time alone with Katie and glean the details he needed to understand her character in the movie. It would be weird with their managers tagging along.

Katie pondered for a few moments. "You know what? Let's drive and help you practice driving stick."

"Oh, I can drive a stick just fine," Dae-jung teased. "I've had years of practice—ask any of my partners."

"I'll show you some of California's famous vistas. We can even play a round at Pebble Beach," continued Katie, completely ignoring his salacious comment as she usually did when Dae-jung or one of the younger members said something overtly sexual.

"Thanks, Noona," Dae-jung said, only slightly disappointed that Katie didn't acknowledge what he was implying about his sexual prowess. "You're the best."

"I'm not, but you've been a good sport these last few months. It couldn't have been very much fun."

"It wasn't, but Allen and I got along well enough after I made sure he cleared up the misunderstanding with Gary," Dae-jung shared happily, practically bouncing with excitement. At Katie's furrowed brows, he realized he'd misspoke.

"What did you clear up, Dae-jung?" Katie asked quietly.

Dae-jung rubbed the back of his neck.

"Oh, uh, just how, you know, it was really shitty of Allen to have put you on the spot like that and then not put Gary in his place." Dae-jung presented Katie with his best innocent boxy grin. "Allen is a good guy, so he apologized more and offered to take me around LA and introduce me to his network. He even volunteered to film future M/Vs at a severe discount, so now we're friends."

"Allen is a decent person, but he's definitely always looking out for himself, Dae-jung. Be careful," Katie warned. "Your network is 100% more powerful than his."

"I'm a grown-up, Noona," Dae-jung retorted. "You know I have a good vibe check."

"Hmmmm."

"Plus, he's fun and knows all the cool spots in K-town despite not being Korean."

"Ah, the truth comes out," Katie grinned.

"Someone has to take care of me, Noona," Dae-jung pouted. He stood and stretched, suddenly wanting to look up all the scenic stops up and down California. "You're always working—either with a trainer, learning choreo, or fighting with Woo-jin hyung about music."

"Well, Woo-jin oppa is back in Seoul with Chang-nam oppa so at least you're spared that," she replied. "Want to leave tomorrow? If we head out early, we can grab a late lunch at my favorite Chinese restaurant in Berkeley."

"Sounds good, Noona," Dae-jung replied as he headed inside the house to throw his clothes into a suitcase.

"Oh, and don't forget to pack some warmer clothes! June Gloom is a thing in California—especially along the coasts!"

"Yes, mom!" he hollered back, not bothering to hide his laughter at her indignant "Yah! The disrespect!" She sounded like Ye-jun the more time passed, and it comforted him.

It was going to be great.

It was not great. It wasn't terrible, either. But it wasn't great.

It just was...anticlimactic.

Mostly, Dae-jung was not prepared for the understated wealth Katie had grown up around. He was ridiculously rich now, and still, he was impressed with the house Katie had grown up in. It was massive, filled with art and expensive furniture and rugs.

When he asked if her mother would be upset at her entering the house without her, Katie merely shrugged and said, "It's technically my house. I certainly pay all the property taxes and utilities." She drank in her surroundings greedily. "Besides, my mother can't possibly hate me more."

He let the topic drop, content to soak in the house and its atmosphere. Despite many pictures of Mattie on the wall, there was not a single picture of Katie—a marked contrast to his parents' home where Dae-jung's pictures were everywhere. Katie was invisible.

"Which was your room?" Dae-jung asked quietly.

When Katie indicated the room but made no move toward it, Dae-jung went ahead on his own. If it had ever harbored a teenage Katie, Dae-jung could no longer tell. It was a perfectly appointed guest room, and part of him grieved.

She had been so thoroughly excised. He could not imagine a family that operated as such. Katie might have grown up rich, but to Dae-jung, her family wallowed in poverty.

She soon took him to the local country club and he had a perfectly tasteful country club lunch and then a round of golf in the golden California sun where he summarily trounced Katie (though Dae-jung had a sneaking suspicion she was letting him win).

Dae-jung wondered how he'd never thought to question whether the small, sleepy town Katie had grown up in was awash in money or not. He remembered how Katie had made it seem as if she had grown up in some backwater town and not one filled with huge estates hidden in rolling foothills—as well as the many country club golf courses from which he could choose.

"Noona, you said you grew up in the boonies," he protested.

"It was, in a way," Katie replied as she drove the golf cart along the manicured lawns to the next hole. "It was super white, super sheltered, and super out of touch with reality."

"It doesn't seem so bad," Dae-jung remarked.

Katie cut him a glance. "You of all people should know that the surface is never as it seems. It was stifling. I couldn't wait to escape."

"People seem nice enough."

"My parents received a letter in their mailbox the day after they moved in, telling them to go back to where they came from," Katie said. "We were one of, like, six Asian families in this gated community, and we were constantly treated like shit. It was obvious they didn't want us here."

"Oh," said Dae-jung. He should have known better based on how his band was treated in the US and other western countries.

"Make no mistake, Dae, money only buys you the illusion of being protected from racism. But the instant these people are alone, we're nothing but chinks and gooks."

Dae-jung nodded, chagrined that this was the universal experience of being Asian in the US.

Katie spent the next two days showing him her old high school, her old church, and introducing him to a few more elementary and high school friends. Dae-jung was even happily surprised to see Danny—one of Katie's friends who had visited her in Seoul—and pumped the older man for more embarrassing stories about her.

Before he knew it, they were taking the scenic route back to Los Angeles. The next few days were filled with Katie hugging the curves of Highway 101 at a reasonably thrilling speed as he stared out at the Pacific, stopping to take photos of elephant seals or look at historic landmarks like Hearst Castle or the Madonna Inn. Dae-jung felt inexplicably warm whenever he caught Katie smiling in genuine happiness.

On the last night before returning to Los Angeles, they each checked into their suites at a swanky resort in Santa Barbara. While Dae-jung would never call Katie a relaxed sort of person, he could see Katie get noticeably more tense as the night progressed. After eating lots of rich foods and killing a bottle of wine between them, he suggested a stroll down the beach. Though Katie seemed as if it were the last thing she wanted to do, she agreed.

"Thanks for taking me on this detour and showing me around your home state, Noona," Dae-jung said. The wind carried the scent of salt and tiny water droplets, and he was glad he'd taken off his slippers to feel the wet sand squishing between his toes.

"Of course, Dae-jung," Katie said. After a long silent spell, she added, "The recovery center I stayed at is a few miles down the road, you know."

"Oh," he replied.

Katie never spoke about that time and most days, he could forget that she'd gone through such a devastating period. Most days, he just thought of Katie as his depressed noona who was a lot like how Woo-jin used to be. Bouts of depression still hit Woo-jin sometimes—the winter months, especially—and Dae-jung was used to being more understanding of his bandmate during those periods.

He chided himself for having totally forgotten.

"I would take you to tour the facility, but I don't ever want to go back there," Katie said.

"Were they bad to you?" he asked.

The wind whipped Katie's hair across her face as she shook her head. "It wasn't that they were bad so much as they were culturally ill-equipped." Katie shivered and Dae-jung gave into the urge to wrap his arms around her. He was surprised that she let him. "The house that Ha-joon oppa and I stayed in was a little further away, but that had at least slightly better memories of Oppa."

Dae-jung absentmindedly planted a light kiss on the crown of Katie's head. "I'm so glad you had Alton hyung and Ha-joon hyung to take care of you, Noona."

Katie just nodded and brushed wayward tears off her cheeks. Dae-jung was shocked Katie had let him hold her as long as she did, but he was content. She smelled a little sweaty but also like the citrus shampoo she favored. He would hold her until she pushed him away.

"I have a confession to make," Katie whispered after a few more moments.

"What is it, Noona?" he asked. "You can tell me."

Katie turned around in his arms and flicked her gaze to his before focusing on an indeterminate point behind him. Katie really resembled Woo-jin hyung in more ways than one.

"I—I haven't kissed anyone since Jae-sung and—and I'm worried I'll be awful on screen. The movie rides on our chemistry, Dae," Katie rambled. She was adorable when she was so flustered. "I don't want to kiss just anyone to practice with—and maybe you wouldn't mind since—"

Dae-jung raised a finger to Katie's lips, effectively shushing her. Her face burst into flames as her eyes fixated on his mouth.

The decision was made before he could think it all the way through. After all, they were going to be kissing on set anyway. What difference did it make if they kissed a few weeks earlier? If this was how he could help Katie deal with her anxiety, then he would.

Of course, he had to approach her just right.

Dae-jung smiled softly at Katie. "If you wanted to kiss me, Noona, you could have just said so. You don't have to make up a reason."

"I'm not—"

Dae-jung didn't get to hear the rest of Katie's sentence because he was already pressing his lips into hers. He decided that the less time she had to freak out, the better. Her lips were slightly chapped, but overall, he enjoyed the shape of Katie's mouth slotting with his.

Except though Katie kissed him back, he could tell she was not fully present. For one, her whole body was way too tense—perhaps due to shock. And two, well, he'd figure that out later because quite frankly, he was a little distracted in trying to open Katie up.

"Relax, Noona. You're thinking too much."

"Dae-ju—"

Dae-jung took advantage of Katie's lips parting to risk a little flick of his tongue, and at her throaty "oh," he knew he had her.

"That's it, Noona," he rasped. He lifted a hand to cup the base of Katie's neck and she melted.

Katie let him in, and Dae-jung was determined to make it worth it. She tasted like the cabernet they'd shared at dinner and a hint of salt from the sea. Every now and then, a tiny gasp would escape, and Dae-jung would feel the sighs go straight to his groin.

She was going to be trouble.

Eventually, the wind became too much and Dae-jung broke away, however reluctantly. Katie stumbled back a step, eyes glassy and lips swollen, hand touching her mouth reverently.

And then, before Dae-jung could gather his bearings, Katie closed the distance between their bodies and devoured him whole.

Dae-jung was so utterly fucked.

CHAPTER 8

July 2026

Dae-jung of DOYEN was seen on set at "Landslide" though he is not slated for any scenes until filming moves to Korea. Sources close to the movie claim Dae-jung is often in Katie Wu's trailers and is even staying at her Malibu and San Marino residences. Is romance brewing between the attractive co-stars?

- The National Enquirer, July 2026

The thing of it was, Dae-jung didn't technically need to be on set, let alone in the country. All the flashback scenes they were shooting had nothing to do with him except he found himself really wanting to be present.

After their trip up and down California—not to mention that massive makeout session on the beach—he felt much closer and possibly even more protective of Katie than before. So if his only purpose was serving as her moral support, it was enough for him.

Katie was required on set because quite simply, she was the source material. Also, she and the Asian American actresses portraying the younger iterations of Vikki Yu needed to have a consistent narrative as well as continuity of mannerisms.

Dae-jung watched as all the actresses grew to rely on and trust the actor playing the character based on Katie's father. He was a kind gentleman who constantly checked in on the actresses after portraying particularly abusive scenes, adamant on ensuring everyone knew he was acting and in no way an actual threat—especially for the young actresses playing Vikki's elementary, middle, and high school versions.

When Katie wasn't needed for consultation, Dae-jung helped as she ran her lines repeatedly in a quick, monotone voice. He wasn't necessarily the fastest at reading English lines but she mostly needed him to provide an auditory stop as she memorized thousands of words. He tried his best, though he wasn't sure why she chose him to run lines with instead of Ha-joon or the Asian American actor playing Roland Tan, the character based on Alton Kuang and other love interest in the movie.

He hoped it was because Katie found him to be a source of serenity and not because she was looking for ways to occupy him due to him being otherwise in the way. He was used to being part of a group, but he usually had an equal role to play. Here, Dae-jung was relegated to the sidelines until filming would begin in Seoul. He was growing increasingly frustrated.

He supposed his frustration could have all been avoided had he just shown up when he was actually needed instead of so preemptively.

The free time provided way too many opportunities for Dae-jung to overthink and chat with Ha-joon in the trailer. He wondered if he was betraying Jae-sung with his tumultuous feelings about Katie, and so, he tucked them away until they could serve him.

Katie grew increasingly anxious as her scenes with the character based on her father and those depicting her recovery approached. Every cell of her being vibrated with terror—a fact she unsuccessfully attempted to hide from Dae-jung and Ha-joon.

It got worse after her filming started.

Katie often required Dae-jung to gently be a touchstone so she could snap out of that dark place she sank into for those sequences. Ha-joon was also there to help, but her stocky manager often reminded her of the past, so more often than not, Dae-jung had to bring her back to the present.

"Hey, Noona," he would say in Korean as she'd blink slowly, surprised at his presence. "It's me, your Dae-jung. You're safe, Noona. No one can hurt you here."

Katie would come back, slightly embarrassed but still grateful. But as the days dragged on, she disappeared more and more into herself, and Dae-jung and Ha-joon worried, unsure of how to call her back.

Some days, Katie was so emotionally worn that she would toss him the keys to her yellow Lamborghini while Ha-joon followed in the rental. She'd only pipe up occasionally that he was grinding her gears into dust despite all her efforts to teach him how to drive stick properly. Dae-jung knew he was actually a pretty good driver—even with the manual shift—so he just let her blow off steam.

Those nights, Dae-jung knew to leave her alone on her balcony as she smoked blunt after blunt. She was a little worse for wear the next morning, but she was always on set by the first call time like the professional she was.

How Dae-jung wished he could cradle Katie in soothing murmurs and kisses, except ever since the trip, she'd been exceedingly cautious about crossing any physical boundaries with him. She'd even pulled back on hugging and general touching—which Dae-jung missed something fierce.

He was starving for any sort of human contact, and thus, he found himself taking the Lamborghini out every now and then to party with Allen. If he occasionally took a person—male or female, he wasn't picky—to a hotel for a few hours before he drove back to San Marino, that was his own business.

At least his English rapidly improved due to daily usage.

Dae-jung not only gained more American friends, he gained more insight into Katie's character's background so that he could ponder how Choi Eun-seong could possibly push Vikki Yu's buttons with his own particular mannerisms in his future scenes. He took notes so he could refer to them when he was back in Korea.

Dae-jung bent all his energy into preparing his lines, making sure Katie wasn't spiraling too terribly, and channeling any pent-up emotions into humming the occasional melody or scrawling a few incoherent lyrics and sending them to Woo-jin.

Except, Dae-jung couldn't help but feel as if everything was crashing forward to a head—and he didn't know who would emerge from the rubble.

After three months in Los Angeles, Dae-jung of K-pop band DOYEN landed today at Taoyuan International Airport in Taiwan. He greeted fans in a loose linen shirt and pants set, Gucci slides, and a green beret. Katie Wu was on the same flight as her "Landslide" co-star, fueling rumors of their budding romance. Wu was a fashion disappointment in, as predicted, gray sweats and a Warriors cap.

- Soompi, July 2026

"You seem happier, Noona," Dae-jung commented as Katie and Ha-joon settled into the air-conditioned car SB Entertainment had sent to pick them up in.

"I love Taiwan," Katie murmured as she leaned against the leather seat. The brief minutes of being in the wet, muggy air of Taiwan was more than enough to remind her why she chose to spend as much time inside as possible. Despite the failing in weather, she said, "Some part of my soul feels at ease here—like, oh, this is the land of my people. I belong here. I have a right to this place despite being born an ocean away."

"Do you not feel the same in Seoul? Even after all these years?" Dae-jung sounded hurt, and it puzzled her.

She listened with half an ear as Ha-joon talked to Sung-mo on the phone from the front passenger seat. Sung-mo had returned to Seoul to take care of some business for the company and would be meeting them at the hotel later. As much as she enjoyed Dae-jung's company, she was grateful for Ha-joon's grounding presence. It helped, too, that Ha-joon was a logistics king whereas Dae-jung's freewheeling personality, while fun, could get frustrating when it came to accomplishing things.

Katie regarded Dae-jung again. He was so earnest, his eyes so soulful and deep. He was hard to look at without her heart squeezing tighter.

"Seoul is..." She sighed. "Seoul is hard," she settled on saying.

"You have a right to Seoul, too. Because we're your people, Noona," he said. "We're always your people."

Katie stared at him again, knowing that he was referring to himself and the rest of his bandmates. She wasn't sure if Dae-jung was including Jae-sung, but given the generosity of Dae-jung's personality, he probably was.

"Ah," she replied, voice thick. "Yes, well. Want me to take you to a Taiwanese night market tonight?"

Dae-jung slid Katie a look as if to say that he knew what she was up to. But then, he had mercy on her. "Yeah, that sounds awesome, Noona."

They were quiet for the remainder of the thirty-minute drive to The Floating Orchid, Alton's boutique hotel in Taipei. She always loved the light scent of citrus, rose, and vetiver in the lobby. It followed them into the glass elevator as they rode up to her and Dae-jung's adjacent suites after Ha-joon checked them in.

Katie casually mentioned how the launch party for her first album had been set in the hotel's sky bar. Before Dae-jung could comment more than a "that's so cool," her phone vibrated. She fished her phone out of her purse and checked her texts.

"Everything okay?" asked Dae-jung.

Katie's whole body felt heavy. "Yeah, it was my big aunt. She said my grandfather asked to see me."

"Is that bad?"

"No," she replied quietly. "He's always been kind to me. I may have to cancel on the night market though. They want me to have dinner with them tonight."

The elevator dinged and the doors opened to the tastefully understated hallway, the deep violet of the carpet contrasting with gold accents in the wallpaper and art frames.

Dae-jung gestured for Katie to exit first as he and Ha-joon followed. "Oh, that's alright. Family first, Noona."

"Yeah, I have to pretty much leave as soon as I drop my shit off in the suite and catch a High Speed Rail to Kaohsiung," she said, scanning the room numbers for her own. Katie cleared her throat. "They invited you to come along, if you wish."

Dae-jung seemed startled then delighted. "Oh! I would love to, Noona! Grandparents and aunties love me!"

"If you're not too tired, I can ask my cousins to take us to a night market there," Katie said as they stopped in front of her suite. "Or we can ride the Ferris wheel and go on the rooftop rides on one of the big hotels there."

"Sounds great."

"We can take the High Speed Rail back tomorrow morning or I can ask to use Alton's jet." Katie paused to consider logistics a bit more. "I may have to request the jet now though so I guess it depends on how you want to travel tomorrow."

"Folks in Taiwan generally know how to behave, right? Like in Japan and Korea?" Dae-jung checked.

"Yeah," she said. "They're good about respecting boundaries and privacy. Also, I've never had a problem, but you're a lot more famous than I am."

Dae-jung nodded. "Just seeing if our managers need to come along and if we need security."

Katie unlocked her door and stepped into the suite. Dae-jung followed her even as Ha-joon left for his own quarters, telling them to update him when they decided on a plan. They slipped off their shoes in the tiny alcove and she looked around at the rich cream carpet, the pleasing curve of the royal purple chaise lounge, and the plush ovals of the magenta sofa. Everything from the end tables to the floor lamps felt luxuriously round and indulgent.

"I feel like CHIMERA is usually really good about pretending not to see any of you in the wild," Katie added as she sat on the sofa and welcomed its support.

"Let's do the High Speed Rail then, Noona. I love trains," Dae-jung said, still standing and leaning against the gold and cream patterned wall. "We can tell our managers to take a break. After all, you're visiting family and it's not work-related." As always, Dae-jung's good humor was infectious.

"Hopefully there are business class seats available, too. That way we have ticketed seats versus searching until we find open ones."

"And miss out on a good deal? Never!" he exclaimed. "Besides, we probably wouldn't be recognized in a hat and face mask, right? Especially since no one is expecting us to take the train?"

Katie smiled. He really was very enthusiastic. "The price difference is negligible, Dae. And then we won't have to keep switching seats."

"Ah, true. I suppose it's better to have guaranteed seating."

"Sorry to ruin your dreams of a good deal. We can haggle extra at the night markets," she said.

Dae-jung beamed at Katie. "Thanks, Noona. You always know how to take care of me."

Katie felt her stomach curl in pleasure at his praise. She shifted and cleared her throat, catching the way Dae-jung was suppressing a smile at her obvious discomfort. She sniffed and dug through her purse for her wallet to tip the bellhop when they eventually brought up her luggage.

Tipping wasn't expected, but she stayed at The Floating Orchid often enough that she tried to treat the staff extra well. Katie didn't want them to think that Alton's good friend was a cheapskate.

She passed a $1,000 note to Dae-jung, knowing that he never carried cash. Besides, he had four large suitcases to her single one. She couldn't believe Sung-mo would be bringing an additional suitcase for Dae-jung because he was getting bored of his current clothes. This despite the fact that one of the four suitcases was full of clothes he'd purchased while in Los Angeles.

Ridiculous man.

"Is Ah-Gong okay?" Katie asked as she followed her first aunt into the tiny elevator they'd installed after her grandparents had gotten too old to climb multiple flights of stairs.

"Ah, Katie-ah, he's getting old and eats and sleeps really early now. He hasn't left the house in a while except for doctor visits," her aunt replied.

"Oh," Katie said. At Dae-jung's concerned face, she translated her aunt's comment to Korean. He squeezed her arm softly, and she flashed him a grateful smile.

She tried to settle the roiling in her stomach. It had been building since she received the text from her aunties, and now, it was all coming to a head. Katie hadn't seen her grandfather in two years—not since she came through Taiwan for the book tour. But even then, it had been a hurried affair.

If Katie was honest, it had been so rushed because she hadn't wanted to face her ah-gong. She wasn't sure how much her aunties had told him, but he wasn't stupid or an invalid. He had to have known. And yet, he never alluded to any of the scandals she'd been involved in. Her ah-gong had just carried on as if nothing had ever happened.

Katie supposed that was the best she could hope for.

The only reason she was agreeing to see him again was because he was aging. She didn't know how much time she had left with him. Her ah-ma had passed away while she'd been in college and Katie'd always regretted that she'd only met her a handful of times.

The elevator doors opened to reveal her grandfather's main living area, which looked frozen in time from her earliest memories. It seemed larger in her memories, though the room was smaller than she recalled even from her last visit a few years ago.

The floors were still a dark green marble tile throughout the house, a worn tan leather sofa was against one of the wood-paneled walls, and a standing fan was rotating in the corner. There were few decorations, and the sparse living space reminded her of her own utilitarian preferences. The flat-screen television played a news program on mute, and her ah-gong sat in a wicker rocking chair. A Southeast Asian helper was sitting near him, and Katie nodded to acknowledge her.

Her ah-gong seemed frail, his face long and narrow with thin, gold-wire glasses perched on his nose, his wiry body clad in a thin white tank top, loose pajama shorts, and old house slippers. His complexion was more sallow, but other than a few more liver spots on his light brown skin, he was only slightly diminished from the image she always held in her mind.

"Hello, Ah-Gong," Katie said.

"Katie, come let me look at you," her ah-gong said in thick, accented Mandarin.

She dutifully sat next to him.

"They tell me you're here to film a movie?"

"Yes, Ah-Gong," she said. "We're starting in a few days. This is my friend, Pǔ Dàzhōng."

Katie spoke as formally and politely as she could, but it was so rare to use honorifics in Chinese that it sounded strange to her ears. Plus, it was odd saying Dae-jung's name in Chinese, and she was surprised she remembered it. But she was even more surprised when Dae-jung greeted her grandfather in very polite Mandarin.

"I'm very sorry my Chinese is not very good, but if you happen to know Japanese or English, I can speak those a bit better," Dae-jung said.

Katie did not appreciate the way Dae-jung's dark locks curled or the way his obsidian eyes sparkled kindly at her ah-gong as Dae-jung reached out to hold the old man's hands. It was unfair for a man to be so pretty. She unexpectedly choked up.

To her astonishment, her grandfather and Dae-jung conversed for a few minutes in rudimentary Japanese. After her brain caught up, it made sense. After all, the Japanese had occupied Taiwan, and her grandfather would have had to learn it in order to survive.

And Dae-jung? Well, Dae-jung had to learn snippets of several languages in the course of being an idol, and if she recalled correctly, he and Jae-sung had been responsible for Japanese. Plus, Akihiro was his bestie. Dae-jung had attempted Chinese, but his pronunciation was almost as bad as Woo-jin's, so he'd stuck to Japanese.

Katie spoke quietly with her big aunt as she waited for them to finish chatting and exhaust Dae-jung's limited Japanese.

"Baba," her auntie finally said, continuing in Taiwanese that Katie only sort of caught bits and pieces of.

"What are they saying?" asked Dae-jung.

Katie shrugged. "My parents only spoke Taiwanese when they didn't want us to understand them. I never really learned it, though I had every intention and opportunity when I lived here."

They discussed tentative plans for after dinner and waited patiently for her elders to finish their conversation.

"Kǎi Tíng-ah," her ah-gong said suddenly, his dark eyes intense. "I also refused to give your father money."

"What?" Katie replied, the wind knocked out of her.

"Your father asked me multiple times and eventually, so did your mother," said Ah-Gong. "I refused every time."

"I see," Katie said, reeling.

"You're a good daughter, Kǎi Tíng-ah." Her grandfather patted her knee twice.

"I—" Katie choked. She hadn't realized she'd needed her family's approval until she'd gotten it. "Thank you, Ah-Gong." Her throat closed and she couldn't say anything more.

"Ah, come on, Kǎi Tíng," her first aunt said. "Baba, we're going to be late for dinner. I'll bring Kǎi Tíng back to see you before she leaves tomorrow."

Katie jerkily hugged her grandfather in the most awkward and bony hug she'd ever experienced. On a whim, she whispered "I love you, Ah-Gong" in Taiwanese and kissed him on the cheek. He seemed taken aback but not upset.

She followed her aunt and Dae-jung out to the awaiting car, silently grateful for the space they gave her. Of course she'd known her father had asked her grandfather for money, but she'd never made the connection between her ah-gong's refusal with her own. Her grandfather didn't feel responsible for her father's death; perhaps she could let that weight go.

Dinner with Katie's aunties and uncles went well. They were polite and friendly and so was Dae-jung. He was lovely with her family and Katie's heart couldn't help but constrict at the sight of him trying so very hard with his English and the few Chinese phrases he remembered. Her small aunt also had learned Japanese, so they'd carried on a brief conversation. Katie answered the questions her elders peppered her with and ate everything they ordered for her until her stomach was near to bursting.

Katie's Kaohsiung cousins dropped by during dinner, the noise in the private dining room gradually increasing until she could barely think. Some of her younger cousins even volunteered to take her and Dae-jung to the night markets and the amusement park at the top of a big department store.

Dae-jung charmed them, too.

Somehow, Katie got conned into riding the Ferris wheel alone with Dae-jung and when he clapped in happiness at the view, her heart stuttered at how beautiful he looked under the faint lights of the city. The sight more than made up for her slight nausea due to sitting in the tiny, stuffy cabin.

She couldn't remember the last time she had so much fun.

Katie did not know why it filled her with such terror.

HALP!
> - Text from Ahn Mi-ran to Katie Wu, July 2026

If it has to do with Jae-sung's dick, I don't want to know.
> - Text from Katie Wu to Ahn Mi-ran, July 2026

You could have warned me.

>   - Text from Ahn Mi-ran to Katie Wu, July 2026

It's been over a year. How is this still a surprise?
>   - Text from Katie Wu to Ahn Mi-ran, July 2026

I think I love him. He's fucked my brains out and in its absence, my heart is now making decisions.
>   - Text from Ahn Mi-ran to Katie Wu, July 2026

Why are you telling me this? I'm not Jae-sung?
>   - Text from Katie Wu to Ahn Mi-ran, July 2026

WHAT DO I DO?
>   - Text from Ahn Mi-ran to Katie Wu, July 2026

TELL HIM. OBVIOUSLY HE LOVES YOU, TOO. IT'S BEEN A MOTHERFUCKING YEAR.
>   - Text from Katie Wu to Ahn Mi-ran, July 2026

Hmph. What's it like making out with not one but three super hot men for work? Ohohoh and are you going to tell Dae-jung you want him to fuck you six ways til Sunday?
>   - Text from Ahn Mi-ran to Katie Wu, July 2026

STOP DEFLECTING. GO DEAL WITH YOUR FEEL-
INGS. IF YOU'RE NOT GOING TO TAKE MY ADVICE,
GO ASK YOUR GOD AND STUFF.
                    - Text from Katie Wu to Ahn Mi-ran, July 2026

There's no need for yelling. Jesus. You sure you're okay with this?
(Also, you need to get laid. You're way too uptight.)
                    - Text from Ahn Mi-ran to Katie Wu, July 2026

I SET YOU TWO UP. I AM VERY HAPPY FOR YOU. GO
GET YOUR MANZ. (Also, no, I do not. I'm fine.)
                    - Text from Katie Wu to Ahn Mi-ran, July 2026

Right. You know who actually is fine? Park Dae-jung.
                    - Text from Ahn Mi-ran to Katie Wu, July 2026

HOW DARE YOU KEEP ME ON READ?
                    - Text from Ahn Mi-ran to Katie Wu, July 2026

Dae-jung couldn't quite put his finger on it, but Katie was different after her visit with her family—like some sort of freight had shifted. He'd figured it had something to do with what her grandfather had said to her, but he hadn't wanted to pry.

Except it wasn't just that.

Katie seemed a little distant—as if she'd pulled herself back from him. She wasn't cold or mean. She was still 99.9% the same. He couldn't pinpoint it exactly, which annoyed him.

It ate at the back of his mind when Dae-jung was running his lines with the translator. It poked at him when he saw Katie on set with Asian American actors Christopher Cheng and Kevin Gao, the men playing her other two love interests. It corroded whatever interactions he had with them—despite all her efforts to draw Dae-jung into their conversations.

Dae-jung was pretty certain he was the consummate professional with Chris and Kevin. He even really liked them and enjoyed his individual interactions with them for the most part. And yet, he keenly felt his Koreanness—an aspect of himself he'd never really thought of in relation to Katie except that she was so very not. He wondered if she'd felt the same years ago, like an outsider, despite all his members' efforts to the contrary.

Dae-jung wondered if Katie still felt the same, if Korea could ever be her home.

He did not know why it suddenly seemed so very important. He did not care to examine it.

"Dae-jung, do you want to come out to dinner with me, Chris, and Kevin?" Katie asked as she entered his trailer. She looked disdainfully at the mess of clothes and half-empty soda bottles. "I think it's omakase?"

Dae-jung set aside his phone. Katie peered at him, brow wrinkled in concern.

"Are you okay, Dae? You haven't seemed like yourself lately. Is the shoot getting to you?"

Dae-jung felt guilty for making Katie worry, as if she didn't have enough on her plate. Although he got the feeling that at least for this portion of the movie, she was in a much better place. He was relieved, of course. And yet, he also felt extraneous and adrift.

This was highly unlike him. He had to get a grip.

"I'm fine, Noona," he said, cracking his trademark boxy smile.

Katie considered him carefully. "How about we go to a pet cafe and take pictures of puppies instead? There's a new one in Ximending I overheard the staff discussing."

"What about Kevin and Chris?"

"They'll survive one night without me," Katie replied breezily. "I need a serotonin boost anyway, and they mostly annoy me."

"I thought you got along with them really well," Dae-jung blurted out.

Katie's eyes scrunched. "Yeah, they're great. But I miss you, Dae-dae."

"You see me every day," he protested.

Katie pouted and batted her eyelashes. "If you don't want to go, then just say so," she whined in pitch-perfect aegyo.

Dae-jung slipped into a genuine smile. "Alright, Noona," he said, his heart aching unexpectedly. "I'll go with you. But only because you begged so nicely."

Her eyes flashed something indecipherable. "You like when a person begs, huh?" Katie's voice dropped low and rough, and Dae-jung felt a kick in his gut. He wondered when she stopped ignoring sexual innuendo around him. Then her face switched to as greasy a look as possible and she waggled her brows. "Kinky," she teased, laughing at his expression.

Sometimes, Katie was incredibly aggravating. Dae-jung did not know why he was going with her after all.

"You seem happier here," Dae-jung said later, after rolling around on the tiled floor with several fluffy puppies. They were so cute.

Katie had nonstop squealed and giggled and made kissy faces at the puppies though she'd stayed clear of the kittens because she was allergic. It didn't stop her from gazing longingly at their tiny paws or clapping at their squeaky mewls.

"What's not to love about baby animals?" she answered.

"No, I mean filming in Taiwan. I'm glad."

"Mmmmmm," Katie acknowledged as she concentrated on the little black and tan dachshund in her hands and nuzzled its face, smooching it loudly.

Dae-jung figured Katie was letting the subject drop until she scooched next to him, a wiggly poodle mix in his lap.

"I never thanked you, Dae," Katie said as she leaned her head onto his shoulder. She smelled like oranges and the boba tea she'd been steadily sipping. "I didn't expect the filming in LA to take so much out of me. Thank you for being such an anchor."

Katie looped an arm through his and squeezed his bicep with her other hand. Dae-jung felt butterflies overtake his belly, fluttering about and making general nuisances of themselves.

"I couldn't have done it without you and I'm so grateful you're in this movie with me," she continued. "I know I was awful for most of your trip in the US. Hopefully, it's been better since we've gotten to Taipei."

Dae-jung kissed Katie softly on her temple, gratified at the way her eyes unfocused for a few seconds. "You're not awful, Noona. You're just going through a lot, and I'm happy to be here with you."

Katie blinked rapidly and tilted her face up, lips parted. For a moment, Dae-jung thought he could see straight into her heart.

"Oh, naughty puppy!" she scolded suddenly.

The black and tan dog she'd played with earlier had begun to pee on Katie and she helplessly winced as it continued to relieve itself on her. Dae-jung couldn't help but laugh even as he rued the timing.

"It is a pup-pee, Noona," Dae-jung jested.

"It really is! And that's terrible, Park Dae-jung. I don't deserve this!"

He tucked an errant lock behind her ear. "You're right. You only deserve good things, Noona," he said huskily.

Dae-jung moved aside as a staff member brought over pee pads and paper towels. Katie smiled graciously and waved off all apologies.

When Katie was mostly cleaned up, she collected her purse and they walked the few short blocks to her favorite shaved ice spot specializing in almond jello shaved ice. Now that the sun had set, Ximen was bustling with tourists. He heard so much Korean in passing that if he closed his eyes, he could almost think he was back in Seoul. Back home, he had his own go-to bingsu order of strawberry and matcha, but the Taiwanese shaved ice was still quite the treat—especially when Katie paid.

"You spoil me," Dae-jung commented as he shimmied happily in his seat. He liked the mango shaved ice in Dongmen better, but the almond jello, mung bean, and grass jelly toppings Katie recommended hit the spot all the same.

"What's the point of having a noona if they don't spoil you a bit, hmmm?" Katie crinkled her eyes and patted him on the arm, her hand lingering longer than necessary. "You ready to head back? We have an early call time tomorrow."

"Sure thing, Noona," Dae-jung replied, grabbing her hand and weaving his fingers between hers. He was pleased to note that she did not let go.

Dae-jung held her hand even as he felt her slight tremble.

He held Katie's hand the entire taxi ride back to The Floating Orchid, his thumb lightly stroking hers. He held her hand through the lobby, up the glass elevator ride, and as he walked her to her suite.

He held her hand even as she swiped the keycard to her suite, and since she didn't let go, he held her hand as he followed Katie into her quarters.

"Thanks for taking me out tonight, Noona," Dae-jung said, still holding onto Katie. "I guess I needed more cheering up than I'd thought."

"You know you can talk to me, right? I know I'm broken all to pieces, but I can still listen. I can still hold space for you."

Katie stared up at him, eyes dark and tender. He wanted to taste her.

"I know, Noona. I know," Dae-jung said as he stroked her cheek with his free hand.

Katie's eyes slowly drifted closed as she leaned into his touch, holding her breath. She was so, so beautiful.

Dae-jung made a decision.

He thumbed over her bottom lip and she gasped, eyes and mouth fluttering open. He kept his thumb heavy on her and held her molten gaze through hooded eyes, the two of them frozen on the cusp of desire.

And then, Katie slipped her tongue, all wet and hot against him, and the balance was tipped.

"You sure you want this?" he asked, his mouth a hair's breadth from hers. Dae-jung was so drunk on Katie he didn't even recall moving.

"I trust you to keep me safe," she breathed.

That was all the encouragement Dae-jung needed. Katie opened and he entered, leaving no crevice unplundered. He only knew the hint of almond jello and her familiar taste. And then, he knew just how soft and sweet Katie could be. He knew her whimpers and mewls and the difference between her falling apart on his tongue versus her falling apart on his cock.

Dae-jung knew, and when he woke beside Katie early the next morning, he knew he was in for ruin.

August 2026

CHOI EUN-SEONG: Nothing in this life is guaranteed, Vikki. *(Choi Eun-seong is holding both of Vikki Yu's hands.)* There is no perfect time, no perfect person. There is only now, only you and me.

VIKKI YU: Are you saying I'm not perfect? This is a terrible confession, Eun-seong. *(Vikki's lips tremble and her eyes are wet.)*

CHOI EUN-SEONG: I love you, Vikki. I have always loved you and I will always love you.

VIKKI YU: How do you know I won't hurt you again? That I won't run away? *(Tears stream down Vikki's face, fear and yearning warring over her features.)*

CHOI EUN-SEONG: I don't, but that's the risk I would take with anyone. So if I'm to risk my heart anyway, I'd rather risk it all on you.

    - Scene excerpt, "Landslide" (SB Entertainment)

Katie knew she was being stupid and yet, she could not stop. Fucking Dae-jung was a Bad Idea except it had been so long—so very long since a man had fucked her. Once she'd gotten a taste, she was not strong enough to quit.

She knew, too, that she was falling—and falling hard.

Though Dae-jung had known she hadn't slept with anyone since Jae-sung, he hadn't quite made the connection that it wasn't just because her head had been a mess after the breakup. She fundamentally could not fuck without catching feelings. Except if Katie was honest with herself, she knew her feelings had been caught long before.

Dae-jung was the brightest part of her days.

Katie was so very selfish and stupid.

She was imprudent every moment of her grueling schedule. Witless when the sparks between them were visceral manifestations captured on film for everyone to witness.

Katie was convinced Dae-jung knew just how gone she was for him. How could he not when he consumed all of her waking thoughts and likely all her sleeping ones, too?

Even after filming moved to Seoul and Katie's rooms were no longer down the hall from him, she and Dae-jung spent almost every free moment together, oblivious to anyone and anything outside the fragile bubble of happiness she constantly inhabited.

And yet, Dae-jung never took advantage of the fact that he knew her body and all its tells, always careful to follow the intimacy coach's detailed blocking. His hands and eyes never wandered. He never overstepped within the bounds of their working moments.

Katie knew that though she was so incredibly foolish, her heart would always be safe with Park Dae-jung.

It never once occurred to her that perhaps she was so very, very wrong.

September 2026

They say do not go gentle into that good night
To rage, rage against the dying of the light

But I could do with a little more gentleness
With a little more serenity than fight
I am so tired
So very tired
To say I haven't earned my rest—whose right
To judge my sorrows, however slight
- Draft lyrics from Katie Wu to Hwang Woo-jin, September
2026

Audio_clip_03_260831.wav sent
Audio_clip_09_260807.wav sent
Audio_clip_21_260816.wav sent
Audio_clip_01_260824.wav sent
Audio_clip_04_260903.wav sent
Audio_clip_13_260905.wav sent
 - Audio files from Katie Wu to Hwang Woo-jin, September
2026

I thought our time had passed
No longer chiasmatic
Now anaphasic
Cleaving into cytokinesis
You were once my nucleus
But now we are two

Yet perhaps instead
You were my sine
And I your cosine

And this phase was just a tangent
And we were too young
Too obtuse
- "The Science of Love," from Katie Wu to Hwang Woo-jin,
September 2026

All love songs are the same
Gone the way of happy families
Like how every song of heartbreak thinks
Their unhappiness smashes the mold

Alas, the analogy eventually folds
Tolstoy cannot be universally applied
They are all the same
And mine is no different

As before, and so it will repeat
I loved you
I love you, will love you
And when it ends, it will not be neat

Yet, convince me your eyes are not the kindest
Tell me your mouth's not the sweetest
At turns, filthiest, most beguiling
You fill in all my cracks and I yours

How can you and I not hold?
- "Anna Karenina," from Katie Wu to Hwang Woo-jin, September 2026

Are you okay?
      - Text from Hwang Woo-jin to Katie Wu, September 2026

"What are you doing, Dae-jung?" Ye-jun asked on a rare night all seven of them had convened for Korean fried chicken and beer in Woo-jin's dining room.

Dae-jung raised a brow and waved absently at his chimaek. "Eating?"

"Don't play dumb," Ye-jun retorted, his voice uncharacteristically serious. "Why am I hearing from all sorts of my actor friends that you and Katie are dating?"

"Uh," was all Dae-jung's unhelpful brain supplied.

"Well? Are you and Katie dating?"

All of a sudden, Dae-jung did not find the dinner quite as friendly. He especially resisted the urge to glance at Jae-sung. Dae-jung would not be able to bear the disappointment on his leader's face.

"I wouldn't say we're dating, Hyung," Dae-jung mumbled into his chicken wing.

Ye-jun scoffed. "Don't tell me you're doing some sort of method acting? Staying in character for the sake of the show?"

"Ah, Ye-jun-ah," Woo-jin interjected. "It's none of our business. They're both adults."

"Like hell it's none of my business," Ye-jun scowled. "And how dare you not call me hyung? Do you know how much shit Mina noona is going to give me if he hurts Katie?"

"First of all, Ye-jun, it's been fifteen years. This 'early '92' business is not going to happen. I don't care if we were in the Joseon period or whatever where you'd be my hyung because of your January birthday—we're both '92s, so fuck off," Woo-jin challenged. "Second of all, your wife is always giving you shit."

Dae-jung wanted to sink into the floor. This was not how he wanted his members to find out. In fact, he had never intended for his bandmates to find out—especially Jae-sung, who was suspiciously quiet.

"That's not fair, Hyung," Dae-jung responded quietly. "I'm sure she could hurt me just as easily."

Ye-jun would not be deterred. "You do know you're the first person Katie's been with since—"

"Ye-jun!" shouted Woo-jin. "I think we're all getting a little too heated. I'd like to reiterate that it's none of our fucking business."

Dae-jung felt like shit. "I'm not taking advantage of her, Hyung. No matter what you may all think."

"No one thinks that," Akihiro said loyally. He leaned across the dining table to squeeze Dae-jung's forearm. Thank goodness for Akihiro.

Dae-jung caught a glimpse of Soo-min's face, which told him everything. He was a coward for refusing to look at Jae-sung, like the worst sort of betrayer. He wouldn't be able to bear it.

"We're just worried you might get hurt, Dae-jung-ah," said Do-won kindly. "Noona is—well, Noona can be a lot."

"What's that supposed to mean, Hyung?"

Guilt flashed across Do-won's face. "I just—I just don't want us to be fighting about Noona again."

"I don't recall there being any fighting about Katie," said Jae-sung suddenly, his beer mid lift.

Now that Dae-jung had finally looked at his leader, Jae-sung's face was perfectly bland. Dae-jung's spirits sank even further. It was the face Jae-sung put on for particularly contentious interviews. Jae-sung was pissed.

"Well, obviously you weren't included, Hyung," Do-won retorted, irritation prominent on his normally happy face. "And I'm telling you, it was shitty to go through—not only because you were having a hard time, but because all of us were. You lost a girlfriend and we lost a friend, and we didn't know how to deal with our warring loyalties."

Jae-sung sucked in his cheeks. "I didn't realize I had caused such difficulty for all of you."

"Well you did," confirmed Ye-jun brusquely. "If you'd thought about it for any amount of time, you would have figured it out. And Dae-jung was there! He knows firsthand!"

"Ye-jun," Woo-jin repeated, this time laying a solid hand on their eldest member's thigh. "Come on, let's go on a walk."

"I don't—"

"It wasn't a request, Ye-jun," Woo-jin stated.

"You're on the 33rd floor!" Ye-jun protested, but Woo-jin was undeterred.

Woo-jin dragged Ye-jun out of his chair. "Ye-jun-ah, you're not helping. Come on, now. Let's take a breather and you can tell me all about Soo-hwan and Soo-mi and how they're smarter than all the other babies in the world."

Ye-jun's response was lost to the other room and Dae-jung suddenly wished Woo-jin had drawn him away instead. The dining area was stifling.

"Was that the purpose of the team dinner? Some sort of intervention?" Dae-jung was furious. He was ashamed.

"No, Dae-jung," insisted Akihiro, his kind eyes distressed. "We would never."

"So it's just a coincidence? Is there a separate group chat where I'm not included? Or maybe both Jae-sung hyung and I are excluded this time?"

The misery on Akihiro's face was all Dae-jung needed for confirmation.

"Do you love her?" Soo-min asked, finally participating in the discussion, and Dae-jung didn't know what to make of it.

"Of course I love her. We all love her. You know this, Soo-min," Dae-jung answered irritably.

Soo-min shook his head. "No, Hyung. I mean, do you *love* her?"

Dae-jung ran an exasperated hand through his hair. "Seems a bit early for that, no? We're just having a bit of fun—all that chemistry we're building on set has to go somewhere. Why not with me?" he answered. "She knows I'm safe—that I would never hurt her."

Soo-min merely stared at him mournfully and remained silent.

"It doesn't have to be more serious than that," Dae-jung insisted. "Not that I have to justify myself to any of you. Co-stars have romances all the time. We're professionals."

"We know, Dae-dae," assuaged Akihiro. "How is filming going? Is it like when you filmed 'Memories of Moonlight' or 'Love's Eternal Melody'?" he added in an obvious pivot.

Dae-jung shot Akihiro a muted smile, grateful yet annoyed that he was grateful. He allowed the conversation to shift, mostly because he was starting to feel backed in a corner and he hated how defensive he felt. This was exactly why he hadn't mentioned Katie to any of his bandmates. This was why he barely thought beyond the next moment with her.

He could not parse through all his myriad feelings; better to let sleeping dogs lie.

He was a hypocrite.

"Noona," Dae-jung panted above Katie, his palm heavy on her head. "Fuck, I'm gonna miss your fucking mouth."

Katie pulled off his cock with a pop. "Wait, what?"

Shit.

"Noona, I—I didn't mean that the way it sounded," Dae-jung scrambled. Granted, there wasn't much blood going to his brain so he could be forgiven for his lack of articulation.

Katie stood from her place at the foot of his sofa chair and wiped her mouth. She slipped back into the cocktail dress she'd discarded on his bedroom floor earlier. She wrapped her arms around themselves as if she was cold.

"How did you mean it then? Are you going on a trip?" she asked quietly.

Dae-jung tugged his boxer briefs back on and tucked himself back in. He was glad for the rumpled button-down and loosened tie Katie never got around to removing. He, too, wiped the corners of his mouth. Funny how just moments ago, he was drooling over the sight of Katie on her knees and now, his mouth was all dried up.

"I—" He shut his mouth—something he should have done mere minutes ago. "No, Noona. I'm not going on a trip."

Katie seemed to dim in front of his eyes. Gone was the hazy desire and joyful celebration present from the wrap party earlier that evening.

"It's been fun, hasn't it, Noona?" Dae-jung said lightly, running his hand through his hair.

Katie did not speak, content to wait him out like a hunter waiting for a trap to be sprung.

He swallowed hard. He forced himself to look Katie in the eyes. "You don't need me to be a safe place to deal with all that built-up sexual tension on set anymore, right?"

She flinched ever so minutely. He would've missed it had he not been watching her so intently. Had he read the situation all wrong? He was usually better than this.

"Ah," Katie exhaled faintly.

"That's what you'd intended, right? Like it was with Jae-sung hyung—I was hot, available, and asked?"

Dae-jung wanted to cringe at how crass that had sounded, but what could he do? Wasn't that what it was? All it had been? He hurriedly continued. "But now that shooting's over, you're probably leaving Korea, right? To go back to your life in America?"

Katie nodded feebly. "Right," she murmured.

"I normally don't go for friends with benefits situations—I'm such a romantic that I tend to blow them up into more than they are. No problem with one-night stands, though—isn't that weird?"

Dae-jung was babbling. He did not know why he was babbling. Likely because Katie was so quiet he was desperate to fill in the spaces.

"Except in your case, I wasn't worried at all! Not that you're not lovable—you're very lovable, Noona. I'm just nothing like Jae-sung hyung and I could never betray him—and the members don't really approve of us, and I just..." He finally tapered off his rambling.

Dae-jung wasn't even quite sure what he'd said. If he was honest, it was closer to word vomit than an actual conversation.

"Noona, please say something."

"Your members don't approve?" Katie whispered, holding trembling fingers to her swollen lips. "I—I suppose they wouldn't. I don't want to cause trouble between you and your bandmates—especially Jae-sung."

"Well, it was always going to be short-term, Noona. They were worried you'd break my heart, and that I'd hurt you, too—especially Jun hyung—but they didn't understand. Please don't worry about it," Dae-jung assured. He didn't like the expression on Katie's face. "I was glad to help you out."

Katie cleared her throat. "I appreciate your kindness, Dae-jung-ah," she rasped.

"Of course, Noona. I love you."

The corner of Katie's mouth lifted as she huffed a small laugh. "Yeah. I love you, too, Dae-jung." She smoothed out her blue dress and inhaled deeply, then exhaled slowly. "I, uh, I just realized that amidst wrapping the shoot and the party, I completely forgot to pack for my trip home."

Dae-jung's face fell. "Noona?"

Katie backtracked through his penthouse, gathering her things with great alacrity. He followed her and before Dae-jung registered what she was doing, she'd already slipped on her heels by his front door.

"Noona—did I—"

"Take care of yourself, Dae-jung," Katie interrupted tenderly. "I'll be seeing you—if not soon, then at the press junket and premiere for whenever they release the movie."

He tried to hug her goodbye but by the time he'd moved, Katie was already gone. Dae-jung could not help but think that his evening had ended drastically differently than he'd imagined.

He wasn't stupid. His noonchi, that preternatural Korean ability to read a room, was top-notch. He could tell he'd hurt Katie with his ill-timed slip. Except when Dae-jung objectively examined the past few weeks, he knew their situationship had run its course.

It didn't matter how desperately Dae-jung wanted to beg Katie to stay, to give him a shot at something real. Guilt lanced through him, his mind flashing to Ye-jun's disappointment, Do-won's blistering warning, and Jae-sung's hidden fury.

It was kinder to let Katie go. Dae-jung knew himself to be a fool.

But I was, all of me, deceived
Willfully complicit
I should have known
Did I not speak it unto existence?
There was another
And they were not me
- Draft lyrics, September 2026

Who hurt you more:
○ *I'll Smile Even If It Hurts - Ladies' Code*
○ *Drive You Home - Jackson Wang*

                        - Katie Wu, X, September 2026

While we're at it:
○ *Don't Speak - No Doubt*
○ *Cool - Gwen Stefani*

                        - Katie Wu, X, September 2026

Last one, I promise:
○ *A Rush of Blood to the Head - Coldplay*
○ *The Scientist - Coldplay*

                        - Katie Wu, X, September 2026

I lied:
○ *Stay - DOYEN*
○ *Yuki-onna - Kitahara Akihiro*

                        - Katie Wu, X, September 2026

Mei, you okay? If that pretty boy hurt you, I will end him.
   - Text from Alton Kuang to Katie Wu, September 2026

"Babe, is everything okay?" Jae-sung heard Mi-ran ask in English.

"What?" he mumbled, a little disoriented, thinking she was speaking to him.

At Mi-ran's irritated shushing, Jae-sung woke up a little more. He did not remember falling asleep in his bed, but he supposed he wasn't as young as he used to be and Mi-ran had worn him out.

"Honey, slow down. I can't understand what you're—" Mi-ran stopped speaking. "HE WHAT?"

Jae-sung shot Mi-ran a concerned look, but she just glared at him as if he just told her god was an old white man.

"Oh, Katie," she said compassionately. "Please don't do anything drastic. I'll be right over."

"Katie?" Jae-sung mouthed.

Mi-ran summarily ignored him even more. He couldn't decide whether that was aggravating or hot. His dick twitched and he settled on both. He really was a simple man when it came to Mi-ran.

Then, his brain finally caught up. Was Katie okay? Why would she feel the need to do something drastic? Was she spiraling again?

Jae-sung found himself breaking out into a cold sweat, his stomach filled with dread. He abruptly sat up in bed.

Mi-ran ended the call and before he had a chance to say anything, she whirled on him and poked him in the chest. "What. Did. You. Do?"

"What?" he asked as he held up his hands.

"What did you guys say to Dae-jung?"

"I—uh, I mean, we say a lot of things to Dae-jung?" he stumbled.

Mi-ran narrowed her eyes at him. "Wrong answer, Park Jae-sung."

"What happened?"

"I couldn't really understand much from Katie's incoherent sobbing, but from what I gathered, Dae-jung dumped her mid-fellating—"

"I did not need to know that detail—"

"I don't fucking care—that's pertinent and exceedingly shitty—and went on some rant about how he could never love her and that he could never betray you and that you and your members don't approve of her or whatever—"

Jae-sung startled at that and whatever flickered on his face was enough to convince Mi-ran.

"You fucking asshole." Mi-ran threw off the covers as she got out of bed and pulled on a hoodie draped over a nearby chair.

"Wait—wait a second—I don't know that we said all *that*, Mi-ran. Give me *some* credit."

"Do you still love her, Oppa?" Mi-ran's voice belied her calm demeanor. "I can handle it if you are."

"No, baby," Jae-sung replied immediately. "I love you."

She held his gaze and he almost lost himself. "They're not mutually exclusive."

"I don't. Not in that way anymore, and not for a long time," he insisted.

Mi-ran sucked in a deep breath and exhaled slowly. "Alright. I've gotta go. I've already wasted enough time as it is."

"I'm going with you," he said, getting out of bed.

"No. Absolutely not."

"What if Katie's hurt herself by the time you get there? What if you need to call Alton or the company?" Jae-sung stopped. He did not need to work himself up even more.

"I would probably call the hospital first, Oppa," Mi-ran replied.

"Right, right," he agreed inanely. "Either way, someone would need to notify the company."

Mi-ran regarded him carefully. "I need you to be brutally honest with yourself right now. Katie is in a bad way and we don't know how badly. If you're going to be triggered into a spiral of your own, you need to stay home." She caressed his cheek gently. "I cannot take care of you both."

"I'll be fine. I've dealt with it." And as if Jae-sung could ever cajole Mi-ran into going against her better judgment, he added, "I promise."

"Okay, Oppa. I trust you."

Jae-sung didn't believe in any gods, but he still prayed that Katie was safe, that she'd found enough comfort to hold her over until they arrived. He wouldn't be too late again. Jae-sung rebuked any timeline that made it so.

Chapter 9

September 2026

Sometimes, I wonder if I deserve a happy ending. If I'm honest with myself, I don't even know what that would look like. I feel broken, like I'm just earthenware shattered into pieces.

If someone tries to comfort me with the Japanese art of kintsugi—like every mediocre white Christian megachurch pastor appropriating an East Asian culture for their own image of Jesus—I will vomit. I don't want to be patched up, gilded over with pretty platitudes. I want to be someone else entirely. I want to disappear.

I want to be obliterated, no longer shards, but fine dust, scattered in the wind.
- "Telling a Truth Is a Slippery Slope" (Red Lantern Publishing House, October 2023)

Jae-sung didn't know what he expected when he and Mi-ran entered Alton's penthouse, but Katie calmly sipping a steaming cup of tea in her kitchen was not it.

"Katie, are you okay?" he asked gently as he sat at her wooden table.

Katie's eyes were red-rimmed and puffy as she flicked her gaze to his. "I've been better, but I'll be okay," she reassured.

He was not reassured. Jae-sung knew more than anyone just how good Katie was at acting. "You don't have to pretend for me," he said.

A snarl throttled in her throat. "And you don't have to pretend to feel bad for me, Jae-sung. I know you don't approve."

Jae-sung was silent. He supposed he deserved that.

"Unnie," Mi-ran interjected with a soft hand on Katie's, "I'm so sorry."

Katie nodded at Mi-ran and resumed sipping her tea sullenly.

Jae-sung was still stuck on Mi-ran calling Katie "unnie." The two of them usually forwent honorifics, content to live in a faux-American bubble of informality, and it was odd for this bit of real Korean life to slip in.

Jae-sung did not know why he found it strange. What did that say about him? Did he think of Katie and Mi-ran as foreigners? As people who did not belong, despite Mi-ran being born and raised in South Korea? Or was it more that it was unexpected and hammered in the gravity of the situation? He felt ashamed and uncomfortable. He did not like it.

What was he even doing here? Mi-ran had been right to object to his presence.

"It's not that I disapprove, Katie," he started as Mi-ran cut him a glance that was full of disbelief. "More that I was caught off guard. I didn't know what to say to Dae-jung, and so I said nothing."

Jae-sung watched as Katie pulled in on herself and shrank. He felt a strange pricking behind his eyes.

"And now that you're not surprised?" Katie asked.

"Dae-jung was my biggest supporter when you came back to Korea—not that the others didn't support me. I don't even know how to explain it." He sighed and examined his fingers a bit before he continued. "He just wasn't the hyungs or Soo-min, okay?"

Katie nodded in understanding. "They gave me a lot of shit about you, Jae-sung. They were on your side, too."

Jae-sung's throat tightened, that stinging feeling increasing in his eyes. He swallowed. "I loved you for a long time, Katie. Even when we were over—even after you came back."

"Oh," Katie replied. "I'm sorry."

He was terrified of meeting Mi-ran's eyes to see how she was taking this—but he had to continue. Katie and Dae-jung deserved to hear him say it. Maybe Mi-ran did, too.

Mi-ran reached out and squeezed his hand. His heart filled with gratefulness even as tears spilled over onto his cheeks.

"Dae-jung was so kind and gracious. He didn't lie to me or tell me I was right for treating you the way I had. He didn't make excuses for me. He just listened and let me be a person. He made sure I knew I was loved, that I was human." Jae-sung took a deep, steadying breath. "So when I found out about you two—I guess I felt a little betrayed? But then, I felt immediate guilt. We had both moved on, and you both were consenting adults. What business was it of mine?"

"I'm sorry," Katie whispered again.

"You have nothing to be sorry for though, Katie," Jae-sung insisted. "Like, why wouldn't you want to be with Dae-jung? He's beautiful, kind, and so lovable. And why wouldn't he want to be with you? You're who I dreamed of until I got a new dream."

Katie sniffled and then scowled. Jae-sung thought she was adorable.

"He thought I was using him—and maybe I was," Katie said finally. "Maybe I'm no good for him. I'm no good for anyone."

"Unnie," Mi-ran said again, gently. "No good can come from this line of thinking. We can't convince you otherwise if you don't believe it, and you will only make yourself feel worse."

Katie just shrugged. "I'm heading to Singapore tomorrow," she said instead, changing the subject.

"I thought you were going to stay in Korea for a bit," Mi-ran said. "Weren't you looking at apartments?"

"It was a stupid idea," Katie murmured.

"You could just talk to him," Jae-sung said.

"And say what, Jae-sung? Sorry I made you feel like I was using you? Please don't leave me? I'm a wreck and ruin everything I touch but take a chance on me anyway?" Katie's voice was like shattered glass. Jae-sung's heart wanted to break.

"Yes," he replied. "Say that. Be honest for once, Katie."

Katie flinched.

"Oppa," Mi-ran said with unconcealed censure.

"I still have to work with him on the soundtrack and for all the press and promotions for the movie," Katie said.

"What does that have to do with anything?"

Katie rolled her eyes. "It has to do with everything! Dae-jung thought I just needed a safe and warm body for sex—and he offered under those circumstances. He doesn't want anything more than that, otherwise he would have offered. If I talk to him about this, it will just make things weirder, and I really don't want to do that."

"Dae doesn't do friends with benefits," Jae-sung argued. "And it's already weird."

"So he told me. But he said it was surprisingly easy with me and also has no problem with one-night stands. What does that tell you, Jae-sung?"

"That he has feelings for you, Katie," Jae-sung retorted. "I don't know why that's so hard for you to get."

"It means he sees me as a one-night stand—just strung out over a period of time," she returned, voice raising. "It was easy because he knew there was a defined beginning and end! There are no complications."

"That's some deft mental gymnastics, Katie. Use your brain for something other than strawman excuses to protect yourself from fabricated realities."

It wasn't until Mi-ran put a hand on his knee that Jae-sung realized he was breathing hard. That perhaps he was way out of line.

"I'm sorry, Katie," he said. "I'm not helping."

"It's what I deserve," Katie mumbled.

"You deserve grace," Mi-ran interjected. "You deserve love, compassion, and honesty. I might not agree with how Oppa delivered the information, but I think there's a lot going on that you're willfully not seeing."

"You're biased. You and Jae-sung are basically married," Katie grumbled.

Jae-sung's breath hitched. He hated how Katie could still render him into nothing with a few well-placed words.

Mi-ran replied with grace and aplomb. He was struck again by just how much he loved her.

"We're all biased, babe. It's the human condition, after all. But just because we're biased doesn't mean we are not also correct. Or at least, closer to the mark than you are." Mi-ran smiled sadly as she got up. "We love you, Katie. You're good and worthy even if you don't believe it at the moment." She hugged Katie from behind and kissed her hair. "Do you want us to stay?"

Katie shook her head. "I'm fine, really. I appreciate you both coming over."

"Don't be a stranger."

"I won't."

Katie got up from her seat and walked Mi-ran and Jae-sung to the front door where she wrapped herself tightly around his girlfriend. "Thank you, Mi-ran," she whispered wetly. Then she turned to Jae-sung and hugged him as well. "I love you, Jae. I'm so lucky to have you in my life again."

Before he knew it, they were ushered out the door and in Mi-ran's car.

"Well, that went better than expected," he said, trying to cut the tension.

"Yeah, it did." Mi-ran smirked as she started the car. "You got a new dream, huh?"

Jae-sung refused to be embarrassed. "Yeah, I do."

"Who are they?" she teased. "Anyone I know?"

He debated teasing back but then decided that it was too important. Mi-ran was too important.

"It's you, Ahn Mi-ran. It will always be you."

Mi-ran's features softened and she grinned. "Don't you forget it, Park Jae-sung. You're my dream, too, and I don't give up what's mine."

Jae-sung reached for Mi-ran's hand over the console and drew it into his lap. One day, maybe one day very soon, her ring finger would be occupied real estate. He could not wait.

Has Katie Wu ditched Dae-jung of DOYEN for his bandmate Lambent? Former labelmates Lambent and Katie were seen exiting a private jet together and looking cozy in Singapore.
                                        - Allkpop, September 2026

Lambent of DOYEN and Katie Wu seen socializing with Empyrean Group heir Alton Kuang around Singapore hotspots. Kuang and Katie are longtime family friends. Could Katie be seeking his approval of Lambent?
                                        - Netizen Buzz, September 2026

It's not what it looks like, Dae-jung.
        - Text from Hwang Woo-jin to Park Dae-jung, September 2026

*I certainly hope it is—you both should have all the fun together!
I give you both my blessings!*
    - Text from Park Dae-jung to Hwang Woo-jin, September
2026

You are such an idiot.
    - Text from Hwang Woo-jin to Park Dae-jung, September
2026

I love you, too, Hyung!
    - Text from Park Dae-jung to Hwang Woo-jin, September
2026

Dae-jung had never been a jealous sort, and he was not about to make an exception this time. Katie and he had been a strictly temporary solution to the temporary quandary of riled up hormones and sexual tension. That was it.

What did he care that all his friends kept sending him links and pictures of Katie leaning into the crook of Woo-jin's arm or him kissing her on the forehead? What was it to him if she was in Singapore when he'd thought she was heading back to Los Angeles? What did it matter that he'd meant so little, that any hot, available, and forward DOYEN member would do?

Maybe Soo-min would be next.

Woo-jin's overly cautious texts were unnecessary, unwanted, and unbelievable.

Dae-jung had seen it coming, right? Hadn't he imagined her with Woo-jin hundreds of times? Hadn't he assumed the two of them would be perfect together? They were closer in age, super tsundere, had similar interests, and were ridiculously talented. How could Dae-jung have possibly been more than a fleeting stop gap?

So, no. Dae-jung wasn't jealous. Friends didn't get jealous of each other's happiness—and dammit if Katie didn't seem happy.

"Are you okay, Dae?"

Dae-jung jerked his head up as Jae-sung's deep voice interrupted his brooding—not that Dae-jung had been brooding. Nope.

"Yeah," Dae-jung replied unconvincingly.

"I thought I would find you here," Jae-sung said amiably as he entered the rooftop garden, an iced Americano in one hand and a lemonade in the other. It was Dae-jung's favorite spot at the SB Entertainment headquarters and he often stole away to the semi-hidden enclave to decompress.

He resisted the urge to scream. "Well, you found me."

Jae-sung peered at him closely before handing him the lemonade. "You sure you're okay? You haven't been answering any of our texts."

Damn his members and their overly concerned reactions. Dae-jung sipped the drink, pleased to note it was his favorite kind: lemonade with added passionfruit syrup. He loved sweet drinks.

"I haven't been answering anyone's texts," he said. "Everyone keeps sending me pictures of Hyung and Noona, asking if I'm okay."

Jae-sung's eyes were far too understanding. "Can I sit here?" he asked and then sat next to Dae-jung on his favorite wooden bench. After Dae-jung's permission, Jae-sung asked again. "Well, are you?"

Dae-jung didn't deserve any of his sympathy—or was it empathy? Either. Neither. Both. He could never keep them straight.

"Yes."

"Okay," said Jae-sung.

Dae-jung eyed his leader suspiciously. "That's it? That's all you have to say?"

"Uh, yes?" sputtered Jae-sung. "Unless you're, um, not actually fine?"

"I'm fine. Finer than fine. The finest, in fact."

Jae-sung failed at suppressing a grin. "I can see that."

Dae-jung didn't think it was funny and suddenly, an ugly thought wormed its way into his mind and out his mouth. "I bet you think this is hilarious, huh?"

Jae-sung seemed a bit taken aback. "No? I mean sort of? I am not sure exactly what you mean?"

"I bet you think it's exactly as I deserve—that Noona did exactly what you and the other members thought she would." Dae-jung could not keep the bitterness from his voice.

Jae-sung's eyes widened a fraction as his face fell. "Oh, Dae-jung. Have I hurt you so terribly that you'd think I want you to be miserable?"

"I'm sorry I slept with Noona," Dae-jung blurted out. "I didn't mean to betray you, Hyung. I was just so lonely, and she was just so sad."

Jae-sung sank into the spot next to Dae-jung. "You didn't stab me in the back, Dae-jung," he said, loudly slurping his iced Americano that was more ice than coffee. "I'm sorry I made you feel that way."

"But you are her ex—"

"So? It's been like five years. Katie and I are adults. We've clearly both moved on. And why wouldn't Katie want to be with you? Your soul shines so bright, Dae-jung. You are easy to love."

Whatever unsettled feeling that had slightly dissipated after Jae-sung absolved him of any guilt vanished as soon as Jae-sung said "easy to love."

"It wasn't like that, Hyung."

"You're telling me Katie doesn't love you?"

Dae-jung sighed. "Not like *that*, she doesn't."

"And why would that bother you?" Jae-sung persisted.

"It doesn't," replied Dae-jung.

"Then why are you so upset about the pictures?"

Dae-jung pouted. "Didn't I just say I was fine?"

Jae-sung wrapped a heavy arm around Dae-jung's shoulders. "Katie is easy to love," he commiserated.

Dae-jung could not help but think of Woo-jin and his similar sentiments on the flight to Los Angeles all those months ago. If only he had taken his hyung more seriously. Hubris always had a cost.

"You stopped eventually, though," insisted Dae-jung, still feeling prickly. "I know you still loved her—even after everything that happened. Why didn't you chase after her, Hyung?"

Dae-jung felt Jae-sung shift his body in discomfort. The petty part of him rejoiced that he was not the only one feeling awkward and out of sorts.

"Sometimes, sometimes, Katie would open just a little bit and I could see straight into her—and her heart. Her heart was so beautiful," Jae-sung started, his voice husky and wistful. "Those glimpses were enough to keep me going. But in the end, I don't know that it would have been enough."

Dae-jung let Jae-sung's words seep into his being and become his own. He, too, knew what it was like to see into Katie's depths during those rare moments she bloomed. He did not know if it was enough to carry him from slightly north of platonic—he could admit that, right?—into the territory of true love. He wanted true love. Had always craved it.

Maybe Katie could be it?

"I think I made a mistake, Hyung," Dae-jung admitted.

To his credit, Jae-sung didn't rub it in. "Then apologize and see if it can be made right."

"But what about Woo-jin hyung?"

His leader rolled his eyes. "You know Hyung is dating Alton, right? Katie went as a distraction."

"Why would any reporter think Hyung and Alton were dating?" wondered Dae-jung. "The media is very heteronormative—it's totally worked in our favor."

"Perhaps Alton is also petty and wanted you to think a certain direction."

Dae-jung shuddered involuntarily. "Alton's terrifying."

"Don't I know it," agreed Jae-sung.

"What if it's too late?" Dae-jung chewed his bottom lip. "And are you sure you're okay with this, Hyung?"

"Life isn't a scripted movie, Dae-jung. If you love her, you don't need my permission."

"I don't know if it's love yet, Hyung."

"Well, whatever it is, Katie doesn't belong to me; she belongs to herself. And if she's willing to open her heart to you—to give it to you because you're safe and not because you're the safe choice—that means Katie trusts you to keep her heart safe," replied Jae-sung. "If she's willing to open herself to you all the time, you'd be stupid to let her go. You would regret it for the rest of your life."

"You wouldn't hate me?"

Jae-sung raised an incredulous brow. "For what possible reason?"

"If Katie noona trusted me and not you to keep her heart safe, I mean," Dae-jung clarified. It sounded ridiculous when he said it out loud.

Jae-sung sighed. "I won't lie to you, Dae. Part of me—that ego we all have inside of us—is a little like, 'Why not me?'"

Dae-jung cast his eyes to the floor. He forced himself not to be upset.

"Except, I don't know that I was ready for who Katie was at the time. I remember so many tiny instances where she tried to tell me or at least give me hints, but each time, I just said something trite that missed the mark entirely," continued Jae-sung. "Maybe I would be worthy of it now, but I'm not interested in being her person anymore—and I don't think she's interested in having me be that, either."

"Is it only because you have Mi-ran?"

Jae-sung paused, picking up a fallen leaf and fiddling with it. "You know, for the longest time after Katie left, I thought I must be a monster—I must have been so horrible that Katie had to pull a full-on disappearing act to get rid of me." The rapper's voice wobbled. "I thought no one would ever love me again."

"I'm sorry, Hyung," Dae-jung said softly.

The older man shrugged. "'I'm not saying I don't still feel that way sometimes, but with Mi-ran, I feel settled. I feel sure."

"I'm glad," Dae-jung said, feeling a little lost.

"Anyway, I don't know how to answer your question because I can't live another life where I don't have Mi-ran in my life to compare. I can only tell you that now, in this life, I am not, nor will I be, mad at you for pursuing a relationship with Katie."

"Oh," mumbled Dae-jung.

"Besides, who cares if I did get mad about it? It's none of my business and you deserve to live your life however you see fit," added Jae-sung. "I do, however, reserve the right to be mad at you about other things." The older man giggled as he winked saucily at Dae-jung.

Dae-jung's mouth lifted in the corner. "Thanks, Hyung."

"Think nothing of it."

"I gotta go catch a plane to Singapore," said Dae-jung.

Jae-sung gawped. "Oh, shit, really?"

"Nah, I'm just kidding," Dae-jung laughed, "but you've given me a lot to think about."

"Anytime, Dae-jung." Jae-sung reached over and embraced him tightly. "You're my brother, and I love you."

Suddenly, Dae-jung had a thought. "Actually, hold on a second. I have something for you but it's in Woo-jin hyung's studio."

"Why is it in Hyung's studio?" Jae-sung asked as they both got up and started walking toward the elevator bank.

"I just figured it would be the last place you'd consider snooping."

They chatted about random things until they got to Woo-jin's studio and Dae-jung let himself in.

"I don't see why Hyung bothers having a keycode since we all know it anyway," commented Dae-jung.

"Well, not all of us take advantage of it quite like you do, Dae," chuckled Jae-sung.

Dae-jung hoped the bag was still where he put it last and opened the various drawers of Woo-jin's desk until he saw the familiar packaging. He gently lifted the slightly crushed gift bag out and handed it to Jae-sung.

"This is from Noona," he said. "She asked me to give it to you when the timing was right. I think the timing is right."

Jae-sung crinkled open the bag and removed a rich brown knitted scarf with orange-gold accents.

"Oh," murmured Jae-sung as he unfolded the accessory to its full length. "There's a bonsai tree on either end."

"Yeah, Noona handmade these for us. We each have one."

"How come I've never seen them?" asked Jae-sung.

Dae-jung shifted uncomfortably. "We try not to wear them around you—in case you asked questions."

"Ah. I really have made it hard on you all these past years, haven't I?"

"Nothing we weren't willing to bear, Hyung," replied Dae-jung.

Jae-sung's eyes filled as he stroked the material tenderly. "When?" he croaked out.

"When she first came back to Korea," he answered.

"She'd forgiven me even then?"

"I don't think Noona ever thought she had anything to forgive."

"No, I suppose she wouldn't." Jae-sung cleared his throat. "Thanks, Dae."

"You're welcome, Hyung." The moment felt too fraught—too emotional—so Dae-jung did what he always did in moments such as this. He let it stretch until breaking and then, he threw out a non sequitur. "Let's get some bingsu."

His bandmate startled at the abrupt subject change and then smiled. "Sounds great."

And just like that, Dae-jung knew everything was going to be okay.

April 2027

Katie Wu seen all over Asia in the company of various male heirs, actors, and celebrities. Is something in the works or is she living up that single life in the wake of her breakups with Dae-jung and Lambent of DOYEN?

- Soompi, April 2027

As expected from the #1 wh0r3 of K-pop.

- X user, April 2027

Y'all really can't just let a person live, huh?

- X user, April 2027

Interesting how the media never mentions all the female heiresses, actresses, and celebrities Katie has been seen with, too. But go off, I guess.

- X user, April 2027

Here's the thing. Dae-jung had meant to call or text Katie, but he kept waiting for the perfect moment and it never arrived.

First, he'd thought she'd return to Seoul with Woo-jin but she ended up in Taipei instead to film a last-minute guest judge stint on "The Singer Songwriter." Then, Katie went to Tokyo and Kyoto to do a press tour for the Japanese translation of her book.

He recalled that Katie had been surprised about the demand for it since she didn't particularly have a lot of Japanese fans. She'd theorized it had to be him being in the movie that'd generated buzz for the book, and had promised him a dinner in Tokyo from the Japanese royalties. But now that it had come to it, she did not bring it up so neither did he.

It wasn't even that they weren't communicating. Katie was both perfectly civil and normal in all the group chats. They even occasionally texted each other privately, but it would be a stretch to call it the same as before.

And yet, Katie was everywhere, even if not in actual person. He heard her voice on the soundtrack recordings when he and DOYEN listened to her vocal guides or added their parts. Though the lead single of the soundtrack featured all the members of the band, the M/V concept only told the story of Choi Eun-seong and Vikki Yu. Though Katie had filmed her part separately, her presence was still felt.

Sometimes, Dae-jung wondered if Katie had engineered it so intentionally.

As promotions ramped up for the December movie release, he resigned himself to the inevitable awkward reunion. As such, he was therefore wholly unprepared to see Katie tucked between Woo-jin and Ye-jun in the private room he was to meet his bandmates at for lunch.

"Noona?" Dae-jung said, voice cracking.

Katie's lack of shock was enough to inform Dae-jung that she'd known he was coming. He did not know how he felt about her having this advantage, however slight.

"Dae-jung, could you please tell your hyungs that they're wrong and full of shit?" Katie requested in lieu of a greeting.

Dae-jung swallowed once and gathered himself. He knew the way of such things. "I suppose it depends on what exactly they're wrong and full of shit about."

"These idiots here think there is unresolved tension between us." Katie turned away from Ye-jun and Woo-jin to take a casual sip of soju—it clearly was turning out to be that kind of lunch already—and licked her lips. "Of course, the only unreleased tension is that in my fingers just itching to squeeze their very attractive necks."

"If you're into that kinky shit you should have just told us, Katie," quipped Ye-jun. "It wouldn't be the first time Woo-jin and I have shared."

"That was one time, Ye-jun."

"Ah," Dae-jung interrupted before he couldn't unhear something. But first, would he be brave or would he retreat the way Katie offered? "I'm afraid we'll have to agree to disagree, Noona."

Katie's mouth formed a surprised "O" as the two older men burst into delighted cackling. He vaguely registered them demanding Katie KakaoPay them each some ridiculously high amount. He resolved to murder his hyungs as soon as it was expedient.

"I think I hurt you terribly, Noona," Dae-jung continued, grabbing an empty seat across from Katie.

"Because you agree with your meddling hyungs?" Katie scoffed, obviously trying to wrest back some control over the discourse and ignoring Woo-jin jabbing her in the side with his elbow. "I can handle a minor disagreement. I'm used to being surrounded by fools."

"I made a mistake. I wanted more with you but instead, I gave you the impression that I was doing you a favor," Dae-jung said, not caring that there was an audience. He had apologized enough to his bandmates in group settings. "I was afraid. I'm so sorry."

Katie waved a careless hand without meeting his gaze. "It's all in the past, Dae-jung. As the Chinese say, don't put it on your heart."

"Katie-yah, why are you like this?" Ye-jun grumbled exasperatedly.

"Seriously," added Woo-jin. "Your stupid pride causes you so much unnecessary suffering."

"Who's suffering?" Katie parried back. "I'm not suffering. Are you suffering, Dae-jung?"

Dae-jung took Katie's measure. He knew what she wanted him to say, to patch things over superficially. Her offer was tempting, but he recalled Jae-sung's words. He did not want to regret it for the rest of his life.

"Noona, I still want to be with you. Do you think you can forgive me? Do you think you would be willing to give me a chance to be more than what we were?"

Katie blanched.

"There's nothing to forgive, Dae-jung," she insisted. She added no other words.

Perhaps he'd misread her again. Perhaps Katie had already moved on. It had been months after all. He was an arrogant fool. Except, why would Woo-jin and Ye-jun go through all this trouble if she was all sorted?

He refused to buy Katie's act. Woo-jin's obvious wink helped.

"I want you, Noona. I want to be with you and find out if we could love each other the way people in love with each other do."

"I—" Katie snapped her mouth shut. She took a shaky breath. "What if I was just using you? What if you were just really convenient?"

"Then you were just using me, and I was just really convenient," Dae-jung said. "I understood what was being offered at the time," he added softly. "But even so, I'd like to know if you'd want to try with me now, at this moment in time."

"And if I say no?"

"Then you say no, and we move on from this as you wish."

"I'm seeing someone," Katie blurted out.

"Bullshit," exclaimed Woo-jin. "Alton would have told me."

Ye-jun nodded in agreement. "Mina noona would've told me, too. Lying does not become you."

"If you want to say no, just say no. You aren't doing Dae-jung any favors. You're better than this," Woo-jin scowled.

Dae-jung watched as Katie's face colored. He decided he would let his hyungs interrogate her on his behalf.

"I—I'm not lying. My uncle set it up and—"

"What does he do? How old is he? How long has this been going on? What does he look like? How much money does he make? Can he provide for you? Will he be a good father?"

Dae-jung idly admired how rapid-fire Ye-jun could get when he was riled up. He did not envy Katie's position despite the circumstances.

"Uh, the fuck? He's an accountant and he's your age. I met him a few weeks ago," Katie stumbled out, her voice rising in both pitch and volume. "He's alright-looking, I guess? I don't know how much he makes. I don't need providing for—I literally just met him."

"Do you like him?" asked Woo-jin. "Does he like you?"

"I guess? He seems a decent sort."

Ye-jun leaned into Katie's space, ears and neck red with exertion. "You guess? You don't seem very sure about him at all! Does he even exist?"

"Of course he exists! I could make up someone more interesting than a fucking accountant!"

"So you admit he sounds boring as fuck," Ye-jun gloated.

Dae-jung was gratified to see Katie angrily turn away to sip her soju.

"What could you possibly have in common?" asked Woo-jin, his dark eyes narrowing in suspicion.

"Why, because how could a dumb pop star have anything intelligent to say to an accountant?" Katie snarled. "I graduated UCLA *summa cum laude*. I was a muggle for years longer than you all. I know how to talk to normal people."

Woo-jin held up his hands in a conciliatory manner. "I'm sorry, Katie. That's not what I meant. He just doesn't seem like your type is all."

"I don't have a type."

Ye-jun snorted. "You absolutely have a type. I believe you're fond of hot and famous pop stars. Most of whom are in DOYEN. You might be familiar with the band."

Even Dae-jung chuckled at that.

"You don't know everything about me, Lee Ye-jun."

Dae-jung decided her torture had gone on enough. "You never said no, Noona."

Katie's eyes flew to his. "What?"

"You never said no."

"About what?"

"About whether or not you wanted to try again with me," Dae-jung clarified. He purposely ignored the smug looks on Ye-jun and Woo-jin's faces. He did not need them to muck it up any more than they already had.

"I just told you I'm seeing someone," Katie said.

"Yes, Noona. You did," he replied. "But you didn't say no."

Katie tugged on her collar. "I fail to see the difference."

"Do you have feelings for this accountant?"

"Dae-jung-ah, you cannot frame it so vaguely," interrupted Ye-jun. "Polite disinterest is a feeling, and Katie will absolutely take advantage of such a technicality."

Dae-jung conceded to Ye-jun's superior slippery logic. "Very well, Hyung. Noona, do you want to date this accountant? Do you see yourself falling in love with him, marrying him, and having his children?"

"No," Katie whispered.

"No, you don't see yourself with this accountant? Or no, you do not want to try with me?" he clarified. "Or both, I guess. Both is an option, too."

"What do you want from me, Park Dae-jung?" Katie croaked out. He noted how her hands were balled into fists.

Dae-jung gentled his tone even more. "I want you to be honest and tell me what you want." He reached out for her hands with his, wrapping his long fingers around her own. "Whatever you want, I will respect your decision."

Katie stilled so much that Dae-jung wasn't sure she was breathing. In fact, Dae-jung wasn't sure he was breathing either.

Finally, finally, Katie spoke.

"I want to believe you, Dae-jung," she said, retracting her hands. "I really do."

"I sense a 'but' coming on," Dae-jung said. He noted the commiserating sympathy in his bandmates' eyes.

"And I'm sure you mean it—or at least believe you mean it."

Ye-jun sank his entire face into his awaiting hands. Woo-jin just gaped in disbelief.

"You think I'm mistaken?" Dae-jung asked, an edge creeping into his voice. "I assure you. I know my own mind."

"Yeah? Well, I wouldn't want you to change it again with your dick in my mouth."

Dae-jung heard one of his members choke. He supposed he deserved that. "You said you'd forgiven me. That it was all in the past."

"I guess I didn't know my mind as well as I thought."

"You're mean, Noona." Dae-jung glared at Katie.

"I am. Just ask Park Jae-sung." She lifted her chin a half-notch.

Dae-jung recognized when her stubbornness kicked in. He knew he had lost this conversation. But he could be stubborn, too. "Then say it. I want to hear you say it."

"Say what?"

"Say no. Say you do not want another shot at us. I want to hear you say it." And since Dae-jung was being daring, he added, "I want you to look me in the eyes and tell me."

"This is ridiculous. You're all ridiculous." Although their food had yet to arrive, Katie gathered her phone and purse to leave.

"I'm onto you, Noona. I know you hate lying," Dae-jung said evenly. "Except you lie all the time by telling the truth." She was a master at latching onto a nugget of truth and engineering a bulletproof case around it to justify her narrative.

Katie stood. "I trust between the three of you, you can cover the bill. I'll see you all later when you've come to your senses." She left in an indignant rush.

The three men stared after her and Ye-jun whistled to release tension. "Well, that went well."

"You think?" snarked Woo-jin, downing several shots of soju in quick succession.

"I, personally, think it went great," Dae-jung commented.

Ye-jun and Woo-jin exchanged concerned glances.

"Were we at the same disastrous lunch?" asked Ye-jun.

"She didn't say no, Hyung," grinned Dae-jung as he hit the service button at their table. "Noona never said no."

August 2027

After a six-year hiatus from making music, Katie Wu is back with the new LP "After Midnight." Longtime fans are de-

lighted that Wu has signed back up with SB Entertainment, and the quality of the album speaks for itself. Wu explores our nightmares and what happens when monsters show their true selves after the glittering party's over.

Cynical and wounded out the gate with "The House of Ways and Means," the album never loses that sense of foreboding. Track after track thrums with dread, resignation, and seemingly misplaced hope. The Lambent-produced "Monster's Ball" is unnerving, slinky with eerie strings and plaintive vocals.

But without a doubt, "I've Lost You" featuring labelmate KJ is what every song of heartbreak aspires to be. It is sublime. KJ's rapping is subdued and full of regret while Wu rages and wails on the hook and her verses. The interplay between their two styles in conjunction with the agonizing topline and grounding bassline makes a perfect ballad of love gone wrong.

It doesn't even begin to cover the 23-minute hidden track that is actually an entire cello concerto—but I will leave that for you to discover on your own. Though the wait was long, "After Midnight" is totally worth it. Fantastic from concept to execution.

- NME, August 2027

I don't know shit about classical music but that hidden track on "After Midnight" destroyed my heart. Is it about God or love or both? I don't know. I only know that the physical album is worth getting for this track alone. The entire album is brilliant.

- Consequence, August 2027

[1] The House of Ways and Means [2:07]
[2] Monster's Ball (prod. by Lambent of DOYEN) [3:28]
[3] The Queen Is Dead/Long Live the Queen [3:45]
[4] Hush [3:12]
[5] Masquerade [2:41]
[6] We Return to the Shadows [3:22]
[7] I've Lost You (feat. KJ of DOYEN) [3:19]
[8] A Pumpkin Again [4:02]
[9] To Fit a Glass Slipper [2:34]
[10] It's Always Happy If You End Early Enough [3:01]
[Hidden Track] Doubt [23:17]
- Track list, "After Midnight" (SB Entertainment Music,
2027)

No taxation without representation
But I have been press-ganged
Commandeered
Tariffed like a foreign body
Treated like I made a tempest in a teapot
I am not endeared

Reparations for my heart, now!
Stolen by casual means
You hurt me
You hurt me
We forgive but we do not forget

We forget but we do not forgive
You hurt me
You hurt me
And now, and now
Now, we requite
 - "The House of Ways and Means" (SB Entertainment Mu-
sic, 2027)

The spell is broken
I'm no longer a could but a has been
 - "A Pumpkin Again" (SB Entertainment Music, 2027)

YEESSSSSSSSSSSSSSSSSSSSSSSSSSSS!!! We eating good this
year!!!
- X user, August 2027

the mv omg the mv she is devastating and KJ is just ad;slfjad-
sklfjasdlkjafdladsj is it weird to stan them as a couple?!?
- X user, August 2027

Is she just working through the entire line up of DOYEN? Tell
her to get in line.
- X user, August 2027

Hwaiting, Noona! Hyung, you did so good! #AfterMidnight
                     - Kitahara Akihiro, Instagram story, August 2027

"Katie?"

Katie was retching into a wastebasket, frantically tearing at the corset laces on her back. Tears streamed down her face. She was in a bad way.

"Let me help you," said Jae-sung as he rushed to her side and attempted to undo the double knot that she'd unwittingly tightened. He cursed as his thick fingers fumbled while Katie tried to keep her trembling body still. He couldn't find any purchase. "I need to get a stylist noona."

Katie shook her head. "I don't want them to worry," she gasped.

Jae-sung cast about worriedly and landed on the scissors on the table. "I hope they have a back-up outfit," he said.

He attempted to cut as close to the knot as possible. As soon as the laces were snipped, he pried her from the steel and leather cage as best he could.

"Can you breathe better, Katie?"

Katie nodded as she resumed her vomiting. Jae-sung handed her a water bottle, rubbing soothing circles on her back.

The door opened and he heard a stylist noona exclaim, "Katie-yah! Is it your nerves or are you actually sick? Do we need to call manager-nim?"

"Katie isn't feeling well, but hopefully, she'll be fine in a few minutes," Jae-sung assured. "But, I'm afraid I may have ruined her outfit," he added sheepishly. "She couldn't breathe and I couldn't untie her in time, so I panicked."

The stylist sighed. "We'll figure it out. I'll give you a few moments while I go find another lacing."

Katie panted a few breaths and then rinsed her mouth, spitting into the trash can.

"Thanks," she coughed.

"Of course," he replied. "I didn't realize your panic attacks had gotten worse. Do you always barf before a show?"

Katie flashed a wan smile. "At least once a tour or comeback season," she revealed. "If you wouldn't mind keeping the key to my success to yourself?"

"Ever the deflector."

"Tigers never change their stripes," she quipped breathlessly.

"How come I never knew?" Jae-sung squeezed her shoulder kindly.

Katie snorted an inelegant laugh. "When would you have ever found out? You were always on tour and even when you weren't, it's not like you could've been seen with me."

"Ah," he sighed. "I suppose you're right." Jae-sung leaned back against the sofa. "Well, I'm here now, Katie. I'm here now."

She flushed slightly and tugged the much abused corset higher. "Thanks, Jae."

Not for the first time did Jae-sung wonder what else he didn't know about Katie. Not that it was his business anymore other than friendly curiosity. He was relieved that things between them had evolved into this peaceable collegiality. Jae-sung couldn't remember the last time he'd had more fun collaborating with another artist than with Katie. And now, he was getting the chance to perform with her at a music show and support her in ways he hadn't been able to before.

It was funny how life worked out. Jae-sung had thought Katie was the love of his life and when he'd lost her, he'd despaired. Instead, he found Mi-ran—his future wife—in great part thanks to Katie. Jae-sung selflessly hoped that she, too, would find the kind of love he'd found with Mi-ran.

December 2027

If you had told me in January that SB Entertainment's "Landslide" would be the best movie of 2027, I would have laughed in your face. Despite all expectations, this trilingual semi-autobiographical movie has succeeded for Katie Wu much in the way "8 Mile" did for Eminem. Wu is shockingly raw and gentle in her acting, and her chemistry with Park Dae-jung (yes, of the Korean boy band DOYEN) sets fire to the screen.

The story is heartbreaking, believable, and a study of human suffering and triumph in the face of adversity—both self-made and inflicted. The acting is top-notch and not once do you notice that languages are being traded one after another. The fact that Wu was so good in three separate languages is of particular note, and she deserves any and all acting awards.

The soundtrack, too, is grounding and stunning, featuring Asia and Asian America's top singers and rappers. Produced by Lambent (also of DOYEN), the twelve tracks are sure to light up the airwaves and clubs for the next year. Scheduled for limited release on Christmas day, get your tickets now. Superb.

- Entertainment Weekly, December 2027

Crammed full of features from top-selling pan-Asian and Asian American superstars, the Lambent-produced "Land-

slide" soundtrack enhances and drives the movie forward, never stalling out with even a single dud. Whether it's pop, hip-hop, a ballad, or a club banger, there are no skips.

- Rolling Stone, December 2027

As SB Entertainment changed the K-pop music landscape, so they are trying to change the way movies are made and stories are told. What at first seemed a case of extreme nepotism and self-interest now looks like a prescient bet on an astounding film. "Landslide" is the movie to beat.

- The New York Times, December 2027

Can it be considered acting when you're just playing yourself?

- X user, December 2027

My new addiction is checking this ex-bird app for new DJ x Katie interactions and edits. What a time to be alive!!!

- X user, December 2027

Love watching PDJ be a smooth motherfucker even as Katie is the most awkward panda to ever awkward!

- X user, December 2027

Katie and Dae-jung were sharing a cozy love seat on the set of England's top morning show, answering easy questions during the European leg of their press run for "Landslide," when Susie Carmichael, the peppy blond co-host, giggled and leaned eagerly toward them from her easy chair.

Katie had always found morning show personalities grating and Susie was no exception. Katie would take a cynical, sarcastic, and mean late-night host over the relentless cheer and affected goodwill of their early morning counterparts in a heartbeat.

"As we all know, Vikki Yu, the character Katie plays in 'Landslide,' is based on Katie in real life," Susie stated. "Dae-jung, since you know Katie both in real life and played opposite her in the movie, what do Vikki and Katie have in common?"

Katie sighed internally. With that sort of lead-in, Katie had hoped for a truly original question, but she should have known better. Such was the nature of the press junket, but that didn't mean she had to like it.

She listened with half an ear, expecting some variation of Dae-jung's typical drivel of "oh, they're both so talented and passionate." She was preparing herself to react accordingly when Dae-jung said in a silky baritone, "The way they both make my heart flutter."

Katie's mouth involuntarily dropped open as Susie, her co-host Brad Crenshaw, and the audience alternately swooned at Dae-jung's answer then laughed at Katie's dazed shock. What was Dae-jung doing?

"Oh, stop," Katie forced out as lightly as she could endeavor. "Don't be ridiculous."

Dae-jung reached for her hand, and she couldn't help but turn to face him. Katie tried not to mind him inadvertently drawing attention to the cast encasing her arm, but she already knew the hosts would ask about it. The stage lights were so hot and Katie could tell her face was flushed.

"How could I, Noona?" he crooned, his thumb smoothing over her knuckles. "It's the truth. You're so talented and kind, it's impossible not to fall for you."

Katie's face scrunched in pained mortification as she snatched her hand back. Dae-jung was laying it on a bit thick, and she couldn't believe he was pulling out the "noona" card in an English interview. The internet was going to eat this clip up.

"Oh, before I forget, how did you break your arm, Katie?" Brad asked, right on cue. "Does it still hurt?"

Katie resisted the urge to roll her eyes. "I slipped on set while filming a variety show in Seoul a few weeks ago. I'm fine, though. Thank you so much for asking," she answered, hoping that would be the end of it.

Dae-jung, however, had other plans. "Noona," he purred, "you're forgetting the most important part." Katie could hear everyone sigh and had to begrudgingly admit that Dae-jung was a master at commanding an audience.

Well, he wasn't the only star on the stage. She hooded her eyes and dropped into her best bedroom voice. "And what is that, Dae-jung-ah?"

Dae-jung's face lit in delight. "So," he said with a clap of his hands, "picture this: Katie and I are on opposing teams and we have to do some relay race involving running and lots of water and—oh, I'm spoiling it." Dae-jung paused for cinematic effect before flashing his boxy smile. "I'm sure the producers won't mind. You'll all promise to watch anyway?"

A chorus of yeses from the audience made Katie smile even though she knew Dae-jung was setting her up.

After being assured, Dae-jung continued hamming it up. "Great, what was I saying?" He pouted fetchingly. "Oh, yes. So we're passing water down the line and there's water everywhere. Katie and I are matched against each other—she can get really competitive, you know," he revealed conspiratorially, leaning in closer to Susie. Katie swore the TV personality melted, and Katie resisted the urge to elbow Dae-jung in the ribs. "So Noona is racing against me but slips, and because she's a cheater, she grabs my shirt to pull me down with her."

"What happened next?" Susie asked breathlessly even as Brad winked at Katie, saying, "Atta girl, Katie. That's the way to win."

Katie chuckled, replying, "I know, right? What Dae-jung didn't say was that he was cheating the entire show. I was just trying to even the score."

"You can prove nothing!" Dae-jung protested laughingly, his eyes sparkling in mischief. "But I did what anyone would have done—I pulled away hard! It's not my fault Katie fell backwards even harder."

"Hey, that hurt! I made a complete fool of myself in front of all these other celebrities," Katie rued, unconsciously rubbing her arm.

Susie's face flashed understanding. "Ugh, that's the worst!" she commiserated. "That's just adding insult to injury."

"Maybe I should start telling everyone Park Dae-jung of DOYEN broke my arm," Katie teased. "Think of all the fanwars."

Dae-jung grinned, and Katie knew he wasn't done. "But I didn't tell everyone the best part," he said. His innocent countenance didn't fool Katie for a second. "I happen to know that every bone Katie's broken has been in front of a man she's crushing on."

Brad and Susie cracked up along with the audience. "Really!" exclaimed Brad. "How many bones have you broken?"

"Three," she admitted to more laughter from everyone.

"So, who was on set?" asked Susie. "You must tell us."

Before Katie could reply, Dae-jung interjected. "Me, of course," he smirked. "Tell everyone how much you love me, Noona."

Katie was going to kill Dae-jung. He had everyone eating out of his hand.

Later, when she finally summoned the courage to rewatch the clip after being spammed by all her friends about it, she noted how her entire body had cringed, her desperate lean away from Dae-jung causing the crowd to screech in delight.

But at that moment, she had to right this ship. "Oh, please," she retorted. "Actor Lee Ju-ho was also there, and Susie, let me tell you, he's the most beautiful man I've ever seen."

She took pleasure in Dae-jung's surprised face and winked at him. His boxy smile was her reward.

"Well, there you have it. You all heard it here first: Katie is crushing on Lee Ju-ho," Brad said, trying to keep a straight face.

Susie laughed and playfully swatted Brad with her cue cards. "Oh, you all are terrible," she tittered before wrapping up their segment.

Katie smiled and thanked the hosts and tried valiantly not to die of embarrassment on live TV. Her plan to one-up Dae-jung had spectacularly backfired.

Katie would never know peace on this press tour again.

Once other producers saw how this morning show had struck viral gold, they all included questions designed to encourage Dae-jung to praise and fawn over Katie. The number of easy layups they passed to him was truly astounding.

A late show host asked Dae-jung if it was weird to do love scenes with a longtime friend, and Dae-jung replied, "Katie's an excellent kisser. Five out of five stars. Ten out of ten would try again."

When the host asked Katie to respond, her brain betrayed her by completely exiting the chat. Later, Mi-ran gleefully described her garbled answer as belabored bleating and blathering. Katie appreciated the alliteration, but that was it.

The worst part was: Katie could not prevent her instinctual squirm when trapped by compliments. She was furious that she could endure an onslaught of degradation with a blank face, but a well-timed declaration of sincere affection from Dae-jung could reduce her to a spluttering idiot.

The internet ate it up; Katie hated how she did, too.

Katie was nursing a gin and tonic, resting in a burgundy tufted leather booth of the San Francisco Ritz-Carlton lounge while longing for a joint, when Dae-jung suddenly blocked her light.

"You're avoiding me," he declared.

Even amidst the old-world splendor and decadence, Dae-jung looked expensive. His artfully tousled hair showed off the curl in his hair, and he'd styled his bangs off his face so Katie could look directly into his intense gaze. His skin was golden against his white Polo Ralph Lauren shirt, and Katie had the sudden urge to lick him.

"That's absurd. You're here, aren't you?" Katie replied, waving her glass haphazardly, the clink of her ice more felt than heard over the swanky jazz standards playing in the background. "Besides, I've seen you every day for the last four weeks."

Even if she wanted to ignore him, she couldn't. Katie, Dae-jung, and the other two actors had been making the talk show rounds in Europe, Los Angeles, and New York to pre-record promotions for "Landslide," and were bound to Seoul and Taipei after their San Francisco stop to continue more of the same. They were always on the shows together for ease of booking and frankly, she and the other two actors needed Dae-jung's superior star power.

Dae-jung rubbed his chin as he chuckled. Katie could see a few days' growth of stubble and forced away the memory of it scratching her thighs.

"You know what I mean."

His dark eyes flashed amusement as he lazily took her in. She felt oddly vulnerable and mentally shook herself. The strange game Dae-jung had played these last few weeks was affecting her more than she wanted to admit.

It would be one thing if his flirtations and extreme attentiveness were limited to their interviews. To Katie's incredible consternation, he turned every interaction into an opportunity to praise her acting, her talents, her beauty, and her personhood. Combined with the sheer volume of viral compilations Mi-ran and Mattie sent of Dae-jung flustering her, Katie was inundated by the unstoppable charm and charisma of Park Dae-jung, professional idol and actor.

Katie hated every second.

Someone must have tattled about her ending things with that accountant, and Katie resented all their meddling. It was masterful.

In comparison, Katie was a drunk toddler. All she could do was pretend she didn't secretly store Dae-jung's comments in a shorn-off corner of her heart.

"Well, since you're here, do you want to grab dinner? I think this is our last free moment before the press junket starts tomorrow and we have to attend the SF premiere," Katie said, unprovoked. That would show him.

Dae-jung shrugged. "I can always eat."

"Great! I want to eat at Rintaro but they only take reservations two weeks in advance—"

"And you want to use my celebrity status to get a table and skip the line?" he interrupted.

Katie smirked. "I mean, you might as well be useful, right?" She downed the remainder of her cocktail.

"Right."

"Besides, don't I owe you Japanese food? It's not Tokyo, but it's still amazing."

Dae-jung raised an eyebrow. "I'll be the judge of that."

Later, when Dae-jung was busy gorging himself on fresh sushi and throwing back hot sake with Katie in a private booth at Rintaro, she couldn't help but crow, "See? Isn't it amazing?"

He nodded, handsome even with his mouth stuffed full. "You were right, Noona. This place is probably the best Japanese food I've had in the US."

Katie giggled. "I don't know about that, but it's definitely high up there." Clearly the sake was hitting her harder than she had anticipated because then, she added, "If I was avoiding you, I wouldn't have asked you out for dinner."

The instant her words were out of her mouth, Katie knew that she'd made a tactical error. Dae-jung's eyes lit up and his lips slanted at a dangerous angle.

He leaned over the table so closely she could feel the heat of his breath. "It's been eight months, Noona. I've decided I'm done waiting."

Katie shivered. "I didn't ask you to wait for me."

"I know." His velvety baritone caressed her skin.

"Then why did you?" Katie could not help how breathless she sounded.

Dae-jung leaned back to meet her eyes. He was rarely so serious. "Because I wanted to."

Katie couldn't help herself. "Why?" she asked.

"I listened to your new album very carefully, Noona. And I think I've got you figured out." Dae-jung ran a long finger along his sensuous lips. "You think you're a monster who no one will ever love. You preemptively left Jae-sung before he could notice just how mean or cruel you believed yourself to be."

Dae-jung tilted his head and examined Katie closely. She resisted the urge to squirm. She wanted to leave.

"With us, I think at first we both might have thought it was situational before it became more. Except I, being foolish, chose to believe convenience was all you wanted." He tapped his chin. "I didn't think someone as talented, educated, and amazing as you would want someone like me."

"Dae-jung—" Katie made to interrupt. She hated when he belittled his talents.

"Ah, let me finish, please," he said.

She swallowed her words and allowed him to continue despite her every cell thrumming with energy.

"I couldn't fathom how you could go from Jae-sung hyung—who is so brilliant and smart—to me. What can I do other than sing, act, or dance?" He held up his hand to forestall Katie's inevitable objection. "And so I left you. I convinced myself you couldn't possibly want me and so, I hurt you. I'm so sorry I hurt you, Noona."

"I thought we already settled this, Dae-jung." Her voice had dropped to a whisper.

"We did. Sort of. But I don't think you believed me."

Dae-jung would not allow Katie to avert her gaze, and if not for the fortifying sake coursing through her veins, she would have long fled.

"I asked for you to give me another chance, but now I see that you couldn't possibly have trusted my word. Not because you think I'm untrustworthy—or maybe not just because of that."

"I trust you, Dae-jung," Katie breathed.

"I appreciate that, Noona," he smiled. "I think you were relieved though. Relieved that I didn't have enough time to figure out who you really are—or rather, who you really believe yourself to be."

Dae-jung's eyes were impossibly kind. Katie's whole being ached at being perceived.

"I think who you really don't trust is yourself."

"Is that right?" Katie hated how her tone lacked the bite necessary for that line to hit. It was too late to reel her words back.

"I think it's exactly right," he parried back knowingly. "That's why you fill every moment with work and people you have no chance of falling in love with."

"And you think you're the kind of person I could fall in love with?"

"I actually don't know," Dae-jung said, rubbing the back of his neck shyly. "I certainly hope so. But that's not why I'm telling you this."

Compelled by the lilt and lull of Dae-jung's voice, Katie asked, "Why are you telling me this then?"

"Because it pains me. Because I want you to ask yourself: If you actually believed you were such a monster, why do you love so much? Why do you expose Mattie, Alton hyung, Mi-ran noona, Woo-jin hyung—there really are too many of us to list—why do you risk our hearts, Noona?"

"What?" Katie did not know where Dae-jung was going with this line of thought.

"If you really thought any of us were in danger from you, you would disappear like you did a few years ago. Except you would never resurface. You would brick yourself off from the world. You would even be willing to harm yourself so that you couldn't harm anyone ever again."

"But I promised Mattie I wouldn't," Katie cried.

Dae-jung reached out and gripped her hands tightly. "A monster wouldn't care what they promised to anyone, Noona. You are brash and you are brave, and sometimes, you are afraid. You are many things, but you have never been a monster."

Katie felt split asunder.

Katie knew Dae-jung was handling her expertly, but she didn't care. She had not been understood so deeply in years—if ever. And then Katie had the humbling realization that her friends had indeed understood her; they'd just had the grace to let her believe otherwise because it was the only way to keep her.

She marveled that Dae-jung didn't care to keep her. That he was willing to let her go even if it hurt him. Even if he could be the love of her life.

Above all else, Katie knew Dae-jung just wanted her to be free.

Katie wanted to believe him. She chose to believe him.

"Ask me again, Dae-jung," she said.

"What?" he whispered.

The hope that suddenly sprang into Dae-jung's eyes grieved Katie. She had done this to him. It would end tonight.

"Ask me again," Katie said.

"Noona," he murmured, eyes bright. "Will you give me another chance?"

"Yes," she replied. "Yes, I will."

Chapter 10

February 2028

As expected, "Landslide" is a major contender at the Oscars tonight! It's swept all the major award ceremonies thus far with multiple nominations and wins across categories and award shows, such as the 2028 Golden Globes for Best Motion Picture – Drama. Among the prestigious awards, what sticks out most so far is the triumphant cast winning the 2028 SAG Award for Outstanding Performance by a Cast in a Motion Picture. The exuberant joy as a multi-Asian/Asian American cast celebrated both on and off stage has been the highlight of the award season.

- PopSugar, February 2028

Oscar speculation for "Landslide" is running rampant! Will the film snag another Best Motion Picture like it did at the Golden Globes, or will it be snubbed like it was at the BAFTAs? Can the film's original song, "Luck Favors the Prepared," win another award? Though newcomer actress Katie Wu was nominated for multiple best actress awards, she has only managed to nab the 2028 SAG Award for Outstanding Performance by a Female Actor. Will she win the Oscar for that same nomination? We'll find out tonight.

- E! News, February 2028

What will K-pop global sensation DOYEN and Katie Wu have in store for Oscar viewers tonight? We hear the performance will be one for the history books—and if it's anything like their SAG and Golden Globes performances, we're in for a treat. The group and Katie have already won the 2028 Golden Globe for Best Original Song – Motion Picture. Will they make it a repeat and win an Oscar—a first for K-pop?

- Us Weekly, February 2028

Y'all know the original song award is only given to the songwriters NOT the performers, right? That means all members of DOYEN and Katie contributed to writing the song since they won the GGs and are nommed for the Oscars.

- X user, February 2028

SB Entertainment putting that payola to good use.

- X user, February 2028

I don't think that word means what you think it means.

- X user, February 2028

Watch, all the other fandoms are gonna add "Oscar nom" on their streaming goals. That's not how it works. Your faves could never.

- X user, February 2028

Who else is doing it like them? Grammys who?

- X user, February 2028

[Verse 1: Katie Wu]
Never been one for luck
What's it matter when we all die
Memento mori
You crawl until you fly

Luck is a fickle bitch
Life is a constant switch
Carpe noctem, audentes fortuna iuvat
Semper paratus or die in a ditch

Did it for the glory, did it for the story
Waded through the gory, yup!
Gotta be a fighter even for a miter
I always pull through; clutch

[Pre-chorus: Soo-min, DJ]
They say luck favors the prepared
I'm inclined to agree

Don't forget
Fortune smiled on both you and me

[Chorus: KJ, Lambent, Akihiro, Jun]
Where ya bars at though?
We're still ascending but you've plateaued
Don't expect it to last
Only hard work prevails

Luck favors the prepared
Let's get lucky, baby (Let's get lucky)
Luck favors the prepared
Let's get lucky, baby (Let's get lucky)

[Verse 2: Lambent, 1DEL1GHT]
"Has beens" and "never weres" complain
I was born under a lucky star
You fools, you cowards
I'm king of the guttersnipes
Born in a ditch, but clawed my way out
Born a prince, but you still have to bow

Was it luck or hard work
Who cares—it's my life
A dream with my fam, my bros
Fired all the way up and still I run
Want the prize but none of the burn
Want my luck then snatch your turn

[Pre-chorus: Akihiro, Jun]
They say luck favors the prepared

I'm inclined to agree
Don't forget
Fortune spat on both you and me

[Chorus: KJ, 1DEL1GHT, Soo-min, DJ]
Where ya bars at though?
We're still ascending but you've plateaued
Don't expect it to last
Only hard work prevails

Luck favors the prepared
Let's get lucky, baby (Let's get lucky)
Luck favors the prepared
Let's get lucky, baby (Let's get lucky)

[Bridge: Katie Wu]
Mind the gap; your bar is too low
I've played this game for years
One second you're up
The next you're eating crow

[Verse 3: KJ]
A prison of your own making
Manacles all in your mind
Worshiped at the wrong altars
Slinging liquor instead of rhyme

You on top, is your position secure?
You never learn, you stay obscure
Blame it all on bad luck
You shattered the mirror

Bravery faces a blank measure
You fill them with whole rests
No iron sharpening iron
Full of lead, sinking behemoths (good luck)

[Chorus: Katie Wu, Lambent, Soo-min, DJ, Akihiro, Jun]
Where ya bars at though?
We're still ascending but you've plateaued
Don't expect it to last
But hard work prevails

Luck favors the prepared
Let's get lucky, baby (Let's get lucky)
Luck favors the prepared
Let's get lucky, baby (Let's get lucky)
　　　- DOYEN feat. Katie Wu, "Luck Favors the Prepared" (SB
　　　　　　　　　　　　　　Entertainment Music, 2028)

Dae-jung and Akihiro were struggling to keep it together in the stretch SUV. Even though Dae-jung told himself he was used to red carpets by now and had done quite a few this awards season, his stomach was still tied up in knots. After all, despite Bong Joon-Ho calling the Academy Awards a local awards show, it was still a big fucking deal.

"Can you believe we're performing at the Oscars, Dae?" asked Akihiro. His leg kept jiggling and Dae-jung forced himself not to hold Akihiro's thigh down. "It's surreal! You can't even perform unless you're nominated!"

Akihiro knew he was aware of all these facts, but Dae-jung understood the need to say the words out loud. They'd performed at the SAG Awards, but DOYEN the group hadn't been nominated for anything. He had been a wreck, but he hadn't actually anticipated their cast winning the ensemble award. He'd thought "Parasite" and "Squid Games" were flukes.

For that matter, he never once thought he'd be at any Hollywood film award show like the Golden Globes—let alone winning one for Best Original Song – Motion Picture or Best Motion Picture – Drama. (Technically, that last award went to Song PD and a few of the SB Entertainment execs since they were the producers.)

The real wild thing was that "Luck Favors the Prepared" wasn't even the title track! They had been prepared for "Return to Me," the love song featuring Katie and DOYEN, to be the award contender. In fact, the ballad was far more popular in Asia. But in America, the audience loved the harder, rap-focused "Luck." Some dancer had posted their choreo to it on TikTok, and soon enough, the song went viral.

Much like the rest of DOYEN's career, a combination of serendipity and their hard work allowed them to rise to the challenge. After all, how could they have ever imagined having an Academy Award–nominated song when they were preparing for their debut?

Impossible.

Dae-jung wondered how Katie was doing and what she was wearing tonight. At every award show, she'd hit the best dressed lists, but Katie had refused to even send him a selfie before she'd left. He supposed he would see her on the red carpet later with Alton.

He told himself that he was not even a little bit jealous. That Katie had brought Alton because Woo-jin couldn't bring him and Dae-jung couldn't bring her.

He consoled himself with the knowledge that the rest of his members were in the adjoining vehicles, that he was never alone when surrounded by his very best friends. Arriving at the venue, Dae-jung and Akihiro stepped out of their black SUV, straightening their tuxedos and greeting their band mates.

"Alton hyung says he and Katie are only a few cars behind us so if we hang around, we can all walk in together," said Woo-jin after a brief greeting. "Oh, there's Song PD-nim, too. We can be the Korean contingent until Hyung and Katie get here."

Dae-jung busied himself with clapping his members on the back and allowing Soo-min to hang off of him, even if it wrinkled his JayBaek Couture tuxedo. He told himself this was no different than their performances for the Golden Globes and the Grammys. The rooms had been full of people indifferent to them, and still, DOYEN had forced them to their feet. DOYEN would be recognized because they belonged on that stage with Katie by their sides.

Dae-jung felt a sudden jab in his side.

"Manager hyung said they're here," said Jae-sung, dashing in his black rimmed glasses and slicked black hair. "Let's go greet our friends."

Dae-jung watched as Young-sik, Katie's head of security, opened her door, and Katie emerged.

He could not drink her in fast enough. Katie's long black hair was now chopped into a gamine pixie length, the sides shaved into a sharp undercut that highlighted the cut of her jaw and her intensely made-up eyes. Her ears were draped with heavy rubies encircled with countless tiny diamonds. Katie's fingernails were painted a dark gunmetal sheen, fingers ringed with thin bands of mixed metals with a gigantic diamond on her middle finger linked to a heavy chain across the back of her hand, circling her wrist.

But that was not what had caught Dae-jung's eye.

Katie was in a three-quarter-sleeved bolero tuxedo jacket, black and sequinned, shimmering in the setting sun. Underneath, she wore a semi-loose tuxedo shirt that was unbuttoned down to her navel, revealing so much smooth, tan skin. Golden bands circled her neck and curved under her breasts, the rest of the lines disappearing under her top. Dae-jung idly wondered how much tape was required. Then he wondered if the metal curled around her nipples and if they hurt.

Katie wasn't wearing pants—her shirt was just barely long enough to cover the rounds of her ass. Her long, lithe legs seemed endless, and her pointy, bloodred stilettos made his mouth run dry.

"Fuck," Dae-jung whispered in collective with his bandmates.

"Good luck keeping it in your pants until the end," sniggered Akihiro. "If you don't fuck her in the bathroom, I will."

"I'm sure she wouldn't mind," replied Dae-jung absently.

"Just give me the greenlight and I will," Akihiro repeated seriously. "You lucky bastard."

"Don't I know it."

Dae-jung waited his turn as Katie hugged each of his members separately, careful not to muss their carefully pressed tuxes. "Want to be inside you, Katie," he whispered darkly when it was his turn.

"Get in line," Katie chuckled back. "Akihiro already asked me to meet him in the bathroom during the first commercial break."

He resisted the surging desperate need coursing straight to his dick. "Savage little fuck."

"Oh, he assured me he was anything but little, but I trust you know best," Katie replied. And then she was gone, strutting ahead with Alton on her arm, handsome and rich as ever.

"Christ almighty," cursed Do-won. "Noona's got my cock all hard."

"Not you, too," groaned Soo-min. "In case you haven't noticed, we're surrounded by media and a good lot of them are Korean. What the fuck, Hyung?"

Jae-sung threw an arm around Dae-jung and the other around Woo-jin. "Well, I never thought I'd live to see the day when Minnie was the voice of reason. Come on, you fuckheads. You act like you've never seen pussy before."

"After tonight, the whole world will have—"

Dae-jung cut Do-won off. "Finish that thought, Hyung," he said lightly.

Do-won grinned wickedly. "You know, I must've forgotten. All these flashing lights." The dance leader strolled ahead, waving at fans and the paparazzi alike.

Dae-jung straightened his posture and rolled his shoulders back. He was a professional. He could wait, but it would be a near thing.

What a performance! Of course, we expect nothing less from DOYEN, and Katie Wu proves she's in the same league. Their act opened with musicians, dressed in the traditional clothing of their respective countries, playing Korean drums and flutes as well as Chinese violins and lutes. In addition, the funky live band dressed in traditional African clothing and African American Sunday best. The set was a feast for the eyes and ears, as was the explosive and seductive choreography and intricate dance break.

DOYEN showed up and showed out in modern hanboks and Air Jordans, while Katie wowed in modern hanfu complete with bondage accessories. Katie's rapidfire rap paired with the smooth vocals and swaggy bars of DOYEN was a match made in heaven. Most surprising was just how well Katie integrated with DOYEN in their elaborate footwork and coordination. The chemistry between her and each member sizzled. We're in love all over again.

- Teen Vogue, February 2028

We wanted to showcase the backgrounds of our musicians as well as our own. In particular, we wanted to highlight that though our Academy Award arrangement of "Luck Favors the Prepared" mixed in the traditional instruments of Korea and China, the hip-hop genre of the song owed a great deal to Black music and Black history.

- Katie Wu, W Korea (February 2028)

That's how you fucking do a stage!

- X user, February 2028

CHIMERABELLE WE STAY WINNING

- X user, February 2028

Oscars better thank DOYEN for their ratings bump. Of course, like the SCAMMYs, they only use POC for the optics. We'll see how they represent next year.

- X user, February 2028

WAIT WHO WAS THAT GUY WITH THE TINY WAIST I JUST WANNA KNOW HIS NAME

- X user, February 2028

oop there go the locals

                                             - X user, February 2028

It's so obvious they dumbed down the choreo for Katie so she could keep up. What a laughable showing. It was the start of the performance and she was already breathless.

                                             - X user, February 2028

like the oscars even matter who is even watching other than chumera and the jizzies

                                             - X user, February 2028

Stay pressed lol

                                             - X user, February 2028

Thirty minutes before showtime, Katie was in the greenroom, heaving into a wastebasket.

"Are you okay, Noona?" Soo-min asked solicitously.

"She gets like this sometimes," Jae-sung replied. "I was so worried when we were performing at Music Bank."

"I guess it's a good thing Noona's barely wearing anything so her breathing isn't restricted," Do-won observed. If Katie wasn't busy upending her entire earthly remains, she would have laughed. "Hyung, I heard you had to cut her costume."

Akihiro giggled. "Not sure what there is to cut from her outfit tonight, but I'm not objecting."

"Stop trying to get Noona into the bathroom with you, Aki-yah," chided Dae-jung.

"I don't care as long as she brushes her teeth. I suppose we don't have to kiss. I can be quick."

"YAH, Akihiro!" rebuked Ye-jun as he lightly swatted the younger singer. "Isn't that your usual performance?"

Katie choked on her saliva. This was not at all gracious but DOYEN was doing their best to cheer her up. Dae-jung handed her a bottle of water. She took a swig, swished it around, and spat out again.

"Hyung!" complained Akihiro. "Stop all that slander. Noona doesn't know, and I'll not have you poison her with your lies."

"I'm sure your stamina is more than adequate, Hiro," Katie rasped. "Sorry for the vomit."

Woo-jin sat next to Katie and rubbed her back. "You sure you're okay?"

"Yeah, it's just a thing I do. Wonnie takes a pre-concert shit; I take a pre-performance vomit," Katie replied.

"But you didn't do this before the Golden Globes," remarked Soo-min. Katie loved how the lead vocalist always seemed to be aware of her. He was sweet.

Katie started to remove her bolero and slipped off her heels. "That time I made it to the bathroom."

"Quick reflexes, Noona," hummed Do-won in approval. "Alright everyone. Let Noona change, and we'll huddle up backstage. We're up soon."

"I'll try not to shame you guys," Katie added weakly.

"As if you could ever," Jae-sung said gently. He squeezed Katie's shoulder and then she was alone.

Well, alone as she could be in a room full of coordi-unnies and Ha-joon. They swapped out Katie's jewelry, layered on more makeup, stuffed her into a beautiful modern take on hanfu, and then strapped her into more BDSM hardware than she'd seen in a long time.

Soon, Katie was in the wings, drawn into the DOYEN huddle and slapping her hand in the midst of theirs, chanting, "Katie, gaja! DOYEN gaja! Go, go!"

Katie heard the deep bass of the Korean barrel drums, the floating trills of bamboo flutes and piris, the earthy buzz of erhus, and the ringing articulation of pipas above her. Katie leapt onto the rigged trampoline, propelling her on stage from below as her hanfu billowed behind her.

She growled as she prowled the stage. "Never been one for luck / What's it matter when we all die / Memento mori / You crawl until you fly." The rest was a blur as Katie injected as much dynamism as she could, letting loose a blitzkrieg of words.

The real challenge was when the members slowly joined her on stage one by one. Katie seduced them each with all her might, the moves bordering on scandalous as first Soo-min, then Dae-jung, slunk behind her and ground themselves into her, their hands wandering in previously defined paths.

When KJ and the others joined, it was a tantalizing dance, balancing that fine line between teasing and conquering, the power rippling through each of them as they traded off the mic. "Where ya bars at though? / We're still ascending but you've plateaued / Don't expect it to last / Only hard work prevails."

In the back of Katie's mind, she was exceedingly grateful for the other award shows that they'd already performed at—a dress rehearsal, as it were, for the Academy Awards. At the front of her mind though, she was channeling her inner performance beast. Katie wanted to make these seven amazing men proud, not wishing to hold them back. She wanted that rare stamp of approval from Dance God Do-won and, quite frankly, she didn't know when she would ever have this chance again.

So when Katie was being stalked by both Lambent and 1DEL1GHT during their verse, when she was being tossed around like a prop between Jun and Akihiro, and when KJ practically ate her up on stage, she sank deeper and deeper into that pocket all performers wish for. That pocket where every step Katie took, every note she sang, every bar she rapped, every atom of her body was working in alignment with seven other humans toward one common goal.

When the eight of them reached the dance break, it was a rush unlike any Katie had ever experienced. What a joy it was to hit all her marks in unison with some of her favorite people! She prepared for that last chorus and then bowed alongside DOYEN to a standing ovation.

On that fateful night when she'd fled Jae-sung's apartment, Katie could have never imagined such an occurrence. Truly, she marveled at the strange and fortuitous curves of the universe.

Katie opted to stay in her performance outfit for the rest of the award ceremony and the guys opted to stay in theirs as well. When the presenters announced Katie Wu and DOYEN as the winner for Best Original Song, she couldn't contain her mortified delight when as one, the seven members of DOYEN pretended to be her security team on the way to the stage.

"Thank you so much," Katie said as Jae-sung maneuvered her in front of the mic. "We did it, Jezebelles! Thank you for all your hard work! This is for all the Asian American diaspora kids out there, wondering if there's a place for them. Here's a tiny step toward liberation for all!"

Katie bowed slightly and stepped back. She tittered behind a hand when she saw Woo-jin fondle the Oscar lovingly in his huge hands. All was as it should be.

Jae-sung spoke quickly and eloquently next. "Thank you, CHIMERA! We could have never imagined being on this stage fifteen years ago. We have soared because you gave us wings. Thank you to the academy for this honor."

Woo-jin, as the producer of the track and the entire soundtrack, went next. "CHIMEEERRRRRRAAAAAAAA!! Thank you for all your support! Thank you, academy," he said in English before switching to Korean. "Thank you to SB Entertainment and our tireless staff, our families, and everyone who has supported us. I love making music and there is no one I'd rather make music with than my fellow DOYEN members and Katie. May we continue to make music together for a long time."

At that, the time was called and the remaining members called out "Thank you" and "We love you, CHIMERA" and circled up, arms flung around each other's shoulders, jumping for literal joy. Katie helped herd them offstage, thrumming with adrenaline, surely grinning like an idiot the entire time.

Katie's speech was a disgrace. I'm ashamed to be Asian American if she's the face of it.

\- X user, February 2028

At least she's pretty to somebody.

\- X user, February 2028

HOLY FUCKING SHIT DID YOU SEE THAT KISS THAT FUCKING LUCKY BITCH

\- X user, February 2028

I can't believe he took that conniving cunt back
- X user, February 2028

idk why chumera are so mad like their boys haven't always had basic taste
- X user, February 2028

Maybe everyone should just mind their fucking business.
- X user, February 2028

Still in disbelief. Beyond grateful.
- Katie Wu, X, February 2028

THANK YOU CHIMERA, OUR GREATEST LOVE.
- DOYEN Official, X, February 2028

Katie looked ethereal and incandescent onstage with her hanfu and multitude of harnesses strapped to her lissom frame as she accepted her Academy Award for Best Actress. Dae-jung glowed with such pride and joy, he was surprised he hadn't burst into flames.

"Holy fucking shit! Wo cào! Tài niúbī le!" Katie exclaimed into the mic. Dae-jung had no idea what she'd said in Mandarin, but judging from Alton's face it was likely on par with her English expletive at the start. "Ah, ssibal! I don't even have a speech," she continued. "I really didn't think I'd win!"

Alton leaned over to Dae-jung and whispered, "Who would have thought that Katie would be saying 'fuck' in three different languages at the goddamned Academy Awards?" He laughed. "A day for the history books."

Katie clutched the trophy tightly and took a deep breath.

"I apologize in advance if I forget to thank you. Please know that I would have written your names down but I didn't ever think—anyway. To my baby brother Mattie: I love you. You're my favorite. Ha-joon oppa—saranghae! All my love and gratitude to my SB Entertainment fam. Thank you for taking me back and believing in me." She took a deep steadying breath. "Um, shout out to DOYEN for being the best colleagues and friends. Saranghae hyung-nim!"

Dae-jung and the rest of his members snickered and giggled at Katie's grammar slip. If she had only been acknowledging Ye-jun and Woo-jin, it would've been fine. But since the rest of them were her age or younger, it wasn't quite right. He couldn't wait for the shit they were going to give Katie after. Had to keep her humble.

"Thank you to Song PD-nim for believing in me. Thanks to my costars and everyone who worked on the movie. To my fierce Jezebelles, you are my champions! And finally, Alton."

Katie's face crumpled, both her lips and hands trembling.

"Ge—I—"

She gestured futilely in the air as if words would just appear. Tears poured from Katie's eyes. This was ugly crying, and Dae-jung longed to run onstage to comfort her even as he felt the cruel sting of jealousy.

"You're my gravity," Katie finally choked out. "You hold me together, you ground me, and you let me go when I remember how to fly."

Alton clenched the arms of his chair so tightly, his knuckles white as adoration beamed from his face. A camera zoomed in on his handsome visage and Dae-jung did not envy the man for this invasion of privacy even as he acknowledged it made for ratings gold.

"Love is too small a word. I love you, Alton Kuang. You are the very best of men. I hope one day I can make you proud." Katie turned her full body to Alton and bowed Chinese-style, pushing her folded palms out in front of her lowered head. "Everyday—even the worst ones—I'm grateful Ha-joon oppa found my life worth saving. Thank you again, everyone."

Dae-jung stood along with the rest of the theater to clap as Katie exited the stage. He glanced around the theater as he surreptitiously dabbed at his eyes. He noted how Woo-jin handed Alton a handkerchief even though Alton had his own. He wondered at how the older man was keeping it together. If Katie had spoken of Dae-jung like that in her speech, he would be a puddle of tears on the floor.

After the Best Actor and Best Picture winners were announced, the ceremony ended. He was slightly disappointed that "Landslide" didn't win Best Picture, but overall, how could he complain? An Academy Award for DOYEN had never been on their radar and now, here it was.

He would be grateful.

"YAH! Katie! How could you call us all hyung-nim when Woo-jin and I are the only ones older than you?" Ye-jun's ranting pulled Dae-jung out of his thoughts. He hadn't noticed when Katie had come out from backstage. "Hyung-nim? It's just Jun hyung, isn't it?!"

"Shut up! I didn't expect to win!" Katie buried her face into her hands. "I got flustered, okay? I meant to say sunbaenim but I also wanted to be cool and call you hyung to show that we're just friends—I got them all mixed up! I'm so embarrassed!"

His members laughed and teased her some more. Katie, who spoke more languages than all of them, laughed along, too. Dae-jung watched as she sparkled, graciously thanked well-wishers, and introduced everyone to whatever celebrity came up to her. Katie was always so insistent on including him and his bandmates in the conversation, never wishing to exclude them.

And then suddenly, Dae-jung realized that he loved Katie. He loved her with a clarity and depth he never thought he'd reach again—or had at least tucked into the hidden parts of his heart.

Disregarding the press swarming about her, Dae-jung strode the few steps to Katie, dragged her into his space with one arm wrapped around the small of her back, lifted his other hand to her face and kissed her. Dae-jung kissed Katie as if they were the last two people on earth, as if he could breathe new life into her and himself simultaneously.

The best part? Katie kissed him back as if she could never get her fill of him.

She leaned back, breathless, pupils blown. "Dae?" she questioned.

His surroundings gradually filtered back to Dae-jung's senses. He briefly registered the shock on all his members' faces. Fuck.

Ye-jun threw a casual arm around his shoulders and spoke out the side of his mouth. "We'll deal with it, Dae," he assured. "Go get your girl home and fuck her into the mattress."

"Hyung!" Dae-jung protested. "Katie might want to attend the af-ter-parties!"

Ye-jun just poked a nosy finger into Dae-jung's cheek. "Then fuck her in the limo, but for fuck's sake, give her what she deserves," he ordered.

Dae-jung mindlessly agreed and noted how Woo-jin and Alton had now flanked Katie protectively from any other media. She didn't seem upset, but fear gnawed at him. He had outed the two of them without any consideration to how Katie would feel about the additional scrutiny it would bring her.

He didn't care for himself. He was well past the age of 30, and his fans would be stupid to expect him to be alone. But Dae-jung knew that the more delusional factions of the fandom would tear Katie apart. She was by no means averse to controversy—had often courted it out of some bullish contrariness, but that didn't mean she wanted the attention this new scandal would bring. That didn't mean Katie wanted the news of her dating to overshadow her legitimate accomplishments.

Dae-jung hated that he had to consider his love for Katie a scandal, finally understanding how Ha-rin must have felt all those years ago. It tarnished the purity of what she was to him. Katie was true. True like the bond between him and his members. True like what his father felt for his mother. True like how his grandparents had loved each other.

Katie, who had endured so much, who had faltered and then gotten back up. She was the truest person in his life. Dae-jung didn't think it was the adrenaline and endorphins of tonight—after all, they'd all won plenty of awards before.

He just knew.

If Dae-jung ended up being wrong later? Well, that was a chance he was willing to take.

After what felt like an eternity, Katie found her way back to him. "Take me home, Dae-jung-ah," she whispered in his ear, listing precariously.

"Did you have fun, sweetheart?" Dae-jung whispered back, smiling at her drunken nod. "You sure you don't want to go to the after-parties?"

Katie shook her head vehemently. "I'm at just the right bit of buzzed, and I'll be fine once we get home. But if I have any more to drink, I won't be able to fuck you proper. And all I've been thinking about this whole time is how I want to eat you."

Dae-jung felt his balls tighten and flagged Alton down. "I'm taking Katie home. Are you heading to Woo-jin hyung's hotel room?"

Alton smirked knowingly. "You telling me to stay away from my own house, Dae-jung?"

"I don't particularly care whether you overhear or not, Hyung," Dae-jung responded, lobbing a knowing grin of his own. "Maybe you and I can compete to see who makes our partner come first and then how often."

Alton tilted his head back and laughed. "I'm a selfish man, Dae-jung-ah. I plan to keep all of Woo-jin's sounds to myself."

"You know we've all heard each other over the years, right?" Dae-jung teased. "Hyung gets this cute hitch in his voice right before—"

"Alright. Off with you, Dae-jung. Keep my girl safe and rock her fucking world. She deserves it," Alton interrupted.

Dae-jung snapped a sharp salute and began the slow work of guiding Katie to the exit. He had waited years. He could wait a little longer.

Despite Katie's makeup artist's best efforts, by the time Dae-jung got her to Alton's place in Malibu, her makeup was a wreck. Between her tears and the numerous hugs and kisses from friends and strangers alike, it was just a smear of color.

Katie had never been more beautiful.

In the shower, Dae-jung helped her wash her face, though by now, Katie was more than capable of doing so herself. He was pleased that Katie let him care for her, relishing the way she closed her eyes and tipped her face to let him lather her scalp. Dae-jung enjoyed the feel of the short stubble on the sides of her head. He always appreciated a fresh fade even though he himself had not had one in years.

"Did I congratulate you yet, Katie?" he asked in his sonorous baritone. Dae-jung watched Katie shiver at the sound.

"I think so," Katie murmured. "Did I, you?"

"Yes," he affirmed. "But you can congratulate me again."

She huffed, amused. "I've never sucked an Oscar winner's dick before," she pondered.

"And I've never eaten out a two-time Academy Award winner."

Katie stroked his chest lightly. "Seems we both have a lot to experience with an Oscar winner for the first time. It may take us at least a week to be sure we've left no stone unturned."

"Maybe longer," Dae-jung replied as he kissed her jawline. "I think your imagination is getting lazy in your advanced age."

"Impudent ass," Katie teased, pulling him closer so he could feel her breasts heavy against his torso. "Good thing you're my impudent ass."

"Always," he promised.

Dae-jung slid one large palm over her breast and another down her side to grab her bottom. He continued his slow meander along the cut of her jaw and up to her sensitive ear. He slipped her lobe into his mouth and sucked, glorying in the way her hips bucked into him involuntarily.

"Your outfit drove me crazy, Katie," he rasped into her ear. "Just a hint of your fantastic tits and your fucking long legs. All I could think of was plowing into you all night."

Katie gasped, writhing against his breathy confessions. She reached a hand between his legs and palmed his length. He hissed at how cool her hand felt against the heat of his velvety skin.

"Flatterer," she panted. "All eyes were on you and your group. No one was even looking at me."

"I was looking at you," Dae-jung replied. "We were all looking at you. The way Akihiro would have stolen you from me if given half the chance."

Katie shook her head. "Impossible. It's you I love, Dae-jung. You and only you."

Pleasure burned through his veins at her declaration. It didn't matter how often she said it, Dae-jung would never take her love for granted. Not after they almost ruined what they had by not being honest about their feelings.

"I wouldn't mind," he said.

"Liar," she accused as she squeezed his balls. "There's no need to play at generosity, Dae. I don't want it."

"But I want to give you everything, Katie," Dae-jung whined against her dripping hair, the scrape of her sides a delicious contrast.

Katie leaned back and grabbed his chin so that he looked at her. "Please don't, Dae-jung. I appreciate how you're willing to risk yourself to let me be free. Truly." She kissed him, soft and slow. "Don't give away more than you want to give, Dae-jung. You deserve all you want and more, and if it's in my power to give, I will give it to you gladly."

Dae-jung's heart expanded and stretched more than he'd ever thought possible. The water started to turn cold. He shuddered as his flesh prickled.

"Come on, California's always in a drought," Katie said as she slid from his embrace, turning off the water.

Dae-jung dutifully followed her out.

Katie dried herself, draped her towel over a chair, and laid out on the bed. "Lotion me up?" she asked, holding out her very practical tub of CeraVe cream.

He scooped up the thick emollient and slathered her arms first as quickly as possible, then lingered on her glorious tits. Dae-jung loved how his hands glided over Katie's skin and how she turned into putty the moment he began fondling and groping her breasts. He flicked his thumbs over her nipples, and she arched her back. The indents from the metalwork she'd worn earlier were still impressed upon her areola.

Dae-jung decided that even though he would get a mouthful of lotion, it would be worth suckling Katie. He was rewarded with a mewl and Katie's hands pressing his face deeper into her chest.

He spread his hands down the round of her belly and cupped her mound, his fingers tickling at her entrance. Katie was so wet.

"Please," Katie exhaled, no pretense at self-control. "Want you, Dae-jung."

Dae-jung circled her center with light, tortuous touches, determined to hear her beg more. He swirled his tongue on her nipple and alternated biting and soothing. He thumbed wet figure eights over her clit as Katie writhed, desperate for more friction.

Katie sank her fingers into his hair and pushed his head down.

"You're so impatient tonight, Katie," he snickered even as he let her exert even more pressure. He kissed his way down to her heat, eager to taste her cunt.

"You offered," she retorted.

He hummed thoughtfully. "As I recall, you also offered similar services."

"Mean," Katie huffed. "I'm a two-time Academy Award winner, you know."

"Ah, you outrank me then," Dae-jung conceded. He placed a wet kiss right to the side of her clit, chuckling when he could feel Katie's pout radiate through her skin. "Perhaps you could steer me in the right direction?"

Katie huffed again and grabbed him lightly by his ears, maneuvering him until his nose just touched her swollen bud. He nosed her gently and she sighed, sinking deeper into the mattress.

Dae-jung breathed Katie in, the smell of her citrus body wash the most prominent scent, with just hints of her personal notes underneath. He burrowed closer and released a warm breath just to watch her skin react.

"Dae-jung," she whined. "Want you to fuck me with your mouth."

He didn't bother replying. Dae-jung knew it wasn't what Katie wanted. What she wanted was his tongue inside of her, so he got to the business of consuming her. He teased with pointed kitten licks and sweeping strokes between her lips. He lapped at Katie's entrance and swirled her clit.

Katie exerted even more pressure on his head, burying his face into her cunt.

Dae-jung could take a hint. Normally, he would slow down, force her to wait for him until she was a begging, sopping mess. Tonight, he was greedy in a different way. Instead of showing off his prowess in bringing her to the edge, he just wanted to immerse himself in her taste.

He engulfed Katie's core with his entire mouth, drawing her essence into him whole. She sobbed, arching her back and twisting his hair in her fists. He reached up, palmed her breast, and caressed her even as he continued to feed, suctioning her clit the way Katie loved, sinking into the lewd squelch of his mouth against her most private spaces.

"Yes," Katie gasped, "fuck, yes."

Dae-jung moved his other hand from pinning her thigh down and slowly inserted his middle finger. She clenched and throbbed around him as he rubbed her spot in conjunction with his mouth on her clit. He felt one of her hands claw at his back, the primal nature sending a surge of want straight to his cock.

"Please," Katie wept. "Please, Dae, please!"

He slid another finger into her, beckoning her orgasm closer with every crook. Dae-jung played Katie faster and faster until his world narrowed to her broken cries, his aching hand, and the sharp flavor of her melting into his mouth. He flicked her swollen bud rapidly as he tamped down inside her, and then Katie was gone.

Katie unloosed a litany of curses as her arousal flooded his awaiting lips, her hands mauling his face and hair. Dae-jung endured the slight discomfort even as he let her ride his face through her orgasm until she finally pushed him away.

"Fuck," she panted, curling up on her side.

Dae-jung crawled onto the bed and wrapped his body around Katie's, pillowing her weary neck on his arm. She was a sweaty mess. She was his. "I love you, Katie," he said.

"Mmmmm," she mumbled, "I love you, too, Park Dae-jung."

Katie ground her ass into his crotch as she reached behind and pulled him even closer to her.

"You sure you're not too tired?" Dae-jung asked. He knew how worn out she could get after coming from his mouth. Katie was practically boneless.

"Oh, I'm not moving, Dae-jung," she purred. "But if you want to fuck me like this, I'll make it up to you tomorrow."

Dae-jung chuckled. He knew how this would end.

Katie would promise him whatever filth she could conjure as long as it meant she wouldn't have to move. Except, she rarely followed through. Not out of any malicious intent, just that Katie was never quite as enthusiastic about contorting her body into various positions as he would have thought.

Though she was not particularly spoiled in general, Katie was decidedly spoiled in bed. Dae-jung was occasionally tempted to ask Jae-sung if she'd always been a pillow princess, or if something about him in particular brought it out of her. Perhaps that would be weird, but considering he and Jae-sung already acknowledged they were hole buddies (thanks to Katie's crass and cackling insistence), it really wasn't. Few could understand how the years had tied them to one another so intimately. Even Katie found it puzzling on occasion despite rolling with it as best she could.

At any rate, Dae-jung knew that there would be no making it up in the morning. Katie would likely be too hungover or tired to do much other than pout and nap.

"Is that what you want, Noona?" he intoned softly. "If you want my dick inside you, all you have to do is say so."

"You won't think I'm greedy?" Katie asked, grinding against his erection.

Dae-jung snickered. "Oh, you're definitely greedy, Katie. But I don't mind when you're greedy for my dick."

"I want it," Katie said. She grabbed his hand and covered her breast. "Use me, Dae-jung. I want your Oscar-winning come inside me."

He chuckled again. "Is that why you want me? Because I'm an Academy Award–winning singer?"

"Of course," Katie said as she tried to position him at her clenching hole. "Only the best come for me."

Dae-jung nuzzled into the crook of her neck, and she sighed happily. "You're so weird," he said fondly. He felt the head of his penis finally catch at her entrance and pushed in, allowing himself to luxuriate in her tight heat. "Fuck," he breathed.

"Mmmmm, fuck," Katie agreed.

She hooked her leg over his, swiveling her hips as he hooked one arm around her neck to caress a breast as his other hand grabbed the other one. He rested his face at her cheek, mouth open and panting, all the while slowly thrusting into her. When Katie started to flag, Dae-jung repositioned them back to spooning, curling her into a tight angle so he could more easily pump into Katie, caging her in with his arms to provide proper leverage.

"Fuck, Dae-jung," she blathered, "I wish I could suck and fuck you at the same time—god, I love your cock."

"Feel so fucking good, Noona," he moaned. "Love fucking you. Love your tight pussy on my dick. You ride me so well, I'm gonna come soon."

"Want it, Dae. Want you to fill me up," Katie begged.

Dae-jung roughly turned Katie's head and stuffed his tongue in her mouth. She sucked, so wet and messy, and his shaft throbbed. He stuck some of his fingers in her mouth, and she obediently slobbered over them, too.

"Jesus," he groaned. He brought his soaked fingers to her clit and without care to her sensitivity, he massaged her, pinioning Katie deeper onto his cock.

Katie's desperate sounds urged him forward, his hips pistoning faster and faster.

"Gonna come," he warned, and with a few more sloppy thrusts, he shot, pulsing and hot. Though Dae-jung knew he would soften soon, he stayed put as Katie continued to grind. "You're so fucking hot, baby. You think you have it in you to come again for me?"

Katie sounded more decadent than any porn he'd ever watched. She was wrecked. Dae-jung had done this to her, and if he was capable, he would have come again from that thought alone. His fingers continued to press, slippery and sticky, even as he carefully pumped into her. One time, he'd slipped out and her cry of loss still haunted him.

"Come for me, sweetness," he babbled as he splayed a large hand across Katie's collarbones and throat. He added a tiny bit of pressure, and her breath hitched. "I wish everyone could see you now, spread apart for me. So needy. So greedy. Such a good girl for me."

Dae-jung nipped her earlobe and somehow, that did the trick. Katie came, loud, ragged, and all his.

The next few weeks were a consistent blur of more talk shows, interviews, and magazine photoshoots. Sometimes, Katie and Dae-jung were together. Sometimes, it was just Dae-jung. And other times, it was some combination of her, his bandmates, his castmates, and himself.

Katie expertly maneuvered and swerved when hosts and journalists asked her about the very public kiss with Dae-jung, acknowledging only that the kiss had happened, was consensual, and was more than satisfactory. She deflected, teased, and otherwise blatantly ignored more pointed questions about her relationship status.

Dae-jung personally thought it was a missed opportunity to say, "Five out of five stars. Ten out of ten would try again."

SB Entertainment put out a relentlessly bland and professional press release on behalf of both Dae-jung and Katie. Dae-jung grumbled over it, mostly because he wanted to say, "Please mind your own fucking business. We don't comment on our artists' personal lives. Go suck a dick."

The internet fanwars, though. That was a trainwreck and provided ample fodder for SB Entertainment's legal department. It was expected, and still, Dae-jung was disappointed. Why couldn't some people understand? He was not some K-pop avatar of all their fantasies and delusions. He was a person. He wasn't a doll for their amusement.

Of course, Katie bore the brunt of the backlash. Such was the rampant misogyny of the internet. When Dae-jung checked in on her, she merely waved away his concerns.

"I get it," Katie said. "You're an idol in the biggest K-pop band on earth. I'm on a completely different tier—like scraping bottom—and for many of your fans, I will never be good enough for you. No one will."

"That's not true, Noona," Dae-jung insisted.

Katie caressed his face. "I know, Dae-jung. I'm used to this shit. I've dealt with this my entire public life. It doesn't bother me."

He pouted. "How?"

"The same way you got used to all the racism and misogyny directed at DOYEN." Katie kissed him on the nose. "You sucked it up, kept going, and reminded yourself of what your true goal was. You knew your true value."

"I love you, Katie," Dae-jung said quietly. "I know I'm a lot. Being with me comes with a lot."

Katie embraced him, somewhat bone-crackingly tight. "I'm a lot, too. We can be a lot together."

March 2029

Katie Wu seen sporting a large marquise cut ruby ring with pavéd diamonds on her ring finger. Though it's not a traditional engagement ring, when has K-pop's star couple ever been traditional? Are wedding bells in the future?

- Soompi, March 2029

Looks like DOYEN has caught wedding fever. First Jun, then KJ, now DJ! Sorry, CHIMERA. DOYEN is all grown up.

- Koreaboo, March 2029

Wow, seems quick. Good news, though. The sooner they get married, the sooner DJ can get his starter marriage over.

- X user, March 2029

Congratulations, DJ and Katie!!

- X user, March 2029

"You want an elaborate wedding, don't you?" Katie asked Dae-jung. They were cozying on his bed and though she'd moved into his penthouse a few months ago, Katie still thought of the place as his.

Her fiancé winced as he nodded.

"You're lucky I love you, you know?"

"I do," Dae-jung replied.

"So you won't be upset if I let you do whatever you want? I don't care about any of the details," Katie said. "I don't want to do any planning—except that you also have to include a tea ceremony. Otherwise, my family will balk."

"Is your mother going to come?" Dae-jung asked.

Katie sighed. "I really don't know. I've reached out to her a few times, but she's rebuffed all my entreaties. At least Mattie is coming with his wife, and Alton, of course, will be here. My extended family in Taiwan will at least send a few of my cousins as representatives," she said.

Katie tried not to let her mother get to her. She'd had almost a decade to come to terms with her mother and her utter refusal to see reason or the truth. Katie knew it was her mother's way of coping with her own trauma, but it didn't sting any less.

"We might have to swing by Taiwan to see my grandfather, though," she added. "And probably have to have a separate reception there to satisfy that side of the family."

"You sure you don't have opinions about the wedding?" teased Dae-jung. "I think you just added a second ceremony and reception to my plate."

Katie supposed Dae-jung wasn't wrong, but he was the one who wanted a big wedding. And it didn't seem fair that the majority of her family were too elderly to attend in Seoul. It seemed only right to have another reception in Kaohsiung. He was lucky she wasn't insisting on another reception in California!

"You're the one who has too many friends and can't bear to not invite any of them," Katie grumbled. "I wanted to elope!"

Dae-jung grinned and kissed her temple. "I'm sorry that so many people want to celebrate us, love." He kissed down the curve of her cheek and when he got to the corner of her mouth, he licked her.

"Gross!" Katie complained, pushing him away.

He cackled and pounced on her, pinning her to the bed. "You like it," Dae-jung insisted. "You love my tongue."

"Only in certain places, Dae-jung. My face is not one of those places."

"Hmmmm," Dae-jung mused. "Maybe my memory needs to be refreshed. Could you direct me to the places you prefer?"

Katie's cunt clenched. "Don't think you can distract me into taking some of this work off your plate. I refuse! You wanted this wedding and you'll plan it—don't you dare shuffle your responsibility onto me."

"Care to make a wager?" Dae-jung murmured as he dipped his tongue into her ear. She arched involuntarily. "If I can make you come with just my mouth, you'll figure out the Taiwan part."

"I will not be swayed, Park Dae-jung. You chose this!"

"But, jagiya," he protested as he nibbled on her earlobe and his clever hands swept the sides of her body. "It's for the both of us."

Katie could never deny Dae-jung anything. "Fine," she acquiesced. "But if you don't, you owe me the new Porsche 911, too."

Dae-jung nipped Katie sharply. "You already have a Porsche 911!"

"True," Katie said as she palmed his cock through his sweatpants. "But I don't have the new one."

Dae-jung choked as she flicked the rounded head.

"I want it in red."

Katie ended up having to plan the Taiwan portion of their wedding, but Dae-jung, good sport that he was, sent her a red 911 anyway.

EPILOGUE

July 2042

Rumor has it that Katie Wu will be in Singapore next week to film a surprise cameo in acclaimed director Andy Leung's latest action movie. The 64-year-old director is most famous for expanding on the 'gun fu' action genre and we can't wait to see how Wu fits into the story. The 49-year-old Academy Award–winning actress and Grammy-winning singer-songwriter is looking excellent for her age. This is the first major film she's signed onto since the birth of her first child. We can't wait.

- E! News, July 2042

"Appa, what are you making for dinner?" asked Seong-su as Katie brought her eldest son into the kitchen of their Seoul home. After a long day full of activities, all Katie wanted was to collapse onto her bed and sleep for an uninterrupted six hours. "Eomma says she's hungry as fuck."

Dae-jung choked on his soda and tried mightily not to laugh. "Su-su, what did we tell you about saying grown-up words?"

"What you told me or what Eomma told me?" Katie's all-too-honest son said as he dumped his backpack onto the kitchen table. Katie resisted the urge to nag him about putting the bag away in his room.

Her husband arched a judgy brow at her. "What did your eomma tell you?"

"She said that I'm not old enough to say these words in front of adults, and that if I want to say them, to say them in the right context and not in front of anyone who can get me in trouble." Seong-su was far too earnest for his own good. Katie was so fond.

"Is that right?"

"Snitch," Katie hissed at Seong-su even as she laughed. "Am I wrong though?"

Dae-jung joined her in cracking up. "No, you're not wrong, I suppose. But is this really the precedent you want to set with our oldest?"

"Our kids should know how the world works," Katie retorted. "Where are the rest of the kids?"

"Seong-min should almost be done with her Chinese tutor," said Dae-jung, "and Seong-hun and Seong-jin are allegedly watching Chinese videos."

"Allegedly?"

"I haven't checked on them in a while. Who knows what they're really up to," confessed Dae-jung.

"I'll go check on them, Appa," Seong-su said as he scampered off.

Seong-su was guileless most of the time, but he sure knew how to get in good with his father and maybe sneak in some extra screen time while he was at it. He was 12 going on 13, but still such a baby sometimes.

"What are you making? And should I be worried?" Katie teased as she rounded the kitchen island and hugged Dae-jung.

Dae-jung used to be such a disaster in the kitchen, but after Seong-su was born and Katie was sick of takeout, she gave him an ultimatum. Either she was hiring a cook or he was going to learn how. Surprisingly, Dae-jung chose to learn how to cook, somehow conning Ye-jun and Woo-jin into teaching him and then turning it into content for his fans. He thoroughly enjoyed taking real cooking lessons on the side to astonish his hyungs when he actually knew what he was doing.

Katie didn't complain because she just wanted someone else to cook some nights. It seemed like a win-win.

And now, a decade later, she was so grateful that Dae-jung took his fatherly duties so seriously. Even though he and the rest of his DOYEN bandmates were busy preparing for their thirtieth anniversary celebrations next year, he consistently helped with making dinner, packing lunches (always adding his whimsical artistic decorations and cute little notes), and was far more involved than most men of his generation.

"I picked up your dry cleaning for your trip next week, yeobo," Dae-jung said as he stirred the kimchi jjigae on the stove. "Don't forget to say hi to Woo-jin hyung and Alton hyung for me."

Even after all these years, Katie still had to quell the urge to tell him not to call her "yeobo." Her husband was likely the only man she'd ever allow such a term of endearment. If she had married anyone else, she would have murdered them before letting them call her such a diminutive. But Dae-jung was such a honey bear himself, how could she not allow it?

"How could I forget?" Katie said as she mentally checked an item off her massive to-do list. "Thanks for picking it up, Dae," she added. "I would have totally forgotten and then had to show up in meetings in sweatpants."

"You probably would prefer that," Dae-jung laughed.

"The look on Alton's face would be priceless. Woo-jin wouldn't care though," Katie mused. "Are you sure you don't need me to hire temporary help or snag one of Jae-sung's nannies?"

Dae-jung shook his head as he began to grab various banchan out of the fridge. Katie would help, but she was still weary from last-minute business meetings and shuttling Seong-su and the other kids around.

"I cleared my schedules already, so we're good on that front. And I promised the kids a pizza night, a movie night, and a hot pot night, so I think we should be good on the dinner front, too."

Dae-jung beamed his trademark boxy smile at Katie and all of a sudden, she was hurtled back in time to when she was 21 and meeting him for the first time in Taipei before their concert. He had been so quiet and polite back then. And then when she'd met him again at SB Entertainment a few months later, Dae-jung had been such a source of brightness, easing Katie's loneliness by treating her as the big sister he'd never had.

Katie's eyes teared up suddenly.

"Yeobo, what's wrong?" Dae-jung asked as he rushed around the kitchen counter to hug her. "You're only going to be gone a week—no need to worry so much, love."

Katie sniffled and sank into his comforting hug. He always knew how to love her and ground her in the moment.

"Ah, Dae-jung. I'm so lucky to have you," she mumbled into his chest. "I don't know what country I saved in a past life, but—"

His baritone chuckle rumbled through her. "You're so ridiculous, yeobo. We're lucky to have each other."

Katie sniffled some more. "You're right you're lucky. Who else would overlook your goofy ears and big eyes and the ability to ruin thousand-dollar shoes?"

She leaned back, content to gaze at the man who still consistently topped the world's most handsome man lists every year. The years had been kind to him and he was looking more and more like his father every year.

Katie's mind flashed to those few days in the suicide recovery center and how hopeless she'd felt then. How her entire life had seemed stuck and irrevocably shattered. And now, here she was, married to *the* Park Dae-jung, with four healthy children, and more love than she knew what to do with.

It was a good life.

The End (of this timeline).

Coming soon in 2025:
Inevitable

Catch up on the Her Multiverse Series:
Illusive
Weightless

Acknowledgments

Part of me feels ridiculous since I only just finished writing the acknowledgments in my debut novel a few months ago. Not much has changed since then—and I am both grateful for the continued support and somewhat bemused at what new words to say to many of the same people.

Of course, it goes without saying (but I will anyway because it's important to name and thank people publicly), that once again, my creative team is impeccable. I am so grateful for their labor and thoughtful critiques and contributions.

Jacquelin Cangro, every time I send you my work, I know that I will learn something new about craft and my story will improve markedly. Also, it cracks me up how no matter how hard I try to fill in location details, you're always asking for more. Thanks to your gentle instruction, my characters are not just floating heads in empty space.

Diane Park, I don't even know what to say. You are my second (and better) brain. Thank you for championing me, for your tireless effort in keeping my work culturally accurate and factual, and for just being an outstanding person and friend. How lucky I am to have you in my life. I adore you.

Melody Ip, our comments back and forth in Google docs are some of my favorite moments. Thank you for your excellent suggestions, your immaculate grammar checking, and your friendship. I always learn so much (and promptly forget) about copy and grammar. You are so kind and generous with time and knowledge.

Joyce Park, your mind! I am always in awe at the gorgeous covers you create to bind my story, series, and aesthetic together. Thank you for being the Visual Queen of my book! I so enjoy our random conversations about K-pop, kids, life, and how we have definitely done multiple cost-benefit analyses on divorcing our husbands to marry our faves.

Aeri Kim, thank you so much for bringing my characters to life in your joyful illustrations. They have so much movement and feel so real. What a consummate and professional artist you are!

Carmie Zhang, thank you for your art, your unending patience with my inability to articulate a physical vision, and your incredible illustrations for my characters. I adore being concert buddies and look forward to our mutual enabling to buy questionable amounts of merch and tickets.

Jessica Robinson, Leslie Hartje-Dunn, Rei, and Grid, thank you all for listening to me as I brainstormed and tried to figure out plot, motivations, and the heart of this book. Your insights and support meant the world to me and this book would not exist without you.

Jessica Rosenberg, your patient generosity with your time and knowledge has been such a safe harbor as I figured out this publishing business. Your calm, wisdom, and practical help were and are huge reasons I am not screaming and sobbing in an overwhelmed corner somewhere. Thank you.

To the Boba Ramen Crew: Rose Nieh, Andrea Siu, Patti Chang, and Amy Lee. As always, I love you. We don't see each other nearly often enough, but when we do, it's like nothing has changed.

To my fellow Degenerates, Hasina Rashed and Blessing Gana, you both continually elevate and inspire me. Your talent, brilliance, and consistent support constantly show me how to be a better person.

Erica Howard, thank you for being a friend who shows up. Your unending love and support for your internet nieces and nephews brightens my days. Your funny candor, vulnerability, and pursuit of your dreams make me marvel at how tenacious and fantastic you are.

Marsha Ungchusri, thank you for being such a fun and consistent presence in my life. Where would I be without our weekly writing sessions and chats? Love watching you embrace stan life as the best life.

Stella Won, I'm so grateful for the way you entertain and go along with all my wild ideas—and even go as far as recording a podcast with me. Thank you for your brilliant mind, your quippy catchphrases, and for being a fellow toddler mom at our big age.

To my village: Brandi Riley, Lizz Porter, E, Cindy Chiang, Jenn Yoo, Nancy Lin, Sophia Lai, Emily Lai, Sandi Francioch, Cathy Barger, Sarah Poon, Jie Gao, Po-wen Chen, Vicky Tai, Chris Wong, Joe Chang, Jeff Harry, Damion Taylor, Anita Jackson, Susanna Stroberg, Jenny Park, DJ Peter Lo, PD-nim Michaela, my fellow Possums, the Barricades or Bust group chat, the Unnies Afterlife group chat, the Kpopcast fam, my Mochi Magazine colleagues, and countless others. Thank you. Your conversation, support, and encouragement helped raise both me and my children.

To BTS, anything I write here sounds at once too cliché, trite, pathetic, and thirsty. I mean it all. I am grateful I live in the same timeline as you and get to witness just part of your journey. May you all have happy and healthy lives.

And finally, many thanks to my mother Sarah Huang, my brother Alex Duan, my husband James, and my ridiculous crew of little sweethearts. Cookie Monster, Gamera, Glow Worm, Sasquatch, and Kitsune, you are my joy and light. May my love cover you for all lifetimes.

Glossary

Aegyo (애교): acting cute or childish by pitching the voice cuter or higher, and changing speech patterns, facial expressions, or gestures to seem cute. Common among K-pop idols for their fans.

Ah-gōng (阿公): Taiwanese for grandfather

Appa (아빠): Korean for dad (informal/casual)

Audentes fortuna iuvat: Latin for "fortune favors the bold"

Bàba (爸爸): Mandarin for father

Babo (바보): Korean for fool, stupid

Bǎobèi (寶貝): Mandarin for treasure, darling, baby

Carpe noctem: Latin for "seize the night"

Chaebol (재벌): in South Korea, a large conglomerate owned by a family, usually very rich individuals or family

Daepyo (대표): Korean for CEO

Dongsaeng (동생): younger sister/brother, what Koreans call a younger person if they are close or related

Eomma (엄마): Korean for mom (informal/casual)

Gēgē (哥哥): Mandarin for big brother, can also be used as a term of endearment

Gumiho (구미호): Korean name for a nine-tailed fox that often appears in Korean and East Asian folklore, confer Kitsune (キツネ) in Japanese and Húlí jīng (狐狸精) in Chinese

Gyopo (교포): term for the Korean diaspora, sometimes used in a derogatory manner

Hoobae (후배): junior, what Koreans use to refer to someone younger or with less experience than them

Hyung (형): older brother, what Korean males call older males if they are close or related

Jagiya (자기야): honey, darling, baby, an affectionate way to call your significant other in Korean

Jjang (짱): Korean slang for best, the best, awesome

Maknae (막내): refers to the youngest member in a group of people (e.g., family, friends, K-pop groups)

Meimei (妹妹): Mandarin for little sister, can also be used as a term of endearment

Memento mori: Latin for "remember we must die"

Năinai (奶奶): Mandarin for paternal grandmother

Nim (님): roughly translated as Mr./Mrs./Miss/Ms. When added after a proper noun, "-nim" is the most formal honorific to show politeness and respect to people when in formal or professional settings.

Noona (누나): older sister, what Korean males call older females if they are close or related

Oppa (오빠): older brother, what Korean females call older males if they are close or related

PD: Producer-Director, can be used in film and television as well as music production

Sajaegi (사재기): Korean term used when companies buy their artists' albums in bulk or stream using bots in order to manipulate sales and streaming charts, commonly associated with K-pop

Saranghae (사랑해): Korean for "I love you"

Sasaeng (사생): Korean for an obsessive fan who stalks or invades the privacy of a celebrity

Satoori (사투리): Korean for regional dialect

Semper paratus: Latin for "always prepared"

Shú Gong (叔公): Mandarin for paternal granduncle

Ssi (씨): roughly translated as Mr./Mrs./Miss/Ms., less formal than "nim." When added after a proper noun, "-ssi" is an honorific to show politeness and respect to people/strangers who are generally the same age or social status.

Ssibal (씨발): Korean expletive for fuck or shit

Sunbae (선배): senior, what Koreans use to refer to someone older or with more experience than them

Unnie (언니): big sister, what Korean females call older females if they are close or related

Wá (娃): Mandarin for baby, child, son or daughter, doll

Wo cào! Tài niúbī le! (我肏! 太牛屄了!): Chinese expletives for "Fuck me! That's fucking awesome!" (Literally a cow's cunt.)

Yeobo (여보): honey, Korean term of endearment used only among married couples

About the Author

Virginia Duan is an Asian American author who writes stories full of rage and grief with biting humor and glimpses of grace. Creator of the Her Multiverse series, the novels explore how Asian American singer Katie Wu's choices in love, friends, and family impact her journey of self-discovery, healing from trauma, and choosing the life she wants for herself. Peek behind the glamour of the K-pop industry and discover how Katie learns to love herself and a different band member of global K-pop sensation DOYEN in every timeline.

Her new cozy fantasy series, The Witches' Council, follows several small love stories in a world where magic is real, marriage is a job, consummation rituals are mandatory, and love is with whom they least expect: their spouse!

Based in the San Francisco Bay Area, Virginia lives with her husband and five children. (Yes, five.) She spends most of her days plotting her next book or article, shuttling her children about, participating in more group chats than humanly possible, and daydreaming about BTS a totally normal amount.

Join Virginia's mailing list to receive sneak peeks, bonuses, and updates on her latest stories at https://virginiaduan.com.

HER MULTIVERSE SERIES

Asian American singer Katie Wu flees to Seoul to rebuild her career after a scandal, befriending the seven members of global K-pop boy band DOYEN, when timelines suddenly diverge.

The series explores how Katie's choices in love, friends, and family impact her journey of self-discovery, healing from trauma, and choosing the life she wants for herself. Peek behind the glamour of the K-pop industry and discover how Katie learns to love herself and a different band member of DOYEN in every timeline.

Each book is a stand-alone emotional rollercoaster in the witty and steamy Her Multiverse series.

Her Multiverse Series

Illusive

Weightless

Inevitable (2025)